CAPPY RICKS:
OR, the Subjugation of matt Peasley

By
PETER B. KYNE

Cappy Ricks:
OR, the Subjugation of matt Peasley

by   Peter B. Kyne

Copyright © 2023

All Rights reserved.
No part of this publication may be reproduced, stored in a retrieval system, or transmitted in any form or by any means, electronic, mechanical, photocopying or Otherwise, without the written permission of the publisher.

The author/editor asserts the moral right to be identified as the author/editor of this work.

ISBN: 978-93-57273-24-4

Published by

DOUBLE 9 BOOKS

2/13-B, Ansari Road, Daryaganj
New Delhi – 110002
info@double9books.com
www.double9books.com
Tel. 011-40042856

This book is under public domain

ABOUT THE AUTHOR

Peter B Kyne was born on October 12, 1880 in San Francisco to John Kyne and Mary Cresham. Peter B. Kyne was one of the best creative writers, for both novels and short stories, in American Literature. He went to business college with the goal to help people at the farm, but his professors noticed his skill for writing and advised him to become a writer. After doing a lot of jobs, Kyne lied about his age and joined the military. After leaving the military, Kyne again got a few suggestions for doing the job, and in 1905 got employed as a reporter in San Francisco Morning Call. He has been writing short stories and started publishing them after getting married in 1910, and also often in some major magazines of the day, for example, Collier's and The Saturday Evening Post. Kyne's first novel, "The Three Godfathers", was published in 1913, where he got major success. It was also made into a few movies, the most popular was featuring John Wayne (3 Godfathers (1948)). Most of his short stories and novels were converted into movies and during the 1930s people over their having thought that it was difficult to go into a theatre and not see a film based on Kyne's story. He likewise also worked on the screenplays of a few of the movies based on his books. In 1940, his last book was published, "Dude woman".

CONTENTS

TO THE IDEAL AMERICAN SAILOR 7
CHAPTER I. – MASTER OF MANY SHIPS AND SKIPPER OF NONE .. 9
CHAPTER II. – THE MAN FROM BLUE WATER 12
CHAPTER III. – UNDER THE BLUE STAR FLAG 16
CHAPTER IV. – BAD NEWS FROM CAPE TOWN 22
CHAPTER V. – MATT PEASLEY ASSUMES OFFICE 26
CHAPTER VI. – WORDY WAR AT A DOLLAR A WORD 30
CHAPTER VII. – CAPPY RICKS MAKES BAD MEDICINE 37
CHAPTER VIII. – ALL HANDS AND FEET TO THE RESCUE 41
CHAPTER IX. – MR. MURPHY ADVISES PREPAREDNESS 45
CHAPTER X. – THE BATTLE OF TABLE BAY 48
CHAPTER XI. – MR. SKINNER RECEIVES A TELEGRAM 58
CHAPTER XII. – THE CAMPAIGN OPENS 63
CHAPTER XIII. – AN OLD FRIEND RETURNS AND CAPPY LEADS ANOTHER ACE 71
CHAPTER XIV. – INSULT ADDED TO INJURY 74
CHAPTER XV. – RUMORS OF WAR 77
CHAPTER XVI. – WAR! 82
CHAPTER XVII. – CAPPY FORCES AN ARMISTICE 87
CHAPTER XVIII. – THE WAR IS RENEWED 92
CHAPTER XIX. – CAPPY SEEKS PEACE 94
CHAPTER XX. – PEACE AT LAST! 98
CHAPTER XXI. – MATT PEASLEY MEETS A TALKATIVE STRANGER 102
CHAPTER XXII. – FACE TO FACE 110
CHAPTER XXIII. – BUSINESS AND – 117
CHAPTER XXIV. – THE CLEAN UP 122

CHAPTER XXV.	CAPPY PROVES HIMSELF A DESPOT	128
CHAPTER XXVI.	MATT PEASLEY IN EXILE	134
CHAPTER XXVII.	PROMOTION	139
CHAPTER XXVIII.	CAPPY HAS A HEART	143
CHAPTER XXIX.	NATURE TAKES HER COURSE	148
CHAPTER XXX.	MR. SKINNER HEARS A LECTURE	155
CHAPTER XXXI.	INTERNAL COMBUSTION	158
CHAPTER XXXII.	SKINNER PROPOSES — AND CAPPY RICKS DISPOSES	169
CHAPTER XXXIII.	CAPPY'S PLANS DEMOLISHED	177
CHAPTER XXXIV.	A GIFT FROM THE GODS	182
CHAPTER XXXV.	A DIRTY YANKEE TRICK	185
CHAPTER XXXVI.	CAPPY FORBIDS THE BANS — YET	192
CHAPTER XXXVII.	MATT PEASLEY BECOMES A SHIPOWNER	198
CHAPTER XXXVIII.	WORKING CAPITAL	202
CHAPTER XXXIX.	EASY MONEY	204
CHAPTER XL.	THE CATACLYSM	211
CHAPTER XLI.	WHEN PAIN AND ANGUISH WRING THE BROW	216
CHAPTER XLII.	UNEXPECTED DEVELOPMENTS	220
CHAPTER XLIII.	CAPPY PLANS A KNOCK-OUT	235
CHAPTER XLIV.	SKINNER DEVELOPS INTO A HUMAN BEING	242
CHAPTER XLV.	CAPPY PULLS OFF A WEDDING	246
CHAPTER XLVI.	A SHIP FORGOTTEN	250
CHAPTER XLVII.	THE TAIL GOES WITH THE HIDE	260
CHAPTER XLVIII.	VICTORY	265

TO THE IDEAL AMERICAN SAILOR

As exemplified in the persons of my good friends,

Captain Ralph E. Peasley, of Jonesport, Maine,

Who skippered the first five-masted schooner ever built, brought her, on that first voyage, through the worst typhoon that ever blew, and upon arriving at the Yang Tse Kiang River for the first time in his adventurous career, decided he could not trust a Chinese pilot and established a record by sailing her up himself!

Captain I. N. Hibberd, of Philadelphia, Pennsylvania,

Sometime master of the American clipper ship, Cyrus Wakefield, who, at the age of twenty-five, broke three world's records in one voyage: San Francisco to Liverpool and back, eight months and two days; Liverpool to San Francisco, one hundred days; from the equator to San Francisco, eleven days. The clipper ship is gone but the skipper remains, an undefeated champion.

Captain William P. Cantey, of San Francisco, California,

Sometime mate of the brig Galilee, who, with his naked hands, convinced in thirty-five minutes nine larger men than himself of the incontrovertible fact that you cannot keep a good man down.

TO THE AMERICAN SHIPOWNER

As exemplified in the persons of my good friends,

John H. Rossiter, Manager of W. R. Grace & Co., of San Francisco.

Edwin A. Christenson, President of the Sudden & Christenson S.S. Line, of San Francisco.

John R. Hanify, President of the John R. Hanify Company, of San Francisco.

TO THE PACIFIC COAST LUMBERMAN

As exemplified in the person of my good friend,

Augustus J. ("Gus") Russell, California Manager for the Portland Lumber Company, and my personal representative, without salary, in the wholesale lumber trade, ever since I abandoned lumber for literature.

TO FREIGHT, SHIP, AND MARINE INSURANCE BROKERS

As exemplified in the persons of my good friends,

Messrs. E. B. Smith, Oscar J. Beyfuss, and Allan Hayes.

This volume is dedicated, without charge for the advertising but with profound appreciation of the part they have made in making this book possible. With the author they must bear an equal burden of whatever of praise or censure shall entail.

CHAPTER I.
MASTER OF MANY SHIPS AND SKIPPER OF NONE

A psychologist would have termed Alden P. Ricks an individualist, but his associates in the wholesale lumber and shipping trade of the Pacific Coast proclaimed him a character.

In his youth he had made one voyage round Cape Horn as a cabin boy, his subsequent nautical experience having been confined to the presidency of the Blue Star Navigation Company and occasional voyages as a first-cabin passenger. Notwithstanding this apparent lack of salt-water wisdom, however, his intimate knowledge of ships and the men who go down to the sea in them, together with his very distinct personality, had conduced to provide him with a courtesy title in his old age.

It is more than probable that, had Alden P. Ricks been a large, commanding person possessed of the dignity the average citizen associates with men of equal financial rating, the Street would have called him Captain Ricks. Had he lacked these characteristics, but borne nevertheless even a remote resemblance to a retired mariner, his world would have hailed him as Old Cap Ricks; but since he was what he was—a dapper, precise, shrewd, lovable little old man with mild, paternal blue eyes, a keen sense of humor and a Henry Clay collar, which latter, together with a silk top hat, had distinguished him on 'Change for forty years—it was inevitable that along the Embarcadero and up California Street he should bear the distinguishing appellation of Cappy. In any other line of human endeavor he would have been called Pappy—he was that type of man.

Cappy Ricks had so much money, amassed in the wholesale lumber and shipping business, that he had to engage some very expensive men to take care of it for him. He owned the majority of the stock of the Ricks Lumber and Logging Company, with sawmills and timberlands in California, Oregon and Washington; his young men had to sell a million feet of lumber daily in order to keep pace with the output, while the vessels of the Blue Star Navigation Company, also controlled by Cappy, freighted it. There were thirty-odd vessels in the Blue Star fleet—windjammers and steam schooners; and Cappy was registered as managing owner of every one.

Following that point in his career when the young fellows on the Street, discovering that he was a true-blue sport, had commenced to fraternize with him and call him Cappy, the old gentleman ceased to devote his attention to the details of his business. He was just beginning to enjoy life; so he shifted the real work of his multifarious interests to the capable shoulders of a Mr. John P. Skinner, who fitted into his niche in the business as naturally as the kernel of a healthy walnut fits its shell. Mr. Skinner was a man still on the sunny side of middle life, smart, capable, cold-blooded, a little bumptious, and, like the late Julius Caesar, ambitious.

No sooner had Cappy commenced to take life easy than Skinner commenced to dominate the business. He attended an efficiency congress and came home with a collection of newfangled ideas that eliminated from the office all the joy and contentment old Cappy Ricks had been a life-time installing. He inaugurated card systems and short cuts in bookkeeping that drove Cappy to the verge of insanity, because he could never go to the books himself and find out anything about his own business. He had to ask Mr. Skinner—which made Skinner an important individual.

With the passage of five years the general manager was high and low justice in Cappy's offices, and had mastered the not-too-difficult art of dominating his employer, for Cappy seldom seriously disagreed with those he trusted. He saved all his fighting force for his competitors.

However, Cappy's interest in the Blue Star Navigation Company did not wane with the cessation of his activities as chief kicker. Ordinarily, Mr. Skinner bossed the navigation company as he bossed the lumber business, for Cappy's private office was merely headquarters for receiving mail, reading the newspapers, receiving visitors, smoking an after-luncheon cigar, and having a little nap from three o'clock until four, at which hour Cappy laid aside the cares of business and put in two hours at bridge in his club.

Despite this apparent indifference to business, however, Mr. Skinner handled the navigation company with gloves; for, if Cappy dozed in his office, he had a habit of keeping one eye open, so to speak, and every little while he would wake up and veto an order of Skinner's, of which the latter would have been willing to take an oath Cappy had never heard. In the matter of engaging new skippers or discharging old ones Mr. Skinner had to be very careful. Cappy always declared that any clerk can negotiate successfully a charter at the going rates in a stiff market, but skippers are, in the final analysis, the Genii of the Dividends. And Cappy knew skippers. He could get more loyalty out of them with a mere pat on the back and a kindly word than could Mr. Skinner, with all his threats, nagging and driving, yet he was an employer who demanded a full measure of service, and never permitted sentiment to plead for an incompetent. And his ships were his pets; in his affections they occupied a position but one degree removed from that occupied by his only child, in consequence of which he was mighty particular who hung up his master's ticket in the cabin of a Blue Star ship. Some idea of the scrupulous care with which he examined all applicants for a skipper's berth may be gleaned from the fact that any man discharged from a Blue Star ship stood as much chance of obtaining a berth with one of Cappy Ricks' competitors as a celluloid dog chasing an asbestos cat through Hades.

The reader will readily appreciate, therefore, the apprehensions which assailed Cappy Ricks when the Blue Star Navigation Company discovered it had on its payroll one Matthew Peasley, a Nobody from Nowhere, who not only had the insufferable impudence to apply for a job skippering the finest windjammer in the fleet, but when rebuffed in no uncertain terms, refused to withdraw his application, and defied his owners to fire him. Such a preposterous state of affairs borders so closely on the realm of fancy as to require explanation; hence, for the nonce let us leave Cappy Ricks and Mr. Skinner to their sordid task of squeezing dividends out of the Blue Star Navigation Company and turn the searchlight of inquiry upon the amazing Matthew.

CHAPTER II.
THE MAN FROM BLUE WATER

If, instead of advancing the theory that man sprang from a monkey, Darwin had elected to nominate the duck for that dubious honor, there is no doubt but that he would have pointed to the Peasley family, of Thomaston, Maine, as evidence of the correctness of his theory of evolution. The most casual student of natural history knows that the instant a duckling chips its shell it toddles straightway to the nearest water. The instant a male Peasley could cut his mother's apron strings, he, also, made for the nearest water, for the Peasleys had always been sailors, a statement which a perusal of the tombstones in Thomaston cemetery will amply justify. Indeed, a Peasley who had not acquired his master's ticket prior to his twenty-fifth birthday was one of two things — a disgrace to the family or a corpse. Consequently, since the traditions of his tribe were very strong in Matthew Peasley VI, it occasioned no comment in Thomaston when, having acquired a grammar school education, he answered the call of his destiny and fared forth to blue water and his first taste of dog's body and salt horse.

When he was fourteen years old and very large for his age, Matt commenced his apprenticeship in a codfisher on the Grand Banks, which, when all is said and done, constitutes the finest training school in the world for sailors. By the time he was seventeen he had made one voyage to Rio de Janeiro in a big square-rigger out of Portland; and so smart and capable an A.B. was he for his years that the Old Man took a shine to him. Confidentially he informed young Matt that if the latter would stay by the ship, in due course a billet as third mate should be the reward of his fealty. The Old Man didn't need a third mate any more than he needed a tail, but Matt Peasley looked like a comer to him and he wanted an excuse to encourage the boy by berthing him aft; also it sounds far better to be known as a third mate instead of a mate's bosun, which was, in reality, the position the Old Man had promised Matt. The latter promptly agreed to this program and the skipper loaned him his copy of Bowditch.

Upon his return from his first voyage as third mate Matt went up for his second mate's certificate and passed very handily. Naturally he expected prompt promotion, but the Old Man knew the value of experience in a second mate—also the value of years and physical weight; so he informed young Matt he was entirely too precocious and that to sail as second mate before he was nineteen might tend to swell his ego. Consequently Matt made a voyage to Liverpool and back as third mate before the Old Man promoted him.

For a year, Matt Peasley did nicely; then, in a gale off the Orinoco River, with the captain too ill to appear on deck, the first mate went by the board, leaving the command of the ship to young Matt. She was dismasted at the time, but the lad brought her into Rio on the stumps, thus attracting some little attention to himself from his owners, who paid his passage back to Portland by steamer and found a second mate's berth for him in one of their clipper ships bound round the Horn.

Of course Matt was too young to know they had their eyes on him for future skipper material and were sending him around Cape Horn for the invaluable experience he would encounter on such a voyage. All he realized was that he was going round the Horn, as became one of the House of Peasley, no member of which would ever regard him as a real sailor until he could point to a Cape Horn diploma as evidence that he had graduated from the school for amateurs.

Matt Peasley lacked two months of his twentieth birthday when he stepped onto a San Francisco dock, in his pocket a highly complimentary discharge as second mate from the master of the clipper ship—for Matt had elected to quit. In fact, he had to, for on the way round the mate had picked on him and called him Sonny and Mother's Darling Boy; and Matt, having, in the terminology of the forecastle, come aboard through the hawse pipes, knew himself for a man and a sailor, despite the paucity of whiskers on his big, square boyish chin.

Accordingly he had advised the mate to address him only in the line of duty, on which occasions he desired to be referred to as Mr. Peasley, and, the mate demurring from this program, the customary maritime fracas had ensued. Consequently, somebody had to quit on arrival at San Francisco; and since, Matt was the last to come, he was the first to go. On the strength of his two previous discharges he shipped as second mate on the bark Andrew Welch, for a voyage to Honolulu and back; then, his services as second mate being all in, he went before the inspectors for his first mate's ticket and was awarded an unlimited license.

Matt was now past twenty; and, though not fully filled out, he was big enough to be a chief kicker anywhere. Six feet three in his bare feet; two hundred pounds in the buff; lean, lithe and supple as a panther, the mere sight of his big lumpy shoulders would have been sufficient to have quelled an incipient mutiny. Nevertheless, graduate that he was of a hard, hard school, his face was that of an innocent, trusting, good-natured, immature boy, proclaiming him exactly what he knew his men called him—a big, over-grown kid. He hated himself for his glorious youth.

"You're pretty much of a child to have an unlimited ticket, my son," the supervising inspector informed him. "However, you've had the experience and your record is far above the average, so we're going to issue the license; but if you'll take a bit of advice from an old sailor you'll be content to go as second mate for a year or two more, until your jowls blacken up a bit and you get a trifle thicker in the middle."

With the impudence and irreverence of his tender years, however, Matt Peasley scorned this well-meant advice, notwithstanding the fact that he knew it to be sound, for by shipping as second mate and remaining in the same ship, sooner or later his chance would come. The first mate would quit, or be promoted or drowned, or get drunk; and then his shoes would be waiting for Matt tried and true, and the holder of a first mate's ticket.

However, there is an old saw to the effect that youth must be served, and young Matt desired a helping totally disproportionate to his years, if not to his experience; hence he elected to ignore the fact that shipmasters are wary of chief mates until they have first tried them out as second mates and learned their strength and their weaknesses. Being very human, Matt thought he should prove the exception to a fairly hard-and-fast rule.

He had slept one night on a covered dock and skipped three meals before it occurred to him that he had pursued the wrong tactics. He was too far from Thomaston, Maine, where the majority of sailors have gone to school with their captains. Back home there were a dozen masters who knew his people, who knew him and his proved ability; but out here on the Pacific Coast the skippers were nearly all Scandinavians, and Matt had to show them something besides his documents.

He had failed signally to procure a single opportunity to demonstrate his fitness for an executive position. After abandoning his plan to ship as chief mate he had sought a second mate's berth, but failing to find one, and with each idle day making deeper inroads into his scant savings, he had at length descended to the ignominy of considering a job as bosun. Even that was not forthcoming, and now his money was entirely dissipated.

Now, when a big overgrown kid finds himself penniless three thousand miles from a friend and minus three meals in succession, the fourth omission of the daily bread is not likely to pass without violent protest. Matt was still a growing boy, with a growing boy's appetite; consequently on the morning of his second day of fasting he came to the conclusion that, with so much of his life before him, a few months wasted would, after all, have no material bearing on his future; so he accepted a two months advance from a crimp and shipped aboard the American barkentine Retriever as a common A.B. — a most disgraceful action on the part of a boy, who, since eighteenth birthday, had been used to having old sailors touch their foretop to him and address him as "Mr. Peasley, sir."

CHAPTER III.
UNDER THE BLUE STAR FLAG

Matt had been attracted to the barkentine Retriever for two very potent reasons — the first was a delicious odor of stew emanating from her galley; the second was her house flag, a single large, five-pointed blue star on a field of white with scarlet trimming. Garnished left and right with a golden wreath and below with the word Captain, Matt Peasley knew that house flag, in miniature, would look exceedingly well on the front of a uniform cap; for he now made up his mind to enter one service and stick to it until his abilities should receive their inevitable reward. To ship as a foremast hand and rise to captain would be a proud record; so Matt throttled his pride and faced the future with confidence, and a stomach quite filled with very good beef stew.

From the cook he learned that the Retriever carried a million feet of lumber; that she was owned by Cappy Ricks; that Cappy Ricks was the president of the Blue Star Navigation Company, and the most contemptible old scoundrel in all the world; that the skipper was a blue-nose and a devil and a fine man rolled into one; that the barkentine could sail like a yacht; and that presently they would up-hook and off to Grays Harbor, Washington, there to load a cargo of fir lumber for Cape Town. And would Matt mind slipping ashore and buying the cook a bottle of whiskey, for which the latter would settle very minute he could get an advance out of the Old Man. No? Disgusted, the cook rattled his pans and dismissed Matt as one unworthy of further confidence.

Just before the tug came alongside to snake her outside the Heads, the mate came aboard with his lee rail pretty well under and was indiscreet enough to toss a piece of his lip at the Old Man. Five minutes later he was paid and off and kicked out on the dock, while the cook packed his sea bag and tossed it overside after him. The captain, thereupon, bawled for the second mate, who came running. Matt noticed this and decided that should the Old Man ever bawl for him he would come running too.

"Mr. Swenson, you have a chief mate's license, have you not?"

"Yes, sir."

"Very well. You're the first mate. Mr. Lindstrom"—turning to the bosun—"you've waited a year for your chance, and here it is. You're the second mate. Bosun!" He was looking straight at Matt Peasley as he spoke. Matt did not stir. "Hey, there," the skipper roared, "you big mountain of meat, step lively!"

Matt stepped lively.

"I am not the bosun, sir," he explained. "I'm just A.B."

"How dare you contradict me?" the Old Man growled. "I tell you, you don't know what you are yet, barring the fact that you're an American, and the only one, with the exception of myself, in the whole damned Scowegian crew. Do you think you could get away with a bosun's job?"

"I could get away with your job if I had the chance, sir," Matt declared, almost impudently.

"There she blows!" the Old Man declared. "Bless me, if you're not a Native Son! Nobody but a Native Son would be that fresh. I suppose this is your second voyage, you puling baby?"

Matt Peasley's dander was up instantly.

"I'm sailor enough to know my way alow or aloft in any weather, sir," he retorted.

The captain saw his opening and struck.

"What's the ring-tail?" he demanded.

"It's a studdin'-s'l on the gaff of a fore-an'-aft, sail, sir. You haven't got one on the Retriever, sir."

"Huh! You've been reading W. Clark Russell's sea yarns," the skipper charged. "He was quite a pen-an'-paper sailor when it came to square-rigged ships, but he didn't have much to say about six-masted schooners. You see, they didn't build them in his day. Now then, son, name the sticks on a six-legged schooner, and be sure and name 'em right."

"Fore, main, mizzen, spanker, jigger and driver, sir," Matt fired back at him.

"Bully for you, my son. You're the third mate. Cappy Ricks allows me the luxury of a third mate whenever I run across a young fellow that appears to be worth a whoop in hell, so grab your duds, and go aft, and don't bring any cockroaches with you. I'll dig up a bosun among the squareheads."

"Thank you, sir."

"Name?"

"Mr. Peasley, sir."

Since he was no longer an A B., young Matt concluded he might as well accord himself the respect due him as a ship's officer; so he tacked on the Mister, just to show the Old Man he knew his place. The master noted that; also, the slurring of the sir as only a sailor can slur it.

"I shouldn't wonder if you'd do," he remarked as Matt passed him on his way to the forecastle for his dunnage.

On his way back he carried his bag over his shoulder and his framed license in his left hand. Two savages were following with his sea chest.

"I do declare!" the skipper cried. "If that lubberly boy hasn't got some sort of a ticket! Let me see it, Mr. Peasley." And he snatched it out of his grasp.

"So, you're a first mate of sail, for any ocean and any tonnage, eh?" he said presently. "Are you sure this ticket doesn't belong to your father?"

"Sir," declared the exasperated Matt, "I never asked you for this job of third mate; and if I've got to stomach your insults to hold it down I don't want it. That's my ticket and I'm fully capable of living up to it."

"I'm glad to hear that, Mr. Peasley, because if you're not I'll be the first one to find it out — and don't you forget it! I'll have no marine impostors aboard my ship. Where do they ship little boys before the mast, Mr. Peasley?"

"On the Grand Banks, sir."

"I beg your pardon," said the skipper; "but really I thought you were a Native Son. My father was drowned there thirty years ago."

"The Peasleys have all died on the Banks sir," Matt replied, much mollified.

"We'll go down into my cabin and drink a toast to their memory, Mr. Peasley. It isn't often we skippers out here meet one of our own."

It is hard for a Down-Easter, even though he may have lost the speech of his people, not to be, partial to his own; and Captain Noah Kendall, of the barkentine Retriever, was all the cook had declared him to be. He scolded his Norsk mates so bitterly while the vessel was taking on cargo at Grays Harbor that both came and asked for their time an hour before the vessel sailed. However, the old man was aware they would do this, for he had handled that breed too long not to know that the Scandinavian sailor on the Pacific Coast quits his job on the slightest pretext, but never dreams of leaving until he knows that by so doing he can embarrass the master or owners. Even if the mates had not quit, Kendall would have discharged them, for it had been in his mind to try Matt Peasley out as chief mate, and acquire a second mate with a sweeter disposition than that possessed by the late incumbent.

No sooner had the Norsk mates departed than Captain Noah Kendall paid a visit to Captain McBride in command of the schooner Nokomis (also a Blue Star vessel), which had arrived that day and was waiting for the Retriever's berth at the mill dock, in order to commence loading.

"Mac," quoth Captain Noah, "what kind of a second mate have you got?"

"A no-good Irish hound named Murphy," McBride replied promptly, for he had heard rumors of war aboard the Retriever and something told him Kendall had come to borrow his second mate, in order that the Retriever might tow out immediately. A canny, cunning lad was McBride, but for all his Scotch blood he was no match for Captain Noah Kendall.

"I heard he wasn't worth two squirts of bilge water," Captain Noah lied glibly. "However, I'll take him off your hands and reimburse you for the expense of bringing his successor down from Seattle or up from San Francisco. My two mates have just asked to be paid off, and despite the fact that they have signed articles, I've let them go. No use going to sea with a pair of sulky mates, you know. Fortunately, I had a young Down-Easter aboard and I've put him in as first mate—"

"Noah," urged McBride. "I wouldn't advise you to take this man Murphy."

"Beggars can't be choosers," Captain Noah replied mournfully. "The tide serves in half an hour and the tug is alongside the Retriever now. If I have to wire to Seattle for a second mate I may not be able to get one—and if I am forced to wire to San Francisco I may be stuck here a week. I've shipped my crew and paid them all in advance, and if I don't get to sea in an hour I'll lose every man Jack of them, and have it all to do over again."

"Well, I'll speak to the fellow for you, Noah," McBride suggested, and darted out of the cabin to interview the said Murphy. Two minutes later he was back.

"Sorry, Noah, but Murphy says he wouldn't sign up for a trip to Cape Town at chief mate's wages."

"I'm sorry, too, Mac," Captain Noah answered resignedly. "I'm sorry you're such a liar. My grief is only compensated by the knowledge that Murphy is not aboard the Nokomis at this minute, and, if you did any talking while you were out on deck a minute ago you must have talked to yourself. Do I get this man, Murphy and thus save the Blue Star Navigation Company five hundred dollars or must I wire Cappy Ricks to wire you to do your duty by the company?"

"You infernal thief," shouted McBride, "you're taking the best second mate I've had in years."

"Never mind that. Do I get Mike Murphy peaceably or—"

"You've got him already" McBride charged.

"You're better at telling the truth than you are at lying, Angus McBride. You'll have plenty of time to get a second mate while the Nokomis is loading, and you can send the bill for his railroad fare to Cappy Ricks and tell him to charge it to the Retriever."

McBride tried to appear aggrieved, but failed. He burst out laughing, and reached for the locker in which he kept the schooner's supply of grog.

"Would it was prussic acid," he growled.

"Don't say I went behind your back and stole your mate," Kendall retorted. "And if your second mate is as poor as your whiskey," he added, piling insult on to injury, "you can have him back when I return from Cape Town."

Matt Peasley felt that he was going to like Michael J. Murphy. The latter was Irish, but he had left Ireland at a very tender age and was, to all intents and purposes, a breezy American citizen, and while he wore a slight cauliflower in one ear, his broad, kindly humorous face and alert, bustling manner was assurance that he would be an easy man to get along with. When the Old Man introduced him to Matt, he extended a horny right hand that closed on Matt's like the jaws of a dredger, the while he ran an equally horny left hand up and down the chief mate's arm.

"I'm sure we'll get along famously together, Mr. Murphy," Matt suggested.

Again Mr. Murphy ran his hand over that great arm.

"You know it!" he declared with conviction.

Captain Noah laughed aloud, and as Matt scampered forward over the deckload, herding his savages before him, to receive the tug's breast line and make it fast on the bitts the skipper turned to Mr. Murphy.

"There's a lad for you," he declared.

"He has manners and muscle, and those are two things that seldom go together," Mr. Murphy rejoined. "He's Down-Easter, I see. Did Cappy Ricks send him to you, sir?"

"No—not that he wouldn't, however, if he'd ever met the boy. The crimp brought him aboard with the sweepings and scrapings of San Francisco."

"I hope he wasn't drunk—like the rest," Mr. Murphy answered anxiously. "'Twould be a sin to desecrate that lovely body with whiskey."

"He was bung up and bilge free—and that's why he's chief kicker now. The hawser's fast for'd, Mr. Murphy. Cast off your stern line."

"All clear for'd, sir," Matt Peasley's shout came ranging down the wind, and the tug snatched the big barkentine out from the mill dock into the stream where she cast her off, put her big towing hawser aboard, paid it out and started for Grays Harbor bar.

CHAPTER IV.
BAD NEWS FROM CAPE TOWN

On a certain day in February Mr. Skinner, coming into Cappy Ricks' office with a cablegram in his hand, found his employer doubled up at his desk and laughing in senile glee.

"I have a cablegram—" Mr. Skinner began.

"I have a good story," Cappy interrupted. "Let me tell it to you, Skinner. Oh, dear! I believe this is about going to kill the boys up on 'Change when I tell them." He wiped his eyes, controlled his mirth and turned to the general manager. "Skinner," he said, "did you know I had gotten back into the harness while you were up at the Astoria mill? Well I did, Skinner. I had to, you know. If it was the last act of my life I had to square accounts with that man Hudner, of the Black Butte Lumber Company."

Mr. Skinner nodded. He was aware of the feud that existed between Cappy and Hudner, and the reasons therefor. The latter had stolen from Cappy a stenographer, who had grown to spinsterhood in his employ—one of those rare stenographers who do half a man's thinking for him. Cappy always paid a little more than the top of the market for clever service; and whenever, a competitor stole one of his favorite employees, sooner or later that competitor paid for his sins, "through the nose."

"While you were away," Cappy went on, "I met Hudner a luncheon. 'Hudner,' I said, 'It's been my experience that nobody gets anything good in this world without paying for it—and you stole the finest stenographer I ever had. So I'm going to make you pay for her. See if I don't.' Well, sir, Skinner, he laughed at me and told me to go as far as I liked; and, a number of my youthful friends being present, they each bet Hudner a five-dollar hat I'd hang his hide on my fence within sixty days.

"Well, Skinner, you know me. Any time it's raining duck soup you'll never catch me out with a fork; and, of course, when the boys showed such faith in my ability to trim Hudner I had to make good. I have a letter from Hudner to prove it; and to-day at luncheon, when we're all gathered at the Round Table, I'm going to read that letter and my reply to the same; and Hudner will have fifty dollars' worth of hat bills to pay!"

"How did you tan his pelt?" Skinner queried.

"Easy! While you were away I chartered his steamer Chehalis for a load of redwood lumber from Humboldt Bay to San Francisco at three dollars and a half a thousand feet. Of course, you know a boat like the Chehalis, with a big pay-roll, will break just even on such a low freight rate; but inasmuch as he was going to lay the Chehalis up in Oakland Creek, owing to lack of business, when I offered him a load of redwood he concluded to take it, just to keep the vessel moving and pay expenses. I stipulated discharge in San Francisco Bay.

"Well, sir, when the Chehalis got to our mill, Skinner, I ordered them to load her with sinkers — oh! oh, this will be the death of me yet, Skinner. And we gave her poor dispatch in loading. Then she had to lay behind the bar two days longer before she could cross out; and when she got here I ordered her to discharge into the British bark Glengarry — and discharging from one vessel in to another is the slowest work in the world. And Hudner — he's — written — me, Skinner, declaring he'll never charter a boat to me again; says the Chehalis lost two thousand dollars on the voyage." And Cappy went off into a gale of laughter, and handed Skinner the letter to read.

For the benefit of the reader, who may desire a closer insight into Cappy's Machiavellian nature, be it known that a sinker is a heavy, close-grained clear redwood butt-log, which, if cut in the spring, when the tree is alive with sap, is so heavy it will not float in the millpond; hence the term sinker. A vessel laden with lumber sawed from sinkers, therefore, will carry just fifty per cent. of her customary cargo; and unless the freight rate be extremely high, she cannot make money.

"Do you know, Skinner," Cappy announced presently, "I think you'd better hunt up a steady job for me! Dadding it, boy, I never knew there was so much fun in business until I had practically retired! Really, Skinner, I must take more interest in my affairs."

"Here's something to sharpen your teeth on, Mr. Ricks," the general manager replied, and presented the cablegram he had been holding for five minutes.

Cappy took it and read, thereby becoming aware for the first time, that he had in his employ an individual by the name of Matthew Peasley.

Cape Town, February 15, —.

Bluestar, San Francisco:

Captain knifed Kru boy argument boat fare. Instruct consignees honor my drafts as captain.

Matthew Peasley, Mate.

"The murdering black hound!" Cappy murmured in an awed voice. "If he hasn't gone and killed the best skipper I ever had! Poor Kendall! Why, Noah and I were good friends, Skinner. Every time the Retriever touched in at her home port I always had Noah Kendall up to the house for dinner, and we went to the theatre together afterward. Thank God! It isn't a week since his life insurance premium fell due and I had the cashier pay it."

Cappy sat gazing dejectedly at the carpet.

"Poor old Cap'n Noah!" he soliloquized aloud. "Twenty-five years you sailed under the Blue Star, and in all that time there was never once when I had to jack up and tell you to 'tend to business. And, Noah, you could make a suit of sails last longer than any man I ever knew; but you did have a hell of a temper." And having delivered this touching eulogy on the late Captain Kendall, Cappy roused himself and faced Skinner.

"I should say I have a job on my hands," he announced, "with the finest sailing ship in the fleet down in South Africa without a skipper! Skinner, I'll tell you what you do, my boy: You dictate the nicest letter you know how to dictate to Noah's widow, up in Port Townsend. Tell her how much we thought of Noah and extend our sympathy, and a check for his next three months' salary. Put her on my private pension list, Skinner, and send her Cap'n Noah's salary every quarter-day as long as she lives. Tell her we'll attend to the collection of the life insurance and will bring Noah's body home to Port Townsend at our own expense. It's the least we can do, Skinner. He was the only skipper I ever had who did not, at one time or another, manage to embroil me in a lawsuit. Who are our consignees at Cape Town?"

"The Harlow & Benton Company, Limited."

"Cable them for confirmation of the mate's message, and request them to have Cap'n Noah's body embalmed and shipped to Port Townsend, Washington, prepaid, deducting charges from our invoice."

CHAPTER V.
MATT PEASLEY ASSUMES OFFICE

The death of Captain Noah Kendall, while profoundly deplored by his next in command, first mate Matthew Peasley, had not been permitted by that brisk young man to interfere in the least with the task of getting the cargo out of the Retriever, for sailoring, like soldiering, is a profession in which sentiment is a secondary consideration. Each day of demurrage to a ship like the Retriever, even at the prevailing low freight rate, meant a loss of at least a hundred dollars to the owners, and since navigating a ship safely and expeditiously is the least of a good skipper's duties, and since, further, Matt Peasley was determined to be a skipper in the not very distant future, he concluded to give his owners evidence of the fact that he was, in addition to being a navigator, also a first-class "hustler." If the Retriever made a loss on that voyage he was resolved that no blame should attach to him.

"Skipper's dead, Mike," he announced to Mr. Murphy, the second mate. "Policeman in a small boat alongside says the old man got into a row with the Kru boy that rowed him ashore and the black scoundrel skewered him. I'm going ashore to look after his body and order a tug to kick us into our berth. I guess the old man didn't get time to attend to the business that brought him ashore, poor fellow."

"Very well, Sir," Mr. Murphy replied, and murmured some commonplace expression of regret. He was not particularly shocked for he had lost shipmates in a hurry before now.

Matt Peasley proceeded to the beach, attended to the necessary details incident to the skipper's untimely removal, was informed by the Harlow & Benton Company, Limited, of the location of the berth he was to discharge, ordered a tug for that afternoon, went to the cable office, registered his cable address, sent a cablegram to the owners and returned to the ship.

"Well, Mike," he announced to the second mate, "I guess I'm the skipper; following the same line of deduction, I guess you're the chief mate, so I'll move my dunnage into the old man's cabin and you move into mine. I'll pick up a second mate in Cape Town before we leave."

Mr. Murphy eyed his youthful superior with mild curiosity, not untempered with amusement. "Thank you for the promotion, Captain Matt," he replied. "However, if you'll excuse my apparent impudence on the grounds that I'm about fifteen years older than you and have been longer in the Blue Star employ, I'd like to make a suggestion."

"Fire away, Mike."

Mr. Murphy hitched his belt, walked to the rail, spat tobacco juice from between his fingers and came back. "You're the youngest chief mate I've ever seen, and this is your first berth in that capacity," he began. "Suppose you hang on to it and don't be so infernally generous."

"But you have a first mate's license, haven't you?"

"Certainly. But—"

"No ifs or buts, Mike. The skipper's dead; I was first mate; consequently I take command of the ship, and by virtue of my authority I appoint you first mate. That goes. You'll do one of two things, Mike. You'll be first mate or get out of the ship."

Michael J. Murphy grinned. "You mean that?"

"Naturally."

"If you stick by that determination you'll find yourself on the beach in Cape Town, unless you conclude to take my recently vacated berth as second mate. And I'd hate like the devil to have you do that. There's neither sense nor profit for you in swapping jobs with me."

"But I tell you I'm going to be skipper."

"I know—until old Cappy Ricks sends down a relief captain. If you promote me now, the relief captain may conclude to retain me as first mate and then you'd have to take my job or quit the ship; and of course I wouldn't care to have that happen. I'd have to quit the ship, too. I wouldn't care to do that. I've made up my mind to sail under the Blue Star flag for the rest of my natural life and I'd hate to have to change my mind."

"I've made up my mind to the same thing, Mike, and I know I'm not going to change my mind."

"Well, then, Matt, you stick in your first mate's berth and I'll be satisfied with my second mate's berth."

"I suppose you'll say next that the relief skipper will be happy in poor old Captain Noah's berth, eh?" Matt interrupted. He grinned at Mr. Murphy.

"Mike, listen to me. There isn't going to be any relief skipper. You're going back to Hoquiam, Grays Harbor, Washington, U. S. A., as chief kicker of the barkentine Retriever, and you're going to take orders from me all the way. In fact, you might as well begin right now. Take your duds and move into my cabin."

"Matt," Mr. Murphy pleaded earnestly, "you don't know Cappy Ricks, do you?"

"No, but I'll get acquainted with him in due course. Don't let that worry you Mike."

"All right, I won't. But what does worry me is the fact that Cappy Ricks doesn't know you.

"Does he know you?"

"No."

"Do you know him?"

"Yes, by proxy. I've heard a lot about him, and that's why I'm in his employ and resolved to stay there. If a man sails under the Blue Star flag long enough and behaves himself and displays a little human intelligence from time to time sooner or later he gets his chance. Cappy Ricks does all the hiring and firing for the fleet, and whenever he has a good job to fill, he never goes outside his own employ to fill it. He always promotes the deserving. You cabled him, of course, that Captain Kendall has been killed."

"Yes, I did. And I cabled him also to cable me authority to draw drafts, as skipper, in order to disburse the vessel."

"Just like a kid! Just like a kid!" Mr. Murphy groaned. "That finishes you, Matt. Cappy'll think you're fresh and you'll be ten years proving to him you are not."

"It proves I'm on the job," Matt protested doggedly.

"No matter, Matt. Cappy Ricks will go over the list of his skippers due for promotion into a larger ship and more pay, and right away he'll start Captain Noah's successor for Cape Town to bring the ship home."

"If he does, Mike, he's crazy."

"Oh, he's crazy enough, Matt, like a fox—so blamed crazy he will not consider handing over this Retriever to an untried and unknown man who has been in his employ for less than a voyage. Why, I wouldn't myself."

"Maybe you think he'll hand her over to you?" Matt asked, with the suspicion and impetuosity of youth.

"Boy," said Mr. Murphy patiently, "you're getting into deep water close to the shore. Starboard your helm and put her on the other tack. If he gives her to me—which he will not—I'll take her. I've been three years in his employ. I'm capable—"

"Mike," Matt interrupted. "I like you fine, but I want to tell you that if Cappy Ricks cabled you to take charge, I wouldn't let you. I'm next in command, and it's only etiquette that I should have my chance."

"Then," Mr. Murphy murmured sententiously, "there'd be a fight with skin gloves and I'm afraid you'd get licked, son. I wasted a good many years in the navy, Matt, and there I learned two things—how to obey and how to fight with my fists. I was the champion amateur light-heavy-weight of the Atlantic fleet, and every once in a while something happens to prove to me that I'm far from being a slouch even at this late date."

"No offense, Mike. We're crossing our bridges before we come to them, and besides, I didn't intend to be offensive."

"I understand. Our conversation was entirely academic," Murphy admitted graciously.

"You said you learned to obey in the navy," Matt suggested. "What's the matter with obeying my last order?"

"All right, Matt. I'll obey. But remember, I have given you fair warning. If I move into your cabin to-day, I'll not move out when the relief skipper comes."

"I'll take a chance," said Matt Peasley.

CHAPTER VI.
WORDY WAR AT A DOLLAR A WORD

While the capable Mr. Skinner was preparing the reply to Matt Peasley's cablegram, and dictating for Cappy Ricks' signature a letter to Noah Kendall's widow, Cappy was busy at the telephone. First he retailed the news to the Merchants' Exchange, to be bulletined on the blackboard and read by Captain Noah's friends; next he called up the secretary of the American Shipmasters' Association, of which the deceased had been a member, and lastly he communicated the sad tidings to the water-front reporters of all the daily papers. This detail attended to, Cappy's active mind returned to more practical and profitable affairs, and he took up Matt Peasley's cablegram. He was deep in a study of it when Mr. Skinner entered with the letter to Mrs. Kendall.

"'Captain knifed, killed, Kru boy argument boat fare,'" Cappy read aloud. "Skinner, my dear boy, what is the cable rate per word to Cape Town?"

"Ninety-eight cents per word," replied Mr. Skinner, who had just looked it up.

"We will if you please, Skinner, confine ourselves to round numbers. There is such a thing as being too exact. Call it a dollar. Figuring on that basis, I see this garrulous mate has squandered five dollars of our money to no purpose—yes, by jingo, more than that. He might have used the code book! Hum-m-m! Ahem! Harump-h-h-h! Skinner, this fellow will not do. He is too windy. Skinner, he tells the story in eight words, and forgets to use his code book. Give me a skipper, Skinner, my boy, who always has his owner's interest at heart and displays a commendable discretion in limiting the depredations practiced by the cable company. For instance, the man Peasley might have omitted the word knifed; also the explanatory words, argument boat fare, and the word mate. Though regretting Noah's demise most keenly, as business men we are not cable-gramically interested in the means employed to accomplish his removal. Neither do the causes leading up to the tragedy interest us. The man Peasley should merely have said "Captain murdered." Also, he might have trusted to us to realize that when the captain dies the first mate takes charge. He need not have identified himself—the infernal chatter-box!"

Cappy read the next sentence. "Instruct consignees honor my drafts as captain."

"H'm! Harum-ph! He might have said 'please,' Skinner! Sounds devilishly like an order, the way he puts it. Though he is temporarily in command I challenge his right to handle our money until I know more about him. Harum-ph! Reading between the lines, Skinner, I see he says: 'If you send a skipper to Cape Town to bring the Retriever home while I'm on the job, you're crazy.' Look over the vouchers in Cap'n Noah's last report and let us ascertain how long this forceful mate has been in our employ."

Now, the ordinary form of receipt to which a seaman puts his signature when signing clear bears upon its reverse side a series of blank spaces, which the captain must fill in. These blanks provide for mention of the date of signing on, date of discharge, station held on vessel and remarks. On none of the vouchers of the Retriever's last voyage, however, did the name of Matthew Peasley appear.

"Must have shipped in San Francisco just before the vessel sailed for her loading port," Cappy announced. "Send in a boy."

One of Cappy's young men was summoned.

"Son," said Cappy, "you run down, like a good boy, to the office of the Deputy United States Shipping Commissioner and tell him Mr. Ricks would like to see the duplicate copy of the crew list of the barkentine Retriever."

When an American vessel clears for a foreign port the law required that her crew shall be signed on before a Deputy United States Shipping Commissioner, who furnishes a certified copy of the crew list to the captain and retains a duplicate for his own files.

The Blue Star youth returned presently with his duplicate list, on consulting which, to his unspeakable amazement, Cappy Ricks discovered that Matthew Peasley had shipped aboard the Retriever as an able seaman, and that the first mate was one William Olson — which goes to prove that in the heat of passion a skipper will often discharge a mate on the eve of sailing for a foreign port and forget to tell the Deputy Shipping Commissioner anything about it.

"Remarkable," Cappy declared. "Ree-markable!"

"Dirty work here," Mr. Skinner announced. "Captain dead and a common A.B. cabling us for authority to draw drafts as captain, while posing as first mate. Nigger in the woodpile somewhere, Mr. Ricks."

"I'll smoke him out in five minutes, Skinner. Ring up the local inspectors and inquire if, by any chance, they have ever issued a captain's license to one Matthew Peasley."

Skinner obeyed. After a brief wait he was informed that the said Peasley had an unlimited license as first mate of sail, and was entitled to act as second mate of steam vessels up to five hundred tons net register.

"Nothing doing!" Cappy piped. "Skinner, when a mate with an unlimited license ships before the mast, THERE'S A REASON!"

"Drunkard!" Mr. Skinner suggested without an instant's hesitation.

"Eggs-actly, Skinner. Good seaman, I daresay, but worthless and unreliable in an executive capacity, and I can't trust a ripping fine barkentine like the Retriever with that kind of man. I suppose he feels the hankering for a spree coming on right now. Skinner, if we gave the man Peasley permission to draw drafts he'd paint Cape Town red. I feel it in my bones."

"So do I, sir."

"What vessels have we in port at this moment, Skinner?"

"McBride is discharging the Nokomis at Oakland Long Wharf."

"The ideal man." Cappy smote his desk. "I've been wanting to promote Mac into a larger vessel and pay him twenty-five dollars a month more for the past two years. He's too good for a little hooker like the Nokomis, and he's got a steady-going Norwegian mate that's been with him in the Nokomis for three years. Time to take care of that mate. Skinner, I have an idea. See that it is carried through. McBride's mate shall buy out Mac's interest in the Nokomis. If he hasn't the money, tell him I'll lend it to him, secured by the insurance, provided he and McBride can come to terms. See that they do. Tell Mac he's to have the Retriever, and I'll arrange to get Cap'n Noah's interest for him from the estate at a fair figure. Give him expense money and his credentials and tell him to start for Cape Town tomorrow night; and cable the man Peasley to retain charge of the vessel at captain's pay until McBride arrives to relieve him."

Mr. Skinner retired to his office and got down his code book. The general manager knew what he desired to say and hoped he might find something in the code book to help him say it at cut rates, but despairing after a diligent search he finally evolved and dispatched this cablegram to Matt Peasley, addressing it to the cable address of the Retriever.

San Francisco, Feb. 16th, 19 — .

Rickstar,

Cape Town.

Peasley, your meager maritime experience renders prohibitive compliance request. Retain charge master's pay pending arrival successor.

Bluestar.

Having dispatched his message to Matt Peasley, Mr. Skinner, as he thought, had dismissed Peasley from his thoughts forever. It would appear, however, that in this particular the general manager was counting Mother Carey s chickens before they were hatched. He little suspected, in his desire to be fair, even at considerable expense, to inform Matt Peasley just why the Blue Star Navigation Company couldn't possibly hand over its fine barkentine to a stranger, that he had only reopened the controversy; that his unfortunate reference to "meager maritime experience" had flicked Matt Peasley on a raw spot and been provocative of this reply, received the same day:

Cape Town, Feb. 16, 19 — .

Bluestar,
San Francisco.

Skipper dying sea foreign port unwritten maritime law stipulates mate succeeds. Yankee can sail anything afloat. This my chance. Grant it or insure successor's life. Will throw him overboard on arrival.

> Peasley.

Mr. Skinner promptly carried this defi to Cappy Ricks.

"He's a sea-lawyer," Cappy piped angrily. "The scoundrel! The un-mi-ti-ga-ted—scoundrel! Cable him instantly, Skinner, that if he spends another cent of our money in unnecessary cablegrams I'll fire him." He snapped his fingers. "Attend to it, Skinner, attend to it."

Mr. Skinner attended to it, and the following morning he found this reply on his desk when he came down to work:

> Cape Town, Feb. 17, 19—.
>
> Bluestar,
> San Francisco.
>
> Holler when you're hit. Paid for it myself.
> Am I to bring Retriever home?
>
> Peasley.

"I dare say the fellow did," Mr. Skinner informed Cappy. "He has four months' wages coming to him at sixty dollars a month—and if he didn't, why, I'll instruct McBride to deduct the cable charges from his wages when he pays him off."

"I think your reference to his meager maritime experience annoyed him, Skinner," Cappy suggested thoughtfully. "It may be that he is a most excellent sailor. At least, he spends his money like one."

Cappy had no further comment to make, and the reply to this impudent communication was accordingly left to Mr. Skinner, who cabled:

> San Francisco, Feb. 17th, 19—.
>
> Rickstar,
> Cape Town.
>
> No!
>
> Bluestar.

"I think that will settle the upstart," Mr. Skinner declared confidently as he rang for a messenger boy.

It did not. Four hours later he received this:

> Cape Town, Feb. 17, 19—.

> Bluestar,
> San Francisco.
> Why?
>
> > Peasley.

Now it was a custom of Mr. Skinner's, when a subordinate laid claim to an inalienable right which the general manager was not willing to concede, to regard with very grave suspicion that subordinate's loyalty to the company. If the subordinate protested Mr. Skinner would warn him, kindly, quietly, but none the less forcefully; and if he persisted Mr. Skinner would dispense with the services of that subordinate so fast the offender, nine times out of ten, would be left standing in a sort of fog and blinking at the suddenness with which the metaphorical can had, metaphorically speaking, been tied to his caudal appendage. Every large business office has its Skinner—a queer combination of decency, honesty, brains and brutality, a worshiper at the shrine of Mammon in the temple of the great god Business, a reactionary Republican, treasurer of his church and eventually a total loss from diabetes, brought on by lack of exercise and worry over trifles.

However, to return to our particular Mr. Skinner and Matt Peasley, the rebellious. In all justice to Skinner it must be admitted that his first impulse with reference to Matt Peasley was eminently fair. He really desired to convey to this persistent person an intimation to the effect that the latter was, colloquially speaking, monkeying with the buzz-saw and in imminent danger of having his head lopped off; and he would have given it, too, provided the delivery of the ultimatum should not have cost the Blue Star Navigation Company ninety-eight cents a word, including the address. Consequently, Skinner, always efficient and realizing that McBride would doubtless be enabled to pick up another mate in Cape Town, or in a pinch, could dispense with a first mate altogether, made answer to Matt Peasley as follows:

> San Francisco, Feb. 17th, 19—.
>
> Rickstar,
> Cape Town.
>
> Peasley, you are hereby discharged. Turn over command second mate, call consignees your wages immediately.
>
> > Bluestar.

Having dispatched this cablegram and ended it all, as it were, Mr. Skinner next cast his cold gray glance adown the duplicate crew list borrowed from the deputy shipping commissioner, and discovered that the second mate shipped at San Francisco was one Christian Swenson.

"I do hope he's not a drinking man," Skinner sighed. "The Retriever is quite a responsibility to entrust to a man we have never seen or heard of before, but the man Swenson can scarcely be as vicious and insubordinate as this fellow Peasley, and under the circumstances we'll have to run the risk."

And having wotted the which, Mr. Skinner cabled Christian Swenson to take charge of the Retriever, at master's wages, until the arrival of his successor. Next he cabled The Harlow and Benton Company, Limited, requesting them to pay off Matt Peasley and, if necessary, invoke the authorities to remove him from the vessel.

"That fellow is a tough one to handle," he remarked to Cappy Ricks, to whom he showed all the cablegrams, "but I guess this will about cut off his wind."

"A sea lawyer is the curse of the Seven Seas!" Cappy declared waspishly. He was very bitter against Matt Peasley, whom he now regarded as an ally of the piratical cable company.

CHAPTER VII.
CAPPY RICKS MAKES BAD MEDICINE

That afternoon Mr. Skinner herded Captain McBride of the Nokomis and his Norwegian mate into Cappy Ricks' office. Cappy brought them to terms very promptly, and the captain started for New York on the Overland the same night. From New York he was to take passage to Liverpool, thence via the A. D. line to Cape Town. Cappy almost had a bloody sweat when he reflected on the expense for provisions and wages for the crew during the weeks of idleness while McBride was on the way to join the Retriever. Both he and Mr. Skinner had decided that nothing could be gained by informing McBride, who was a little, mild-mannered gentleman with gold eyeglasses, of the potential ducking that awaited him at the hands of Matt Peasley; for just before McBride said good-bye and started for the train Cappy and Mr. Skinner discovered that their apple cart again had been upset. The following cablegram received from Matt Peasley knocked into a cocked hat all their high hopes of ridding themselves of the incubus.

> Cape Town, Feb. 17, 19—.
>
> Bluestar,
>   San Francisco.
>
> *Swenson fired before leaving San Francisco. Second mate Murphy declines take your orders, claiming me superior officer; I decline also, claiming captain en route my superior officer. Owner can fire captain but only captain can fire or disrate ship's officers. Besides I shipped for the round trip.*
>
>   *Peasley.*

"Well," said Cappy, "what do you know about that? He clings to us like a barnacle or a poor relation—and the worst of it is the damned sea lawyer is absolutely right. We have no authority to fire him, Skinner. Just think of a government that will permit such a ridiculous state of affairs as that to exist! Think of it, Skinner! We hire the man Peasley but we can't fire him—and in the meantime he'll roost in Cap'n Noah's cabin and run up bills on us and consume our groceries and draw master's pay until McBride arrives and discharges him."

For geographical and financial reasons Cappy Ricks was barred from quarreling with Matt Peasley. However, he was as cross as a setting hen and just naturally had to vent his displeasure on somebody, and as he paid Mr. Skinner a very large salary to be his general manager, he figured he could afford to quarrel with Skinner. So he said:

"Well, Skinner, if you hadn't butted in on the shipping end of the business the man Peasley would not have been given this opening to swat us. It's nuts for a sailor any time he can trip up a landsman, and particularly his owners—"

"You O.K.'d the cablegrams, Mr. Ricks," Skinner reminded him coldly.

"Don't talk back to me!" Cappy piped. "Not another peep out of you, sir! Not another word of discussion about this matter under any circumstances! I don't want to talk about it further—understand? It's driving me insane. Now, then, Skinner, tell me: If the man Peasley should decline to recognize McBride's authority, what course would you advise pursuing?"

"I do not think he will be that arbitrary, Mr. Ricks. In the first place—"

"Skinner, please do not argue with me. The man Peasley would do anything—"

"Well, in that event, McBride can call in the civil authorities of Cape Town, to remove Peasley by force from the ship."

"Skinner, you'll drive me to drink! I ask you, has a British official any authority over an American vessel lying in the roadstead? Will a foreign official dare to set foot on an American deck when an American skipper orders him not to do so?"

"I am not a sea lawyer," Mr. Skinner retorted, "I do not know."

"The Retriever will have discharged her cargo weeks before McBride arrives. Then suppose Peasley takes a notion to warp his vessel outside the three-mile limit. What authority has McBride got then?"

"I repeat, I am not a sea lawyer, Mr. Ricks."

"Don't equivocate with me, Skinner! Let's argue this question calmly, coolly and deliberately. Don't lose your temper. Now then. Peasley said he'd throw his successor overboard, didn't he?"

"Oh, merely a threat, Mr. Ricks."

"Skinner, you're a fine, wise manager! A threat, eh?" Cappy laughed—a short, scornful laugh. "Huh! Threat! Joke!"

"You do not think it is a threat?"

"No, sir. It's a promise. McBride is a splendid little man and game to the core; but no good, game little man will ever stay on a deck if a good, game big man takes a notion to throw him overboard, and the man Peasley is both big and game, otherwise he would not defy us. Why, Skinner, that fellow wouldn't pause at anything. Hasn't he spent over a hundred dollars arguing with us by cable? Why, he's a desperate character! Also, he would not threaten to throw his successor overboard if he didn't know that he was fully capable of so doing. Paste that in your hat, Skinner. It isn't done." Skinner inclined his head respectfully. Cappy continued: "What I should have done was to have sent a good, game, big man—"

He paused, and his glance met Skinner's wonderingly as a bright idea leaped into his cunning brain and crystallized into definite purpose. He sprang up, waved his skinny old arms, and kicked the waste-basket into a corner of the room.

"I have it, Skinner! I've solved the problem. Go back and 'tend to your lumber business and leave the man Peasley to me. I'll tan that fellow's hide and hang it on my fence, just as sure as George Washington crossed the Delaware River."

Mr. Skinner, glad to be excused, promptly made his escape. When Cappy Ricks stripped for action, Mr. Skinner knew from long experience that there was going to be a fight or a foot race; that whenever the old gentleman set out to confound an enemy, the inevitable result was wailing and weeping and gnashing of teeth, in which doleful form of exercise Cappy Ricks had never been known to participate.

"Send in a boy!" Cappy ordered as the general manager withdrew.

The boy appeared. "Sonny," said Cappy Ricks, "do you know All Hands And Feet?" The boy nodded and Cappy continued: "Well, you go down on the Embarcadero, like a good boy, and cruise from Folsom Street to Broadway Wharf Number Two until you find All Hands and Feet. Look in front of cigar stands and in the shipchandlery stores; and if you don't find him in those places run over to the assembly rooms of Harbor Fifteen, Masters' and Pilots' Association, and see if he's there, playing checkers. When you find him tell him Mr. Ricks wants to see him at once."

CHAPTER VIII.
ALL HANDS AND FEET TO THE RESCUE

Captain Ole Peterson was known to the coastwise trade as All Hands And Feet. He was a giant Swede whose feet resembled twin scow models and whose clenched fists, properly smoked and cured, might have passed anywhere for picnic hams. He was intelligent, competent and belligerent, with a broad face, slightly dished and plentifully scarred, while his wide flat nose had been stove in and shifted hard a-starboard. Cappy Ricks liked him, respected his ability and found him amusing as one finds an educated bear amusing. He had a reputation for being the undefeated rough and tumble champion of Sweden and the United States.

"You ban vant to see me, sir?" he rumbled as, hat in hand, he stood beside Cappy Ricks' desk half an hour later. Compared with the huge Swede, Cappy looked like a watch charm.

"Sit down, captain," Cappy replied amiably. "I hear you're out of a job. Why?"

Briefly All Hands And Feet explained what Cappy already knew; that his last command, being old and rotten and over-loaded, had worked apart in a seaway and fallen to pieces under him. The inspectors had held him blameless.

"I have a job for you, Ole," Cappy announced. "But there's a string attached to it."

"Aye ban able to pull strings, sir," Ole reminded him.

Cappy smiled, and outlined to the Swede the conditions surrounding the barkentine Retriever. "I'm going to give you command of the Retriever," he continued confidentially. "You are to bring her home from Cape Town, and when you get back I'll have a staunch four-masted schooner waiting for you. I was going to send McBride of the Nokomis on this job, but thought better of it, for the reason that Mac may not be physically equipped to perform the additional task I have in mind and I believe you are. Peterson, if you want a steady job skippering for the Blue Star Navigation Company you've got to earn it, and to earn it you've got to give this fellow Peasley a good sound thrashing for the good of his immortal soul. The very moment you step aboard the Retriever let him know you're the master."

"Do you tank he ban villin' to fight?" Ole demanded.

"Something tells me he will. However, in case he doesn't, don't let that embarrass you. Man-handle him until he does. Let me impress upon you, captain, the fact that I want the man Peasley summarily chastised for impudence and insubordination."

"All right, sir," said Ole. "Aye ban work him over." To be asked to fight for a job was to this descendant of the Vikings the ne plus ultra of sportsmanship. "Aye never ban licked yet," he added reminiscently.

"When we cabled we were sending a man to relieve him," Cappy complained, "he replied, telling us to insure his successor's life, because he was going to throw him overboard the minute he arrived."

All Hands And Feet swept away any lingering fears Cappy might chance to be entertaining. "Aye ban weigh two hundret an' saxty pounds," he announced.

"Which being the case," Cappy warned him, "should he succeed in throwing YOU overboard I should consider you unfit for a job in my employ." (The old fox had not the slightest idea such a contretemps was possible, but in order to play safe he considered it good policy to hearten Ole for the fray.) "Should he defeat you, captain, I have no hesitancy in saying to you now that such a misfortune would have a most disastrous effect on your future in my employ. You know me. When I order a job done, I want it done, and I want it done well. Understand! I don't want you to maim or kill the man, but just give him a good sound—er—commercial thrashing; and after you've tamed him I want you to—"

All Hands And Feet nodded his comprehension.

"An'," he interrupted, "after aye ban slap him once or twice aye ban give good kick under de coattail an' fire dis fresh guy—eh?" he suggested.

"Fire nothing!" shrilled Cappy. "You follow instructions, Ole, or I'll fire you! No, sir. After you've thrashed him I want you to bend a rope round him amidships and souse him overside to bring him to! Remember, we fired him once and he would not be fired. The damned sea lawyer quoted the salt-water code to us and said he'd shipped for the round trip; so we'll take him at his word. He's your first mate, captain. Bring him back to Grays Harbor with you; and then, if you feel so inclined, you may apply the tip of your number twenty-four sea boot where it will do the most good; in fact, I should prefer it. But by all means see to it that he completes his contract with the barkentine Retriever."

"Aye skoll see to it," Ole promised fervently.

"I thank you, captain. Come out in the general office now and I'll introduce you to the cashier, who will furnish you with expense money. Meantime, I'll have Skinner fill out a certificate of change of masters and have it registered at the custom-house. Can't send you down there without your credentials, you know."

All Hands And Feet mumbled his thanks; for, indeed, he was grateful for this chance to prove his metal. Calm in the knowledge of his past performances, he took no thought of the personal issue with Matt Peasley, for never had he met a mate he could not thrash. He followed Cappy out to the cashier's desk; and while the latter equipped All Hands And Feet for his journey to South Africa, and Mr. Skinner departed for the custom-house to have the certificate registered, Cappy wired McBride, aboard the Overland speeding east, instructing him to come back to San Francisco.

When Skinner returned to the office he found Cappy clawing nervously at his whiskers.

"The man Peasley has completely disrupted our organization," he complained bitterly. "Here I go to work and promote McBride to the Retriever to make room for his mate in the Nokomis, and now I have to recall Mac and give the Retriever to All Hands And Feet until she gets back to Grays Harbor; in consequence of which Mac hasn't a thing to do for four months and draws full pay for doing it, and later I've got to provide a permanent place for All Hands And Feet! Skinner, if this continues, I shall yet fill a pauper's grave." He was silent for several seconds; then: "By the way, Skinner, have you replied to that last cablegram from the man Peasley?"

"No, sir. I didn't think it required an answer."

"You mean you didn't know what answer to give him," Cappy snarled. "Well, neither do I; but since the cuss has got us into the spending habit, I'm going to be reckless for once and send him a cable myself, just to let him know I'm calling his bluff."

And, with that remark, Cappy squared round to his desk and wrote, in a trembling hand: "Special messenger big as horse carries reply your last cablegram."

"There," he said, turning to his general manager; "send that to the man Peasley, and sign my name to it."

CHAPTER IX.
MR. MURPHY ADVISES PREPAREDNESS

Matt Peasley said nothing to Mr. Murphy when Cappy Ricks' cryptic cablegram was received. Insofar as Matt was concerned, that cablegram closed the argument, for even had it seemed to demand a reply the master of the Retriever would not—nay could not, have answered, for the controversy had already ruined him financially. So he went on briskly with his task of discharging the Retriever and when the A. D. liner pulled out for Liverpool with Captain Noah's body on board, he laid off work merely long enough to dip the ensign and run it to half mast again until the steamer was out of sight; then he furled the flag, stored it in the locker in Captain Noah's stateroom, into which he had now moved, and went on superintending the discharging. When the vessel was empty he had a tug tow him out into the roadstead, where he cast anchor and set himself patiently to await the arrival of the special messenger "as big as a horse."

Somehow Matt didn't relish that little dash of descriptive writing. In conjunction with the noun horse Cappy Ricks had employed the indefinite article a, and while a horse was a horse and Cappy might have had a Shetland pony in mind when he coined the simile, nevertheless, a still small voice whispered to Matt Peasley that at the time Cappy was really thinking of a Percheron. The longer Matt chewed the cud of anticipation the more acute grew his regret that he had threatened to throw his successor overboard. He traced a certain analogy between that threat and Cappy Ricks' simple declarative sentence, and finally he decided to take Mr. Murphy into his confidence.

"Mike," he said, "did you ever hear any gossip to the effect that Cappy Ricks will swallow a bluff?"

"No, I never have," Mr. Murphy replied. "Why do you ask? You been trying to bluff him, Matt?"

"No, I really meant it when I said it, and if I'm crowded I'll make good, but somehow I wish I hadn't said it. It wasn't dignified."

"What did you say, Matt?"

"I cabled the owners that if they sent a skipper down here to relieve me they had better insure his life, because I'd throw him overboard upon arrival."

"Why, that's war talk," Mr. Murphy declared, highly scandalized. "I don't think Cappy Ricks will stand for that. I know blame well I wouldn't."

"What would you do, Mike, if you stood in Cappy's shoes and I sent you that cablegram?"

"Well," Mr. Murphy mused, "of course I'd be a little old man weighing about a hundred and thirty pounds ring-side, and I wouldn't be able to thrash you myself, but if it took my last dollar I'd send somebody down here to do the job for me."

"Well, I guess that's just about what Cappy has done," Matt admitted, and handed his mate Cappy's cablegram.

"Hah-hah!" Mr. Murphy commented. "That threat got past the general manager, right up to headquarters. Why, the old man signed this cablegram and they do say that when Cappy takes personal charge the fur begins to fly. Matt, if I was a drinking man I'd offer to bet you a scuttle of grog it's a case of die dog, or eat the meat-axe. Your bluff has been called, my son."

"Then," Matt averred impudently, "the only thing for me to do is to call Cappy's."

"How?"

"Why, give his messenger a good trouncing, of course. You don't suppose I'm going to stand by and take a thrashing or let the other fellow heave me overboard, do you? I should say not!"

Mr. Murphy puffed at his pipe, in silence for several minutes, the while he pondered the situation. Presently he arrived at a solution.

"He wouldn't send a prize-fighter down here, just to lick you," he announced. "The old man is the wildest spendthrift on earth when you get him started, but as a general rule his middle name is Tight Wad. He would select a combination of scrapper and skipper, and there are any number of such combinations on the beach of 'Frisco town. I could name you a dozen off-hand, and any one of the dozen would make you mind your P's and Q's, big as you are. Still, they all fight alike—rough and tumble, catch-as-catch-can. They come wading in, swinging both arms and you could sail the Retriever through the openings they leave. Know anything about boxing, Matt?"

"Not a thing, Mike. I've always had to climb the big fellows."

"Then I'll teach you," Mr. Murphy announced with conviction. "You're in fine shape now—as right as a fox and fit to tackle the finest, but there isn't any sense in getting mauled up when you don't have to. I'll go ashore and buy a set of six-ounce gloves, a set of two-ounce gloves and a punching bag. For the next three weeks you won't have anything to do except prepare for the battle, and I can teach you a lot of good stuff in three weeks. To be fore-warned is to be fore-armed, Matt, and if Cappy has sent a Holy Terror to clean you, give him a regular fight, even if he licks you."

Matt Peasley nodded. He entertained a profound respect for Mr. Murphy's judgment.

CHAPTER X.
THE BATTLE OF TABLE BAY

In due course Captain Ole Peterson arrived at Cape Town. As the steamer which bore him slipped up Table Bay to her pier All Hands And Feet saw a big barkentine, flying the American flag, at anchor just inside the breakwater and rightly conjectured she was his future command. Three hours ashore proved ample time to consummate all of the Retriever's neglected business. He discovered that the man to whom he was to administer a good, sound, commercial thrashing, as per Cappy Ricks' instructions, had already purchased and gotten aboard stores and water for the voyage back to Grays Harbor, so All Hands And Feet drew some money from the consignees, to be deducted from the freight money, paid off all the vessel's bills, O.K.'d the consignees' statement of account to be forwarded to the owners, received a ninety-day draft on London, in payment of the freight, mailed it to his owners, cleared his vessel, procured a reliable man to witness the formal transfer of authority from Matt Peasley to himself, engaged a launch and set out for the Retriever. All Hands And Feet had had ample time to plan his campaign, and he had planned it well. Immediately upon setting foot on the deck of the Retriever he planned to attack; then, this duty accomplished, he would send his witness ashore, up hook and away. The attack having taken place in British waters All Hands And Feet hoped Matt Peasley would have no redress in American waters; and if he took the complainant to sea with him the man Peasley would, of a certainty, have no legal redress in British waters!

Mr. Murphy was the first to sight All Hands And Feet. The worthy fellow had observed the arrival of the steamer and it had occurred to him that possibly Cappy Ricks' messenger might be aboard her. He had been on the lookout for two hours, accordingly, and the instant he saw a launch coming toward the Retriever his suspicions were fully aroused. He ran below and returned with the two ounce gloves and Captain Kendall's powerful marine glasses, which latter he leveled at the approaching launch, and while the new skipper was still a couple of cable lengths distant, Mr. Murphy recognized him. Instantly he secured the two ounce gloves and ran aft to where Matt Peasley, dressed in slippers, duck trousers and undershirt, sat under an awning reading Sinful Peck.

"Matt," he declared, "the special messenger will be aboard in about three shakes of a lamb's tail. I recognize him."

"Who is he?" Matt demanded coolly.

"All Hands And Feet—and believe me, he's there! He isn't a man, Matt, he's a bear—he's a devil, and if he ever gets his hands on you it's Kitty bar the door! Get into the gloves, boy, get into the gloves. You could smash that big Swede to your heart's content, but you wouldn't even stagger him with the first few punches. You'd just break your hands on him before you could knock him out and then he'd walk over you. Into the gloves, Matt, and save your knuckles."

"All right, Mike. Don't be in such a hurry. Call a couple of hands and let down the companion ladder so the special messenger can bring his dunnage aboard. I'll fight him after I've finished this chapter— that is, if he insists on being accommodated."

"He'll insist," Mr. Murphy declared. "He likes it, and the reason he likes it is because he does it well, and that's the reason he's here. He won't waste any ceremony on you, Matt. He's always up and doing."

Matt finished his chapter of Sinful Peck just as All Hands And Feet, followed by a Cape Town gentleman and two Kru boys, bearing respectively a brown canvas telescope basket and a sea chest, bore down upon him, convoyed by Mr. Murphy.

"A big Swede skipper," Matt Peasley soliloquized, as he eyed the stranger with alert interest. "Thunder, but he's big. He's the biggest thing I ever saw walking on two legs, with the exception of a trick elephant." He rose, put down his book and advanced to greet his visitors. While All Hands And Feet was still fully thirty feet from him he bawled aloud:

"You ban Mr. Peasley?"

"Captain Peasley," young Matt corrected him. "Since the death of Captain Kendall I have been in charge of the vessel; hence, for the present, I am known as Captain Peasley. What can I do for you, gentlemen?"

All Hands And Feet glanced appraisingly at Matt Peasley and did him the honor to remove his coat and vest.

"Yes; it's pretty hot down in these latitudes," Matt remarked, by way of being pleasant and making conversation.

All Hands And Feet removed an envelope from his coat pocket and handed it to Matt; and while the latter perused it the big Swede strode to the scuttle butt and helped himself to a drink of water. Matt opened the envelope and read this communication from Cappy Ricks:

San Francisco, California.
February 20, 19 — .

Mr. Matthew Peasley,
Chief Mate Barkentine Retriever,
Cape Town, South Africa.

My Dear Mr. Peasley:

Cast your eye along the lines of the bearer of this note, Captain Ole Peterson, who comes to Cape Town to take command of the Retriever. Within five minutes he will, acting under instructions from me and without the slightest personal animus toward yourself, proceed to administer to you the beating of a lifetime. By the time he gets through wiping the deck with you perhaps you will realize the necessity, in the future, of obeying orders from your owners.

In your cablegram received to-day, you take occasion to remind us that no manager or owner has authority to disrate a ship's officer. This is quite true. Such authority is vested only in the master of the ship. You need have no fear for your job, however. We believe you to be a clever first mate, otherwise Captain Kendall would not have dug you up out of the forecastle; and believing this, naturally we dislike the thought of disrating you. We have, therefore, instructed Captain Peterson to retain you in your berth as first mate.

However, in view of the fact that we have informed him of your amiable intentions of throwing him overboard, he will first inculcate in you that spirit of respect to your superiors which you so manifestly lack. He will then dip you into the drink, to bring you to, and after that you will kindly go forward and break out the anchor. You signed for the round trip and you're going to complete your contract. Remember that.

Cordially and sincerely yours,
Blue Star Navigation Company,
By Alden P. Ricks,
President.

Matt Peasley read this extraordinary communication twice, then folded it and calmly placed it in his pocket.

"May I inquire, sir," he said, facing the gentleman who had accompanied All Hands And Feet aboard the Retriever, "who you are and the nature of your business?"

"I am the American consul, Mr. Peasley, and I am here at the invitation of Captain Peterson, the master of this ship, to witness the formal transfer of authority from you to him. I was given to understand by Captain Peterson that you might offer some slight objection to this arrangement."

"Slight objection!" Matt Peasley replied with a rising inflection, and grinned maliciously.

The consul had his Yankee sense of humor with him and chuckled as Matt lifted his big body on his toes and stretched both arms lazily. Then Matthew Peasley turned toward All Hands And Feet.

"I have a letter from the owners of the Retriever," he said respectfully, "which leads me to presume that you are to supersede me in command of the vessel." All Hands And Feet nodded. "Which being the case," Matt Peasley continued, "as a mere matter of formality, you will of course present your credentials as master."

"Sure!" Ole replied pleasantly, and sidled toward Matt Peasley with outstretched arms. Could Cappy Ricks have seen his skipper then, he would have reminded the Old Man more than ever of a bear.

Matt Peasley needed no blueprint of the big Swede's plans. All Hands And Feet, depending on his sheer horse power and superior weight, always fought in mass formation, as it were. His modus operandi was to embrace his enemy in those terrible arms, squeeze the breath out of him with one bearlike hug, then lay him on the deck, straddle him, and pummel him into insensibility at his leisure. Matt gave ground rapidly and held up a warning hand.

"One moment, my friend," he requested. "Before you get familiar on brief acquaintance, don't you think you had better present your credentials?"

All Hands And Feet shook his two great fists and grinned good-naturedly.

"How dese ban suit you for credentials?" he queried.

"Fine," Matt Peasley answered; "only, before you present them, our first duty is to the ship. I take it that you have cleared the vessel and that after trimming me you intend to put to sea."

"You ban guess it," the Swede rumbled. "Put up de dooks. Anyhow, I ban't have to fight little feller. Dat ban one comfort."

"You cleared the ship, eh? Well, Swede, I'm glad to hear that. I should have cleared her myself and sailed long ago if I had only had a skipper's ticket; but these British custom-house officials are great sticklers for red tape and they wouldn't clear me. And, of course, a man can't sail without his papers. When he does they send a gunboat after him. However," he added brightly "the ship is cleared and the skipper—so I am unofficially informed—is aboard. By the way, Swede, I left a lot of O.K.'d bills for stores and provision up at the office of the Harlow & Benton Company, Limited. Did you square up for them?"

"Yah; everything ban shipshape," All Hands And Feet assured him.

"And you insist on presenting your credentials in bunches of fives, eh?"

All Hands And Feet nodded and once more commenced sidling toward Matt Peasley, who backed away again, meantime addressing himself to the United States consul:

"You heard what he said, Mr. Consul. He may be my superior officer, but I have not been informed of that fact officially; and meantime, so far as I am concerned, he is merely a fine, big squarehead who has climbed aboard my ship uninvited and attacked me. Did you ever see a sea bully licked, Mr. Consul?"

"I have never had that pleasure, Mr. Peasley."

All the time Matt Peasley was circling around the deck, with All Hands And Feet sidling after him.

"Then you've got something coming, sir," Matt replied. "Help yourself to a reserved seat on the rail and watch the joyous procedure. Mr. Murphy?"

"Here, sir," Mr. Murphy replied promptly.

"I'm going to thrash the big fellow, Mr. Murphy. Stand by to see fair play and keep the crew off him. I observe you have equipped yourself with a belaying-pin. Thank you, Mr. Murphy. You anticipate the situation."

He turned to All Hands And Feet, who was still crowding him as they circled the deck. "Stop where you are, my friend; otherwise, Mr. Murphy will crack you on the head with the belaying-pin."

All Hands And Feet grinned patronizingly and paused.

"Vell?" he queried.

"On my ship," Matt continued, "all fights are pulled off under my rules. Kicking, choking, biting, gouging and deadly weapons are prohibited. If you get me down you can use your fists on me, but anything else will necessitate the interference of the referee with his trusty belaying-pin."

"Vell?" All Hands And Feet queried again. He was very eager for the fray.

"We have procured a set of two-ounce gloves in anticipation of this physical culture exhibition," Matt replied. "Unfortunately, however, I fear your hands will not fit them. Would you care to try them on?"

"Cut it oud! Cut it oud!" the enemy rumbled contemptuously, and again commenced his advance.

"One minute, then, my friend, until I put on—"

"Fight mit your bare hands like a man!" the big Swede bellowed scathingly.

"You forget. I told you all fights on my ship are pulled off under my rules. I always fight with two-ounce gloves."

"All righd. Suit yourself." All Hands And Feet felt he could afford to give the enemy a trifle the better of the argument without the slightest prejudice to his own chances for success.

Accordingly, Mr. Murphy skillfully bandaged Matt Peasley's hands, drew on the gloves and gently shoved his young champion toward the center of the deck. "Let 'er go!" he announced.

"Come Swede! Present your credentials!" Matt taunted. His long left flashed out and cuffed All Hands And Feet on the nose.

It was a mere love-tap! All Hands And Feet grinned pityingly, and with his left arm guarding his face, rushed.

"Lower deck!" Mr. Murphy warned, and laughed as Matt planted left and right in the midriff and danced away from the Swede's swinging right. All Hands And Feet grunted—a most unwarriorlike grunt—and dropped both hands—whereupon a fog suddenly descended upon his vision. Faintly he made out a blur that was Matt Peasley; bellowing wrathfully he rushed. Matt gave ground and the Swede's vision cleared and he paused to consider the situation.

"No rest for the wicked," Mr. Murphy declared. "At him, boy, at him!"

All Hands And Feet realized he faced a desperate situation, and as Matt stepped in he ducked and leaped upon his antagonist.

"By yiminy," he yelled. "I got you now!" and his great hands closed around Matt Peasley's neck.

"Lower deck!" Mr. Murphy yelled shrilly, and a volley of short arm blows commenced to rattle on the big Swede's stomach. For at least seven seconds Matt worked like a pneumatic riveter; then—

"Swing your partner for the grand right and left," Mr. Murphy counseled, and Matt closed with All Hands And Feet, and managed to shake the badly winded champion off.

"All off," Mr. Murphy declared to the American consul and dropped his marline-spike, as Matt Peasley ripped left and right, right and left into Ole Peterson's dish face. "Watch the skipper—our skipper, I mean. Regular young human pile-driver." He raised his voice and called to Matt Peasley. "He's rocking on his legs now, sir; but keep away from those arms. He's dangerous and you're givin' him fifty pounds the best of it in the weights. Try the short ribs with your left and feel for his chin with the right, sir. Very nicely done, sir! Now—once more!"

Mr. Murphy nodded politely to the American consul.

"Excuse me," he said. "The bigger they are the harder they fall, and the Retriever's deck ain't no nice place to bump a man's head. I'll just skip round in back and catch him in my arms."

Which being done, Mr. Murphy laid All Hands And Feet gently on deck, walked to the scuttle butt, procured a dipperful of water and threw it into the gory, battered face. Matt Peasley had simply walked round him and, with the advantage of a superior reach, had systematically cut Captain Ole Peterson to strings and ribbons.

He held up the blood-soaked gloves for Mr. Murphy to untie the strings, the while he sniffed a little afternoon breeze that had just sprung up, blowing straight for the open sea.

"When he comes to, Mr. Murphy," he ordered calmly, "escort him to your old room. Have one of the men stow his dunnage there also; and tell him if he shows his nose on deck until I give him permission, he shall have another taste of the same. Mr. Consul, I should be highly honored if you would step into my cabin and hoist one to our own dear native land."

"With pleasure," the consul replied. "Though I cannot, in my capacity as a citizen of the United States, endorse your—er—mutiny, nevertheless, as a United States consul at Cape Town I shall take pleasure in certifying to the fact that the fallen gladiator was the aggressor, that he did not present his credentials, and that you had no official knowledge of his identity."

"I wish you would make an affidavit to that effect, under the seal of the Consulate, and mail it to me at Hoquiam, Washington, U. S. A.," Matt pleaded, as they reached his cabin. He reached into poor old

Cap'n Noah's little private locker. "I've a suspicion, sir, I'm going to need your affidavit very badly."

"I shall do so, Mr. Peasley. May I inquire what you purpose doing with Captain Peterson?"

"Captain Peasley—if you please, Mr. Consul." Matt looked up and grinned. "I think," he continued, as he inserted the corkscrew, "I shall ship that boy as second mate if he's willing to work. If he's sullen, of course he'll have to remain in his room—and I shall not permit him to present his credentials now."

"Captain Peasley," the consul warned seriously. "I'm afraid you're in very, very Dutch."

"I wouldn't be surprised. However, it will be about three months before I commence to suffer, and in the meantime I'm going to be supremely happy skippering the barkentine Retriever back to Grays Harbor, if they hang me for it when I get there. Say when!"

"When!"

"Here's success to crime, Mr. Consul."

"Good luck to you, you youthful prodigy; good luck and bon voyage, Mr.—I mean Captain Peasley."

"Thank you, Mr. Consul. I hate to hurry you away; fact is, I'd like to have you stay aboard and have dinner with us, but if this breeze holds good I can save my owners an outward towage bill, and I'll have to hustle. So I'll bid you good-bye, Mr. Consul. Glad to have had you for the little exhibition. Here is my name and address—and please don't forget that affidavit."

When the American consul left the ship Matt Peasley was on the poop bawling orders; up on the topgallant forecastle the capable Mr. Murphy and his bully boys were walking around the windlass to the bellowing chorus of Roll A Man Down! while the boatswain, promoted by Matt Peasley to second mate, was laying aloft forward shaking out the topsails and hoisting her head-sails. When the consul looked again, the American barkentine Retriever had turned her tail on Cape Town and was scampering down Table Bay with a bone in her teeth; heeling gently to the freshening breeze, she was rolling home in command of the boy who had joined her five months before as an able seaman.

Matt Peasley rounded the Cape of Good Hope nicely, but he had added materially to his stock of seamanship before he won through the tide-rips off Point Aghulas and squared away across the Indian Ocean. Coming up along the coast of Australia he had the sou'east trades and he crowded her until Mr. Murphy forgot the traditions of the sea, forgot that Matt Peasley was the skipper and hence not to be questioned, and remembered that the madman was only a boy.

"Captain Matt," he pleaded, "take some clothes off the old girl, for the love of life! She's making steamer time now, and if the breeze freshens you'll lift the sticks out of her."

"Lift nothing, Mike. I know her. Cap'n Noah told me all about her. You can drive the Retriever until she develops a certain little squeak up forward—and then it's time to shorten sail. She isn't squeaking yet, Mike. Don't worry. She'll let us know," and his beaming glance wandered aloft to the straining cordage and bellying canvas. "Into it, sweetheart," he crooned, "into it, girl, and we'll show this Cappy Ricks what we know about sailing a ship that can sail! Meager maritime experience, eh? I'll show him!"

Oh, Sally Brown, I love your daughter,

I love your daughter, indeed I do,

he caroled, and buck-and-winged his way back to the poop, for he was only a boy, life was good, he was fighting a fight and as Mr. Murphy remarked a minute later when Matt ordered him to bend the fore-staysail on her; "What the hell!"

Day and night Matt Peasley drove her into it. He stood far off shore until he ran out of the sou'east trades, fiddled around two days in light airs and then picked up the nor'east trades; drove her well into the north, hauled round and came romping up to Grays Harbor bar seventy-nine days from Cape Town. A bar tug, ranging down the coast, hooked on to him and snaked him in.

CHAPTER XI.
MR. SKINNER RECEIVES A TELEGRAM

Cappy Ricks was having his customary mid-afternoon nap in his big swivel chair and his feet on his desk, when Mr. Skinner came in and woke him up.

"I just couldn't help it, sir," he announced apologetically, as Cappy opened one eye and glared at him, "I had to wake you up and tell you the news."

"Tell it!" Cappy snapped.

"The Retriever arrived at Grays Harbor this morning, Mr. Ricks. She's broken the record for a fast passage," and he handed Cappy Ricks a telegram.

"Bless my withered heart!" Cappy declared, and opened his other eye. "You don't tell me? Well, well, well! All Hands And Feet is making good right off the bat, isn't he?" Cappy chuckled. "Skinner, my dear boy," he bragged, "did you ever see me start out to pick a skipper and hand myself the worst of it?"

"No, sir," Mr. Skinner maintained dutifully, and turned away to hide a wicked little smile, which under the circumstances Skinner was entitled to.

"And you never will, Skinner. Paste that in your hat, boy. That big Swede, Peterson, can handle a ship as well as he can handle a refractory mate — and that's going some, Skinner — going some! I'm not surprised at his fast passage. Not at all, Skinner. Come to think of it, I'm going to fire that Scotchman in the Fortuna and give All Hands And Feet his berth. He has earned it."

He adjusted his spectacles and read:

Hoquiam, Washington,

June 27, 19—.

>Blue Star Navigation Company,
>258 California St.,
>San Francisco.
>
>Arrived this morning, seventy-nine days from bar to bar, all hands well, including your special messenger. Offered him job as second mate, just to show I had no hard feelings, but he would not work, so I brought him home under hatches. Permitted him present his formal credentials this morning and turned over command of ship to him. Declined responsibility and left, saying you had promised him command four-masted schooner. Seemed trifle hurt, although it is seventy-nine days since I thrashed him. Consequently I am still in command and awaiting your instructions.
>
>>Peasley.

For a long time Cappy Ricks kept looking sternly at Mr. Skinner over the tops of his spectacles. There was blood on the moon again, and the silence was terrible. He kept rocking gently backward and forward in his swivel chair, for all the world as though preparing for a panther-like spring at Mr. Skinner's throat. Suddenly he exploded.

"I won't have another thing to do with the man Peasley!" he shrilled. "The fellow is a thorn in my side and I want peace! Understand, Skinner? I—want—peace! What in blue blazes do I pay you ten thousand a year for if it isn't to give me peace? Answer me that, Skinner."

"Well you said you wanted to attend to the shipping—"

"That'll do, Skinner—that'll do! You're an honorary member of the I-told-you-so Club and I'm thoroughly disgusted with you. Rid me of this man—immediately. If I ever get another telegram from the scoundrel I shall hold you personally responsible."

Forthwith Mr. Skinner acted. He went up to the office of the United States District Attorney and swore out a Federal warrant for the arrest of Matthew Peasley on a charge of mutiny and insubordination, assault and battery on the high seas, and everything else he could think of. The authorities promptly wired north to send a United States marshal down to Grays Harbor to arrest the culprit; and the following afternoon, when Cappy Ricks got back to his office after luncheon and picked up the paper, the very first thing his glance rested on was the headline:

MATE CHARGED WITH MUTINY!

Mutiny and sundry other crimes on the high seas are out of the ordinary; hence the United Press correspondent at Hoquiam had considered the story of Matt Peasley's arrest worthy of dissemination over the Pacific Coast.

Cappy Ricks read it, the principal item of interest in it being a purported interview with Matt Peasley, who, in choice newspaperese, had entered a vigorous denial of the charge. The story concluded with the statement that Peasley was a native of Thomaston, Maine, where he had always borne a most excellent reputation for steadiness and sobriety.

Cappy Ricks laid the paper aside.

Thomaston, Maine! So the man Peasley was a Down-Easter! That explained it.

"Well, I hope my teeth may fall into the ocean!" Cappy murmured. "Thomaston, Maine! Why, he's one of our own town boys — one of my own people! Dear, dear, dear! Well now, it's strange I didn't know that name. I must be getting old to forget it."

He sat in his swivel chair, rocking gently backward and forward for several minutes, after a fashion he had when perturbed. Suddenly his old hand shot out and pressed the push button on his desk, and his stenographer answered.

"Send Mr. Skinner in!" he commanded.

Presently Mr. Skinner came, and again Cappy eyed him over the tops of his spectacles; again the terrible silence. Skinner commenced to fidget.

"Skinner," began Cappy impressively, "how often have I got to tell you not to interfere with the shipping? Tut, tut! Not a peep out of you, sir — not a peep! You had the audacity, sir, to swear to a Federal warrant against the man Peasley. How dare you, sir? Do you know who the man Peasley is? You don't. Well, sir, I'll tell you. He's a Down-East boy and I went to school with his people. I'll bet Ethan Peasley was a relative of this boy Matt, because Ethan had a cousin by the name of Matthew; and Ethan and Matt and I used to hell around together until they went to sea.

"Lord bless you, Skinner, I can remember yet the day the Martha Peasley came up the harbor, with her flag at half-mast—and poor old Ethan was gone—whipped off the end of her main yard when she rolled!

"We were great chums, Ethan and I, Skinner; and I cried. Why—why, damn it, sir, this boy Matt's people and mine are all buried in the same cemetery back home. Yes, sir! And nearly all of 'em have the same epitaph—'Lost at Sea'—and—you idiot, Skinner! What do you mean, sir, by standing there with your infernal little smile on your smug face? Out of my office, you jackanapes, and call the dogs off this boy Matt. Why, there was never one of his breed that wasn't a man and a seaman, every inch of him.

"All Hands And Feet thrash a Peasley! Huh! A joke! Why, Ethan was six foot six at twenty, with an arm like a fathom of towing cable. Catch me turning down one of our own boys! No, sir! Not by a damned sight!"

In all his life Mr. Skinner had never seen Cappy Ricks so wrought up. He fled at once to call off the dogs, while Cappy turned to his desk and wrote this telegram:

San Francisco, California.
June 28, 19—.

Matt Peasley,
Care United States Marshal,
Hoquiam, Washington.

Congratulations on splendid voyage. You busted record. Lindquist, in the John A. Logan, did it in eighty-four days in the spring of ninety-four. Draw draft and pay off crew, render report of voyage, place second mate in charge, and proceed immediately to Seattle to get your master's ticket. Will telegraph Seattle inspectors requesting waive further probation as first mate and issue license if you pass examination in order that you may accept captaincy of Retriever. Skinner, my manager, had you arrested. Would never have done it myself. I come from Thomaston, Maine, and I knew your people. Would never have sent the Swede had I known which tribe of Peasley you belonged to — though, if he had licked you, no more than you deserved. I want no more of your impudence, Matt.

Alden P. Ricks.

* * * * *

For a week business droned along in Cappy Ricks' office as usual, interrupted at last by the receipt of a telegram from Matt Peasley to Cappy. It was sent from Seattle and read:

"Have now legal right to be called captain. Rejoin ship tomorrow. Wire orders. Thank you."

"God bless the lad!" Cappy murmured happily. "I'll bet he's going to make me a skookum skipper. Still, I think he's pretty young and sadly in need of training; so I'll have to take some of the conceit out of him. I'm going to proceed to break his young heart; and if he yells murder I'll fire him! On the contrary, if he's one of Ethan's tribe — well, the Peasleys always did their duty; I'll say that for them. I hope he stands the acid."

Whereupon Cappy Ricks squared round to his desk and wrote:

San Francisco, July 5, 19 – .

*Captain Matthew Peasley,
Master Barkentine Retriever,
Hoquiam, Washington.*

Glad you have legal right to be called captain. Sorry I have not. Proceed to Weatherby's mill, at Cosmopolis, and load for Antofagasta, Chile. Remember speed synonymous with dividends in shipping business.

Blue Star Navigation Company.

When Cappy signed his telegrams with the company name it was always a sure indication he had discharged his cargo of sentiment and gotten down to business once more.

"A little creosoted piling now and then is bully for the best of men," he cackled. "For a month of Sundays that man Peasley will curse me as far as he can smell the Retriever. Oh, well! Every dog must have his day — and I'm a wise old dog. I'll teach that Matt boy some respect for his owners before I'm through with him!"

CHAPTER XII.
THE CAMPAIGN OPENS

When Matt Peasley's Yankee combativeness, coupled with the accident of birth in the old home town of Cappy Ricks, gained for him command of the Blue Star Navigation Company's big barkentine, Retriever, he lacked eight days of his twenty-first birthday. He had slightly less beard than the average youth of his years; and, despite the fact that he had been exposed almost constantly to salty gales since his fourteenth birthday, he did not look his age. And of all the ridiculous sights ashore or afloat the most ridiculous is a sea captain with the body of a Hercules and the immature features of an eighteen-year-old boy.

Indeed, such a great, soft, innocent baby type was Matt Peasley that even the limited sense of humor possessed by his motley crew forbade their reference to him, after custom immemorial, as the Old Man. The formal title of captain seemed equally absurd; so they compromised by dubbing him Mother's Darling.

"If," quoth Mr. Michael Murphy, chief kicker of the Retriever, over a quiet pipe with Mr. Angus MacLean, the second mate, as the vessel lay at anchor in Grays Harbor, "Cappy Ricks had laid eyes on Mother's Darling before ordering him to Seattle to go up for his master's ticket, the old fox would have scuttled the ship sooner than trust that baby with her."

"Ye'll nae be denying the lad kens his business," Mr. MacLean declared.

"Aye! True enough, Mac; but 'twould be hard to convince Cappy Ricks o' that. Every skipper in his employ is a graybeard."

"Mayhap," the canny MacLean retorted. "That's because t'owd boy's skippers have held their berths ower long."

But Mr. Murphy shook his head. He had come up from before the mast in the ships of the Blue Star Navigation Company, and since he had ambitions he had been at some pains to acquaint himself with the peculiarities of the president of that corporation.

"Give Cappy Ricks one look into Matt Peasley's face and I'll be skippering the Retriever," he declared.

And in this he was more than half right, for Cappy Ricks had never met Matt Peasley, and when the Old Man made up his mind that he wanted the boy to skipper his barkentine, the Retriever, he was acting entirely on instinct. He only knew that in Matt Peasley he had a man who had shipped out before the mast and returned from the voyage in command of the ship, and naturally such an exploit challenged recognition of the most signal nature—particularly when, in its performance, the object of Cappy's admiration had demonstrated that he was possessed of certain sterling attributes which are commonly supposed to make for success in any walk of life.

Since Matt Peasley had accomplished a man's work it never occurred to Cappy Ricks to consider that the object of his interest might be a boy. Young he knew him to be—that is to say, Cappy figured the rascal to be somewhere between thirty and thirty-five.

Had he known, however, that his prospective captain had but recently attained his majority the Old Man would have ascribed Matt Peasley's record-breaking voyage from Cape Town to Grays Harbor as sheer luck, and forthwith would have set Master Matthew down for a five-year apprenticeship as first mate; for Cappy was the product of an older day, and held that gray hairs and experience are the prime requisites for a berth as master.

Any young upstart can run coastwise, put in his service sailing a ship from headland to headland, and then take a course in a navigation school, where in six weeks he can cram sufficient navigation into his thick head to pass the inspectors and get a master's ticket; but for offshore cruising Cappy Ricks demanded a real sailor and a thorough business man rolled into one.

Mother's Darling had returned to Grays Harbor from a flying visit to Seattle, where two grizzled old ex-salts, the local inspectors, had put him through a severe examination to ascertain what he knew of Bowditch on Navigation and Nichols on Seamanship. Naturally he did not know as much as they thought he should; but, out of sheer salt-water pride in the exploit of a stripling and in deference to a letter from Cappy Ricks requesting them to waive further probation as chief mate and issue Mr. Peasley his master's license if they found him at all competent—this in order that the said Peasley might take command of his barkentine, the Retriever, forthwith—the inspectors concluded to override the rules of the Department of Commerce, and gave Matt Peasley his master's license.

Upon his return from Seattle, Matt called at the telegraph office in Hoquiam and received his loading instructions from the owners. His heart beat high with youthful importance and the joy of victory as he almost ran to the water front and engaged a big gasoline launch to take him aboard the Retriever and then kick her into the mill dock at Cosmopolis. His ship was not where he had left her, however, and after an hour's search he discovered her several miles up the Chehalis river. Murphy was on deck, gazing wistfully at the house and wishing he had some white paint, when Matt Peasley came aboard. Even before the latter leaped to the deck Mr. Murphy knew the glad tidings—knew them, in fact, the very instant the boy's shining countenance appeared above the rail. The skipper was grinning fatuously and Mr. Murphy grinned back at him.

"Well, sir," he greeted young Matt, "I see you're the permanent skipper. I congratulate you."

"Thank you, Mike. And I hope you will have no objection to continuing in your berth as first mate. I realize I'm pretty young for an old sailor like you to be taking orders from—"

"Bless your soul, sir," Mr. Murphy protested; "of course I'll stick with you! Didn't you whale the big Swede Cappy Ricks sent to Cape Town to kick you out of your just due?" He reaffirmed his loyalty with a contemptuous grunt.

"What are you doing way up the river?" the captain demanded.

"Oh, that's a little liberty I took," the mate declared. "You're new to this coast; and, of course, when they ordered us to Grays Harbor I knew we weren't going to be able to go on dry dock, because there isn't any dry dock here. So, while you were in Seattle, I had a gasoline tug tow us up-river. We've been lying in fresh water four days, sir, and that'll kill most of the worms on her bottom."

"Hereafter," said Matt Peasley, "you get ten dollars a month above the scale. Thank you."

Mr. Murphy acknowledged his appreciation.

"Any orders, sir?" he continued.

Matt Peasley showed him Cappy Ricks' telegram and Mr. Murphy nodded his approval. He had been in port nearly a week and the whine of the sawmills and the reek of river water had begun to get on his nerves. He was ready for the dark blue again.

"There's something wrong about our cargo, I think," Matt remarked presently.

"Why, sir?"

"Why, down at the telegraph office this morning I met the master of the schooner, Carrier Dove, and when I told him my orders he snickered."

"Huh! Well, he ought to know what he snickered about, sir. The Carrier Dove just finished loading at Weatherby's mill," Mr. Murphy replied. "She's a Blue Star craft and bound for Antofagasta also. Her skipper's Salvation Pete Hansen, and it would be just like that squarehead to dodge a deckload of piling and leave it for us."

"Well, whatever it was it amused him greatly. It must be worse than a deckload of piling."

"There's nothing worse in the timber line, unless it's a load underdeck, sir. You take a sixty-foot pile with a fourteen-inch butt and try to shove it down through the hatch, and you've got a job on your hands. And after the hold is half filled you've got to quit loading through the hatch, cut ports in your bows, and shove the sticks in that way. It's the slowest loading and discharging in the world; and unless you drive her between ports and make up for the lost time you don't make a good showing with your owners—and then your job's in danger. Ship owners never consider anything except results."

"Well," the captain answered, "in order not to waste any more time than is absolutely necessary, call Mr. MacLean and the cook, and we'll go for'd and break out the anchor."

Immediately on his arrival from Cape Town, Matt Peasley had paid off all his foremast hands, leaving the two mates and the cook the only men aboard the vessel. He joined them now in a walk around the capstan; the launch hooked on and the Retriever was snaked across the harbor to Weatherby's mill. And, while they were still three cables' length from the mill dock, Mr. Murphy, who had taken up his position on the topgallant forecastle, to be ready with a heaving line, suddenly raised his head and sniffed upwind.

The captain had the wheel and Mr. MacLean was standing aft waiting to do his duty by the stern line. Presently he, too, raised his head and sniffed.

"I see you got it too, Mac," Mr. Murphy bawled.

"Aw, weel," Mr. MacLean replied; "Why worrit aboot a bridge till ye hae to cross it? D'ye ken 'tis oors?"

"What are you two fellows talking about and why are you sniffing?" Matt Peasley demanded.

"I'm sniffing at the same thing Salvation Pete Hansen laughed about," the mate answered. "I'll bet you a uniform cap we're stuck with a cargo of creosoted piling—and hell hath no fury like a creosoted pile."

When the vessel had been made fast to the mill dock Matt Peasley walked forward to meet his mate.

"What about this cargo of ours?" he demanded. "Remember, I'm new to the lumber trade on this coast. I have never handled any kind of piling."

"Then, sir, you're going to get your education like the boa constrictor that swallowed the nigger—all in one long, slimy bite."

He gazed at his boyish skipper appraisingly.

"No," he murmured to himself; "I can't do it. I like you for the way you whaled that big Swede in Cape Town, but this is too much."

"Why, I don't find the odor so very unpleasant," the master declared; "in fact, I rather like it, and I know it's healthy, because I remember, when my brother Ezra had pneumonia, they burned creosote in the room."

"Oh, nobody objects to the smell particularly, sir, though it's been my experience that anybody can cheapen a good thing by overuse—and we have three months of that smell ahead of us. It's the taste that busts my bobstay."

"Why, what do you mean?"

"Well, you see, sir, the odor of creosote is so heavy it won't float in the air, but just settles down over everything, like mildew on a pair of boots. So it gets in the stores and you taste it. You can store flour below deck aft and creosoted piling on deck for'd—and you won't be out two weeks before that flour is spoiled. Same way with the tea, coffee, sugar, mush, salt-horse—everything. It all tastes of creosote; and then the damned stuff rubs off on the ship and ruins the paintwork. And if the crew happen to have any cuts or abrasions on their hands they're almost certain to get infected with the awful stuff, and you'll be kept busy doctoring them. Then, the first thing, along comes a gale and you're shorthanded, and there's the devil to pay."

"Aye!" Mr. MacLean interrupted solemnly. "I dinna care for creosote mysel', sir; so, wi' your kind permission, I'll hae ma time—an' I'll hae it noo."

Matt Peasley bent upon the recalcitrant Scotchman a withering glare. "Very well, Mr. MacLean," he said presently, "I never could sail in the same ship with a quitter; so you might as well go now, when we can part good friends." He turned to Mr. Murphy. "How about you, Mike? Are you going to run out on me, too?"

Now, as between the Irish and the Scotch, history records no preponderance of courage in either, for both are Gaels and a comparison is difficult.

However, Scotchmen are a conservative race and will walk round a fight rather than be forced into it, while all that is necessary to make an Irishman fight is to impugn his courage.

Mr. Murphy had seen the fight ahead of the Retriever and he did not blame Mr. MacLean for side-stepping it. Indeed, he had intended pursuing the same course; but Matt Peasley, by his latest remark, had rendered that impossible. To desert now would savor of dishonor; and, moreover, Matt Peasley, though master, had called him by his Christian name. Mr. Murphy touched his forelock respectfully.

"I am not Scotch," he announced, with a slight emphasis on the pronoun. "Shame on you, Angus MacLean—ditching the skipper like that!"

"Sticks an' stones may break ma bones, but names'll never hurrt me," Mr. MacLean retorted. "I tell ye I dinna care for creosote in ma porridge." And he followed Matt Peasley aft, where the latter paid him off and gave him five minutes to pack and get off the ship. Immediately after supper the cook followed the second mate; but, since the former was a Jap and probably the worst marine cook in the world, his departure occasioned no heartache.

"We'll board at the mill cook-house until we're loaded, Mike," Matt Peasley informed the mate. "They have a good Chink up there."

Mr. Murphy sighed as he loaded his pipe and struck a match for it.

"It does look to me, sir," he replied, with that touch of conscious superiority so noticeable in the Celt, "as though Cappy Ricks might have slipped this cargo to a Dutchman."

The Retriever commenced taking on cargo at seven o'clock the following morning, with Mr. Murphy on shipboard and Matt Peasley on the dock superintending the gang of stevedores. Ordinarily the masters of lumber freighters ship their crews before commencing to load, in order that sailors at forty dollars a month may obviate the employment of an equal number of stevedores at forty cents an hour; but Mr. Murphy, out of his profound experience, advised against this course, as tending to spread the news of the Retriever's misfortune and militate against securing a crew when the vessel should be loaded and lying in the stream ready for sea. Men employed now, he explained, would only desert. The thing to do was to let a Seattle crimp furnish the crew, sign them on before the shipping commissioner in Seattle, bring them aboard drunk, tow to sea, and let the rascals make the best of a bad bargain.

The hold was about half filled, and the ship carpenters were at work cutting ports in the Retriever's bows, when Matt Peasley discovered that the mill did not have in hand any order for lumber to be used as stowage to snug up the cumbersome cargo below decks and keep it from rolling and working in a seaway. Accordingly he wired his owners as follows:

Cosmopolis, Washington, July 7, 19 – .

Blue Star Navigation Company,
258 California St.,
San Francisco, California.

No stowage.

Peasley.

Cappy Ricks having deliberately conspired to hang a series of dirty cargoes on his newest skipper, for the dual purpose of teaching Matt Peasley his place and discovering whether he was worthy of it, grinned evilly when he received that two-word message; and, not to be out-done in brevity, he dictated this answer:

San Francisco, California, July 7, 19—.

Captain Matthew Peasley,
Master Barkentine Retriever,
Care Weatherby's mill, Cosmopolis, Wash.

Know it.

Blue Star Navigation Company.

Matt Peasley's cheeks burned when he read that message. Indeed, could Cappy Ricks have been privileged to hear the terse remarks his telegram elicited, there is no doubt he would have sent Mr. Skinner up to the custom-house immediately to file a certificate of change of master.

"Ha!" Mr. Murphy snorted when Matt showed him the message. "I get the old sinner now. This is to be a grudge fight, Captain Matt. You wished yourself onto him in Cape Town against his will, and now he's made up his mind that so long as you wanted the job it's yours—only he'll make you curse the day you ever moved your sea chest into the skipper's cabin. He's going to send us into dogholes to load and open roadsteads to discharge; and if he can find a dirty cargo anywhere we'll get it. But it's carrying a grudge too far not to give us stowage."

"Well, it's his ship," Matt Peabody declared passionately. "If the old thief can gamble on good weather I guess I can gamble on my seamanship—and yours."

The mate inclined his head at the delicate compliment; and Matt, observing this, decided that a few more of the same from time to time would do much to alleviate a diet of creosote.

CHAPTER XIII.
AN OLD FRIEND RETURNS AND CAPPY LEADS ANOTHER ACE

Three days before the Retriever finished loading, the captain wired a trustworthy Seattle crimp recommended by Mr. Murphy, instructing him to send down a second mate, eight seamen and a good cook—and to bring them drunk, because the vessel was laden with creosoted piling. Captain Noah Kendall, Matt's predecessor on the Retriever, had been raised on clipper ships and as he grew old had allowed himself the luxury of a third mate, to which arrangement Cappy Ricks, having a certain affection for Captain Noah, had never made any objection; but something whispered to Matt Peasley that the quickest route to Cappy's heart would be via a short payroll, so he concluded to dispense with a third mate and tack ten dollars a month extra on the pay-check of the excellent Murphy.

The Retriever was lying in the stream fully loaded when the crew arrived, convoyed by the crimp's runner. In accordance with instructions they were drunk, the crimp having furnished his runner with a two-gallon jug of home-made firewater upon leaving Seattle. One man—the second mate—was fairly sober, however, and while the launch that bore him to the Retriever was still half a mile from the vessel the breezes brought him an aroma which could not, by any possibility, be confused with the concentrated fragrance of the eight alcoholic breaths being exhaled around him. Muttering deep curses at his betrayal, he promptly leaped overboard and essayed to swim ashore. The runner pursued him in the launch, however, and gaffed him by the collar with a boat-hook; the launch-man, for a consideration, aided the runner, and the unwilling wretch was carried struggling to purgatory.

"Oh, look who's here!" Mr. Murphy yelled to the skipper, as the bedraggled second mate was propelled forcibly up the ship's companion-ladder to the waiting arms of the first mate. "Welcome home, Angus, my lad."

It was Mr. MacLean, their quondam second mate, cast back on the deckload of the Retriever by the resurgent tide of maritime misfortune. Mr. Murphy sat down and held himself by the middle and laughed until the tears ran down his ruddy cheeks, while Matt Peasley joined heartily in the mirth. The unfortunate Mr. MacLean also wept — but from other causes, to wit — grief and rage.

"I'm happy to have you with us again, Mr. MacLean," Matt saluted the second mate. "While your courage and loyalty might be questioned, your ability may not. So the crimp swindled you, eh? Told you he wanted you for another ship and then switched the papers on you, eh?"

"You should never trust a crimp, Angus," Mr. Murphy warned him. "And you should never do business with them unless you're cold sober. Let this be a lesson to you, my lad. Never be a drinking man and you'll never have to go to a crimp for a snug berth. Run along to your old room, now, Angus, and shift into some dry clothes, if you expect to finish the voyage."

"I'll gie ye ma worrd I'll desert in th' discharrgin' port!" Mr. MacLean burred furiously. "Ye hae me noo, body an' bones —"

"Aye, and we'll keep you, Angus. Have no fear of that. And you'll not desert in the discharging port. I'll see to that," Matt Peasley assured him.

When the last man had been assisted aboard Matt signaled for the tug he had engaged. By the time she had hooked on and towed them over the bar three of the seamen were sober enough to assist the skipper and the mates in getting all plain sail, with the exception of the square sails, on her, and, with a spanking nor'west breeze on her quarter she rolled away into the horizon.

Despite the fact that the Retriever's bottom was rather foul with marine growth, and the further fact that her master had to lay her head under her wing in a blow which, with an ordinary cargo, he would have bucked right into, the run to Antofagasta was made in average time. And when Matt Peasley went ashore to report by cable to his owners he discovered that Cappy Ricks had provided him with a cargo of nitrate for Makaweli.

"What did I tell you, sir?" Mr. Murphy growled when the captain informed him of the owners' orders. "I tell you, sir, the dirtiest cargo Cappy Ricks can find is too good for us. Praise be, the worst we can get at Makaweli is a sugar cargo."

Mr. Murphy's grudge against nitrate lay in the annoyance incident to taking on the cargo properly. Nitrate is very heavy and cannot, like sugar, be loaded flush with the hatches, thus rendering shifting of the cargo impossible. In loading nitrate a stout platform must be erected athwart ship, above the keelsons, in order that the foundation of the cargo may be laid level; for, as the sacked nitrate is piled, the pile must be drawn in gradually until the sides meet in a peak like a roof. It must then be braced and battened securely with heavy timbers from each side of the ship, in order that the dead weight may be held in the center of the ship and keep her in trim. Woe to the ship that shifts a cargo of nitrate in a heavy gale; for it is a tradition of the sea that, once a vessel rolls her main yard under, she will not roll it back, and ultimately is posted at Lloyd's as missing.

When the cargo was out Mr. Murphy went ashore and purchased a lot of Chinese punk, which he burned in the hold, with the hatches battened down, while Mr. MacLean, who had once been a druggist's clerk, and who, by the way, had concluded to stay by the ship, sloshed down the decks with an aromatic concoction mixed by a local apothecary. The remnant of their spoiled stores Matt Peasley, like a true Yankee, sawed off to good advantage on a trustful citizen of Antofagasta, and credited the ship with the proceeds; after which he got his nitrate aboard and squared away for the Hawaiian Islands.

The run to Makaweli was very slow, for the ship was logy with the grass and barnacles on her bottom. At Makaweli he found a sugar cargo awaiting him for discharge at Seattle; and, thanks to the northwest trades at her quarter, the Retriever wallowed home reasonably fast.

CHAPTER XIV.
INSULT ADDED TO INJURY

When Matt Peasley's report of that long voyage reached the Blue Star Navigation Company it was opened by Mr. Skinner, who, finding no letter enclosed, had a clerk check and verify it, and then pass it on to old Cappy Ricks.

"Where's the letter that came with this report, Skinner?" Cappy piped.

"He didn't enclose one, Mr. Ricks."

"Im-possible!"

"All of Captain Peasley's communications with this office since he entered our employ have been by wire."

"But—dad-burn the fellow, Skinner—why doesn't he write and tell us something?"

"About what?"

"Why, about his ship, his voyage—any old thing. An owner likes to have a report on his property once in a while, doesn't he? Unless we happen to charter the Retriever for a cargo to her home port, you know very well, Skinner, we may not see her for years. Besides, I've never seen the man Peasley, and if he'd only write now and then I could get a line on him from his letters. I can always tell a fool by the letter he writes, Skinner."

"Well, then," Skinner replied. "Peasley must be a wise man, because he never writes at all. The only specimen of that fellow's handwriting I've ever seen is his signature on the drafts he draws against us. You will notice that he has even engaged a stenographer—at his own expense, so the clerk informs me—to typewrite his statement of account."

"Then that explains it, Skinner. The big-fisted brute can't write a hand that anybody could read. But, still, he should have dictated a letter, Skinner. The least he might have done was to say: 'Enclosed herewith find my report of disbursements for last voyage.' And then he could have slipped in some mild complaint about the creosote, the trouble he had in getting a crew, and so on."

"I don't see why you complain about a lack of correspondence, sir," Mr. Skinner protested. "For my part, I think it a profound relief to have a captain that isn't writing or wiring in complaints about slow dispatch in loading or discharging, his private feuds with marine cooks and walking delegates from the Sailors' Union. Confound these fellows that are always unloading a cargo of woe on their owners! It strikes me that they're trying to square themselves for incompetence."

"I agree with you, Skinner. But then, all the Thomaston Peasleys were quick-tempered and wouldn't be imposed on; and I hate to think I've picked the only one of the tribe who will dog it and never let a peep out of him."

"Oh!" said Mr. Skinner. "I see! You want him to start something with you, eh?"

Cappy evaded this blunt query, however, and turned his attention to the report.

"Hello!" he said. "I'm blessed if he hasn't anticipated the very question I should have asked. Here's a footnote in red ink: 'Decided not to carry third mate. Two mates ample.' And so two mates are ample, Skinner, though I used to humor Cap'n Noah with three. This confirms me in the belief that Peasley must be a young man, Skinner, and not afraid to stand a watch himself if necessary. And here's another footnote: 'Chief Mate Michael J. Murphy very gallantly declined to leave when he smelled the creosote, and was a tower of strength when it came to stowing the nitrate. He holds an unlimited mate's license, is sober, intelligent, courageous, honest and a hard worker. He goes up for his master's license this week!"

"Ah-h-h!" Cappy Ricks looked up, smiling. "Skinner," he declared, "it is as hard to keep a good man down as it is for a camel to enter the Kingdom of Heaven — I mean for a rich man to enter a camel — bother! I mean you can't keep a good man down, Skinner. And this is the reason: The first mate, Murphy, wanted to leave, but his loyalty would not permit it. Hence the man Peasley must be a good, fair, decent man, to inspire such loyalty. He is, and this report proves it. His action in bringing Murphy to our attention indicates appreciation and a sense of justice. Good! Skinner, make a note of the qualifications of Michael J. Murphy for a master's berth and give him the first opening."

He returned to a perusal of the report.

"Huh! Harump-h-h-h! 'Credit by skipper's rake-off on stores, and so on, $57.03.' Skinner, that proves the man Peasley is too decent and honest to accept a commission from the thieves who supply his vessel, because he knows that if they give him a commission they'll only tack it on to the bill, where he can't see it. Well! All the Thomaston Peasleys were honest, Skinner. No thanks to him. Still, it's a shame to give him another rough deal, for apparently he has — er — many — er — commendable qualities. Still — er — Skinner, I've just got to have a letter from the man Peasley, if it is only a letter of resignation. Get him another dirty cargo, Skinner, the dirtier the better."

The dirtiest cargo Mr. Skinner could think of, with the exception of a load of creosoted piling, was another cargo of the same. So he scoured the market and finally he found one on Puget Sound, whereupon he sent Matt Peasley a telegram ordering him to tow to the Ranier Mill and Lumber Company's dock at Tacoma, and load for Callao. At the same time he wired the Ranier people requesting them to be ready to furnish cargo to the Retriever the following day — this on the strength of a telegram from Matt Peasley received the previous day informing his owners that he was discharged and awaiting orders.

CHAPTER XV.
RUMORS OF WAR

When four days had elapsed the manager of the Ranier mill wired the Blue Star Navigation Company that the Retriever had not yet appeared at their dock.

Now four days wasted means something to a big barkentine like the Retriever; and in the absence of any excuse for the delay Cappy Ricks promptly came to the conclusion that Matt Peasley was ashore in Seattle, disporting himself after the time-honored custom of deep-sea sailors home from a long cruise. There could be no other reason for such flagrant inattention to orders; for, had the man Peasley been ill, the mate, Murphy, whom the captain vouched for as sober and intelligent, would have had his superior sent to a hospital and wired the office for orders.

"Skinner," said Cappy, "send in a stenographer."

When the girl appeared Cappy Ricks dictated this wire:

> Captain Matthew Peasley,
> Master Barkentine Retriever,
> Colman Dock, Seattle, Washington.
>
> Are you drunk, dead or asleep? You have your orders. Obey them P.D.Q. or turn over command to Chief Mate Murphy.
>
> Alden P. Ricks.

"There!" he shrilled. "I've signed my name to it. Sign a telegram Blue Star Navigation Company and these infernal skippers think a clerk sent it; but when they know the boss is on to them they'll jump lively. Bring me the answer to that as soon as it comes, Skinner."

However, the answer did not come that day. Indeed, the next day had almost dragged to a close before Mr. Skinner appeared with this telegraphic bomb:

> Alden P. Ricks,
> 258 California St.,
> San Francisco.
>
> Neither! Been waiting my turn to go on dry dock. On now. Didn't reply yesterday because too busy driving toothpicks in vessel's bottom to plug up wormholes. If Murphy hadn't hauled into fresh water last time on Grays Harbor while I was in Seattle getting my ticket, her bottom would look like a colander now. Sixteen months in the water. You ought to be ashamed to treat a good staunch ship like that. Off dock day after to-morrow; will tow to Tacoma immediately thereafter. Meantime expect apology for insulting telegram.
>
> *Peasley.*

Sixteen months without dry-docking! Why, her bottom must look like the devil! Cappy Ricks gazed long and earnestly at his general manager.

"Skinner," he said, "you're an ass! Why was not this vessel dry-docked before you sent her to Antofagasta?"

Mr. Skinner lost his temper.

"Because I didn't send her to Antofagasta," he replied sharply. "You did! And the reason she wasn't docked is because there isn't a dock on Grays Harbor. If you wouldn't interfere in the shipping, Mr. Ricks, and spoil my plans to satisfy your personal whims, the vessel would never have gone on that long voyage without being cleaned and painted."

"Enough!" Cappy half screamed. "It's a disgrace! Not another word, sir! Not another peep out of you. Why didn't you order the man Peasley to dock her? Why did you leave the decision to him? He knew his vessel was foul—he thought we ought to know it, also; and naturally he expected that when we ordered him to Seattle we would have made arrangements to put him on dry dock. Instead of which he had to make them himself; and I'm shown up as a regular, infernal—er—er—baboon! Yes, sir! Regular baboon! Nice spectacle you've made of me, getting me into a scrape where I have to apologize to my own captain! Baboon! Huh! Baboon! Yes; you're the baboon!"

"Well, I can't think of everything, Mr. Ricks—"

"Everything! Good Lord, man, if you'd only think of something! Send in a stenographer."

Mr. Skinner rang for the girl and retired in high dudgeon, while Cappy Ricks smote his corrugated brow and brought forth the following:

> Captain Matthew Peasley,
> Master Barkentine Retriever,
> Hall's Dry Dock, Eagle Harbor, Wash.
>
> "Yes; that was a grave oversight sending you to Antofagasta without docking you first. Express my appreciation of Murphy's
> forethought in killing some of the worms. Am not kind of owner
> that lets a ship go to glory to make dividends. Keep your vessel in top-notch shape at all times, though I realize this instruction unnecessary to you. Give the old girl all that is coming to her, including two coats X. & Y. copper paint. Replace all planking that looks suspicious.
>
> Alden P. Ricks.

"I guess that's friendly enough," he soliloquized. "I think he'll understand. I don't have to crawl in the dirt to let him know I'm sorry."

Cappy had recovered his composure by the following morning and was addressing Mr. Skinner as "Skinner, my dear boy," when another telegram from Matt Peasley created a very distinct variation in his mental compass. It ran as follows:

> Alden P. Ricks,
> 258 California St.
> San Francisco.
>
> X. & Y. copper paint no good. That brand used last time; hence worms got to her quickly. Giving her two coats O. & Z. Costs more, but does the business. Renewed about a dozen planks. Repair bill about offsets profit on that infernal nitrate. Your apology accepted, but do not say that again!
>
> Peasley.

"'Your apology is accepted!'" Cappy's voice rose, shrill with anger. "Why, the infernal — er — er — porpoise! Me apologize to a man

I employ! By jingo, I'd fire him first! Yes, sir—fire him like that!" The old man snapped his fingers.

"Really, Skinner, I don't know what I'm going to do about the man Peasley. I want to befriend him, because he's one of my own people, so to speak; but I greatly fear, Skinner, I shall have to rough him. Here he is, disputing with me—with me, Skinner—the relative merits of copper paint. And not only disputing, sir, but disobeying my specific instructions. Also, he permits himself the luxury of criticism. Well! I'll not fire him this time; but, by the gods, I'll give him a blowing-up he'll remember. Skinner, send in a stenographer."

"Take letter," the old man ordered presently, and proceeded to dictate:

> *Captain Matthew Peasley,*
> *Master Barkentine Retriever,*
> *Care Rainier M. & L. Co.,*
> *Tacoma, Washington.*
>
> *Sir:— Your night letter of the fifth is before me and treasured for its unparalleled effrontery.*
>
> *Please be advised that in future, when an extraordinary outlay of cash for your vessel's accounts is contemplated, this office should first be consulted. When, in your judgment, your vessel requires docking, repairs, new spars, canvas, and so on, you will apprise us before proceeding to run up a bill of expense on your owners. Your business is to navigate your vessel. Spending money judiciously is a fine art which no sailor, to my knowledge, has ever acquired.*
>
> *Though admitting that the vessel needed docking, I maintain you*
> *should have wired us of that fact, whereupon we would have ordered you to the dry dock patronized by this company. It is customary for owners to express a preference for dry docks and copper paint; and in presuming to go counter to my specific instructions in the matter of paint you are prejudicing your future prospects with this company.*

Another exhibition of your arrogance, impudence, general bad manners and lack of knowledge of the ethics of your profession will result in prompt dismissal from the service of the Blue Star Navigation Company.

Yours, and so on,
Alden P. Ricks, President

CHAPTER XVI.
WAR!

The receipt of Cappy Ricks' letter actually frightened Matt Peasley for about thirty seconds. Then he reread the last paragraph. Like a dutiful servant he forgave Cappy the letter's reference to arrogance, impudence and general bad manners; but the reference to his lack of knowledge of the ethics of his profession made him fighting mad.

Cappy Ricks might just as well have passed him the supreme insult of the seas: "Aw, go buy a farm!" He showed the letter to Mr. Murphy.

"Why, that's adding insult to injury!" the mate declared sympathetically.

The youthful master threw up both hamlike hands in token of complete surrender and profound disgust.

"There's the gratitude of an owner!" he raved. "He wires me my loading orders and never says a word about docking—though as managing owner it's up to him to know when the vessel needs docking. I can't plan her comings and goings so that at the proper time she'll find herself at a port with a dry dock. Of course when he wired me my loading orders I realized he wasn't going to dock me; so I took matters into my own hands. Why, Mike, I wouldn't skipper a ship so foul she can hardly answer her helm. How could I know he'd forgotten she needed docking? I'm not a mind reader."

"I suppose he's been so busy hunting another dirty cargo for us he hadn't time to think of the vessel," Mr. Murphy sneered, and added: "The dirty old skin-flint!"

"Well, I'll just tell Cappy Ricks where to head in!" Matt stormed. "Let him fire me if he wants to. I don't care to sail a ship—particularly a dirty ship—for any man who thinks I don't know my business.

Mike, I'm going to send him a telegram that'll burn his meddling old fingers."

"Give him hell for me!" pleaded Mr. Murphy. "If he fires you I'll quit, too."

The result of this colloquy was that Cappy Ricks received this night letter the following morning:

>Alden P. Ricks,
>258 *California St.,*
>San Francisco.
>
>Referring your letter. Men that taught me nautical ethics expected things done without orders, minus thanks for doing them well, plus abuse for doing them poorly. Regard your criticism as out of place. Am not the seventh son of a seventh son. How could I know you had overlooked fact that vessel needed docking? Your business to plan my voyages to get me to dry-dock port at least once a year. When you wired loading orders, concluded you were cheap owner; hence decided dock her without orders. Expect to be fired sooner or later, but will leave good ship behind me so my successor cannot say, "Peasley let her run down." Had I waited orders, vessel would have been ruined. Yet you have not sufficient grace to express your thanks. Had I not acted in this emergency, you would have fired me later for incompetence, and blacklisted me for not telling you what you know you ought to know without being told.
>
>Referring copper paint, I know from practical experience which brand is best; you know only what paint dealer tells you. Will not stand abuse for knowing my business and attending to it without instructions from landlubber! When you appointed me you said remember speed synonymous with dividends in shipping business. How can I make fast passages with whiskers two feet long on my keel? Send new flying jib and spanker next loading port. Send new skipper, too, if you feel that way about it.
>
>>Peasley.

"Well, Skinner," Cappy Ricks declared, "this is the first time a skipper in my employ ever talked back — and it'll be the last. I've had enough of this fellow's impudence, Skinner. He's right at that — blast him — but he's too much of a sea lawyer; and I won't have any employee of mine telling me how to run my business. Send in a stenographer."

When the stenographer entered Cappy Ricks said:

"Ahem-m! Harump-h-h-h! Take telegram: 'Captain Matthew Peasley, care Rainier Mill and Lumber Company, Tacoma, Washington. You're fired! Ricks.' Ahem! Huh! Har-ump! Take 'nother telegram: 'Mr. Michael J. Murphy, First Mate Barkentine Retriever'— same address as Peasley—'Accept this telegram as your formal appointment to command of our barkentine, Retriever, vice Matthew Peasley, discharged this day; forwarding to-morrow certificate of change of master.' Sign that: 'Blue Star Navigation Company, per Alden P. Ricks,' and get both telegrams on the wire right away."

Cappy turned to Mr. Skinner and chuckled sardonically.

"I'll bet that will gravel the man Peasley," he declared. "There's nothing harder on a captain than being fired, and succeeded by his own mate—particularly after he has so recently recommended that mate! Peasley will be wild—the pup!"

"Well," Mr. Skinner replied, "appointing Mr. Murphy certainly has this advantage,—he's there on the ground and we are thus spared the expense of sending a man from here."

"That's one of the reasons why I appointed him—one of three very excellent reasons, in fact. Now we'll wait and see what the man Peasley has to say to that telegram."

They had to wait about two hours, and this was what Matt Peasley had to say:

> "Many thanks. The second mate and the cook quit the minute they discovered it was to be another cargo of creosoted piling; and now that I am fired Mr. Murphy has concluded that he might as well quit also. Will stick by ship, however, until you send my successor; meantime loading continues as usual."

"Well, that's what the man Peasley says!" Cappy snapped. "Murphy's quit, eh? Well, I guess Mr. Murphy hadn't received my telegram when Peasley sent this message. It'll take more than a cargo of creosoted piling to keep Murphy out of the master's cabin when he hears from me."

The stenographer entered with another telegram.

"Ah!" Cappy remarked, and rubbed his hands together in pleased anticipation. "I dare say this is from Mr. Murphy."

It was; and this is what the loyal Murphy had to say:

> "I thank you for the consideration. Very sweet of you; but I wouldn't work for you again on a bet. You couldn't hand me a ripe peach! Master or mate, creosote tastes the same to me. At Captain Peasley's request am staying by vessel until new master arrives and hires new mate. Would have stuck by vessel for Old Man's sake if you'd slipped us cargo of uncrated rattlesnakes; but since I encouraged him to tell you things for good of your soul and you fired him for it I must decline to profit by his misfortune."

Silently Cappy Ricks folded that telegram and laid it on his desk; his head sagged forward on his breast and he fell to meditating deeply. Finally he looked up and eyed Mr. Skinner over the rims of his spectacles.

"Skinner," he said solemnly, "do you realize, my boy, that we have two extremely remarkable men on the barkentine Retriever?"

"They are certainly most remarkably deficient in respect to their superiors, though in all probability exceedingly capable seamen," Mr. Skinner answered sympathetically, for he had great veneration for the creator of the pay roll.

"I know," Cappy replied sadly; "but then, you know, Skinner, the good Lord must certainly hate a bootlicker! Skinner, I simply cannot afford to lose those two damned scoundrels in the Retriever. They're good men! And a good man who knows he's good will not take any slack from man or devil; so I cannot afford to lose those two. Skinner, I've got myself into an awful mess. Here I've been running by dead reckoning and now I'm on the rocks! What'll I do, Skinner? I'm licked; but, dang it all, sir, I can't admit it, can I? Isn't there some way to referee this scrap and call it a draw?"

"I see no way out of it now except to send another captain to Tacoma."

"Skinner," he declared, "you're absolutely no use to me in an emergency. When I made you my general manager, on a bank president's salary, I thought I'd be able to take it easy for the rest of my life." He wagged his head sadly. "And what's the result? I work harder than ever. Skinner, if I hadn't any more imagination than you possess I'd be out there on the corner of California and Market Streets peddling lead pencils this minute. Leave this problem to me, Skinner. I suppose I'll find a way out of it, with entire honor to all concerned. Holy sailor!" he added. "But that man Murphy is loyal—and loyalty is a pretty scarce commodity these days, let me tell you!"

CHAPTER XVII.
CAPPY FORCES AN ARMISTICE

During the week that succeeded, Cappy Ricks did not once mention the subject of the Retriever and her recalcitrant skipper and mate; and Mr. Skinner argued from this that all was well. Finally one day Cappy came into the office and paused beside the general manager's desk. He was grinning like a boy.

"Well, Skinner," he piped. "I've just come from the Merchants' Exchange and I see by the blackboard that our Retriever cleared for Antofagasta yesterday."

"Indeed!" Mr. Skinner replied politely. "So you found a captain for her. Whom did you send?"

"Nobody," the old man cackled. "Matt Peasley took her out, and the manager of the Rainier mill wires me that Murphy went with him as chief kicker. What do you think of that?"

"Why, I'm—er—satisfied if you are, sir."

"Well, you can bet I'm satisfied. If I wasn't I'd have a revenue cutter out after the man Peasley and his mate right now. By golly, Skinner," he piped, and slapped his wizened flank, "I tell you I've worked this deal pretty slick, if I do say it myself. And all on dead reckoning—dead reckoning, and not a single day of demurrage!"

"Oh! So you wired Peasley and the mate and asked them to go back to work and forget they were discharged?" Mr. Skinner suggested witheringly.

"Skinner, on my word, you grow worse every day. You've been with me, man and boy, twenty-odd years, and in all that time you never saw anybody cover me with blood, did you?"

"No, sir."

"And you never will. Why, I managed this affair by simply forgetting all about it! When you're in a jam, Skinner, always let the other fellow do the talking. I just sat tight until I had a telegram from the man Peasley, informing me that the vessel would be loaded in two days and that his successor had not appeared as yet. I threw that telegram in my wastebasket; and when the vessel was loaded I had another telegram from Peasley, saying that the vessel was loaded, that his successor was still missing, and the mill manager was kicking and insisting that the ship be hauled away from the dock to make room for a steam schooner which wanted to load. So I filed that telegram in the wastebasket also. It was a night letter, delivered in the morning.

"When Peasley didn't get an answer by noon he wired again, saying that, as a favor to me, he would haul the Retriever into the stream, but would accept no responsibility for delay thereafter. He said further that, as a courtesy to me and his successor, he was shipping a crew that day in order that there might be no delay in sailing when the new captain arrived; so I thought I had better reply to that telegram, Skinner — and I did!"

"What did you say, Mr. Ricks?"

"I said: 'Please do not annoy me with your telegrams. You were fired a week ago, but it seems difficult for you to realize that fact. If demurrage results through my failure to get new skipper there in time, that is no skin off your nose. Your pay goes on until you are relieved, and you will be relieved when I get good and ready.' That telegram did the business, Skinner. He received it the day before yesterday and yesterday he towed out!"

Cappy Ricks burst into a shrill senile cackle that was really good to hear. As they grow old most men lose that capacity for a hearty laugh, but Cappy's perversity had kept him young at heart. The tears of mirth cascaded down his seamed old countenance now, and he had to sit down and have his laugh out.

"Oh, thunder!" he panted. "Really, Skinner — there's so much fun in business I wonder why a man can retire — just because he's made his pile! Skinner, I had it on the man Peasley a thousand miles — and he never guessed it! Dear, dear me! You see, Skinner, when he wired me he would not accept responsibility for demurrage to the vessel after she was loaded and hauled into the stream, he forgot that he had to accept responsibility for the vessel himself until his successor should arrive!

"Of course, the man Murphy could quit any time he desired; but if the skipper deserted the ship before being properly relieved, and then something happened to the vessel and I preferred charges against him, the inspectors might be induced to revoke his license—and he realized that. The knowledge made him hopping mad, Skinner; and when he got my telegram I knew he would begin to figure out some plan to make me mad! And, of course, I knew Murphy would help him out—the Irish are imaginative and vindictive; and—oh, dear me, Skinner—read that!" And Cappy handed his general manager the following telegram:

> You are right. I will be relieved when I get good and ready, and I will not be ready until I get back from Antofagasta. Shipped crew yesterday afternoon. All arrived drunk. Next morning all hands sober. Realizing predicament, riot resulted. Fearing lose crew, Murphy and I manhandled and locked in fo'castle. When your telegram arrived it found Murphy minus front tooth, myself black eye. Can stand injury, but not insult. Hence you are stuck with us for another voyage, whether you want us or not. Will have towed out by time you receive this. Go to Halifax!
>
> Peasley.

Mr. Skinner's face was cold and austere as he handed this telegram back to Cappy.

"So you made peace with honor, eh?" he sneered.

"Peace your grandmother!" Cappy chirped. "This war goes on until I get a letter from the man Peasley. Skinner, he and Murphy think they've done something wonderfully brilliant. When I wired him he would be relieved when I got good and ready it did him an awful lot of good to throw the words back in my face. Sure, Skinner! They think they're giving Cappy Ricks the merry ha-ha!"

"Well, of course, sir,'" said Mr. Skinner, "if this sort of horseplay is your fun—if it's your notion of business—I have no comment. You own fifteen-sixteenths of the Retriever, and you can afford to pay for your fancies; but if it was the last act of my life I'd fire that man Peasley in Callao and let him get home as best he could."

"Yes; I know," Cappy replied bitterly. "You fired him in Cape Town once—and how did he come home? He came home in the cabin of the Retriever—that's how he came home; and the Terrible Swede I sent to thrash him and fire him came home under hatches. Yes; you'd do a lot of things, Skinner—in your mind."

Mr. Skinner pounded his desk savagely. Cappy's retort made him boiling mad.

"Well, I'll bet I'd do something," he rasped. "I'd make that bucko suffer or I'd know the reason why."

"Skinner, that's just what we're going to do—just what we're doing, in fact. One of my ancestors sailed with the late John Paul Jones and ever since the Ricks' family motto has been: 'I have not yet begun to fight.' Now listen to reason, Skinner. The Retriever just came off dry-dock, didn't she? Well, it stands to reason she was dirty after that last cargo of creosoted piling; and it stands to reason, also, that the man Peasley slicked her up with white paint until she looked like an Easter bride. A Scandinavian doesn't give a hoot if his vessel is tight, well found and ready for sea; but a Yankee takes a tremendous pride in his ship and likes to keep her looking like a yacht. And just think, Skinner, how the man Peasley must have felt when he came off dry dock, all clean and nice, and then had to slop her up with another cargo of creosoted piling? Just think of that, Skinner!" and again he commenced his insane cackle.

"I have other, and more important things to think about," Mr. Skinner retorted icily. As a business man he was opposed to levity in the office. "What are your plans with reference to the Retriever? Do you wish to bring her back from Antofagasta in ballast?"

"Why, certainly not. Hunt a cargo for her, Skinner. We might just as well let the man Peasley know that though he's gone he's not forgotten. Use the cable freely and see if you can't pick up something for the return trip that will make those two firebrands sick at the stomach."

A month later Mr. Skinner stepped into Cappy's sanctum.

"Well," he announced. "I've got a return cargo for the Retriever."

"What have you got?" Cappy demanded anxiously; and Mr. Skinner told him.

"No?" said Cappy incredulously.

"Yes!" Mr. Skinner assured him.

Cappy's laughter testified to his hearty approval.

"Skinner, my dear boy," he cried. "I don't know what I'd do without you."

And then he laid his wicked old head on his desk and laughed until he wept. Indeed, Mr. Skinner so far forgot his code as to laugh with him.

"We'll stink those two vagabonds — those maritime outlaws — out of the ship," he declared.

CHAPTER XVIII.
THE WAR IS RENEWED

The belief that they had come off victorious in their skirmish with Cappy Ricks cheered Matt Peasley and his mate for the first two weeks out from Puget Sound; after which the creosote commenced to season their food, and then the victory began to take on the general appearance of a vacuum. However, thanks to a clean keel and fair winds, they made a smashing passage and their sufferings were not unduly prolonged.

Immediately on his arrival at Antofagasta the young skipper reported by cable to his owners, thereby eliciting the following reply from Cappy Ricks:

> "You stole ship. If you value your ticket bring her back with cargo agent provides."

Naturally this somewhat cryptic cablegram roused Matt Peasley's curiosity. He could not rest until he had interviewed the agent—and after that sop to his inquisitiveness he returned to the Retriever a broken man. The loyal and disgusted Murphy read the trouble in the master's face.

"What new deviltry's afoot now, Matt?" he demanded, in his eagerness and sympathy forgetting the respect due his superior.

"Green hides, Mike!" the skipper answered, in his distress failing to notice the mate's faux pas and making one himself. "Green hides, old pal; and they stink something horrible. Back to Seattle with the dirty mess, and then another cargo of creosoted—"

"King's X!" yelled Mr. Murphy. "I crossed my fingers the minute your face appeared over the rail. I quit—and I quit as soon as this piling is out. I tell you I won't keep company with green hides. No, sir; I won't. I tell you I will—not—do it! Why, we might as well have a dead hog in the hold! Captain Matt, I hate to throw you down in a foreign port; but this—is absolutely—the finish!"

"Do you value your ticket, Mike?" the captain queried ominously.

"What's a ticket when a man's lost his self-respect?" Mr. Murphy raved.

Matt handed him Cappy's cablegram and the mate read it.

"I think that bet goes double, Mike," the skipper warned him. "You signed for the round trip. I've got to go through—and there's strength in numbers."

"Well," said Mr. Murphy reluctantly, "I suppose I do attach a certain—er—sentimental value to my ticket."

"I thought you would. Cappy's got us by the short hair, Mike; and the only thing to do is to fly to it, with all sails set. We must never let on he's given us anything out of the ordinary."

Mr. Murphy shivered; for, as Cappy had remarked to Mr. Skinner, the mate was Irish, hence imaginative. He imagined he smelled the green hides already, and quite suddenly he gagged and sprang for the rail. Poor fellow! He had stood much of late and his stomach was a trifle sensitive from a diet of creosote straight.

Somehow they got the awful cargo aboard, though, at that, there were not sufficient hides to half load her; in consequence of which all hands realized that Cappy had merely given them this dab of freight to sicken them. They cursed him all the way back to Seattle, where the crew quit the minute the vessel was made fast to the dock.

CHAPTER XIX.
CAPPY SEEKS PEACE

"Here's a telegram for you, sir," Mr. Murphy remarked when Matt Peasley came aboard after cashing a draft on the Blue Star Navigation Company to pay off his crew. It proved to be from Cappy Ricks and said merely:

"Discharge that cargo of hides or take the consequences!"

"The old sinner thought I'd dog it, I suppose," Matt sneered, as he passed the message to Mr. Murphy, who shivered as he read it. "I guess you're elected, Mike," the skipper continued. "The second mate has quit. However, it isn't going to be very hard on you this time. I was speaking to the skipper of that schooner in the berth ahead of us, and he gave me a recipe for killing the perfume of a cargo of green hides."

"If he'd given it to us in Antofagasta, I'd name a ship after him some day," Mr. Murphy mourned.

"Well, we've gotten it in time to be of some use," Matt declared. "You don't suppose I'm going to let this old snoozer Ricks get away with the notion that he put one over on us, do you? Shall we haul Old Glory down? No! Never! I'll just switch off the laughing gas on Cappy Ricks," and the young skipper went ashore and wired his managing owner as follows:

> "Green hides are the essence of horror if you do not know how to handle them. Fortunately I do. Pour water on a green hide and you muzzle the stink. I judge from your last telegram you thought you handed me something."

When Cappy Ricks got that telegram he flew into a rage and refused to believe Matt Peasley's statement until he had first called up a dealer in hides and confirmed it. The entire office staff wondered all that day what made Cappy so savage.

By the following day, however, Cappy's naturally optimistic nature had reasserted itself. He admitted to himself that he had fanned out, but still the knowledge brought him some comfort.

"He's walloped me so," Cappy soliloquized, "he just can't help writing and crowing about it. If I didn't do anything else I bet I've pried a letter out of him. It certainly will be a comfort to see something except a telegram and a statement of account from that fellow."

However, when the report of the voyage arrived, Mr. Skinner reported that it contained no letter. Cappy's face reflected his disappointment.

"I guess you'll have to go stronger than green hides to get a yelp out of that fellow," Mr. Skinner predicted.

"Why, there isn't anything stronger than a cargo of green hides, Skinner," Cappy declared thoughtfully. He clawed his whiskers a moment. Then: "What have you got for her on the Sound, Skinner?"

"Nothing nasty, sir. We'll have to give him a regular cargo this time—that is, unless he quits. I've got a cargo for Sydney, ready at our own mill at Port Hadlock."

"Well, he hasn't resigned yet," Cappy declared; "so we might as well beat him to it. Wire him, Skinner, to tow to our mill at Port Hadlock and load for Sydney. If he believes we're willing to call this thing a dead heat he may conclude to stick. Tell him this is a nice cargo." Again Cappy clawed his whiskers. "Sydney, eh?" he said musingly. "That's nice! We can send him over to Newcastle from there to pick up a cargo of coal, and maybe he'll come home afire! If we can't hand him a stink, Skinner, we'll put a few gray hairs in his head."

These instructions Mr. Skinner grudgingly complied with; and Matt Peasley, with his hatches wide open and buckets of punk burning in the hold to dispel the lingering fragrance of his recent cargo—concluding that, on the whole, he and Mr. Murphy had come through the entire affair very handsomely indeed—towed down to Hadlock and commenced to take on cargo. If Cappy Ricks was willing to declare a truce then Matt Peasley would declare one too.

Matt's peaceful acquiescence in his owner's program merely served to arouse Cappy Ricks' abnormal curiosity. The more he thought of Matt Peasley the greater grew his desire for a closer scrutiny. The most amazing man in the world had been in his employ a year and a half, and as yet they had never met; unless the Retriever should happen to be loaded for San Francisco years might elapse before they should see each other; and now that he had attained to his allotted three score years and ten Cappy decided that he could no longer gamble on the future.

He summoned Mr. Skinner.

"Skinner, my dear boy," he announced with the naive simplicity that made him so lovable. "I suppose it's very childish of me, but I have a tremendous desire to see this extraordinary fellow Peasley."

"You can afford to satisfy your slightest whim, Mr. Ricks," he replied. "I'll load her for San Francisco after she returns from Australia. I daresay if he ever gets through the Golden Gate he'll call up at the office."

"Skinner, I can't wait that long. Many things may happen. Ahem! Harump-h-h-h! Wire the man Peasley, Skinner, to have his photograph taken and forwarded to me immediately charging expense."

"Very well, sir," Mr. Skinner responded.

"Well, I'll be keel-hauled and skull-dragged," Matt Peasley declared to Mr. Murphy. "Here's a telegram from the owners demanding my photograph."

Mr. Murphy read the amazing message, scratched his raven poll, and declared his entire willingness to be damned.

"It's a trap," he announced presently. "Don't send it. Matt, you look about twenty years old and for the next few years, if you expect to work under the Blue Star flag, you must remember your face isn't your fortune. You've got to be pickled in salt for twenty years to please Cappy Ricks. If he sees your photograph he'll fire you, Matt. I know that old crocodile. All he wants is an excuse to give you the foot, anyhow."

"But he's ordered me to send it, Mike. How am I going to get out of it?"

As has been stated earlier in this tale, Mr. Murphy had an imagination.

"Go over into the town, sir," he said, "and in any photograph gallery you can pick up a picture of some old man. Write your name across it and send it to Cappy. He'll be just as happy, then, as though he had good sense."

"By George, I'll just do that!" Matt declared, and forthwith went ashore.

He sought the only photographer in Port Hadlock. At the entrance to the shop he found a glass case containing samples of the man's art, and was singularly attracted to the photograph of a spruce little old gentleman in a Henry Clay collar, long mutton-chop whiskers, and spectacles.

Moreover, to Matt's practiced eye, this individual seemed to savor of a Down-Easter. He was just the sort of man one might expect to bear the name of Matthew Peasley; so the captain mounted the stairs and sought the proprietor, from whom he purchased the picture in question for the trifling sum of fifty cents. Then he bore it away to the Retriever, scrawled his autograph across the old gentleman's hip and mailed the picture to Cappy Ricks.

CHAPTER XX.
PEACE AT LAST!

Mr. Skinner entered Cappy Ricks' office bearing an envelope marked "Photo. Do not crush or bend!" From the announcement in the upper right-hand corner the general manager deduced that the photograph was from Matt Peasley.

"Well, here's Captain Peasley's picture, Mr. Ricks," he announced.

"Ah! Splendid. Prompt, isn't he?" Cappy tore open the envelope, drew forth the photograph, scrutinized it carefully and then laid it face down on his desk, while he got out his spectacles, cleaned them carefully, adjusted them and gazed at the photograph once more.

"Ahem! Hu-m-m-m! Harump-h-h-h! Well, Skinner, life is certainly full of glad surprises," he announced presently, and added— "particularly where that man Peasley is concerned. I never did see the beat of that fellow."

"May I see his photograph, sir?" Mr. Skinner pleaded.

"Certainly," and Cappy passed it to the general manager, who glanced once at it and smiled down whimsically at Cappy.

"Yes, I agree with you, Mr. Ricks," he said. "Of all the surprises that man Peasley has handed us, this is the greatest."

Cappy nodded and smiled a little prescient smile. "Skinner," he said, "send in a stenographer. I'm going to send him a telegram."

He did. Matt Peasley blinked when he got it, and for the first time since he had commenced exchanging telegrams and cablegrams with the peculiar Mr. Ricks he was thoroughly non-plussed—so much so, in fact, that he called his right bower, Michael J. Murphy, into consultation.

"Mike," he said, and handed the mate the telegram, "what in the world do you suppose the old duffer means by that?"

Mr. Murphy read:

> "Matt, I always knew you were young, but I had no suspicion you were a child in arms until I received your photograph."

"Serves you right," the mate declared. "I told you to send the photo of an OLD man."

"But I did, Mike. I sent him a picture of an old pappy-guy sort of man, with long, mutton-chop whiskers, glasses and an old-fashioned collar as tall as the taffrail."

"It beats my time then what he's driving at, Captain Matt. But then one can never tell what Cappy Ricks is up to. I've heard he's a great hand to have his little joke, so I daresay that telegram is meant for sarcasm."

Matt had a horrifying inspiration. "I know what's wrong," he cried bitterly. "He thinks I'm so old I ought to be retired, and that telegram is in the nature of a hint that a letter, asking for my resignation, is on the way now."

"Why—why—why?" Mr. Murphy stuttered, "did you send him the picture of Methuselah himself? Heaven's sake, skipper, there's a happy medium, you know. I meant for you to pick yourself out a man of about fifty-five, and here you've slipped him a patriarch of ninety. Sarcasm! I should say so."

They stared at each other a few seconds; then Mr. Murphy had an equally disturbing inspiration.

"By Neptune!" he suggested, "maybe you sent him the picture of somebody he knows!"

"Well, in that case, Mike, I'm not going to hang on the hook of suspicion. Maybe I can find out whose picture I sent," and away Matt went up town to the photograph gallery. When he returned ten minutes later Mr. Murphy, sighting him a block in the offing, knew the skipper of the barkentine Retriever for a broken man! Beyond doubt he had shipped a full cargo of grief.

"Well?" he queried as Matt hove alongside. "Did you find out?"

Matt nodded gloomily.

"Who?" Mr. Murphy demanded peremptorily.

"Cappy Ricks!" Matt almost wailed.

"NO!" Mr. Murphy roared.

"Yes! The old scoundrel was up here three years ago, visiting this mill—you know, Mike, he owns it—and the Retriever was here loading at the time. He and Captain Kendall were close friends, and they went over to that photograph shop, had their pictures taken and swapped—and like a poor, helpless, luckless boob I had to come along and buy the sample picture the photographer hung in his case. It never occurred to me to ask questions—and I might have known nobody but a prominent citizen ever gets into a show-case—"

"Glory, glory, hallelujah," Mr. Murphy crooned in a deep, chain-locker voice, and fled from the skipper's wrath.

An hour later, in the privacy of his cabin, Matt Peasley took his pen in hand and wrote to Cappy Ricks:

> Mr. Alden P. Ricks,
> Dear Sir:—
>
> I herewith tender my resignation as master of the barkentine Retriever, same to take effect on my return from Sydney—or before I sail, if you desire. If I do not hear from you before I sail I shall assume that it will be all right to quit when I get back from Australia.
>
> I will not be twenty-three years old until the Fourth of July. I was afraid you wouldn't trust me with a big ship like the Retriever if you knew; so I sent you a photograph I purchased for fifty cents from the local photographer. I guess that's all—except that you couldn't find a better man to take my place than Mr. Murphy. He has had the experience.
>
> Yours truly,
> Matt Peasley.

There were tears in his eyes as he dropped that letter into the mail box. The Blue Star Navigation Company owned the Retriever, but—but—well she was Matt Peasley's ship and he loved her as men learn to love their homes. It broke his heart to think of giving her up.

"Skinner," said Cappy Ricks, "I've got a letter from the man Peasley at last; and now, by golly, I can quit and take a vacation. Send in a stenographer." The stenographer entered. "Take telegram—direct message," he ordered, and commenced to dictate:

> Captain Matthew Peasley,
>
> Your resignation accepted. You are too almighty good for a windjammer, Matthew. You need more room for the development of your talent. Give Murphy the ship, with my compliments, and tell him I've enjoyed the fight because it went to a knock-out. Report to me at this office as soon as possible. You belong in steam. A second mate's berth waiting for you. In a year you will be first mate of steam; a year later you will be master of steam, at two-fifty a month, and I will have a four-million-foot freighter waiting for you if you make good. The picture was a bully joke; but I could not laugh, Matt. It is so long since I was a boy.
>
> Cappy.

"Send that right away, like a good girl," he ordered. "He's about loaded and he may have towed out before the telegram reaches him. Or, better still, send the message in duplicate—one copy to the mill and the other in care of the custom-house at Port Townsend. He'll have to touch in there to clear the ship."

He walked into Mr. Skinner's office.

"Skinner," he said, "Murphy has the Retriever, and you're in charge of the shipping. Attend to the transfer of authority before she gets out of the Sound."

CHAPTER XXI.
MATT PEASLEY MEETS A TALKATIVE STRANGER

Cappy Ricks' telegram to Matt, in care of the mill at Port Hadlock, arrived several hours after the Retriever, fully loaded with fir lumber, had been snatched away from the mill dock by a tug and started on her long tow to Dungeness, where the hawser would be cast off. It was not until the vessel came to a brief anchorage in the strait off Port Townsend, the port of entry to Puget Sound, and Matt went ashore to clear his ship, that the duplicate telegram sent in care of the Collector of the Port, was handed to him.

He read and reread it. The news it contained seemed too good to be true.

"I guess I won't clear her after all," he announced to the deputy collector.

The official nodded. "I didn't think you would," he replied. "I have a telegram from the custom-house at San Francisco, apprising me that Michael J. Murphy has been appointed master of the Retriever, so if she's to be cleared Captain Murphy will have to do the job."

"He's my mate, and if you'll wait about half an hour I'll go get the old Siwash," Matt replied happily, and started back to the Retriever in a hurry. He had been gone less than twenty minutes, a fact noted by the astute Murphy, who met his superior at the rail as the latter climbed up the Jacob's ladder.

"Why, you haven't cleared the old girl so soon, have you, sir?" he queried.

"Read that," Matt announced dramatically.

Mr. Murphy read the telegram. "Bust my bob-stay!" he murmured. "The dirty old assassin! The slimy old pile-worm! The blessed old duffer! After treating us like dogs for a year and a half he gives me the ship, sets you down for a two year apprenticeship in steam and says he's going to build you a four-million-foot freighter! The scoundrelly old renegade! Why, say, Matt, Cappy's been spilling the acid all over us and we never knew it. Somehow, I have a notion that if we had yelled murder when he was beating us he'd have had us both out of his employ while you'd be saying Jack Robinson."

"I believe you, Mike. But he needn't think he's going to grab two years of my precious young life before he'll trust me with a steamer. I have an unlimited license for sail, and if I can pass the examination for steam before the inspectors — and I can — I'll get my license immediately. Just consider the old boy's inconsistency, Mike. If a man can handle a square-rigged ship he ought to be trusted with anything; yet, when he gives me a steamer you'd think he was giving me a man's job! Fair weather or foul, you stand on the bridge and control your vessel with the engine room telegraph. Shucks! I wonder if that crotchety old joker thinks it will take me two years to learn how to dock a steam schooner?"

Mr. Murphy hitched his trousers, stuck his thumbs in his belt and glared at Matt Peasley. "See here, you," he declared, "you're a child wonder, all right, but the trouble with you is, you hate yourself too much. Listen to me, kid. I'm the skipper of the Retriever now and you're my friend, young Matt Peasley, so I can talk to you as a friend. You're a pretty skookum youth and I'd hate like everything to mix it with you, but if you start to veto the old man's orders you may look for a fine thrashing from me when I get back from Australia! I won't have you making a damned fool of yourself, Matt. If you are in command of a four-million-foot freighter by the time you're twenty-seven, you'll be the youngest skipper of steam afloat, and you ought to be down on your marrow bones giving thanks to the good Lord who has done so much for you, instead of planning insurrection against Cappy Ricks. The idea!"

"But what sense is there in waiting—"

"When I refereed the scrap between you and All Hands And Feet you took my advice, didn't you? You didn't say to me then: 'What sense is there in waiting? Let me go in and finish the job and have done with it,' did you?"

"But this is business, Mike. For a year and a half Cappy has been having a whole lot of fun out of me—"

"It might have been fun for him, but it came pretty near being the death of me," Mr. Murphy contradicted. "If that jag of green hides from Antofagasta was a joke, beware of Cappy Ricks when he's serious. He's serious about you, Matt. He's picked on you sight unseen, and he's going to do something for you. He's an old man, Matt. Let him have his way and you'll profit by it."

"Well, I'll see what he has to say, at any rate," Matt compromised, and they went below, Matt to pack his sea chest and Mr. Murphy to shave and array himself in a manner befitting the master of a big barkentine about to present himself at the custom-house for the first time to clear his ship.

An hour later Matt Peasley found himself sitting on his sea chest on the cap of the wharf, watching the Retriever slipping down the strait under command of Captain Michael J. Murphy, while a new chief mate, shipped in Port Townsend, counted off the watches. Presently she turned a bend and was gone; and immediately he felt like a homeless wanderer. The thought of the doughty Murphy in that snug little cabin so long sacred to Matt Peasley brought a pang of near jealousy to the late commander of the Retriever; as he reflected on the two years of toil ahead of him before men would again address him as Captain Peasley, he wondered whether the game really would be worth the candle; for he had all of a Down-Easter's love for a sailing ship.

He recalled to mind Mr. Murphy's favorite story of the old sailing skipper who went into steam and who, during his very first watch on the steamship's bridge, ordered the man at the wheel to starboard his helm, and then forgot to tell him to steady it—the consequence being that the helmsman held hard-a-starboard and the ship commenced to describe a circle; whereupon the old sailing skipper got excited and screamed: "Back that main yard!" Matt felt that should anything like that happen to him in steam and the news should ever leak out, he would have to go back to the Atlantic Coast rather than face the gibes of his shipmates on the Pacific.

The passenger boat from Victoria picked him up and set him down in Seattle that night, and the following morning he boarded a train for San Francisco to report to Cappy Ricks.

At luncheon in the dining car that day Matt Peasley found himself seated opposite a man who had boarded the train with him at Seattle. As the young captain plied his knife and fork he was aware that this person's gaze rested with something more than casual interest on his—Matt's—left forearm; whereupon the latter realized that his vis-a-vis yearned to see more of a little decoration which, in the pride of his first voyage, Matt had seen fit to have tattooed on the aforesaid forearm by the negro cook. So, since he was the best-natured young man imaginable, Matt decided presently to satiate his neighbor's curiosity.

"It's a lady climbing a ladder," he announced composedly and drew back his sleeve to reveal this sample of black art. "I have a shield and an eagle on my breast and a bleeding heart, with a dagger stuck through it, on my right forearm."

"I didn't mean to be rude," the other answered, flushing a little. "I couldn't help noticing the chorus lady's shapely calves when you speared that last pickle; so I knew you were a sailor. I concluded you were an American sailor before I learned that you advertise the fact on your breast, and I was wondering whether you belong in the navy or the merchant marine."

"I'm from blue water," Matt replied pleasantly. "You're in the shipping business, I take it."

"Almost—I'm a ship, freight and marine insurance broker." And the stranger handed over a calling card bearing the name of Mr. Allan Hayes. "I'm from Seattle."

"Peasley is my name, Mr. Hayes," Matt answered heartily, glad of this chance acquaintance with a man with whom he could converse on a subject of mutual interest. "I haven't any post-office address," he added whimsically.

"Going over to Columbia River to join your ship, I daresay," Mr. Hayes suggested.

"No, sir. I'm bound for San Francisco, to get a job in steam and work up to a captaincy."

"Wherein you show commendable wisdom, Mr. Peasley," the broker answered. "A man can get so far in a windjammer—a hundred a month in the little coasting schooners and a hundred and twenty-five in the big vessels running foreign—and there he sticks. In steam schooners a good man can command two hundred dollars a month, with a chance for promotion into a big freighter, for the reason that in steam one has more opportunity to show the stuff that's in one."

"How far are you going?" Matt demanded.

"I'm bound for San Francisco too."

"Good!" Matt replied, for, like most boys, he was a gregarious animal, and Mr. Hayes seemed to be a pleasant, affable gentleman. "I suppose you know most of the steam vessels on this coast?" he continued, anxious to turn the conversation into channels that might be productive of information valuable to him in his new line of endeavor.

Mr. Hayes nodded. "I have to," he said, "if I'm to do any business negotiating charters; in fact, I'm bound to San Francisco now to charter two steamers."

"Freight or passenger?"

"Freight. There's nothing for a broker in a passenger vessel. I'm scouting for two boats for the Mannheim people. You've heard of them, of course. They own tremendous copper mines in Alaska, but they can't seem to get the right kind of flux to smelt their ore up there; so they're going to freight it down to their smelter in Tacoma."

"I see. But how do you work the game to pay your office rent?"

"Why, that's very simple, Mr. Peasley. Their traffic manager merely calls me up and tells me to find two ore freighters for him. He doesn't know where to look for them, but he knows I do, and that it will not cost him anything to engage me to find them for him. Well, I locate the vessels and when I come to terms with the owners, and those terms are satisfactory to my clients, I close the charter and the vessel owners pay me a commission of two and a half per cent. on all the freight money earned under the charter. A shipowner generally is glad to pay a broker a commission for digging him up business for his ships—particularly when freights are dull."

Matt Peasley nodded his comprehension and did some quick mental arithmetic.

"Why, you'll make a nice little fee on those ore boats," he said. "I suppose it's a time charter."

"Four years," Mr. Hayes replied, and smiled fatly at the thought of his income. "Of course I'd make a larger commission if the freight rate was figured on a tonnage basis; but on long charters, like these I mention, the ships are rented at a flat rate a day or month. Say, for instance, I negotiate these charters at the rate of four hundred dollars a day, or eight hundred dollars a day for the two boats. Two and a half per cent. of eight hundred dollars is twenty dollars a day, which I will earn as commission every day for the next four years that the vessels are not in dry dock or laid up for repairs."

"And you probably will earn that by one day of labor," Matt Peasley murmured admiringly—"perhaps one hour of actual labor!"

Mr. Hayes smiled again his fat smile. He shrugged.

"That's business," he said carelessly. "An ounce of promotion is worth a ton of horse power."

"Well, I should say so, Mr. Hayes! But you'll have quite a search to find an ore boat on the Pacific Coast. There are some coal boats running to Coos Bay, but they're hardly big enough; and then I suppose they're kept pretty busy in the coal trade, aren't they? It seems to me that what you need for your business would be two of those big steel ore vessels, with their engines astern—the kind they use on the Great Lakes."

"That is exactly why I am going to San Francisco, Mr. Peasley. There are on this Coast two ships such as you describe—sister ships and just what the doctor ordered."

"What are their names?"

"The Lion and the Unicorn."

Matt Peasley paused, with a forkful of provender halfway to his mouth. The S.S. Lion, eh? Why, that was one of Cappy Ricks' vessels! He remembered passing her off Cape Flattery once and seeing the Blue Star house flag fluttering at the fore.

"Were they Lake boats originally?" he queried.

Mr. Hayes nodded.

"What are they doing out here?"

"Right after the San Francisco fire, when fir lumber jumped from a twelve-dollar base to twenty-five, lumber freights soared accordingly," Hayes explained. "Vessels that had been making a little money at four dollars a thousand feet, from Oregon and Washington ports to San Francisco, were enabled to get ten dollars; and anything that would float was hauled out of the bone yard and put to work. Old Man Ricks, of the Blue Star Navigation Company, was the first to see the handwriting on the wall; so he sneaked East and bought the Lion and the Unicorn. It was just the old cuss's luck to have a lot of cash on hand; and he bought them cheap, loaded them with general cargo in New York, and paid a nice dividend on them on their very first voyage under the Blue Star flag. When he got them on the Coast he put them into the lumber trade and they paid for themselves within a year.

"Then, just before the panic of 1907, old Ricks unloaded the Unicorn on the Black Butte Company for ten thousand dollars more than he paid for her — the old scamp! He's the shrewdest trader on the whole Pacific Coast. He had no sooner sawed the Unicorn off on the Black Butte people than the freight market collapsed in the general crash, and ever since then the owners of the Lion and the Unicorn have been stuck with their vessels. They're so big it's next to impossible to keep them running coastwise in the lumber trade during a dull period, and they're not big enough for the foreign trade. About the only thing they could do profitably was to freight coal, coal freights have dropped until the margin of profit is very meager; competition is keen and for the last six months the Lion and the Unicorn have been laid up."

Matt Peasley smiled.

"They'll be hungry for the business," he said, "and I'm sailor enough to see you'll be able to drive a bargain without much trouble."

"I ought to get them pretty cheap," Mr. Hayes admitted. "As you perhaps know, a vessel deteriorates faster when laid up than she does in active service; and an owner will do almost anything to keep her at sea, provided he can make a modest rate of interest on her cost price or present market value."

"Naturally," Matt Peasley observed as they rose from the table.

He purchased a cigar for Mr. Hayes, and as they retired to the buffet car to continue their acquaintance something whispered to Matt not to divulge to this somewhat garrulous stranger the news that he was a sea captain lately in the employ of the Blue Star Navigation Company and soon to enter that employ again. He had learned enough to realize that Cappy's bank roll was threatened by this man from Seattle; that with his defenses leveled, as it were, the old gentleman would prove an easy victim unless warned of the impending attack.

Therefore, since Matt had not sought Mr. Hayes' confidence nor accepted it under a pledge of secrecy, he decided that there could be nothing unethical in taking advantage of it. Plainly the broker had jumped to the conclusion that Matt was a common sailor—above the average in point of intelligence, but so young and unsophisticated that one need not bother to be reserved or cautious in his presence. Some vague understanding of this had come to Matt Peasley; hence throughout the remainder of the journey his conversations with the broker bore on every other subject under heaven except ships and shipowners.

CHAPTER XXII.
FACE TO FACE

In his private office Cappy Ricks sat on his spine, with his old legs on his desk and his head sunk forward on his breast. His eyes were closed; to the casual observer he would have appeared to be dozing. Any one of his employees, however, would have known Cappy was merely thinking. It was his habit to close his eyes and sit very still whenever he faced a tussle with a tough proposition.

Presently an unmistakably feminine kiss, surreptitiously delivered, roused Cappy from his meditations. He opened his eyes and beheld his daughter Florence, a radiant debutante of twenty, and the sole prop of her eccentric parent's declining years.

"Daddy dear," she announced, "there's something wrong with my bank account. I've just come from the Marine National Bank and they wouldn't cash my check."

"Of course not," Cappy replied, beaming affectionately. "They telephoned about five minutes ago that you're into the red again; so I've instructed Skinner to deposit five thousand to your credit."

"Oh, but I want ten thousand!" she protested.

"Can't have it, Florry!" he declared. "The old limousine will have to do. Go slow, my dear—go slow! Why, they're offering random cargoes freely along the street for nine dollars. Logs cost six dollars, with a dollar and a half to manufacture—that's seven and a half; and three and a half water freight added—that's eleven dollars. Eleven-dollar lumber selling for nine dollars, and no business at that! I haven't had a vessel dividend in six months—"

Mr. Skinner entered.

"Mr. Ricks," he announced, "Captain Peasley, late of the Retriever, is in the outer office. Shall I tell him to wait?"

"No. Haven't we been itching to see each other the past eighteen months? Show him in immediately, Skinner." Cappy turned to his daughter. "I want to show you something my dear," he said; "something you're not likely to meet very often in your set—and that's a he-man. Do you remember hearing me tell the story of the mate that thrashed the big Swede skipper I sent to Cape Town to thrash him and bring the vessel home?"

"Do you mean the captain that never writes letters?"

"That's the man. The fellow I've been having so much fun with—the Nervy Matt that tried to hornswoggle me with my own photograph. Passed it off as his own, Florry! He hails from my old home town, and he's a mere boy—Come in!"

The door opened to admit Matt Peasley; and as he paused just inside the entrance, slightly embarrassed at finding himself under the cool scrutiny of the trimmest, most dashing little craft he had ever seen, Miss Florry decided that her father was right. Here, indeed, was a specimen of the genus Homo she had not hitherto seen. Six feet three he was, straight from shoulder to hip, broad-chested and singularly well formed and graceful for such a big man.

He wore stout shoes, without toe caps—rather old-fashioned footgear, Florry thought; but they were polished brightly. A tailor-made, double-breasted blue serge suit, close-hauled and demoded; a soft white silk shirt, with non-detachable collar; a plain black silk four-in-hand tie, and a uniform cap, set a little back and to one side on thick, black, glossy, wavy hair, completed his attire. He had his right hand in his trousers pocket; his left was on the doorknob. He glanced from her to her father.

"He's handsome," thought Florry. "What a beautiful tan on his throat! He looks anything but the brute he is. But he hasn't any manners. Oh, dear! He stands there like a graven image."

Matt Peasley's hand came out of his pocket; off came his cap and he bowed slightly.

"I am Captain Peasley," he said.

Cappy Ricks, leaning forward on the edge of his swivel chair, with head slightly bent, made a long appraisal of the young man over the rims of his spectacles.

"Ahem!" he said. "Huh! Harumph!" Ensued another terrible silence. Then: "Young scoundrel!" Cappy cried. "Infernal young scoundrel!"

"I accept the nomination," said Matt dryly. "You'd never know me from my photograph, would you, sir? I'd know you from yours, though—in a minute!"

Miss Florry tittered audibly, thus drawing on herself the attention of the skipper, who was audacious enough to favor her with a solemn wink.

"None of your jokes with me, sir!" said Cappy severely.

"That's just what I say, sir; none of your jokes on me! Those green hides were absolutely indecent."

"Matt, you're a fresh young fellow," Cappy charged, struggling to suppress a smile.

"And I was raised on salt water too," Matt added seriously.

Cappy laughed.

"You're a Thomaston Peasley," he declared, and shook hands. "Ever hear of Ethan Peasley back there?"

"He was my uncle, sir. He was drowned at sea."

"He was a boyhood chum of mine, Matt. Permit me to present my daughter, Miss Florence."

Miss Florence favored the captain with her most bewitching smile and nodded perkily. Matt held out his great hand, not realizing that a bow and a conventional "Delighted, I'm sure!" was the correct thing in Florry's set. Florry was about to accept his great paw when Cappy yelled:

"Don't take it, Florry! He'll squeeze your hand to jelly."

"I won't," Matt declared, embarrassed. "I might press it a little—"

"I know. You pressed mine a little, and if I live to be a thousand years old I'll never shake hands with you again."

"I'll give her my finger then," Matt declared, and forthwith held out his index finger, which Florry shook gravely.

"Well, well, boy; sit down, sit down," Cappy commanded briskly, "while I tell you the plans I have for your future. I ought to have fired you long ago—"

"I shall always be happy to testify that you tried hard enough," Matt interrupted, and Florry's silvery laugh filled the room. Cappy winced, but had to join with her in the laugh on himself.

"For the sake of your Uncle Ethan, and the fact that you're one of our own boys, Matt," he continued, "I'll retain you if you behave yourself. As I believe I wired you, I'm going to put you in steam."

"You didn't consult me about it, sir; but, to please you, I'll tackle steam. I'm very grateful for your interest in me, Mr. Ricks."

"Huh! That's not true, Matt. You're not grateful; and if you are you have no business to be. I paid you a hundred and twenty-five dollars a month to skipper the Retriever; you earned every cent of it and I made you fight for the job; so, no thanks to me. And I know for a fact that you and Mr. Murphy cursed me up hill and down dale—"

"Oh, Captain Peasley!" Miss Ricks interrupted. "Did you curse my father?"

"She's trying to fluster me," Matt thought. "She thinks I'm a farmer." Aloud he said: "Well, you see, Miss Ricks, I had to work for him. However, Mr. Murphy and I have forgiven him. We're both willing to let bygones be bygones."

"Young scoundrel!" piped Cappy, delighted beyond measure, for he was used to unimaginative, rather dull skippers, who revered their berths and stood before him, hat in hand, plainly uncomfortable in the presence of the creator of the payroll. "Dashed young scoundrel! Well, we had some fun anyhow, didn't we, Matt? And, as the young fellows say, I got your Capricorn. Very well, then. We'll make a new start, Matthew; and if you pay attention to business it's barely possible you may amount to something yet.

"I'm going to provide a berth for you, my boy, as second mate on the dirtiest, leakiest little bumboat you ever saw—our steam schooner Gualala. She's a nautical disgrace and carries three hundred thousand feet of lumber—runs into the dogholes on the Mendocino Coast and takes in cargo on a trolley running from the top of the cliff to the masthead. It'll be your job to get out in a small boat to pick up the moorings; and that'll be no picnic in the wintertime, because you lie just outside the edge of the breakers. But you'll learn how to pick up moorings, Matt, and you'll learn how to turn a steamer round on her heels also."

"I never did that kind of work before," Matt protested. "I stand a good chance of getting drowned, don't I?"

"Of course! But better men than you do it; so don't kick. In the spring I'll shift you to a larger boat; but I want you to have one winter along the Mendocino Coast. It'll about break your heart, but it will do you an awful lot of good, Matt. When you finish in the Gualala, you'll go in the Florence Ricks and run from Grays Harbor to San Pedro. Then, when you get your first mate's license, I'll put you in our Tillicum, where you'll learn how to handle a big vessel; and by the time you get your master's license for steam you'll be ready to start for Philadelphia to bring out the finest freighter on this Coast. How does that prospect strike you?"

Matt's eyes glowed. He forgot the two years' apprenticeship and thought only of the prize Cappy was dangling before him.

"If faithful service will be a guaranty of my appreciation—" he began; but Cappy interrupted.

"Nonsense! Not another peep out of you. You'd better take a little rest now for a couple of weeks and get your stomach in order after all that creosote. Meantime, if you should need any money, Skinner will fix you up."

"I'll not need any, thank you. I saved sixteen hundred dollars while I was in the Retriever—"

"Fine! Good boy!" exclaimed Cappy, delighted beyond measure at this proof of Matt's Yankee thrift and sobriety. "But don't save it, Matt. Invest it. Put it in a mortgage for three years. I know a captain now that wants to borrow a thousand dollars at eight per cent. to buy an interest in one of our vessels. You shall loan it to him, Matt, and he'll secure you with the insurance. Perfectly safe. Guarantee it myself. Bring your thousand dollars round in the morning, Matt. Understand? No fooling now! Make your money work for you. You bet! If I'm not here tomorrow leave the money with Skinner."

"Mr. Skinner is the general manager, isn't he?"

"Yes, and a mighty clever one, too. Don't you monkey with Skinner, young man. He doesn't like you and he doesn't bluff worth a cent; and if you ever have a run-in with him while I'm away and he fires you—well, I guess I'd have to stand by Skinner, Matt. I can't afford to lose him. Cold-blooded dog—no sense of humor; but honest—a pig for work, and capable."

"I'll be very careful, sir," Matt assured him. "Thank you for the vacation, the promised job, and the chance to invest my thousand dollars at eight per cent. And, now that my affairs are out of the way, let's talk about yours. I think I can get you a four-year charter for your steamer Lion—"

"Matt," said Cappy Ricks impressively, "if you can get that brute of a boat off my hands for four years, and at a figure that will pay me ten per cent. on her cost price, I'll tell you what—I'll pay you a commission."

"I don't want any commission, sir, for working for the interests of my employer. What do you reckon it costs a day to operate the Lion?"

Cappy drew a scratch pad toward him and commenced to figure.

"She'll burn a hundred and seventy barrels of crude oil a day, at sixty-five cents a barrel. That's about a hundred and ten dollars. Her wages will average seventy-five dollars a day; it costs twenty dollars a day to feed her crew; incidentals, say twenty dollars a day; insurance, say, four dollars a day; wireless, three and a half dollars; depreciation, say, two dollars and seventy-five cents a day; total in round figures two hundred and thirty-five dollars a day. I ought to get four hundred dollars a day for her; but in a pinch like the present I'd be glad to get her off my hands at three hundred and fifty dollars. But, no matter what the price may be, Matt, I'm afraid we can't charter her."

"Why?"

"Because the Black Butte Lumber Company owns her sister, the Unicorn; she's a burden on their back, as the Lion is on mine, there's war to the finish between Hudner, the Black Butte manager, and myself, and he'll get the business. He's a dog, Matt—always cutting prices below the profit point and raising hob in the market. Infernal marplot! He stole the best stenographer in the United States from me here about three years ago."

"Where is Hudner's office?" Matt queried.

"In this building—sixth floor." Matt rose and started for the door.

"Where are you going now, Matt?" Cappy piped.

"Why, you say the Unicorn will compete against the Lion for this charter I have in mind. That is true enough. I know the Black Butte Lumber Company will be approached for the Unicorn; so I'm going to get the Unicorn out of the way and give you a clear field with the Lion. I figured it all out coming down on the train." And, without waiting to listen to Cappy's protestations, Matt left the office.

CHAPTER XXIII.
BUSINESS AND—

Three minutes later he was closeted with Hudner, of the Black Butte Lumber Company.

"My name is Peasley, Mr. Hudner," he began truthfully. "I arrived from Seattle this morning. I am looking for a steam freighter for some very responsible people and your Unicorn appears to be about the vessel they're looking for. They would want her to run coastwise, and prefer to charter at a flat rate a day, owners to pay all expenses of operating the ship. Would you be willing to charter for sixty days, with an option on the vessel for an extension of the charter on the same terms for four years, provided she proves satisfactory for my clients' purposes?"

Mr. Hudner started slightly. Four years! It seemed almost too good to be true. He was certain of this the next instant when he thought of Cappy Ricks' Lion, also laid up and as hungry for business as the Unicorn. He wondered whether this young broker from Seattle had called on Cappy Ricks as yet; and, wondering, he decided to name a price low enough to prove interesting and, by closing promptly, eliminate his hated competitor from all consideration.

"I should be very glad to consider your proposition, Mr. Peasley," he said. "You say your clients are entirely responsible?"

"They will post a bond if you're not satisfied on that point, Mr. Hudner. What will you charter the Unicorn for, a day?"

Mr. Hudner pretended to do a deal of figuring. At the end of five minutes he said: "Three hundred and fifty dollars a day, net to the vessel."

Matt nodded, rose and reached for his hat.

"I guess you don't want to charter your vessel, sir," he said. "I'm not working for my health, either; so I guess I'll look for some other vessel. I hear the Lion is on the market." And without further ado he walked out.

Mr. Hudner let him go; then ran after him and cornered him in the hall.

"I'll let you have her at three hundred and thirty," he said desperately; "and that's bedrock. And if your clients elect to take her for four years, I'll pay you a thousand dollars commission on the deal. The vessel simply cannot afford to pay more."

After his conversation with Cappy Ricks, Matt realized that Hudner had, indeed, named a very low price on the Unicorn. But Matt was a Yankee. He knew he had Hudner where the hair was short; so he said:

"I'll give you three twenty-five and accept a thousand dollars commission in case my clients take her for four years. That's my final offer, Mr. Hudner. Take it or leave it."

"I'll take it," said poor Hudner. "It's better than letting the vessel fall to pieces in Rotten Row. How soon will you hear definitely from your principals?"

"I'll hear to-day; but meantime you might give me a three-day option on the vessel, in case of unavoidable delays — though I'll do my best to close the matter up at once."

Hudner considered. The Unicorn had paid his company but two dividends since her purchase from Cappy Ricks, while it was common talk on 'Change that the Lion had paid for herself prior to the 1907 panic. In consideration of the fact, therefore, that the Lion did not owe Cappy Ricks a cent, Hudner shrewdly judged that Cappy would be less eager than he for business, and that hence it would be safe to give a three-day option. He led Matt back to his office, where he dictated and signed the option. Matt gave him a dollar and the trap was set.

From Hudner's office Matt returned to that of Cappy Ricks. The heir to the Ricks millions was still there, as Matt noted with a sudden, strange thrill of satisfaction.

"I've waited until your return, Captain Peasley," she said, "to see whether you could dispose of dad's competitor as handily as you disposed of your own that time in Cape Town."

Matt blushed and Cappy chuckled.

"I've bet Florry five thousand dollars you'll dispose of Hudner and the Unicorn, Matt," he said.

"I'm glad of that, sir, because if you hope to win the bet you'll have to help me. I've gone as far as I can, sir. I've got an option on the Unicorn for three days on a sixty-day charter, running coastwise with general cargo, with the privilege of renewing for four years at the same rate. The rate, by the way, is three hundred and twenty-five dollars. I want you to charter her from Hudner; and then—"

"Bless your soul, boy, I don't want her! Haven't I got a boat of my own I'd almost be willing to charter at the same figure to Hudner?"

"You don't understand, sir. The Mannheim people, with copper mines in Alaska, want two boats to freight ore—and their agent came down on the train with me. Don't you see, sir, that you have to control both boats to get a price? If you don't that agent will play you against Hudner and Hudner against you, until he succeeds in tying up both boats at a low price. He wouldn't tell you he wants two boats, but he was fool enough to tell me—"

"God bless my mildewed soul!" said Cappy excitedly, and smashed his old fist down on his desk. "For the man to do things, give me the lad who keeps his ears open and his mouth shut! Of course we'll charter her; and, what's more, we'll give her business ourselves for sixty days just to keep her off the market!"

"Then you'd better hurry and close the deal, sir," Matt warned him. "I only arrived in town this morning; and I checked my baggage at the depot and came up here immediately. The Seattle broker went up to his hotel. He said he had to have a bath and a shave and some clean linen first thing," he added scornfully: "Me, I'd swim Channel Creek at low tide in a dress suit if I had important business on the other side."

"Matt," said Cappy gratefully, "you're a boy after my own heart. Really, I think you ought to get something out of this if we put it through."

"Well, as I stated, I wouldn't take anything out of the Lion charter, because it's my duty to save you when somebody has a gun at your head; but on the Unicorn charter I thought—well, if you can recharter at a profit I thought you might agree to split the profit with me. I'm a skipper, you know, and this sort of thing is out of my regular line; and besides, I'm not on your pay roll at present. I've promoted the deal, so to speak. I supply the ship and the brains and the valuable information, and you supply business for the ship."

"Yes; and, in spite of the hard times, I'll supply it at a profit if I have to," Cappy declared happily. "Of course I'll split the profit with you, Matt. As you say, this Unicorn deal is outside your regular line. It's a private deal; and as the promoter of it you're entitled to your legitimate profit." He rang for Mr. Skinner.

"Skinner, my boy," he said when that functionary entered, "Matt and I are going to unload that white elephant of a Lion and get her off our hands for four years at a fancy figure; but to do it we've got to charter another white elephant—the Black Butte Lumber Company's Unicorn. Here's an option Captain Peasley has just secured on her. Have the charter parties made out immediately in conformity with this option and bring them here for my signature."

Mr. Skinner read the option and began to protest.

"Mr. Ricks, I tell you we cannot possibly use the Unicorn for sixty days, if you are forced to keep her off the market that long. If this thing develops into a waiting game—"

"I'll wear the other side out," Cappy finished for him. "Listen to me, Skinner! How's the shingle market in the Southwest?"

"The market is steady at three dollars and fifty cents, f.o.b. Missouri River common points."

Cappy scratched his ear and cogitated.

"The Unicorn will carry eighteen million shingles," he murmured. "The going water freight from Grays Harbor to San Francisco is how much?"

"Thirty-five cents a thousand," Mr. Skinner replied promptly.

"Therefore, if we used one of our own vessels to freight eighteen million shingles it would cost us—"

"Six thousand three hundred dollars," prompted Mr. Skinner.

"Fortunately for us, however, we do not use one of our own vessels. We use that fellow Hudner's and we get her for three hundred and twenty-five dollars a day. She can sail from here to Grays Harbor, take on her cargo, get back to San Francisco and discharge it in twelve days. What's twelve times three hundred and twenty-five?"

"Thirty-nine hundred dollars," flashed Skinner, to the tremendous admiration of Matt Peasley, who now considered the manager an intellectual marvel.

"Being a saving of how much?" Cappy droned on.

"Twenty-four hundred dollars," answered the efficient human machine without seeming to think for an instant.

"Being a saving of how many cents on a thousand shingles?"

Mr. Skinner closed one eye, cocked the other at the ceiling an instant and said:

"Thirteen and one-third cents a thousand."

"Very well, then, Skinner. Now listen to my instructions: Wire all the best shingle mills on Grays Harbor for quotations on Extra Star A Stars in one to five million lots, delivery fifteen, thirty and forty-five days from date; and if the price is right buy 'em all. We have about ten millions on hand at our own mill. To-night send out a flock of night letters to all the wholesale jobbers and brokers in Kansas, Missouri, Oklahoma, Texas, and all points taking a sixty-cent tariff, and quote 'em ten cents under the market subject to prior acceptance."

He turned to Matt Peasley.

"That clause—'subject to prior acceptance'—saves our faces in case we find ourselves unable to deliver the goods," he explained, and turned again to Skinner.

"We can freight the shingles from Grays Harbor to San Francisco in the Unicorn; re-ship on cars from Long Wharf and beat the direct car shipments from the mills ten cents, and still make our regular profit. Besides, the cut in price will bring us in a raft of orders we could not get otherwise. We can thus keep the Unicorn busy for sixty days without losing a cent on her, and if we haven't come to terms with the Mannheim people at the end of that time we'll find something else for her. And, of course, if we succeed meantime in chartering the Lion at a satisfactory price, we can throw the Unicorn back on Hudner at the end of the sixty days." And Cappy snickered malevolently as he pictured his enemy's discomfiture under these circumstances.

Mr. Skinner nodded his comprehension and hastened away to prepare the charter parties.

CHAPTER XXIV.
THE CLEAN UP

Hudner, manager of the Black Butte Lumber Company, arched his eyebrows as Matt Peasley entered his office half an hour after he had left it and presented for Hudner's signature a formal charter party, in duplicate, wherein the Blue Star Navigation Company chartered from J. B. Hudner, managing owner of record, the American Steamer Unicorn for sixty days from date, at the rate of three hundred and twenty-five dollars a day, said managing owner to pay all expenses of operating said Unicorn.

"Huh!" Mr. Hudner snorted. "I'd like to know what the devil Cappy Ricks wants of my Unicorn when he's got her infernal sister squatting in the mud of Oakland Creek? There's something rotten in Denmark, Mr. Peasley. There always is when that old scoundrel Ricks does incomprehensible things."

"Very likely he's up to some skullduggery, sir," Matt opined.

"I wish you had informed me of the identity of your client, Mr. Peasley," Hudner complained. "I don't like to sign this charter."

"I cannot help that now, sir," Matt retorted. "You have agreed in writing to charter the vessel to any responsible person I might bring to you, and I guess the Blue Star Navigation Company comes under that head."

Mr. Hudner sighed and gritted his teeth. Instinct told him there was deviltry afoot, but in an evil moment he had sewed himself up and he had no alternative now save to complete the contract or stand suit. So he signed the charter party and retained the original, while Matt Peasley, with the duplicate in his pocket, hastened back to Cappy Ricks' office.

"Matt," said Cappy approvingly, "you're a born business man, and it will be strange indeed if you don't pick up a nice little piece of money on this Unicorn deal." He glanced at his watch and then turned to his daughter.

"Florry, my dear," he said, "would you like to go up-town with your daddy and Captain Peasley for luncheon?"

Matt Peasley grinned like a Jack-o'-lantern, all lit up for Hallowe'en.

"Fine!" he said enthusiastically.

Florence withered him with one impersonal glance, saw that she had destroyed him utterly, relented, and graciously acquiesced. When they left the office Matt Peasley was stepping high, like a ten-time winner, for he had suddenly made the discovery that life ashore was a wonderful, wonderful thing. There was such a lilt in his young heart that, for the life of him, he could not forbear doing a little double shuffle as he waited at the elevator with Cappy and his daughter. He sang:

"*The first mate's boat was the first away;*
   But the whale gave a flip of his tail,
And down to the bottom went five brave boys,
   Never again to sail —
     Brave boys,
   Never again to sail!

When the captain heard of the loss of his whale,
   Right loud-lee then he swore.
When he heard of the loss of his five brave boys,
   '*Oh,' he said, 'we can ship some more brave boys —*
   '*Oh,' he said, 'we can ship some more.*'"

Cappy winked slyly at his daughter, but she did not see the wink. She had eyes for nobody but Matt Peasley, for he was a brand-new note in her life. They were half through luncheon before Florry discovered the exact nature of this fascinating new note. Matt Peasley was real. There was not an artificial thought or action in his scheme of things; he bubbled with homely Yankee wit; he was intensely democratic and ramping with youth and health and strength and the joy of living; he could sing funny little songs and tell funny little stories about funny little adventures that had befallen him. She liked him.

After luncheon Cappy declared that Matt should return to the office with him, while Florry instructed the waiter to ring for a taxicab for her. Later, when Matt gallantly handed her into the taxi, he asked innocently:

"Where are you going, Miss Florry?"

"Home," she said.

He looked at her so wistfully that she could not mistake the hidden meaning in his words when he asked, with a deprecatory grin:

"Where do you live?"

"With my father," she said, and closed the door.

When Cappy and Matt returned to the Blue Star offices they were informed that Mr. Allan Hayes was patiently awaiting the arrival of the managing owner of the Lion. Matt concluded, therefore, to remain secluded while Cappy went into his own office and met Mr. Hayes.

Two hours later Cappy summoned Skinner and Matt to his sanctum.

"Skinner," he said briskly, "have you bought any shingles?"

"I have not," said Mr. Skinner.

"Have you sent out those telegrams to the dealers?"

"Not yet, Mr. Ricks. I was going to have them filed just before we close the office."

"Well," said Cappy smilingly, "don't accept any quotations until to-morrow and don't send out those telegrams until further advice from me. I locked horns with that man Hayes, and I think I gored him, Matt. It appeared he called on me first; and when I quoted him four hundred dollars a day on the Lion, he favored me with a sweet smile and said he could get the Unicorn for three-fifty. So, of course, I had to explain to him that he couldn't, because I wouldn't charter her at any such ridiculous figure! That took the ginger out of him and we got down to business, with the result that I've given him a forty-eight-hour option on both boats at four hundred dollars a day each, with a commission of two thousand dollars cash in full to him."

"Why, he told me he would get two and a half per cent. commission!" Matt declared. "He figured he'd have an income of twenty dollars a day for the next four years."

"I daresay he did, Matt," Cappy replied dryly; "but then, in the very best business circles you never pay a broker two and a half commission when you know who his principals are! If he insists, you eliminate him entirely and do business direct. Of course, my boy, if he had put the proposition up to me, and I had agreed to pay him the regular commission while ignorant of the identity of his principals, and he had then reposed confidence in my business honor and told me whom he represented, he would have been perfectly safe. Remember, Matt, that the business man without a code of business honor never stays in business very long. From the office to the penitentiary or the cemetery is a quick jump for birds of that feather."

"Then, why did you offer him two thousand dollars?"'

"Because it never pays to be a hog, my son, and besides I want to close this deal and close it quickly. Naturally Hayes isn't fool enough to toss away two thousand dollars, and something seems to tell me he'll urge his principals to take the boats at our figure, Matthew!" And the graceless old villain chuckled and dug his youngest skipper in the short ribs. "Let this be a lesson to you, my boy," he warned him. "Remember the old Persian proverb: 'A shut mouth catches no flies.'"

Cappy's prediction proved to be correct, for the following morning Hayes telephoned that the Mannheim people desired the steamers at Cappy's figures, the charter parties, signed by Cappy, were forwarded to Seattle, and in due course were returned signed by the charterers; whereupon Cappy exercised his option, procured by Matt from Hudner, to charter the Unicorn for four years additional.

"What did Hudner have to say for himself?" Cappy queried when Matt returned from the latter's office, after finally completing the deal.

"Not a word! He looked volumes, though, sir."

"Serves him right. That man, sir, is a thorn in the side of the market. However, since we're making a daily profit on him we can afford to speak kindly of the unfortunate fellow, Matt; so sit down and we'll figure out where we stand on the Unicorn. She costs us three-twenty-five and we've chartered her at four hundred—a daily profit of seventy-five dollars, of which you receive thirty-seven dollars and fifty cents. That makes eleven hundred and twenty-five dollars monthly income for you, my boy; and, believe me, it isn't to be sneezed at. Meantime you and I, as partners, owe me a thousand dollars commission to that Seattle broker; so I'll have Skinner make a journal entry and charge your account five hundred dollars. There's no need to pay it now, Matt. Wait until the vessel earns it."

"The vessel might sink on her first voyage and that would cancel the charter," Matt replied; "so I guess I'll be a sport and hold up my end. You paid out the hard cash and took a chance, and so will I." And, with the words, Matt drew from his pocket the Black Butte Lumber Company's check for a thousand dollars, indorsed it and passed it over to Cappy Ricks. "We're equal partners, sir," he said, "and I pried that thousand out of Hudner on the side as a commission for chartering the Unicorn to you. Half of it is yours and I owe you the other half; so there you are."

Cappy Ricks threw up his hands in token of complete surrender.

"Scoundrel!" he cried. "Damned young scoundrel! You Yankee thief, haven't you any conscience?" And he laid his old head on his desk and laughed his shrill, senile laugh, while tears of joy rolled down his rosy old cheeks. "Oh-h-h-h, my!" he cackled. "But wait until I get Hudner among my young friends at the Round Table up at the Commercial Club to-morrow! To think of a young pup like you coming in and chasing an old dog like Hudner round the lot and taking his bone away from him!"

He turned to the general manager:

"Oh, Skinner! Skinner, my dear boy, this will be the death of me yet! Remember that old maid stenographer Hudner stole away from us, Skinner? Remember? Oh, but isn't he paying for her through the nose? Isn't he, Skinner? Oh, dear! Oh, dear, what a lot of fun there is in just living and raising hell with your neighbor—particularly, Skinner, when he happens to be a competitor."

When Cappy could control his mirth he handed the money back to Matt.

"Oh, Matt, my dear young bandit," he informed that amazed young man, "I'm human. I can't take this money. It's been worth a thousand dollars to have had this laugh and to know I've got a lad like you growing up in my employ. You're worth a bonus, Matt; I'll stand all the commission. Soak Hudner's thousand away in the bank, Matt; or, better still—Here! Here; let's figure, Matt: You had sixteen hundred saved up and you've loaned a thousand on that mortgage. Now you've made a thousand more. Better buy a good thousand-dollar municipal bond, Matt. That's better than savings-bank interest, and you can always realize on the bond. I'll buy the bond for you."

"Thank you, sir," Matt replied.

CHAPTER XXV.
CAPPY PROVES HIMSELF A DESPOT

Cappy Ricks lay back in his swivel chair, his feet on his desk and his eyes closed. He was thinking deeply, for he had something to think about. Coming in from his club the night before he had observed that Florry was entertaining company in the billiard room, as the crash of pool balls testified. He had scarcely reached his room on the second floor, however, when the pool game came to an end and he heard voices in the drawing room, followed presently by a few random chords struck on the piano, and a resonant baritone was raised in the strangest song ever heard in that drawing room—a deep-sea chantey.

Cappy was no great shakes on music, but before he had listened to the first verse of Rolling Home he knew Captain Matt Peasley for the singer and suspected his daughter of faking the accompaniment. He listened at the head of the stairs and presently was treated to a rendition of a lilting little Swedish ballad, followed by one or two selections from the Grand Banks and the doleful song of the Ferocious Whale and the Five Brave Boys. Then he heard Florry laugh happily.

Cappy was thinking of the curious inflection in that laugh now. Once before he had heard it—when he courted Florry's dead mother; and his old heart swelled a little with pain at the remembrance. He was wondering just what to do about that laugh when Matt was announced.

"Show him in," said Cappy; and Matt Peasley entered.

"Sit down, Matt," said Cappy kindly. "Yes, I sent for you. The Gualala will be in to-morrow and you've had a fine two-weeks' vacation. What's more, I think you've enjoyed it, Matt, and I'm glad you did; but now it's time to get down to business again. I wanted to tell you that the skipper of the Gualala will expect you to be aboard at seven o'clock to-morrow morning."

Matt studied the pattern of the office rug a minute and then faced Cappy bravely.

"I'm obliged to you, Mr. Ricks, more than I can say; but the fact of the matter is I've changed my mind about going to sea again. It's a dog's life, sir, and I'm tired of it."

"Tired at twenty-three?" said Cappy gently.

Matt flushed a little.

"Well, it does appear to me kind of foolish for a man with an income of more than eleven hundred dollars a month to be going to sea as second mate of a dirty little steam schooner at seventy-five dollars a month."

"Well, I can hardly blame you," said Cappy gently. "I suppose I'd feel the same way about it myself if I stood in your shoes."

"I'm sure you would," Matt replied.

Fell a silence, broken presently by Cappy's:

"Huh! Ahem! Harump!" Then: "When I came in from my club last night, Matt, I believe Florry had a caller."

"Yes, sir," said Matt; "I was there."

"Huh! I got a squint at you. Am I mistaken in assuming that you were wearing a dress suit?"

"No, sir."

"Whadja mean by wasting your savings on a dress suit?" Cappy exploded. "Whadja mean by courting my Florry, eh? Tell me that! Give you an inch and you'll take an ell! Infernal young scoundrel!"

"Well," said Matt humbly, "I intended to speak to you about Miss Florry. Of course now that I'm going to live ashore—"

"What can a big lubber like you do ashore?" Cappy shrilled.

"Why, I might get a job with some shipping firm—"

"You needn't count on a job ashore with the Blue Star Navigation Company," Cappy railed. "You needn't think—"

"Have I your permission to call on Miss Florry again?" Matt asked humbly.

"No!" thundered Cappy. "You're as nervy as they make 'em! No, sir! You'll go to sea in the Gualala to-morrow morning—d'ye hear? That's what you'll do!"

Cappy Ricks: OR, the Subjugation of matt Peasley | 129

But Matt Peasley shook his head.

"I'm through with the sea," he said firmly. "I have an income of eleven hundred dollars a month—"

"Oh, is that so?" Cappy sneered. "Well, for the sake of argument, we'll admit you have the income. We don't know how long you'll have it; but we'll credit your account on the books while we're able to collect it from the charterers, and I guess we'll collect it while the Unicorn is afloat. But having an income and being able to spend it, my boy, are two different things; so in order to set your mind at ease, let me tell you something: I'm not going to give you a cent out of that charter deal—"

Matt Peasley sprang up, his big body aquiver with rage.

"You'd double-cross me!" he roared. "Mr. Ricks, if you weren't—" He paused.

"Shut up!" snapped Cappy, undaunted. "I know what you're going to say. If I wasn't an old man I'd let you make a jolly jackanapes of yourself. Now listen to me! I said I wasn't going to let you have a cent out of that charter deal—and I mean it. If you couldn't say Boo! from now until the day you finger a dollar of that income you'd be as dumb as an oyster by the time I hand you the check. What do you know about money?" he piped shrilly. "You big, overgrown baby! Yah! You've had a little taste of business and turned a neat deal, and now you think you're a wonder, don't you? Like everybody else, you'll keep on thinking it until some smart fellow takes it all away from you again; so, in order to cure you, I'm not going to let you have it!"

"I'll sue you—"

"You can sue your head off, young man, and see how much good it will do you. You surrendered to me your option that Hudner gave you on the Unicorn, and you failed to procure from me in writing an understanding of the agreement between us regarding this split. You haven't a leg to stand on!"

Matt Peasley hung his head.

"I didn't think I had to take business precautions with you, sir," he said.

"You should take business precautions with anybody and everybody."

"I thought I was dealing with a man of honor. Everybody has always told me that Cappy Ricks'—"

"How dare you call me Cappy?"

"—word was as good as his bond."

"And so it is, my boy. You'll get your money, but you'll wait for it; and meantime I'll invest it for you. As I said before, you've had a taste of business and found it pretty sweet—so sweet, in fact, that you think you're a business man. Well, hereafter you'll remember, when you're making a contract with anybody, to get it down in black and white; and then you'll have something to fight about if you're not satisfied. Now, by the time you're skipper of steam you'll be worth a nice little pile of money; you can buy a piece of the big freighter I'm going to build for you and it'll pay you thirty per cent. Remember, Matt, I always make my skippers own a piece of the vessel they command. That gives 'em an interest in their job and they don't waste their owner's money."

"I won't be dictated to!" Matt cried desperately. "I'm free, white and—"

"Twenty-three!" jeered Cappy. "You big, awkward pup! How dare you growl at me! I know what's good for you. You go to sea on the Gualala."

"I must decline—"

"Oh, all right! Have it your own way," said Cappy. "But, at the rate you've been blowing your money in on Florry for the past two weeks, I'll bet your wad has dwindled since you struck town. I've put that thousand dollars out on mortgage for you, and Skinner has the mortgage in the company safe, where you can't get at it to hock it when your last dollar is gone. And he has the bond there too; so it does appear to me, Matt, that if you want any money to spend you'll have to get a job and earn it. I have the bulge on you, young fellow, and don't you forget it!"

Matt Peasley rose, walked to the window and stood looking down into California Street. He was so mad there were tears in his eyes, and he longed to say things to Cappy Ricks—only, for the sake of Miss Florence Ricks, he could not abuse her sire. Once he half turned, only to meet Cappy's glittering eyes fixed on him with a steadiness of purpose that argued only too well the fact that the old man could not be bluffed, cajoled, bribed or impressed.

Presently Matt Peasley turned from the window.

"Where does the Gualala lie, sir?" he asked gruffly.

"Howard Street Wharf, Number One, Matt," Cappy replied cheerfully. "I think she had bedbugs in her cabin, but I'm not sure. I wouldn't go within a block of her myself."

Matt gazed sorrowfully at the rug. Too well he realized that Cappy had the whip hand and was fully capable of cracking the whip; so presently he said:

"Well, I've met bedbugs before, Mr. Ricks. I'll go aboard in the morning."

"I'm glad to hear it, Matt. And another thing: I like you, Matt, but not well enough for a son-in-law. Remember, my boy, you're only a sailor on a steam schooner now—so it won't be necessary for you to look aloft. You understand, do you not? You want to remember your position, my boy."

Matt turned and bent upon Cappy a slow, smoldering gaze. Cappy almost quivered. Then slowly the rage died out in Matt Peasley's fine eyes and a lilting, boyish grin spread over his face, for he was one of those rare human beings who can smile, no matter what the prospect, once he has definitely committed himself to a definite course of action. Only the years of discipline and his innate respect for gray hairs kept him from bluntly informing Cappy Ricks that he might forthwith proceed to chase himself! Instead he said quietly:

"Very well, sir. Good afternoon."

"Good afternoon, sir," snapped Cappy.

At the door Matt paused an instant, for he was young and he could not retire without firing a shot. He fired it now with his eyes—a glance of cool disdain and defiance that would have been worth a dollar of anybody's money to see. Cappy had to do something to keep from laughing.

"Out, you rebel!" he yelled. The door closed with a crash, and Cappy Ricks took down the telephone receiver and called up his daughter.

"Florry," he said gently, "I want to tell you something."

"Fire away, Pop!" she challenged.

"It's about that fellow Peasley," Cappy replied coldly. "I wish you wouldn't have that big, awkward dub calling at the house, Florry. He'll fall over the furniture the first thing you know, and do some damage. I think a lot of him as a sailor, but that's about as far as my affection extends; and if you insist on having him call at the house, my dear, my authority over him as an employee will suffer and I'll be forced to fire the fellow. Of course I realize what a pleasant boy he is; but then you don't know sailors like I do. They're a low lot at heart, Florry, and this fellow Peasley is no exception to the general rule."

Cappy paused to test the effect of this broadside. There was a little gasp from the other end of the wire; then a click as his daughter hung up, too outraged to reply.

Cappy's kindly eyes twinkled merrily as he replaced the receiver on the hook.

"What a skookum son-in-law to take up the business when I let go!" he murmured happily. "Oh, Matt, I'm so blamed sorry for you; but it's just got to be done. If you're going to build up the Blue Star Navigation Company after the Panama Canal is opened for business, you've got to know shipping; and to know it from center to circumference. It isn't sufficient that you be master of sail and steam, any ocean, any tonnage. You've got to learn the business from the rules as promulgated by little old Alden P. Ricks, the slave driver. There's hope for you, sonny. You have already learned to obey."

Mr. Skinner bustled in with the mail.

"Skinner," said Cappy plaintively, "what's the best way to drive obstinate people south?"

"Head them north," said Mr. Skinner.

"I'm doing it," said Cappy dreamily.

CHAPTER XXVI.
MATT PEASLEY IN EXILE

From Cappy Ricks' office Matt Peasley went to the rooms of the American Shipmaster's Association, entered the telephone booth and called up Florence Ricks. From the instant he first laid eyes on her, Miss Florry had occupied practically all of Matt's thoughts during every waking hour. He had assayed her and appraised her a hundred times and from every possible angle, and each time he decided that Florry was possessed of more than sufficient charm, good looks, sweetness and intelligence to suit the most exacting. Matt wasn't ultra-exacting and she suited him, and the fact that she was the sole heir to millions was the least of the sailor's considerations as he dropped his nickel down the slot. Neither did the identity of the young lady's paternal ancestor constitute a problem, despite the recent interview with that variable individual. Matt regarded Cappy somewhat in the light of a mixed blessing; while he respected him he was a little bit afraid of him, and just at present he disliked him exceedingly. And lastly, his own social and economic status as second mate of the most wretched little steam schooner in the Blue Star Navigation Company's fleet, failed to enter even remotely into Matt's scheme of things.

The reason for this mental stand on his part was a perfectly simple and natural one. To begin, he was a stranger to caste other than that of decent manhood. The only rank he had ever known was that of a ship's officer, and that was merely a condition of servitude. When ashore he regarded himself as the equal of any monarch under heaven and treated all men accordingly. Since he had never known any of the restrictions of polite conventions behind which society entrenches itself in the world occupied by such pampered pets of fortune as Miss Florence Ricks, Matt Peasley failed to see a single sound reason why he should not indulge a very natural desire for Cappy's ewe lamb—

for a singularly direct and forceful individual was Matthew. It was his creed to take what he could get away with, provided that in the taking he broke no moral, legal or ethical code; and if any thought of the apparent incongruity of a sailor's aspiring to the hand of a millionaire shipowner's daughter had occurred to him—which, by the way, it had not—he would doubtless have analyzed it thusly:

"There she is. Isn't she a queen? I want her and there isn't a single reason on earth why I shouldn't have her, unless it be that she doesn't want me. However, I'll learn all about that when I get good and ready, and if I'm acceptable Cappy Ricks and one of his employees are going to have a warm debate—subject, matrimony. What do I care for him? He's only her father, and I'll bet he wasn't half so well fixed as I am when he got married. I'll just play the game like a white man, and if Cappy doesn't like it he'll have to get over it."

"Miss Florence," Matt began, "this is Matt."

"Matt who?" she queried with provoking assumption of innocence.

"Door Mat," he replied. "Your daddy has just walked all over me at any rate."

"Oh, good morning, captain. Why, what has happened? Your voice sounds like the growl of a big bear."

"I suppose so. I'm hopping mad. The very first day I was ashore I turned a nice little trick for your father. I wasn't on the pay roll at the time, so we went into the deal together and chartered the Lion and the Unicorn to freight ore for the Mannheim people from Alaska to Seattle. I furnished the valuable information and the bright idea, and he capitalized both. The result of the deal was that he has his own steamer, the Lion, off his hands for four years, chartered at a fancy figure. Also he chartered the Unicorn from her owner at a cheap rate and rechartered at an advance of seventy-five dollars a day, and we split that profit between us. That gives me an income of thirty-seven and a half a day for the next four years, provided the Unicorn doesn't get wrecked. Naturally I wanted to stay ashore, when there's money to be made as easy as that—and he won't let me."

"Oh, I'm so sorry, captain."

"Well, that helps."

"You do not have to go to sea, do you?" Miss Ricks queried hopefully.

"Yes, Miss Florry, I do; that's what hurts. Your father induced me to invest all of my savings in a mortgage and a bond, and he has both locked up in the Blue Star safe with that ogre Skinner in charge, so I can't get them to realize on. Of course I could go to law and make him give them to me, but he knows I'll not do that, so he just sits there and defies me. And I neglected to take the proper business precautions about my daily income from the charter of the Unicorn, and because I cannot prove I have a divvy coming on that he says he won't give me a cent of it. He says he'll credit my account on the company's books, and when the Unicorn completes her charter he'll give it to me in a lump. In the meantime he's going to invest it for me, and without consulting me."

"Oh, dear," said Miss Ricks sympathetically. "I'm so sorry dad's such a busybody."

"You're not half so sorry as I am. I'm flat broke, and in order to eat I have to go to work, and in order to go to work I have to get a job, and in order to get the job I have to take what your father offers me—in fact, insists upon my taking. You see, Miss Florry, I'm almost a stranger in Pacific shipping. I don't know any owners except your father and I've never had any coastwise experience. It might be years before I could get another job as master of a sailing ship, and most steamship captains prefer to let some other captains break in their mates for them. So you see I'm helpless."

A silence. Then: "I'm going to sea in the Gualala to-morrow morning, Florry."

It was the first time he had dropped the "Miss," but he dropped it purposely now. Miss Ricks noticed the omission, which probably imbued her with the courage to voice again her excess of sympathy. Said she: "Oh, I'm so sorry, Matt!"

He thrilled at that. "Well," he answered humorously, "for the first time I'm glad I'm not a captain any more!"

Followed another brief silence, while Florry groped for the hidden meaning behind that subtle retort; then he continued: "Your father thinks I was a little presumptuous in calling at the house. He spoke to me about it, Florry, so I'm not going to call any more until he invites me. It's his house, you know. But he didn't say anything about not telephoning to you or seeing you outside his confounded house, so I suppose there's no necessity for me feeling badly about it, is there?"

This was a pretty direct feeler, but Florry parried it with feminine skill.

"Of course you can telephone me whenever you get to port. You mustn't take dad too seriously, Matt. Really he's very fond of you."

"Professionally, yes. Socially, no. I think he wants to give me a good chance to do something for myself in a business way later on, but he made it pretty plain that he is the only member of the Ricks family I'm to take seriously. Of course I expect to have something to say about that myself, Florry, but I didn't tell him so. He's your father, you know, and besides, a man can't make a very good showing on seventy-five dollars a month. But if the Unicorn lives to complete her charter I'll be up on Easy Street, even if I'll only be a plain sea captain when I come into that money. Of course now I'm only a second mate on the worst little steam schooner your father owns and I cannot say the things I want to say—I don't mean to your father, Florry, but to you—"

"But you're a captain now," Florry interrupted, in delicious terror hastening to obstruct any further discussion of what a seventy-five dollar man might have to say were he but in position to say it. "Why should you go to work as a second mate—"

"I've been a captain of sail, Florry. Of course, if I had never been master of a vessel of more than five hundred tons net register, or my sailing license had been limited to vessels of that tonnage, I should have to work up from second mate to master in steam. But any man who has been master of a vessel of more than five hundred tons net register for more than one year is entitled to apply for a license as master of steam vessels, and if he can pass the examination he can get his license."

"Then why don't you do that, Matt?" Florry inquired.

"I have. The idea of two years' probation as second and first mate didn't appeal to me, so while I was waiting round to join the Gualala I went up for my ticket as master of steam. I passed, but when I told your father I had a license to command the largest steam freighter he owns, he only laughed at me and told me the inspectors weren't running his business for him. Just because I'm not twenty-three years old he says I ought to have two years' experience in steam as mate before he gives me command of a vessel. He says I'd better learn the Pacific Coast like he knows his front lawn, or some foggy night I'll walk my vessel overland and the inspectors will set me down for a couple of years."

"Well, that sounds reasonable, Matt."

"Yes, I'll admit there's some justice in his contention, so I'm going to do it to please him, although I hate to have him think I'm a dog-barking navigator."

"Why, what's that?" Florry demanded.

"A dog-barking navigator is a coastwise blockhead that gets lost if he loses sight of land. He steers a course from headland to headland, and every little while on dark nights he stands in close and listens. Pretty soon he hears a dog barking alongshore. 'All right,' he says to the mate; 'we're off Point Montara. I know that Newfoundland dog's barking. He's the only one on the coast. Haul her off and hold her before the wind for four hours and then stand in again. When you pick up the bark of a foxhound you'll be off Pigeon Point.'"

Florry's laughter drowned a further description of the dog-barking navigator's wonderful knowledge of Pacific Coast canines, and after some small talk Matt said good-bye and hung up. When he left the telephone booth, however, he was a happier young man than when he had entered it, for he had now satisfied himself that while Cappy Ricks might arrogate to himself the right of proposing, his daughter could be depended upon to attend to the disposing. He went to his boarding house, paid his landlady, packed his clothes and sent them down to the Gualala, rubbing her blistered sides against Howard Street Pier No. 1. At seven o'clock next morning he was aboard her and at seven-five he superintended the casting off of the stern lines and his apprenticeship in steam had commenced.

CHAPTER XXVII.
PROMOTION

Cappy Ricks was in a fine rage. A situation, unique in his forty years of experience as a lumber and shipping magnate, was confronting him, with the prospects exceedingly bright for Cappy playing a role analogous to that of the simpleton who holds the sack on a snipe-hunting expedition. He summoned Mr. Skinner into his private office, and glared at the latter over the rims of his spectacles.

"Skinner," he said solemnly, "there's the very devil to pay."

Mr. Skinner arched his eyebrows and inclined a respectful ear. Cappy continued:

"It's about the Hermosa. Skinner, that dog-barking navigator you put in that schooner while I was on my vacation has balled us up for fair. I'll be the laughing-stock of the street."

Parenthetically it may be stated that the Blue Star Navigation Company's schooner, Hermosa, had cleared from Astoria for Valparaiso with a cargo of railroad ties, and, for some reason which the captain could not explain but which Cappy Ricks could, the unfortunate man had become lost at sea, finally ending his voyage on a reef on one of the Samoan Islands. The Hermosa had been listed as missing and her owners had been on the point of receiving a check for the insurance on the vessel and her cargo when an Australian steamer brought news of her predicament in Samoa. Her captain sent word that she was resting easily and that he would get her off. Subsequently, Cappy learned that his dog-barking skipper had discharged his cargo of railroad ties on barges, in order to lighten the vessel and float her off with the aid of a launch. Unfortunately, however, he discovered a huge hole in her garboard, and before he could patch it an extra high tide lifted the vessel over the reef and sunk her forty fathoms deep in a place where nobody could ever get at her again.

"Yes, sir," Cappy complained. "I'll be the laughing-stock of the street. Here's a letter from the insurance people, inclosing a check for a total loss on the vessel, but they repudiate payment of the insurance on the cargo."

"Why?" demanded the amazed Skinner. "They insured those ties for delivery at Callao. They can't get out of it."

"I'll bet they can," Cappy shrilled. "I've just called up the Board of Underwriters and they say the cargo hasn't been lost. They say nothing is lost if you know where it is, and the ties are on the beach in Samoa awaiting our pleasure. Skinner, call up our attorneys at once and tell them to enter suit."

"I was just about to call them up on another matter," Mr. Skinner replied. "As secretary of the Blue Star Navigation Company I have just been served with a summons in another suit, entered against the Quickstep."

"What in the fiend's name is the matter with that infernal Quickstep? This is the third suit we've had in two years. Skinner, what is wrong with that steam schooner?"

"She must be hoodooed, Mr. Ricks."

"Another seaman injured by being hit with a cargo block or having a piece of eight-by-eight drop on his foot, I suppose."

"Not this time, Mr. Ricks. One Halvor Jacobsen has sued the Quickstep and owners for five thousand dollars for injuries alleged to have been inflicted upon him by the captain."

"So that Captain Kjellin has been fighting again, eh? Skinner, that man is too handy with his fists, I tell you. He's another one of your favorites, by the way. I only put that fellow in the Quickstep to please you."

"We haven't a better man in our employ," Mr. Skinner asserted stoutly. "He carries larger cargoes and makes faster time than any steam-schooner captain in our vessels of similar carrying capacity. He's a dividend producer, Mr. Ricks, and he is very efficient."

"Don't talk to me of efficiency," Cappy snarled. "What's the sense rushing the vessel round Robin Hood's barn to make dividends, if we lose them in lawsuits?"

"His vessel didn't lay up during the strike of the Waterfront Federation in 1903," Skinner challenged. "You bet she didn't! Kjellin rustled up a scab crew and kept the mob off the vessel at the point of a gun. I understand he's a bit short-tempered, but while there are ships with red-blooded men in them, Mr. Ricks, we must expect the men to pull off a couple of rounds with skin gloves every so often."

Cappy looked over the rims of his spectacles at Mr. Skinner. "Skinner," he said impressively, "listen to me: This is the last suit that's going to be entered against the Quickstep. Was that man Halvor Jacobsen who is suing us second mate on the Quickstep?"

"Yes, sir."

"I knew it," Cappy shrilled triumphantly. "Skinner, with all your efficiency ideas, you fail to see anything remarkable in that fact. Now don't tell me you do, because I know you do not. This is the third suit since Kjellin took charge, and that's proof enough for me that there's something wrong with that big Finn. Those other two suits were for injuries received by men loading cargo in the after hold. The after hold is presided over by the second mate." Cappy waved his hands. "Huh!" he said. "Simple!"

"I believe I comprehend," Mr. Skinner admitted. "But what are you going to do about it? We can scarcely discharge Kjellin without a hearing and without proof that he is to blame."

"What am I going to do about it?" Cappy echoed. "Why, I'm going to send a judge and a jury aboard the Quickstep, try this Finn, Kjellin, and if he's guilty of dereliction of duty I'll bet you a plug hat to one small five-cent bag of smoking tobacco I'll know all about it inside of a week."

"Do you mean to put a secret-service operative aboard disguised as a deckhand?"

"Huh! Skinner, you distress me. I'm going to put Matt Peasley aboard the Quickstep as second mate, and let Nature take its course."

"I wouldn't do that if I were you, sir," Mr. Skinner advised. "That rowdy Peasley and a man like Kjellin will not get along together for one voyage; then Kjellin will fire him, and first thing you know you'll be groping around in the dark again."

"Oh, I know this Finn is a pet of yours," Cappy retorted acidly, "but Matt Peasley is a pet of mine. If we put them together in the same ship maybe we'll have one of those skin-glove contests you referred to a minute ago, but between their mutual recriminations you can bet your hopes of Heaven I'll catch a glimpse of the truth and act accordingly. Matt will not tell a lie, Skinner. Remember that."

"Neither will Kjellin," Skinner declared with equal warmth.

"Well, I don't know whether he will or not. However, that's beside the question. Where is the Florence Ricks?"

"Sailed from San Pedro at noon yesterday."

"Where is the Quickstep?"

"Sailed from Eureka to load shingles last night."

"Good. Wireless the master of the Florence to provide himself with a new second mate. That will give him time to wireless ahead and have one waiting for him when the vessel touches in to discharge passengers from the south. Tell him to inform Peasley he isn't fired, but just transferred. Attend to it, Skinner."

While Mr. Skinner departed to carry out Cappy's order, the old gentleman called up Harbor 15, Masters' and Pilots' Association, and asked for the secretary.

"Ricks of the Blue Star speaking," he announced crisply. "Been furnishing many second mates to the Quickstep lately?"

"Why, yes, Mr. Ricks. Kjellin wires for a new second mate quite frequently. They don't seem to stay with him more than a voyage or two. He's quite a driver, you know, Mr. Ricks."

"I know," Cappy replied grimly. "The next time he wires in to have a second mate join the ship when he touches in here, you might be good enough to call me up. I have a skookum young second mate in the Florence Ricks that I'm training for a captain, and I want to switch him in on the Humboldt Bay run for the sake of the experience. And, of course, you know how it is with masters—they like to think they're selecting their own mates, and always resent any interference from their owners. And if you do ask them to take a certain mate they're apt to suspect he's a spy from the office, and—well, you understand. I'd prefer to have this lad I have in mind go aboard as if you had sent him."

"I understand, Mr. Ricks. I'll let you know the first time Kjellin wires in."

CHAPTER XXVIII.
CAPPY HAS A HEART

"Well, Matt," said Cappy Ricks, cheerfully, as he shook hands with the late second mate of the Florence Ricks. "We don't see much of each other now that you're a mate. But don't worry, you'll be a master again, and then you'll be dropping in here a couple of times a month pestering me for a lot of things for your ship that you could probably get along without. You're looking fit, my boy."

"I'm feeling fit, sir," Matt replied, grinning.

"I'm glad to hear it," was Cappy's grim reply. "Hum! Harump-h-h-h! Let me see now. You've had your course in the Mendocino dog-holes, and that's over. I hope you learned something. You've run for seven months from all the Washington and Oregon ports to Southern California, and—er—that's very nice. But you haven't been over Humboldt Bar yet, have you?"

"No, sir."

"Then you have something coming. Quite a bar in the winter time, Matt, quite a bar! Good many tickets been lost on that bar, Matt, so you ought to have more than a nodding acquaintance with it. You're going second mate in the Quickstep. She's carrying redwood shingles from Eureka to the Shingle Association's air-drying yards up river at Los Medanos at present, and she'll get to Los Medanos Sunday afternoon, so you'd better get there about the same time, in order to turn to discharging bright and early Monday morning. And you'll have to step lively, Matt. The Quickstep lives up to her name, and the way they put shingles into that vessel is a scandal."

"Shingles are nice stuff to handle," Matt ventured.

"Not redwood shingles, Matt. All right after they're dry, but when they come fresh from the saws they bleed a little, so be sure and wear gloves when you handle them. If you have a cut on your hand that redwood sap may poison you. I think you'll like the Quickstep, Matt."

"It doesn't matter whether I do or not," Matt replied humorously. "You always do things for me without consulting me anyhow."

"Why, you don't mind, do you, my boy? It's all for your own good."

"I can bear it, sir, because one of these bright days I'm going to do something without consulting you."

Cappy favored him with a sharp glance. "As the street boys say," he flashed back, "'I get you, Steve!'"

"And having gotten me, Mr. Ricks, do you still want me in your employ?"

"Oh, certainly, certainly. Any time I want to get rid of you I'll fire you or have Skinner do it for me."

Matt looked at his watch and rose. "I have four days' shore leave before me, sir," he said, "so I guess I'll be trotting along and make the most of it. I'll be at Los Medanos Sunday night."

"Her skipper's a big Finn," Cappy warned him. "Behave yourself, Matt. He's bad medicine for young second mates."

"I'll do my duty, sir."

He took his leave. As he went out the door Cappy gazed after him with twinkling eyes: "Young scoundrel!" he murmured. "Damned young scoundrel! You'll be ringing Florry up the minute you leave this office, if you haven't already done it. I'm onto you, young fellow!"

Matt Peasley took Florry Ricks to a matinee that very day. Cappy, suspecting he might attempt something of the sort and desiring to verify his suspicions, went home from the office early that day, and from his hiding place behind the window drapes in his drawing room he observed a taxicab draw up in front of his residence at six o'clock. From this vehicle Matt Peasley, astonishingly well tailored, alighted, handed out the heir to the Ricks millions, said good-by lingeringly and drove away.

"Well," Cappy soliloquized, "I guess I'm going to land the son-in-law I'm after. The matinee is over at a quarter of five, and those two have fooled away an hour. I'll bet a dollar Florry steered that sailor into a tea fight somewhere, and if she did that, Matt, you're a tip-top risk and I'll underwrite you."

That same evening Cappy sneaked into his daughter's apartments and found a photograph of Matt Peasley in a hammered silver frame on Florry's dressing table.

"Holy sailor!" he chuckled. "They think they're putting one over on the old gentleman, don't they? Trying to cover me with blood, eh? Huh! If I'd let that fellow Matt stay ashore he'd have hung round Florry until he wore out his welcome, and I suppose in the long run I'd have had to put up with one of these lawn-tennis, tea-swilling young fellows too proud to work. By Judas Priest, when I quit the street I want to give my proxy to a lad that will make my competitors mind their step, and by keeping Matt at sea a couple of years, I'll get him over the moon-calf period. Deliver my girl and my business from the hands of a damned fool!"

The following evening Cappy questioned his daughter's chauffeur—a chauffeur, by the way, being a luxury which Cappy scorned for himself. He maintained a coachman and a carriage and a spanking team of bays, and drove to his office like the old-fashioned gentleman he was. From this chauffeur Cappy learned that he, the chauffeur, had been out all the afternoon with Miss Florence and a large, light-hearted young gentleman. They had lunched together at the Cliff House.

"What did she call him?" Cappy demanded, anxious to verify his suspicions. "Didn't she address him as 'Matt?'"

"No, sir," the man replied, grinning. "She called him 'dearie.'"

"Holy jumped-up Jehosophat!" murmured Cappy, and questioned the man no further. That evening, however, he decided to have a heart—particularly after Florry had informed him that she was going out to dinner the following night.

"And you'll be all alone, popsy-wops," she added, "so you had better eat dinner at the club."

"Oh, I'm tired of my clubs," Cappy replied sadly. "Still your remark gives me an idea, Florry. If I happen to run across that young fellow Peasley—you remember him, Florry; the boy I'm training for a steamship captain—I'll have him out for dinner with me so I'll not have to eat alone."

"I thought you didn't care for him socially," Florry put forth a feeler.

"Well, he used to remind me considerably of a St. Bernard pup, but I notice he's losing a lot of that fresh, puppy-dog way he used to have. And then he's a Down-East boy. His Uncle Ethan Peasley and I were pals together fifty years ago, and for Ethan's sake I feel that I ought to show the boy some consideration. He's learning to hold himself together pretty well, and if I should run into him to-morrow I'll ask him out."

Florry exhibited not the slightest interest in her father's plans, but he noticed that immediately after dinner she hurried up to her room, and that upon her return she declined a game of pool with her father on the score of not feeling very well.

"You skipped upstairs like a sick woman," Cappy reflected. "I'll bet a hat you telephoned that son of a sea cook to be sure and throw himself in my way to-morrow, so I'll invite him out to dinner. And you're complaining of a headache now so you'll have a good excuse to cancel that dinner engagement to-morrow night so as to eat at home with your daddy and his guest. Poor old father! He's such a dub! I'll bet myself a four-bit cigar I eat breakfast alone to-morrow morning."

And it was even so. Florry sent down word that she was too indisposed to breakfast with her father, and the old man drove chuckling to his office. That afternoon Matt Peasley, in an endeavor to invade the floor of the Merchants' Exchange, to which he had no right, was apprehended by the doorkeeper and asked to show his credentials.

"Oh, I'm Captain Peasley, of the Blue Star Navigation Company," he replied lightly, and was granted admittance as the courtesy accorded all sea captains. He knew Cappy Ricks always spent an hour on 'Change after luncheon at the Commercial Club. When Cappy met him, however, the old man was mean enough to pay not the slightest attention to Matt; so after waiting round for three-quarters of an hour longer, the latter left the Exchange and walked down California Street, where he posted himself in the shelter of a corner half a block south of No. 258, where the Blue Star Navigation Company had its offices. From this vantage point presently he spied Cappy trotting home from the Merchants' Exchange; whereupon Matt strolled leisurely up the street and met him. And in order that Cappy should realize whom he was meeting Matt bumped into the schemer and then begged his pardon profusely.

"Don't mention it, Matt," the old rascal protested. "You shook up a flock of ideas in my head and jarred one loose. If you haven't anything on to-night, my boy, better come out to the house and have dinner with me. I'm all alone and I want company."

"Thank you, sir," Matt replied enthusiastically; "I'll be glad to come."

"You bet you will," Cappy thought. Aloud he said: "At six-thirty."

"Yes, sir. Thank you, sir." And Matt Peasley was off like a tin-canned dog to slick himself up for the party, while Cappy entered the elevator chuckling. "If I ever find the sour-souled philosopher who said you can't mix business and sentiment without resultant chaos," he soliloquized, "I'll boil the kill-joy in oil."

CHAPTER XXIX.
NATURE TAKES HER COURSE

The big steam schooner Quickstep was lying at the Los Medanos dock when Matt Peasley reported for duty. The captain was not aboard, but the first mate received him kindly and explained that Captain Kjellin had gone down to San Francisco by train for a little social relaxation and to bring back funds to pay off the longshoremen.

Early on Monday morning the crew and a large force of stevedores commenced to discharge the vessel. Two winches were kept busy, the first mate being in charge of the work up forward and Matt superintending that aft. The shingles were loaded in huge rope cargo nets, snatched out of the ship and swung overside onto flat cars, which were shunted off into the drying yard as soon as loaded.

The captain returned at noon on Tuesday, and at two o'clock the last bundle of shingles was out of the Quickstep, for the mate had worked overtime Monday night in order that they might finish discharging early enough on Tuesday afternoon to drop down to Oleum and take on fuel oil for the next voyage. This schedule would bring them to the dock at San Francisco about six o'clock, where they would take on stores and passengers and sail at seven for Eureka, on Humboldt Bay, where they would arrive Wednesday night. On Thursday they would commence taking on cargo, but since they had to take shingles from several mills round the bay, they were bound to be delayed waiting for tides to get in and out, and in all probability they would not be loaded and at sea until Saturday night, which would give them Sunday at sea—and in the lumber trade on the Pacific Coast the only profitable way to spend Sunday is to spend it at sea. To spend it in port is a day lost, with the crew loafing and drawing full pay for it. The mate explained to Matt that Captain Kjellin would drive them hard to maintain this schedule, for he prized his job as master of the Quickstep, and had a reputation for speed and efficiency with his owners which he was anxious to maintain.

Despite their best efforts, however, the vessel was doomed to fall behind her schedule. At Oleum they found the oil dock lined with vessels taking on fuel, and in consequence were forced to wait two hours for a berth; seeing which the captain went ashore and telephoned his owners that he would be unable to get to the dock in San Francisco until about eight o'clock. Consequently, Mr. Skinner, realizing that the passengers their agent had booked for the Quickstep, by reason of the cut-rates prevailing on lumber steamers, would not wait on the dock until the Quickstep should arrive, instructed the captain to lay over in San Francisco all night and put to sea at nine o'clock Wednesday morning. In the meantime he said he would send a clerk down to the dock to notify the waiting passengers of the unavoidable change in schedule.

Promptly at eight o'clock Wednesday morning the Quickstep got away from the dock. The minute she was fairly out the Golden Gate, however, she poked her nose into a stiff nor'west gale; and as she was bound north and was empty, this gale, catching her on the port counter, caused her to roll and pitch excessively, and cut her customary speed of ten miles an hour down to five. Every passenger aboard was soon desperately seasick, and off Point Reyes so violently did the Quickstep pitch that even some members of the crew became nauseated, among them Matt Peasley. He had never been seasick before and he was ashamed of himself now, notwithstanding the fact that he knew even the hardiest old seadogs are not proof against mal-de-mer under certain extraordinary conditions. Captain Kjellin, coming up on the bridge during Matt's watch, found the latter doing the most unseamanlike thing imaginable. Caught in a paroxysm at the weather end of the bridge, Matt, in his agony, was patronizing the weather rail! The captain heard him squawk, and ducked to avoid what instinct told him the gale would bring him his way.

"Vat you ban tankin' of?" he roared furiously. "You damned landsman! Don't you know enough to discharge dot cargo over der lee rail?"

Having disposed of a hearty breakfast, Matt raised his green face and stared sheepishly at the Finn. "You didn't get sprayed, did you, sir?" he queried breathlessly.

"No, but who der devil ever heard of a seaman gettin' sick to windward—?"

"I know it looks awful, sir," quavered Matt. "I thought something like this might happen, and in order to be prepared for eventualities I hung a fire bucket over the edge of the weather-bridge railing and set another there by the binnacle. The man at the wheel got me started, sir. He asked me if I liked fat pork. Can't you see that if I had made a quick run for the lee rail while the vessel was pitching to leeward the chances are I'd continue right on overboard? As soon as I get my bearings again I'll empty the bucket, sir."

"Der fire buckets ban't for dot purpose."

"All right, sir. I'll buy you a new fire bucket when we get to Eureka," Matt answered contritely.

Kjellin stayed on the bridge a few minutes, growling and glaring, but Matt was too ill and dispirited to pay any attention to him, so finally he went below.

The Quickstep bucked the gale all the way to Humboldt Bar, and tied up at the first mill dock at half past one o'clock on Friday. It was two o'clock before the passengers and their baggage had been sent ashore, but the minute the last trunk went over the rail the loading began.

"We'll work overtime again to-night," the first mate told Matt at luncheon. "The old man will drive us hard to-morrow, and we'll have more overtime Saturday night so we can get to sea early Sunday morning."

"I don't care," Matt replied. "I get seventy-five cents an hour for my overtime, and I'm big enough to stand a lot of that. But, believe me, I'll jump lively. The old man's out of sorts on account of the delay due to that head wind."

At three o'clock the captain walked aft, where Matt Peasley was superintending the stowing in the after hold.

"Is dot all you've got to do," he sneered—"settin' roundt mit your hands in your poggeds?"

Matt glared at him. True, his hands were in his pockets at that moment, but he was not setting round. He was watching a slingload of shingles hovering high over the hatch, and the instant it was lowered he intended to leap upon it, unship the cargo hook, hang the spare cargo net on it and whistle to the winchman to hoist away for another slingload. He controlled his temper and said:

"I'm doing the best I can, sir. That winchman doesn't have to wait on us a second, sir. We handle them as fast as they swing them in from the mill dock."

"Yump in an' do somedings yourself," Kjellin growled. "Don't stand roundt like a young leddy."

"D'ye mean you want I should mule shingles round in this hold like a longshoreman?"

"Sure! Ve got to get to sea Sunday morning, und every liddle bit helps."

"Well, then you'll get along without my little bit. If you don't know your business, sir, I know mine. Somebody's got to tend that sling, and everybody's business is nobody's business. If I'm not on the job a bundle of shingles may come flying down from above and kill a man, or that heavy cargo block may crack a stevedore on the head. Who's going to look after the broken bundles and see that they're repacked if I don't? I can't do that and mule shingles round in this hold, sir; and what's more I'm not going to do it."

"Den, by yimminy, you get off der ship!" the captain roared. "I don't vant no loafers aboard my boat, und if you tank—"

"Stow the gab, you big Finn! I'm through. Pay me off and help yourself to another second mate." And Matt put on his coat and whistled to the winchman to steady his slingload while he climbed out of the hold. Kjellin followed and Matt preceded him to his stateroom, where the captain paid him the few dollars he had coming to him.

"Sign clear," he ordered, and Matt took an indelible pencil and stooped over the skipper's desk to sign the pay roll. As he straightened up the captain's powerful left forearm came round Matt's left shoulder and under his chin, tilting his head backward, while the Finn's left knee ground into the small of his back. He was held as in a vise, helpless, and Kjellin spoke:

"Ven I get fresh young faler like you, an' he quit me cold, I lick him after I pay him off."

Cappy Ricks: OR, the Subjugation of matt Peasley | 151

"I see," Matt replied calmly. "That makes it a plain case of assault and battery, whereas if you lick him before you pay him off, he can sue your owners. You're a fine, smart squarehead!"

"You bet!" Kjellin answered, and struck him a stunning blow behind the ear. Matt, realizing his inability to wriggle out of the captain's grasp, kicked backward with his right foot and caught the Finn squarely on the right shin, splintering the bone. The captain cried out with the pain of it and released the pressure on Matt's chin, whereupon the latter whirled, picked the Finn up bodily, and threw him through the stateroom door out onto the deck, where he struck the pipe railing and rebounded. He lay where he fell, and when Matt's brain cleared and he came out on deck the captain was moaning.

"Get up, you brute!" Matt ordered. "You got the wrong pig by the ear that time."

"My leg ban broken," Kjellin whimpered.

"I wish it was your neck," Matt replied with feeling, and bent over to examine his fallen foe. When he grasped Kjellin by the right shoulder, however, the Finn screamed with pain, so Matt called the steward, and together they lifted him and carried him to his berth.

"I'll bet a cooky you're a total loss and no accident insurance," Matt soliloquized. "You're not worth it, but for the sake of the owners I'll get a doctor to look you over," and he went ashore at once. When the doctor had looked Thorwald Kjellin over his verdict was a broken tibia, a broken radius and a broken clavicle.

Matt was concerned. "I don't think I ever had any of those things to get broken," he declared humorously, "but if mere words mean anything I'll bet this is a hospital job." The doctor nodded, and Matt turned to the captain: "Do you want to go to the hospital in Eureka or in San Francisco?"

"I ban vant to go home," the Finn moaned.

"Very well, captain; I guess your successor will bring you there. I'm going up to the mill office now to report to the owners by telephone."

"Dot ban't none o' your business, Peasley," Kjellin protested. "Dot is der first mate's job. You ban fired."

"Yes, I know. Now I'm back-firing," Matt retorted.

Fifteen minutes later he had Cappy Ricks on the long-distance telephone.

"Mr. Ricks," he began, "this is Peasley talking from Eureka. I have to report that I'm fired out of the Quickstep. I'm not complaining about that or asking you to reinstate me, because I can get another job now, but I want to tell you why I was fired. The captain got a grouch against me coming up. We had a nor'west gale on our port counter and she rolled and bucked until even some of the crew got seasick. I'm ashamed to say I fell by the wayside myself for a few minutes, and Captain Kjellin caught me draped over the weather bridge railing. So I guess he thought I wasn't much of a seaman. Anyhow he picked on me from then on, and a little while ago he ordered me to mule shingles with the longshoremen in the after hold. I couldn't do that, Mr. Ricks. I'm a ship's officer, and besides you've simply got to have somebody to watch the slings when they're coming into the ship at the rate of two a minute or somebody will get hurt, and then the vessel will be sued for damages. You see we were working overtime and in a hurry to get loaded—"

"I see everything," Cappy retorted. "What happened next?"

"The captain got me foul in his cabin when I went to be paid off, and hung a shanty back of my ear, so I threw him out on deck and hurt him. You'll have to send a new skipper up to bring the Quickstep home, sir. The first mate is a good man but he hasn't a master's license—"

"What did you do to Kjellin, Matt?"

"You'll have to ask a doctor, sir. I didn't intend to break him up, but it seems I damaged all his Latin superstructure, and he'll have to go to a hospital for a couple of months. I'm sorry I hurt your skipper, sir, and I felt I couldn't leave your employ, Mr. Ricks, without an explanation."

"You haven't left my employ at all. Get back on the job and load that vessel, or the first thing you know you'll be stuck in port over Sunday, and that's not the way to make a start as master of the Quickstep. You have a license as master of steam, haven't you?"

"Yes, sir. I can handle her, sir."

"Then do it and don't stand there burning up good money on the long-distance phone. The Quickstep is yours—on one condition."

"I accept it, sir," Matt exclaimed, overjoyed. "What is it?"

"That you stick in her at least six months."

"I will if I live and she floats that long, sir. Thank you. Please have a second mate and an ambulance waiting for me at Meiggs Wharf on Monday. I'll touch in there on my way up river to discharge what's left of your skipper."

CHAPTER XXX.
MR. SKINNER HEARS A LECTURE

Down in the offices of the Blue Star Navigation Company Cappy Ricks, having summoned Mr. Skinner, sat peering whimsically at the general manager over the rims of his spectacles. "Well, Skinner, my dear boy," he announced presently, "sure enough there was something wrong with the Quickstep, and now I know what it is; she has had the wrong master. When he hustles to catch a tide or to get to sea Saturday night or Sunday morning he drives his mates and tries to make them do longshoremen's work. When he bullied a weak mate into doing that, there was nobody to pay exclusive attention to the slingloads as they came into the ship, and naturally accidents resulted. When strong second mates refused he fired them, and after firing them he cornered them in his cabin, held them foul and beat them. You see, Skinner, this skookum skipper of yours didn't realize that with two slingloads of shingles a minute dropping into the ship he had to have a man on the job to watch the loading and do nothing else; and because he didn't realize the error of his way, Skinner, he and Matt Peasley have pulled off that little skin-glove contest, and now Kjellin looks like a barrel of cement that's been dropped out the window of a six-story building. Hum! Ahem! Harump-h-h-h! Call up the attorney for that man Jacobsen that's suing the Quickstep, and tell him to come down here with his man and we'll settle the case out of court. His charge lies against Kjellin for assault and battery, but after all, Skinner, I dare say we are in a measure responsible for our servants. I'll give the attorney about twenty-five dollars for his fee, and er—the man Jacobsen—let me see, Skinner, he had a broken nose, did he not?"

"Yes, sir."

"We'll pay his doctor bill and his wages as second mate since Kjellin fired him, and give him a hundred dollars extra."

"How about Kjellin's hospital bill?"

"I disclaim responsibility, Skinner. Did he settle up with the cashier for his last voyage?"

"Yes, Mr. Ricks."

"Then send him a wireless and tell him he's fired. Also, Skinner, my boy, see that an ambulance is waiting for him at Meiggs Wharf when he arrives on the Quickstep on Monday. We'll show him we're not entirely heartless. Make it clear, however, that this office will not be responsible for the ambulance fee. Matt will bring the vessel down without a second mate, I dare say. He'll stand a watch himself. Better call up Harbor 15 and see if there isn't a second mate out of a job hanging round there, and tell him to join the ship at Meiggs Wharf."

Mr. Skinner's eyes fairly popped. "You don't mean to tell me, sir, that you've given the Quickstep to that rowdy Peasley?"

Cappy relapsed into the colloquialism of the younger generation with which he was wont to associate at luncheon. "Surest thing you know," he said.

"If I may be permitted a criticism, Mr. Ricks—"

"You may not."

"Your sentimental leaning toward your fellow townsman may be the cause of losing one of the best paying ships of the fleet."

"Forget it, Skinner!"

"Oh, very well. You're the boss, Mr. Ricks. But if I were in your place I would have an older and more experienced man to relieve him the moment he comes into the bay. You must remember, Mr. Ricks, that while he may run her very nicely during the summer months, he has had no experience on Humboldt Bay during the winter months—"

"Skinner, the only way he'll ever accumulate experience on that bar is to give him the opportunity."

"He'll take big risks. He's very young and headstrong."

"I admit he's fiery. But I promised him a ship, and he's earned her sooner than I planned, so, even if my decision loses the Quickstep for us, he shall have her. I'll be swindled if I ever did see the like of that boy Matt. He gets results. And do you know why, Skinner?"

"Because," Mr. Skinner replied coldly, "he's a huge, healthy animal, able and willing to fight his way in any ship, and at the same time clever enough to take advantage of your paternal interest in him—"

"Rats! I'll give you the answer, Skinner, my boy: He gets results because he does his duty and doesn't sidestep for man or devil. And he's able to do his duty and do it well because he has a clear understanding of what his duty is—and that, Skinner, is the kind of skipper material I've been looking for all my life. As for the boy's horsepower, let me tell you this: If Matt Peasley wasn't any bigger than I am, he'd fight any man that tried to walk over him. It's in his breed. Damn it, sir, he's a Yankee skipper, and when you've said that you're through. I guess I know. How much have we been paying that bully Kjellin?"

"Two hundred a month."

"Too much! Pay Matt two-twenty-five and attend to the certificate of change of masters."

When Mr. Skinner had departed Cappy sat back in his chair and closed his eyes, as was his habit when his gigantic brain grappled with a problem of more than ordinary dimensions. For fully ten minutes he sat absolutely motionless, then suddenly he straightened up like a jack-in-the-box and summoned Mr. Skinner.

"Skinner," he said plaintively, "I'm feeling a little run down. Will you please be good enough to book Florry and me passage to Europe right away. I've never been to Europe, you know, Skinner, and I think it's time I took a vacation."

Mr. Skinner smiled. "Why all the hurry?" he queried.

"I want to try out a theory," Cappy replied. "I have a great curiosity, Skinner, to ascertain if there is any truth in the old saying that absence makes the heart grow fonder. And if it does, Skinner—why, the sooner I start the sooner I can get back."

Mr. Skinner went out mystified. As Mark Twain's friend, Mr. Ballou, remarked about the coffee, Cappy Ricks was a little too "technical" for him.

CHAPTER XXXI.
INTERNAL COMBUSTION

The Quickstep had arrived in port again before Cappy Ricks and Florry could get away to Europe, so Matt came down by train from Los Medanos and was granted the meager comfort of a farewell with his heart's desire. Thereafter all comfort fled his life, for, with Cappy Ricks away, Mr. Skinner was high and low justice, and he was not long keeping Matt Peasley in ignorance of the fact that it was one thing to skipper a Blue Star ship for Cappy Ricks and quite another thing to skipper the same ship for the Blue Star manager. For Mr. Skinner had never liked Captain Peasley, and, moreover, he never intended to, for the master of the Quickstep was not sufficiently submissive to earn the general manager's approbation as a desirable employee, and Cappy Ricks was the only man with a will and a way of his own who could get along amicably in the same office with the efficient and cold-blooded Mr. Skinner.

Cappy wasn't outside Sandy Hook before Mr. Skinner had Matt on the carpet for daring to bring the Quickstep up river without a pilot. He demanded an explanation.

"I made careful note of all the twists and turns when the pilot took me up the first time," Matt declared. "It isn't a difficult channel, so I decided to save forty-five dollars the next time and take her up myself."

"Suppose you'd buried her nose in the mud and we'd had to lighter her deckload to get her off," Mr. Skinner suggested.

Matt grinned. "If your aunt was a man she'd be your uncle, wouldn't she?" he parried. He had made up his mind not to take Mr. Skinner seriously. Mr. Skinner flushed, looked dangerous, but concluded not to pursue the investigation further.

Three weeks later, when making up to a dock at San Pedro, a strong ebb tide and a mistake in judgment swung the bow of the Quickstep into the end of the dock and a dolphin was torn out. In the fullness of time the Blue Star Navigation Company was in receipt of a bill for $112 dock repairs, whereupon Mr. Skinner wrote Matt, prefacing his letter with the query: "Referring to inclosed bill—how did this happen?" Then he went on to scold Matt bitterly for his inability to handle his ship properly in making up to a dock.

Matt promptly returned Mr. Skinner his own letter, with this penciled memorandum at the bottom of the page: "Referring to inclosed bill for dock repairs—the dock happened to be in my course. That's the only way I can account for it."

For some time, whenever the Quickstep carried shingle cargoes for the Shingle Association, there had been disputes over her freight bill, due to continued discrepancies between the tally in and the tally out, and Mr. Skinner had instructed Matt to tally his next cargo into the ship himself and then tally it out again. Matt engaged a certified lumber surveyor at five dollars a day to do the tallying at the various mills, but at Los Medanos he tallied the cargo out personally. To a shingle it agreed with the mill tally. Subsequently the manager of the drying yard reported a shortage of eight thousand shingles, and again Mr. Skinner wrote Matt for an explanation, to which Matt replied as follows:

"Do not pay any attention to the yard manager's tally. Ours is right. A certified tallyman counted 11,487,250 in, and I counted 11,487,250 out, as I have already reported. Sorry I cannot reverse my decision. However, I have an idea which may account for the shortage: After the vessel is reported down river, the stevedores gather on the dock, and while waiting for us to arrive and commence discharging they whittle shingles to pass the time away. I give you this information for what it may be worth."

Mr. Skinner had the grace to see that he had been rebuked and left standing in a very poor light for one of his noted efficiency, so he did not pursue the subject further; but the next time Matt came to the office he jumped on him for carrying a dead-head passenger from San Pedro in the first cabin.

"Of course I carried him," Matt replied. "When I was before the mast in the Annabel Lee he was her skipper, so when I met him in Pedro minus his ticket and stony broke I gave him a lift to San Francisco. Mr. Ricks informed me that I would be permitted these little courtesies within the bounds of reason."

"When Captain Kjellin had the Quickstep," Mr. Skinner answered, "he never carried dead-heads."

"You mean he didn't have the courage to put the name on the passenger list and write D. H. after it. However, please do not compare me with Captain Kjellin."

"Well, you're not making the time he made in the Quickstep."

"I know it, sir. My policy is to make haste slowly. Kjellin hurried — and see what happened to him. He'll never be fast again, either, with that short leg of his."

"Captain Peasley, I am opposed to your levity."

"Do you want me to worry and stew just because you do not happen to like me and keep picking on me, Mr. Skinner? Why don't you be a sport and give me a fair chance, sir? You have all the best of it in any argument — so why argue?"

"No more dead-heads," Mr. Skinner warned. "Hereafter, pay for your guests."

With the coming on of winter, however, Matt's troubles with Mr. Skinner really commenced, although, in all justice to Skinner, the general manager was merely following out his theory of efficiency, and in respect to the matter upon which he deviled Matt Peasley most he did not differ vastly from many managing owners of steam schooners on the Pacific Coast. The trouble lay in the fact that the Quickstep carried passengers. While she was a cargo boat, and hence had no regular run or sailing schedule, her cabin accommodations were really very good and her steward's department excelled that of the regular passenger boats. By cutting the regular passenger rates from twenty-five to forty per cent. and advertising the vessel to sail at a certain hour on a certain date from a certain pier, free-lance ticket brokers found no difficulty in getting her a fair complement of passengers each trip. There was a moderate profit in this passenger traffic, and Mr. Skinner was anxious to increase it.

The difficulty surrounding the passenger business in the steam-schooner trade, however, lies in the uncertainty of a vessel's arrival and departure. It is all guesswork. Thus Matt Peasley, with his cargo half discharged at San Pedro, would estimate that he would sail from that port, northbound via San Francisco to some Oregon or Washington port for another cargo, at noon on the following day. Accordingly, he would wire his owners, who would immediately advertise the sailing of the vessel from San Francisco forty hours later, the Quickstep's average running time between San Pedro and San Francisco being about thirty-eight hours. If the master's estimate proved correct and there were no strong head winds to retard the vessel, she would sail within an hour or two of the advertised time, whereas a delay of six to eight hours in the arrival of the vessel at San Francisco might mean the loss of all the passenger business garnered for that trip; for competition was keen, and the ticket agents, selling on a commission of one dollar per ticket, would switch the traffic to some other vessel sailing earlier rather than have the tickets canceled and thus lose the commission.

When through delay or miscalculation the vessel lost passenger traffic out of a port other than San Francisco, Mr. Skinner did not feel discouraged. To lose passengers out of San Francisco, where the home office of the Blue Star Navigation Company was located, however, savored of a reflection on his efficiency, and caused him much bitter anguish. Consequently, when Matt Peasley, with a full passenger list from Eureka to San Francisco, wired Mr. Skinner that he would leave his loading port at two P. M. on Wednesday, Mr. Skinner allowed him twenty-two hours for landing his passengers from Eureka to San Francisco and taking on another load for San Pedro, whither the Quickstep was bound on that voyage. As a result the Quickstep was advertised to sail from San Francisco on Thursday at two P. M., and the agents were notified to commence selling tickets. Judge of Mr. Skinner's perturbation, therefore, when he received the following wireless from Matt Peasley at five o'clock on Wednesday:

Bar breaking heavily. At anchor inside. Will cross out as soon as I judge it safe to do so.

Three hours' delay, already, with the prospects exceedingly bright for the Quickstep's lurking inside Humboldt Bar all night! Mr.

Skinner saw his passenger traffic gone to glory for that trip, so he sent a reply to Matt Peasley by wireless, as follows:

> You are advertised to sail from here for San Pedro at two o'clock to-morrow. Hope you will permit nothing to militate against the preservation of that schedule. Answer.

"That's what comes of having an inexperienced man in the vessel," he complained to the cashier. "That fellow Peasley sees a few white caps on the bar, and he's afraid to cross out. Damn! Kjellin had her three years and never hung behind a bar once. Many a time he's come down to Humboldt Bar and found half a dozen steam schooners at anchor inside, waiting for a chance to duck out. Did Kjellin drop anchor too? He did not. Out he went and bucked right through it."

Mr. Skinner waited at the office until six o'clock to get Matt Peasley's answer. He got it—between the eyes:

> I have no jurisdiction over Humboldt Bar.

The Quickstep crossed out next morning, and Mr. Skinner wirelessed her master this message:

> Your timidity has spoiled San Pedro passenger business. Drop Eureka passengers at Meiggs Wharf and continue your voyage.

Now it does not please any mariner to be told that he is timid, and, while Matt Peasley made no reply, nevertheless, he chalked up a black mark against Mr. Skinner and commenced to plan against the day of reckoning.

That was an unusually severe winter. Four times Matt Peasley came down to the entrance to Humboldt Bar and came to anchor. Three times he tried to cross out and was forced to change his mind; seven times did Mr. Skinner upbraid him. The eighth time that Matt Peasley's caution knocked the San Francisco passenger traffic into a deficit, Mr. Skinner sent him this message where the Quickstep lay behind Coos Bay Bar:

> What is the matter with you? Your predecessor always managed to negotiate that bar, and this company expects same of you.

"He's bound to run me out of this ship," Matt soliloquized when he read that terse aerogram, "but I promised Cappy I'd stick six months and I'll do it. That penny-pinching Skinner wants me to cut corners and get myself into trouble so he can fire me. I'll not tell him the things I want to tell him, so I guess I won't say anything — much."

He didn't. He just wired Mr. Skinner as follows:

Any time you want to commit suicide I will furnish a pistol.

About the beginning of March Mr. Skinner opened his cold heart long enough to let in a little human love and get married, and shortly thereafter he found it necessary to make a business trip to the redwood mill of the Ricks Lumber and Logging Company on Humboldt Bay. He went up on the regular P. C. passenger boat and took his bride with him, and while he was at the mill Matt Peasley came nosing in with the Quickstep and loaded a cargo of redwood lumber. He finished loading on the same day that Mr. Skinner discovered he had no further excuse for remaining away from the office, in consequence of which the latter decided to return to San Francisco on the Quickstep. This for several very good reasons: The food on the Quickstep was better than the food on the regular liner, the accommodations were fully as good, the vessel was loaded deeply and would ride steadily — and Mr. Skinner and his bride would travel without charge.

The sight of the Skinners coming aboard was not a pleasing one to Matt Peasley. He did not like Mr. Skinner well enough to care to eat at the same table with him, and he bethought him now of all the mean, nagging complaints of the past six months. In particular he recalled Mr. Skinner's instructions to him anent the carrying of deadhead passengers — and suddenly he had a brilliant idea. He sent for his wireless operator and ordered him to send this message:

Blue Star Navigation Company, San Francisco, Cal.

Please accept my resignation as master of your steamer Quickstep, said resignation to take effect immediately upon my arrival in San Francisco. Kindly have somebody on hand to relieve me.

Matthew Peasley.

Matt had just remembered that his six months in the Quickstep were up. His next move was to call on the steward.

"Go into Stateroom 7," he ordered, "and collect fifteen dollars from that man and woman in there. They came aboard without tickets."

Two minutes later the steward was back with word that the passengers in question were dead-heads, being none other than the manager of the Blue Star Navigation Company and his wife.

"Steward, you go back and tell that man Skinner that Captain Peasley never carries any dead-heads on the Quickstep. Tell him that when Captain Peasley wants to carry a guest he pays the guest's passage out of his own pocket."

"But he'll fire me, sir."

"Do as I order; he will not fire you. I'm the only man that has that privilege, and I'll exercise it if you don't obey me."

Two more minutes elapsed; then Mr. Skinner presented himself at the captain's stateroom.

"Peasley," he said sharply, "what nonsense is this?"

"No dead-heads on this ship, Mr. Skinner. Your own orders, sir. Fifteen dollars, if you please. You're not my guests."

"Of course," said Mr. Skinner, "I shall do nothing of the sort."

"Then get off the ship."

"Sir, are you crazy?"

"No, I am not; I'm just disgusted with you. Fifteen dollars here and now before I cast off the lines, or I'll run you off the ship. Don't tempt me, Skinner. If I ever lay violent hands on you there'll be work for a doctor."

Mr. Skinner was speechless, but he laid fifteen dollars on the captain's desk and returned to his stateroom. His silence was ominous. Five minutes later the Quickstep backed out from the mill wharf and headed down the bay. As she plowed along, the rain commenced falling and a stiff southeast breeze warned Matt that he was in for a wet crossing. He was further convinced of this when the bar tug Ranger met him a mile inside the entrance. She steamed alongside, and, as she passed, her captain hailed Matt.

"Don't try to cross out, Peasley," he shouted. "The bar is breaking."

"The Quickstep doesn't mind it," Matt answered.

"Don't try it, I tell you. I've been twenty years on Humboldt Bar and I know it, Peasley. I've never seen it so bad as it is this minute."

"Oh, we'll cross out without any fuss," Matt called back cheerfully, and rang for full speed ahead. They were down at the entrance, and the Quickstep had just lifted to the dead water from the first big green roller, when Mr. Skinner came up and touched Matt Peasley on the arm.

"Well, sir?" Matt demanded irritably.

"Drop anchor inside, captain. That bar is too rough to attempt to cross out."

"Oh, nonsense!" Matt declared.

"But didn't you hear what that tug-boat captain said? He said it was breaking worse than he had known it for twenty years."

"Bah! What does he know about it?"

"I don't care what he knows, Captain Peasley; I order you not to attempt to cross out. My wife is aboard and I'll take no chances. Come to anchor and wait for the bar to settle."

"You order me?" Matt sneered. "Who in blazes are you to give orders on my ship? I'm at sea, you understand, and you have nothing to say. You'll give your orders and I'll obey them when I'm at the dock, but crossing Humboldt Bar, I'm the master of ceremonies. I can't turn back now. I'd lose my rudder as I came about. Get out. Who invited you up here?"

"How dare you, sir?" Mr. Skinner cried furiously. "Man, have you lost your mind? Obey me, I say."

Matt Peasley laughed blithely. "You miserable, cold-blooded, nagging old woman," he said, and took Mr. Skinner by the nape and shook him. "I've prayed for this day. Do you remember the time you wired me at Coos Bay that my timidity had lost you some passenger traffic? You impugned my courage then, you whelp, and now I'm going to give you a sample of it. All winter long you've been hounding me, trying to make me take chances crossing this bar, just so the vessel might pick up a couple of hundred dollars extra in passenger money. It didn't matter to you what risks other men's wives ran when you were snug in your office, did it? You never thought of the passengers I had aboard, or the lives of my crew or me, did you? You wanted me to cut corners and risk human lives for the sake of your reputation as an efficient manager, you—" And he shook Mr. Skinner until the manager's teeth rattled. "Now you're aboard yourself with your blushing bride, and how do you like it, eh? How do you like it? You know all about navigation, don't you? Well, you and your wife are the only passengers this trip, and I'm going to give you a taste of salt water you'll remember till your dying day," and with a shove he sent Mr. Skinner flying aft until he collided with the funnel.

"You're fired!" Skinner screamed, beside himself with fear and rage. But Matt Peasley was devoting all of his attention to the Quickstep now; and it was well that he did. The vessel rose on the crest of a green comber thirty feet high, and plunged with the speed of an express elevator into the valley between that wave and the next.

A tremendous sea boiled in over the knight heads and swept aft, burying the Quickstep until nothing showed but her upper works. But she was a sturdy craft and came up from under it, rode the succeeding three seas and was comparatively free of water when she shipped the next one. The crest of it came in along the little promenade deck, carrying away the companion that led to the bridge, staving in the doors and windows of all the staterooms on the port side and carrying away the rails and stanchions. There was two feet of water in Stateroom 7, where Mrs. Skinner clung to her husband, screaming hysterically.

But despite the awful buffeting she was receiving the Quickstep never faltered. On she plowed, riding the green billows like a gull, and shipping a sea only occasionally. The deckload, double-lashed, held, although the deckhouse groaned and twisted until Matt Peasley regretted the impulse that had impelled him to do this foolish thing for the sake of satisfying a grudge.

"She'll make it, sir," the man at the wheel called up; but Matt's face was a little white and serious as he tried to smile back.

Another sea came ramping aboard and snatched the port lifeboat out of the davits, smashed in the door of the dining saloon and flooded it, gutted the galley, and drove the cook and the steward to the protection of the engine room. The chief called up through the speaking tube:

"How's the boss making it, captain?"

"It's a wet passage for him, chief. I can hear his wife scream every time we ship one."

"Serves her right for marrying the pest," the chief growled, and turned away.

They crossed out, but at a cost that made Matt Peasley shudder, when he left the bridge in charge of the mate and went below to take stock of the damage. A new boat and four days' work for a carpenter gang—perhaps eighteen hundred dollars' worth of damage, not counting the demurrage! It was a big price to pay for one brief moment of triumph, but Matt Peasley felt that it would have been cheap at twice the money. He passed round on the starboard side of the vessel and found Mr. Skinner wet to the skin and shivering.

"We're over," Matt announced cheerfully. "How did you like the going?"

"You villain!" Skinner cried passionately. "You'll never command another ship in the Blue Star fleet, I'll promise you that."

"I know it, Skinner. But if I were you I'd go down in the engine room and dry out while the cook and the steward straighten things round."

"I'll discharge you the moment we tie up at the dock in San Francisco," Skinner stormed.

"Oh, no, you won't," Matt assured him. "I've beaten you to it. I resigned by wireless before we left the dock at Eureka."

That was a long, cold, cheerless trip for the Skinner family. The Quickstep bucked a howling southeaster all the way down the coast, and the Skinners were knocked from one end of their wet stateroom to the other and slept not a wink. It was a frightful experience, and to add to the discomfort of the trip Mrs. Skinner wept all the way. Eventually, however, the Quickstep tied up at the wharf in San Francisco, and the minute she was fast Matt Peasley, his accounts all made up to date and his clothes and personal effects packed, sprang out on the dock.

"There's your ship, Skinner," he called to the general manager. "I'm through." And he hastened away to the Blue Star office to settle up with the cashier, while Mr. Skinner and his bride entered a taxicab and were driven to their home. And two hours later when Mr. Skinner, warm and dry at last, came down to the office to attend to the task of selecting a new master for the Quickstep, he found Cappy Ricks was back from Europe and on the job.

"I hear you've been having some experience," said Cappy cheerfully as he shook hands with his manager. "Peasley was telling me what he did to you, and all the disrespectful things he said to you. Skinner, my dear fellow, that was an outrageous way for him to act."

"I fired him," said Skinner waspishly. "And while we're on the subject let me declare myself about this man Peasley; as long as I remain in your employ, Mr. Ricks, that man must never command another Blue Star vessel. Do I make myself sufficiently clear?"

"You do, Skinner; you do, indeed," Cappy answered. "I warned Matt that if you ever fired him, I'd have to back you up—and I'll do it, Skinner. I'll sustain your decision, my boy. As long as you're my manager that fellow can never go to sea under the Blue Star flag. The scoundrel!"

"And I wouldn't recommend him to any other owner either," Mr. Skinner suggested.

"I'll not, Skinner. He will never go to sea again. I'm not going to have his license taken away from him—er— Hum! Ahem! Harump-h-h-h! But I'll see that he doesn't use it again. The fact is, Skinner, I'm er—getting—old—and—er—you're pretty hard-worked in the lumber department, so I've—Hum! Harump-h-h-h! decided to relieve you of the shipping entirely and hire Matt for our port captain. He's on the pay roll at three hundred a month. And—er—Skinner, try to be friendly with the boy for my sake. The young rascal is engaged to marry my daughter, and I—er—it's barely possible he'll take up the business—Hum! Ahem! I'll stick round another year and break him into the landward side of shipping and then, Skinner, d'ye know what I'm going to do then?"

"What?" Mr. Skinner asked dully.

"I'm going to learn to play golf," said Cappy.

CHAPTER XXXII.
SKINNER PROPOSES—AND CAPPY RICKS DISPOSES

Having, as he thought, evaded the spirit of Mr. Skinner's ultimatum while conforming to its literal terms, Cappy Ricks hurried home leaving his general manager a stunned and horrified man. In this instance, however, Cappy had erred in his strategy. Skinner was calm, cold-blooded, suave, politic and deferential, but in his kind of fight he never bluffed. He never played his hand until he had sufficient trumps to take the odd trick.

He looked ahead now, into the not very distant future, and saw Matt Peasley, husband of the heiress to the Ricks millions, giving him orders—and the vision did not sit well on the general manager's stomach. Consequently, Mr. Skinner decided for a test of strength at once.

Accordingly, when Cappy Ricks came down to the office the following morning, Mr. Skinner came into the old fellow's sanctum and requested an interview.

"Fire away, my boy," said Cappy amiably, yet with a queer sinking feeling in his vitals, for he did not like the look in Skinner's eye; and something told him there was blood on the moon.

"With reference to this rowdy, Peasley, whom you tell me you are going to make port captain—"

"I also told you, Skinner, my boy, that he is to be my son-in-law," Cappy interrupted, like a good general bringing up his heavy artillery prior to ordering a charge. "I beg of you, Skinner, whatever your animosities, to bear in mind the fact that my daughter could not possibly engage herself to a rowdy."

"Out of respect to you and Miss Florence I shall not indulge in personalities, sir," Mr. Skinner replied smilingly, and Cappy shuddered, for Mr. Skinner never smiled in a fight unless he had the situation well in hand. "I have merely called to tell you that I have invested seventy-five cents of my salary in a stout hickory pick-handle, and the next time Captain Matt Peasley enters my office I shall test the quality of the said pick-handle over his head. I don't care if he is engaged to your daughter; the minute you bring that man into this office I go out. You shall have my resignation instantly. That decision, Mr. Ricks, is final and irrevocable." And without giving Cappy an instant for argument Mr. Skinner bowed himself out.

A month and Cappy Ricks remained minus his port captain; Mr. Skinner was still strongly entrenched in his job as general manager. It was a hard hand to beat, for the fact of the matter was that Cappy Ricks simply could not afford to dispense with Mr. Skinner. The man was too honest, too conscientious, too industrious, too brilliant, too efficient, not to be reckoned with. To part with Skinner was like parting with a dividend-producing gold mine; it was equivalent to unloading on Cappy's shoulders again the burden of work and worry that would have killed him ten years ago had he not surrendered it to Skinner, who handled it as a juggler handles nine balls. Moreover, Skinner knew all of the business secrets of the Ricks Lumber and Logging Company and the Blue Star Navigation Company—why, he was an integral part of the business; and, lastly, Cappy was fond of the man.

Skinner had come to him as office boy at the tender age of ten—and that was twenty-five years before. A daily association for twenty-five years would make a human being like Cappy fond of the devil himself; and, barring the fact that he was cold-blooded, Skinner was a fairly likeable chap, and devoted, body and soul to Cappy Ricks. The longer Cappy pondered the thought of asserting his authority as boss and defying Skinner, the more impossible the alternative became. Also the longer he thought of having Matt Peasley kept out of the business by Skinner, the higher rose his gorge, for Cappy had yearned for a son like Matt Peasley and been denied. Now when he had planned successfully to do the next best thing and have Matt for a son-in-law, to be blocked by Skinner was unbearable. All Cappy could do was to search vainly for an "out," and in the interim, whenever he met Matt

Peasley at his home, he carefully avoided all reference to Matt's future in the Blue Star employ for which, by the way, Matt was eternally grateful. He did not care to talk business with Cappy for a month as yet. He was too happy with Cappy's daughter.

Another month passed. Cappy grew thin and lost his relish for his food. Then Florence, being a woman, began to see, looming out of the rose-tinted mist of her happy dreams, a huge interrogation mark.

She wondered what her father intended doing for her future husband; and since she was accustomed to bossing her parent she spoke to Cappy about it, thereby increasing his mental agony.

About the same time Matt Peasley commenced to wonder also, but forbore to mention the subject to Cappy. Instead, he went down to the Red Stack people and got himself a job skippering a tug; and great was his joy thereat, for the wages were fully as good as he had enjoyed on the Quickstep, and he was enabled to spend nearly every night in port. The two months of idleness, albeit the happiest he had ever known, had commenced to pall on him, and he wanted to be up and doing once more. Also, being a man, he sensed something of the embarrassment of Cappy's position, and, manlike, decided to relieve the old fellow of that embarrassment. Matt concluded that he would retain his job as master of the tug Sea Fox for a few months—say six—and then ask Cappy Ricks for twenty thousand dollars, which amount would by that time be to his credit on the Blue Star books by reason of his half-interest in the seventy-five-dollar-a-day profit he and Cappy had annexed when rechartering the steamer Unicorn. With that amount of money in hand, plus the savings from his salary, he planned to marry Cappy's daughter and go into business for himself as a ship, freight and marine insurance broker.

Mr. Skinner heard of Matt Peasley's appointment as master of the tug Sea Fox several hours before the same information reached Matt himself. The general manager of the tugboat company, scanning Matt's application and having a vacancy to fill, called up Mr. Skinner.

"Say, Skinner," he said, "I have an application for a job as master for one of our tugs from Captain Matthew Peasley. He tells me he was a couple of years under the Blue Star flag, from A. B. to master of steam and sail, with an unlimited license. Is he a good man?"

"We never had a more capable skipper in our employ," said Mr. Skinner truthfully.

"Why did you let him go then?"

"He resigned."

"Under fire?"

"No, he quit voluntarily."

"Honest?"

"Very."

"Then what's wrong with him?"

"He doesn't like me. But he's capable and fearless and a devil on wheels. He'll take a ship anywhere and bring her out again whole."

"Then he's my huckleberry. That's the kind of man for a tugboat skipper," was the reply, and Matt Peasley had the job, greatly to the joy of Mr. Skinner, who realized now that his ultimatum to Cappy Ricks had been a knockout blow. Cappy had surrendered, and the rowdy Matt, having given up hope of a snug berth as port captain of the Blue Star Navigation Company, had in despair sought a job with a tugboat company.

Mr. Skinner was so happy he shelved his office dignity long enough to whistle a popular ballad that had been running through his mind of late. All too gladly had he recommended Matt Peasley for that tugboat job! He would have employed anything, short of dishonorable methods, to rid the Blue Star of that incubus!

Cappy Ricks almost wept with rage when his daughter informed him that Matt had gone back to salt water. She was a little indignant over it, and demanded a show-down from her unhappy father, who looked at her miserably and said he'd think it over.

He did. Every afternoon, upon his return from luncheon he slid down on his spine in his upholstered swivel chair, draped his old shanks over his desk, dropped his chin on his breast, closed his eyes and went into a clinch with the awful problem, with all its dips, spurs and angles. Save for the nervous clasping and unclasping of his hands one would have thought him sound asleep.

For a month no gleam of light filtered through the deep gloom of the old gentleman's predicament. A dozen times had he reached forth to press the push-button on his desk, summon Skinner and force the latter to do one of two things; recede from his position or resign as general manager. Ten times he had paused with his finger on the push-button. He simply could NOT afford to dispense with Skinner! The eleventh time, however, grown desperate from much brooding over his unhappy lot, Cappy pressed the button.

"Send Mr. Skinner in," he commanded bravely to the boy who answered his summons.

Mr. Skinner entered and stood awaiting Cappy's pleasure. On the instant the old fellow was overcome by panic. Frantically he sought an "out."

"Skinner, my dear boy," he purred, "has it occurred to you that young Tommy, the office boy, has been here long enough, and behaved himself well enough, to merit a raise of about ten dollars a month?"

Mr. Skinner was a natural conservative and considerable of a pessimist.

"Well, I daresay he has, although I hadn't given the matter any thought, sir. However, the way lumber has been selling the past few months, we ought to be cutting salaries instead of raising them."

"I know, Skinner, I know. But a boy needs some encouragement; he has to have some concrete evidence of appreciation, er—er—attend to it, Skinner, my boy, attend to it."

Mr. Skinner nodded and retired, leaving Cappy to grit his teeth and curse himself for a poltroon. "It's certainly hell when a man of my age and financial rating stands between his love and duty," he mourned. "Darn that fellow Skinner. If my bluff should fail to work and he got on his high horse and quit, I'd have to climb off my high horse and beg him to return to work. And he knows it. He knows I've been taking it easy so long I never could bring myself to take up the burden of active business again. Money! What does money mean if it can't buy happiness? Drat that devilish Skinner. I wish to jiminy he had the burden of my dollars—"

He paused, overcome by a sudden brilliant thought. "Bully for you, Alden P., you old, three-ply, copper-riveted, reinforced, star-spangled jack-ass!" he murmured. "Why didn't you think of it before and save yourself all this grief?"

His hand shot out once more to the push-button. "Send in Mr. Hankins, sonny," he ordered the office boy.

Mr. Hankins was the cashier; also secretary of all of Cappy's companies, of which Mr. Skinner was first vice president. He entered and stood deferentially beside Cappy's desk.

"Hankins, my dear boy, bring me the stock certificates for my holdings in the Ricks Lumber and Logging Company and the Blue Star Navigation Company. I am going to indorse them, after which I wish you would reissue the stock to me, less one hundred shares of each in the name of Mr. Skinner. Say nothing to Mr. Skinner about this and bring the new certificates to me immediately."

When Hankins had complied with his request Cappy Ricks placed the Skinner certificates in his pocket and went uptown to the office of his attorney. He returned to his office within an hour and immediately sent for Mr. Skinner.

"Skinner, my dear boy," began Cappy affably, "sit down. I want to have a very serious talk with you."

"Nothing wrong, I trust," Skinner began apprehensively, for Cappy's air was very portentous.

"If there was," Cappy snapped, "you wouldn't be here to-day. Some other fellow would be holding down your job, and, I dare say, giving poor satisfaction—by the way, my dear Skinner, something which you have never done."

Mr. Skinner flushed pleasurably and thanked his employer.

"Some twenty-five years ago," Cappy continued, "you entered my employ as a spindle-legged office boy. To-day you are my general manager, and a rattling good one, too, even if we do have our little run-in together every so often. We mustn't pay any attention to that, however, for a fight is good for a man, Skinner. I maintain that it brings out all of his virtues and vices where one can have an unobstructed view of them. However, passing that, I decided a long time ago, Skinner, that you are entitled to more than a mere salary—"

"My salary has been eminently satisfactory, sir—" Mr. Skinner began.

"Don't be an ass, Skinner," Cappy interrupted tartly. "I wouldn't give two hoots in hell for a satisfied man, unless he's his own man—understand. You should have a more vital interest in the Ricks Lumber and Logging Company and the Blue Star Navigation Company. We always make our skippers own a piece of the vessels they command, so they will not be tempted to rob us, for in robbing us they rob themselves. Consequently, thinking it over, Skinner, I have decided to make you own a piece of both the companies you manage, not because you may rob them but because I want to reward you for faithful service. I had planned to do this in my will, but I feel so healthy lately I think I'll live a long time yet, and there isn't any real sense in keeping you waiting. What is the book valuation of the Ricks L. & L. stock?"

"Three hundred eighty-seven thirteen, according to the last annual report," replied Skinner glibly. His eyes glistened.

"And the Blue Star stock?"

"Four hundred thirty-two twenty-seven."

"Hump! Harump-h-h! It will be worth more when the Panama Canal is opened. We'll have a crack at the Atlantic Seaboard market with our Pacific Coast lumber, and the water freight will knock the rail rate silly. Besides, I'm going to buy up a couple of large freighters, or build them, and that stock of yours will pay dividends then. I'll soak you four hundred per share for the Blue Star stock. Is that satisfactory?"

Nobody knew better than Mr. Skinner the fact that the Blue Star stock at the book valuation was appraised very conservatively. He nodded.

"Lumber market's up and down, down and up, and we never know where we stand. Give you that at two-fifty a share. Want it?"

"I should say I do!" Skinner gasped.

"Then you owe me sixty-five thousand dollars. I'll take your promissory note for it at five per cent., and you can pay the note out of your salary and the dividends. You'll be in the clear in ten years at the very latest; the stock I'm selling you now will be worth a hundred thousand—with your management. Here's the contract, which embodies a promissory note. Sign it, endorse the stock to me to secure the payment of the note, and then clear out of here. Not a peep out of you, sir, not a peep. If you say 'Thank you' I'll change my mind about selling."

Mr. Skinner's hand trembled a little as he wrote his name across the backs of the stock certificates and appended the same clear, concise signature to the note. Silently he wrung Cappy's hand.

"Get out," rasped Cappy. Mr. Skinner got out.

CHAPTER XXXIII.
CAPPY'S PLANS DEMOLISHED

Four more months passed, and peace reigned in the offices of the Blue Star Navigation Company. Matt Peasley's name had never been mentioned in Mr. Skinner's presence since that dark day when he had ventured, for the first time in his career, to lay down the law to Cappy Ricks. The pick-handle still reposed behind Skinner's desk, but that was merely because he had forgotten all about it, and nobody ever touched any of his property without his permission. Not once had Matt Peasley's cheerful countenance darkened the Skinner horizon.

This, then, was the condition of affairs when the office boy carried to Mr. Skinner a piece of disquieting information—to wit, that Captain Matt Peasley was without and desired to hold speech with Mr. Ricks.

"Tell him Mr. Ricks is too busy to see him," Skinner ordered. Not having heard anything of Matt for six months he concluded that the latter's affair with the boss' daughter had languished and died a natural death; hence he felt that he could defy Matt with impunity. Judge of his surprise, therefore, when a heavy hand was laid on his shoulder later and Matt Peasley stood glaring down at him.

"Well, sir!" said Skinner coolly.

"I heard you had a pick-handle waiting here for me," Matt replied evenly, "so I just dropped in to tell you that if you ever pull a pick-handle on me I'll take it away from you and ram it down your throat. That's all I have to say to you, Mr. Skinner. If, the next time I call, at Mr. Ricks' invitation, to see him, you intercept my message and try to block my game—"

The great Peasley hand closed over Mr. Skinner's neck and felt of it tentatively.

"Ouch!" gasped Mr. Skinner.

"Admit the brother," Matt called to an imaginary sentry behind Cappy's door. "He has given the password. The lodge has been duly opened and we are now ready for business."

He smiled at Mr. Skinner and passed on into Cappy Ricks' office.

"Well, Matt," the latter hailed him pleasantly, "it's been a long time since I've seen you in this office."

"And it'll be a long time till you see me here again, sir," Matt retorted pleasantly. "I was about to call on you when your message reached me. So suppose you tell me your business first. Then I'll tell you mine."

"No, you won't, Matt," Cappy challenged him, "because hereafter you're not going to have any business unless I have a finger in it too. Matt, my son, do you recall the day you quit the Quickstep?"

"With pleasure," Matt assured him whimsically.

"You're vindictive; but no matter. Skinner declared you should never again command a Blue Star ship while he was in my employ, and I said, by George, that was right—you shouldn't. I said I was going to make you our port captain, and eventually place you in charge of the shipping after I had broken you in."

"I have a curiosity, sir, to know why you didn't go through with that program."

"Skinner wouldn't let me—said he'd quit if I did, and I just couldn't afford to lose him, Matt. However, I have all that fixed up now, so you quit that tugboat job of yours and come to work here as soon as you can. I could have put you to work three months ago, right after I sewed Skinner up, but I thought I'd wait a little while just to save poor Skinner's face." Cappy commenced to chuckle softly. "In-fer-nal rascal!" he declared. "He had me where the hair is short, Matt; he had me where I dassen't defy my own general manager! Yes, sir, that was the long and short of it. I dassen't call his bluff, because he doesn't bluff worth a cent, and I happen to know some of my competitors would like to get him away from me. A good man is always in demand, Matt; never forget that. You see, Skinner has been carrying the burden of this business for the past ten years practically, and he threatened to toss that burden back on me. Well, if he had, Matt, I just couldn't have carried it without competent help—and by the time I had competent help broken in they'd be measuring me for a tombstone."

"How did you whip him into line?" Matt demanded.

"Just like spearing fish in a dry lake, boy," Cappy chuckled. "I just sold Mr. Skinner part of that burden, and now he has to carry it all until he dies, because if he drops it he loses what I sold him. Only one way to whip that boy into line, Matt, and that is to pelt him with dollars."

"But I do not see how that affects me," Matt answered.

"You don't, eh? Why, you're the port captain of the Blue Star Navigation Company, you-you-you bonehead, and Skinner has to stand for you now whether he likes it or not. He'll not sacrifice his future to vent his grudge against you, because he is a business man, Matt, and he knows it's mighty poor business to bite off his nose to spite his face. So you just come to work."

Matt Peasley beamed across at his future father-in-law.

"That was well done, sir," he said, "and I wish I had known you were going to do it. I would have saved you the trouble, because, you see, I never intended to go to work for you in this office anyhow."

"The devil you say!" Cappy interrupted. "Well, you just put some reverse English on those intentions of yours, my boy. I know what's good for you."

But Matt Peasley only shook his head.

"I can't do it, sir," he said. "While deeply appreciative of all you want to do for me, the fact is, if I'm going to marry your daughter—and I am—I'm not going to do it on your money and be dependent upon you for a job. I'll be my own man, Mr. Ricks. I never ask odds of any man, and I don't like to work for a relative."

"Damn your Yankee independence," snapped Cappy angrily. "Why do you oppose me?"

"Because I'll not have anybody saying: 'There goes Matt Peasley. He fell into a good thing. Yes, indeed! Used to be a common A. B. until Alden P. Ricks' daughter fell in love with him—and of course after that he went right up the line in the Blue Star Navigation Company. He's a lucky stiff.'"

"What do you care what people say? I know what I want."

"I do care what they say, and I care what I feel. I want to fight my own way. I want to make a wad of money and build up a business of my own—"

"You're crazy! Why, here's one ready-made, and it will stand all kinds of building up—"

"Then let Skinner build it. I'll build my own. I do not want anybody to think I married your daughter for your money."

"Matt, you poor, chuckleheaded boy, listen to me. I intend doing for you—"

"And that," roared Matt Peasley, smiting the desk, "is the very reason why I shall not permit you to do anything for me. That's final, Mr. Ricks. I hope you will realize it's useless to argue with me."

"I ought to by this time," Cappy replied bitterly. "Very well, I've told you my business with you. Suppose you state your business with me."

"I'd like to draw twenty thousand dollars from my credit on the Blue Star books."

"Huh! So you want to dig into that money the recharter of the Unicorn is bringing you, eh, Matt?"

"If you can spare it, Mr. Ricks."

"Of course I can spare it—only I'll not. If you want that money, Matt, sue for it; and since you haven't any documents to prove you have it coming to you, I suppose you will agree with me that a suit would be useless expenditure of time, money and energy."

"Then you will not give me the money, sir?" Matt Peasley demanded.

"Not a red," said Cappy calmly. "We've fought this whole matter out before, so why argue?"

"Why, indeed," Matt answered, and reached for his hat. He was fighting mad and desired to go away before he quarreled with Cappy.

"I'll go downstairs to the cigar stand and shake you the dice, one flop, to see whether you go into business for yourself or come to work for me," Cappy pleaded.

Matt came to him and placed his great hands on the old man's shoulders.

"You're the finest man I ever knew, Mr. Ricks," he said, "and you're the meanest man I ever knew, so I'll not shake dice with you. You're too fond of having your own way—"

"Yes, and you're the same, blast you!" Cappy shrilled, losing his temper entirely. "Wait till you're my age. There won't be any standing you at all. Get out!"

CHAPTER XXXIV.
A GIFT FROM THE GODS

The barkentine Retriever, lumber laden from Astoria to San Francisco, lay under the lee of Point Reyes in a dead calm. It was a beautiful, moonlit night, with the sea as smooth as a fishpond, and Captain Michael J. Murphy, albeit a trifle surprised at his proximity to the California coast—the result of three days and nights of thick fog, which had suddenly lifted—was not particularly worried. At eight o'clock he turned in, after warning the mate to call him in case the Retriever should drift inshore.

"Never fear, sir," the mate replied. "We'll have a puff of wind about daylight at the latest, and the current sets north and south here rather than toward the beach."

For two hours after Captain Murphy had retired the Retriever rose and fell gently on the slightest swell, her booms and yards swinging idly amidships, her sails and cordage slatting listlessly as the vessel rolled.

Suddenly the lookout shouted: "Steamer on the port bow!" and the mate, following the direction indicated, made out the red and green sidelights and the single white light at the short masthead of the approaching vessel.

"Tug," he announced to the man at the wheel. "Good enough! The lookout at Point Reyes reported us, and the owners have sent a tug out to snake us in."

The mate's prognostication was correct in some particulars, for in about half an hour the tug steamed slowly alongside the Retriever and hailed her.

"Barkentine, ahoy!"

"Ahoy! Retriever, of the Blue Star, Astoria for San Francisco."

"Sea Fox, of the Red Stack Line. Is Captain Murphy on deck?"

"No, but I'll send for him," the mate shouted, and forthwith sent a man below to rout out the skipper. When Murphy came on deck and hailed the tug he nearly fainted at the information that came floating across the water.

"Murphy, this is Matt Peasley speaking."

"Not Matt Peasley that used to command this old box—"

"Don't speak disrespectfully of my first command, Mike—"

"And you're only a tug captain—a dirty, thieving, piratical towboat man, holding up every honest skipper that pokes his nose into San Francisco Bay. Matt, I'm ashamed of you. How are you anyhow?"

"Fine, Mike. Want a tow?"

"I don't need one; I'll have a bit of breeze before long. I'm independent of you!"

The tug crept in closer. "Don't be foolish, Mike; better let me slip you a line."

"How much will it cost, Matt? None of your highway robbery now. Be easy on the Retriever for old times' sake."

"A thousand dollars," Matt Peasley answered pleasantly, and was rewarded with a volley of oaths from Mike Murphy and his crew.

"You're a thief!" yelled Murphy.

"And you're a fool, Mike. You're not more than two miles off the breakers, you're in a calm that may last two days, and when the tide is at flood you'll set in on the beach as sure as death and taxes—and then I'll have a salvage job that will cost your owners not one thousand but ten."

"You go to the devil!" was Murphy's reply to this, and the Sea Fox dropped astern and came round on the starboard bow of the Retriever. In she backed, a foot at a time, and Captain Murphy, up on the topgallant fo'castle, was within easy conversational distance of Matt Peasley, standing on the grating at the stern of the Sea Fox.

"Better grab this heaving line, Mike," Matt suggested.

"Come aboard and have a drink, Matt, but leave your line behind you," Murphy answered hospitably.

The Sea Fox drifted down fifteen or twenty feet, swung slowly, headed out to sea, and then backed gingerly in until her stern was within a few feet of the side of the Retriever.

"Hey, you! What d'ye mean to do? Back into her?" yelled Matt Peasley to his mate. "Full speed ahead! Quick!"

A bell jangled in the bowels of the Sea Fox, her great screw churned the water and she shot out from the Retriever.

"That's right! Go clear over to China, and expect me to haggle with this man through the megaphone, eh?" Matt roared. "Back up again!"

"I tell you, Matt, there isn't the slightest use hanging round for us," Murphy warned the towboat skipper. "I wouldn't let the ship be held up by anybody, least of all a towboat man."

"Well, when the lookout on Point Reyes telephoned into our office that the Retriever was inside the Point, I made up my mind I'd come out and get her, and I don't purpose being disappointed," Matt replied jokingly. "I'll just wait until you drift into the breakers, and then you'll do business with me, never fear."

"G'wan!" snorted Murphy. "How's Cappy Ricks, the old villain?"

"He's fine, Mike. He wanted me to work for him, but I don't like his general manager—Mr. Olson, full speed ahead or you'll smash our stern against this barkentine. Steady! That's better. Astern a trifle. Steady! Mike, how've you been since I saw you last?"

CHAPTER XXXV.
A DIRTY YANKEE TRICK

"Skinner," said Cappy Ricks, "I was called out of my bed at five o'clock this morning by the night operator at the Merchants' Exchange. He told me our Retriever was in the breakers just south of Point Reyes, but that a tug was standing by. What have you heard since?"

"She drifted in there in a calm last night, sir," Mr. Skinner replied. "Fortunately the Point Reyes lookout had reported her early yesterday evening, and one of the Red Stack tugs — the Sea Fox — took a chance and went out seeking. Lucky thing for us—"

"The tug hauled her off then?"

"Got a line aboard just in time. I had a telephone message from Captain Murphy at Meiggs Wharf ten minutes ago. The Retriever is anchored in the fairway."

"What tug did you say it was?" Cappy queried.

"The Sea Fox."

"That's Matt Peasley's command," Cappy mused. "Lucky? I should say we are! It's up to the master of the tug very frequently whether, under such conditions, his task has been a mere towage job at the going rates or a salvage proposition to be settled in court. I dare say Matt will give us the benefit of the doubt and call it towage."

"Don't deceive yourself!" Skinner snapped. "It's salvage; Murphy said so. After he got close in Peasley refused to name a price and came aboard and made Murphy sign a paper acknowledging that his ship was in distress and dire peril, before he would even put a line aboard him—"

"Wow! Wow! The tugboat company will libel the ship now, and sue us for fifty thousand dollars' salvage on vessel and cargo," and Cappy groaned, for he owned both. "By George!" he continued. "I didn't think Matt would do anything like that to me. No, sir! If anybody had told me that boy could be such an ingrate I'd have told him—"

A youth entered Cappy's office uninvited.

"Captain Peasley to see you, sir," he said.

"Show the infernal fellow in," rasped Cappy, and Matt Peasley stalked into the room.

"I should like to see you privately, Mr. Ricks," he announced, and cast a significant glance at Skinner, who took the hint and left the room at once.

Matt sat down. "Well," he said, "I guess the tug Sea Fox and owners, together with her doughty skipper and crew, will finger some of your hard-earned dollars before long, Mr. Ricks. I pulled your barkentine Retriever out of the breakers this morning. In fifteen minutes she would have been on the beach and a total loss—and I have a document, signed by Captain Murphy and his mates, to prove it. I offered the pig-headed fellow a tow at ten o'clock the night before, but he declined it—trying to save a few dollars, of course—so when I had him where he had to have my services—"

"Well!" Cappy snapped, "send your owners round and we'll try to settle out of court. If they're hogs we'll fight 'em, that's all."

"And if you do you'll get licked. We'll get a quarter of the value of that vessel and her cargo. She's easily worth fifty thousand dollars and her cargo is worth thirty thousand more—that's eighty thousand, and a quarter of eighty thousand dollars is twenty thousand."

"You'll have to fight for it, I tell you," Cappy reiterated.

"There is no necessity for a fight, Mr. Ricks. It all rests with me whether this is a salvage job or just a plain towing job at the customary rates."

Cappy looked at his ex-skipper keenly.

"Matt," he charged, "you've got a scheme. You want something."

"I do; I want to save you a lot of fuss and worry and expense. In return I want you to do something for me."

"I'll do it, Matt. What is the program?"

"Give me that twenty thousand dollars you justly owe me—twenty thousand dollars I have to my credit on your books, which you are withholding just because you have the power to withhold it."

"And in return—"

"I'll tear up the deadly document I extorted from Murphy and report a mere towage job to my owners."

Cappy pressed the push-button and a boy appeared.

"Tell Mr. Skinner I want to see him," he ordered, and an instant later Mr. Skinner entered. "Skinner," said Cappy, "draw a check for twenty thousand in favor of Matt Peasley, and charge it to his account."

"And then send it over to the bank and certify it," Matt added, "because before I get through with you, Mr. Ricks, you'll be tempted to stop payment on it, if I know you—and I think I do."

Half an hour later Cappy handed Matt Peasley, a certified check for twenty thousand dollars, and in exchange the latter handed Cappy the only proof the Red Stack people would have had, over and above the contradictory testimony of the crews of the respective vessels, that the services of their tug constituted salvage and not towage. Cappy read it, tore it into shreds and glared at Matt Peasley.

"Matt," he said very solemnly, "I'm glad this thing happened. I've always had a good opinion of you, but now I know that though you have many excellent qualities you do not possess that quality which above all others I require in an employee or a son-in-law.

"You aren't loyal. You had the sweetest case of salvage against our vessel that any man could go into court with, and you kicked it away like that, just for your own selfish ends. You sacrificed your shipmates, who would have been awarded a pro rata of the salvage, and you were false to the trust your owners reposed in you."

Cappy stood up, his face pale with fury, and shook an admonitory finger under Matt Peasley's nose.

"That act, sir, is an index of your true character," he thundered. "A master who will deceive his owners, who will be false to their interests, is a scoundrel, sir; do you hear me?—a scoundrel. You will oblige me, sir, by refraining from any attentions to my daughter in the future. To think that you have descended to such a petty, miserable subterfuge to trick me and rob your owners! Thank God, I have found you out in time!"

"Yes, isn't it fortunate?" Matt answered humorously. "And if you get any angrier you'll bust an artery and die."

"Out of my office!" Cappy raved; for though he was a business man, and never hesitated to do business in a businesslike way, he was the soul of business honor, and in all his life he had never taken a mean or unfair advantage of those who trusted him. The knowledge that Matt Peasley had done such a thing filled him with rage not unmixed with sorrow.

"I'll be gone in a minute," Matt replied gently; "only before I go permit me to tell you something, and on my honor as a man and a sailor I assure you I speak the truth. That wasn't a salvage job at all."

"What?"

Matt repeated the statement. Cappy blinked and clawed at his whiskers.

"Oh," he said presently, "I had forgotten that you and Captain Murphy were once shipmates. And so that fellow Murphy stood in with you to work a hocuspocus game on me, eh?" he thundered. "By Godfrey, I'll fire him for it!" and he rushed to the office door, opened it and called to Skinner: "Skinner, Murphy is to be fired. Attend to it." Then he closed the door again and faced Matt Peasley.

"Murphy is to be reinstated," Matt assured Cappy, "for the reason that Murphy was in deadly earnest when he signed that paper. In five minutes he would have been a skipper without a ship, and he knew it. If you fire Murphy you do a fine man a terrible injustice."

"Well, how in blue blazes did he get so close to the beach and let himself into your clutches?" Cappy raved.

"He couldn't answer that question, sir. He doesn't know. He thinks the current set him in there. It didn't. I set him in there."

"You set him in?" Cappy queried incredulously.

"I set him in. I kept backing up on his starboard counter, ostensibly to dicker with him, and as soon as I had the stern of my tug within a few feet of the Retriever I'd signal my mate at the wheel, he'd give the engineer full speed ahead — why you have no idea of the force of the quick water thrown back from that big towing propeller of the Sea

Fox. The rush of it just swung the Retriever's nose slowly toward the beach and kicked her ahead fifteen or twenty feet, and then her sheer momentum carried her thirty yards farther. By that time I was backed up to her again, bargaining with Murphy, and ready for another kick. It was easier after the flood tide set in, and I kept at her all night long, and gradually kicked her into the breakers, where I wanted her. I knew Murphy would listen to reason then. So you see, Mr. Ricks, it wasn't a salvage job, and I didn't betray my owners at all—"

"You Yankee thief!" Cappy yelled, and dashed at Matt, to enfold the son-in-law-to-be in a paternal embrace. "Oh, Matt, my boy, why do you want to be a tugboat man when I need a man with your brains? Why don't you be sensible and listen to reason?"

Matt held the old man off at arm's length and grinned at him affectionately.

"It's worth twenty thousand dollars to get the better of you, sir," he said.

Cappy sat down very suddenly.

"Ah, yes," he said. "Speaking of money reminds me: What do you intend doing with that twenty thousand dollars?"

"Well, I thought at first I'd go into the shipping business for myself—"

"Skiffs or gasoline launches—which?" Cappy twitted him.

"But you seem bent on having your way, and Florry is making such a fuss, I suppose I'll have to give in to you after all."

Matt stepped to the door, opened it and called: "Mr. Skinner!"

Mr. Skinner looked up from his desk by the window. "Well, sir!" he demanded haughtily.

"Murphy is not to be fired," Matt answered.

"Indeed! And by whose orders?"

"Mine! I'm the port captain of the Blue Star Navigation Company, and, beginning now, I'm going to do all the hiring and firing of captains."

Mr. Skinner turned pale. He started from his chair and made two steps toward Cappy Ricks' office, firmly resolved to present his resignation then and there. At the door, however, he thought better of it, hesitated, returned to his desk and sat down again, for he had suddenly remembered, and, remembering, discovered that Cappy Ricks had laid upon him a burden that must be reckoned with—the burden of his own future. He flushed and bit his lips; then, feeling Matt Peasley's eyes boring into the small of his back, he turned and said:

"I have every reason to believe, Captain Peasley, that you are the right man in the right place."

Matt advanced upon him and held out his hand.

"Mr. Ricks has always bragged that you could think quicker and act quicker in an emergency than any man he ever knew. He's right, you can. Suppose we bury that pick-handle, Mr. Skinner?"

Mr. Skinner's lips twitched in a wry smile, but he took Matt Peasley's hand and wrung it heartily, not because he loved Matt Peasley or ever would, but because he had a true appreciation of Abraham Lincoln's philosophy to the effect that a house divided against itself must surely fall. "I'm sure we'll get along famously together," he said.

"You know it," Matt answered heartily, and stepped back into Cappy's office.

"Well," said Cappy, "that was mighty well done, Matt. Thank you. So you think you'll quit the Sea Fox and be my port captain, eh?"

"I think so, sir."

"Well, I do not, Matt. The fact of the matter is, your business education is now about to commence, and about two minutes ago I suddenly decided that you might as well pay for it with your own money. I have no doubt such a course will meet with the approval of your independent spirit anyhow. You're a little too uppish yet, Matt. You must be chastened, and the only way to chasten a man and make him humble is to turn him loose to fight with the pack for a while. Consequently I'm going to turn you loose, Matt; there are some wolves along California Street that will take your twenty thousand away from you so fast that you won't know it's going till it's gone. But the loss will do you a heap of good—and I guess Florry can wait a while."

He paused and eyed Matt meditatively for fully a minute.

"And you kicked my barkentine ashore with the quick water from your tug's propeller," he mused aloud. "Got her where you wanted her—and Murphy didn't suspect! He laid it to the current!" Cappy shook his head. "A dirty Yankee trick," he continued, "and I love you for it—in fact, it breaks my heart not to make good that grandstand play you just pulled on Skinner, but I've changed my mind about hiring you yet. I'm just going to sit back and have some fun watching you defend that little old twenty-thousand dollars I just gave you. Do you know, Matt, that I never knew a man to save up a thousand dollars, by denying himself many things, that he didn't invest the thousand in a wild-cat mine or a dry oil well? Ah, Matt, it's those first few dollars that come so hard and go so easy that break most men's hearts; but here you are with twenty thousand that came so easy I've just naturally got to see how hard they go! You'll be worth more money to me, Matt, and you'll be a safer man to handle this business when I'm gone, if you go out and play the game for a while by yourself. You have a secret itching to do it anyhow, Matt, and in surrendering to me just now you went down with your colors flying. You just wanted to be kind to the old man, didn't you? Well, I appreciate it, Matt, because I'm an old man, and I know how hard it is for a boy to yield to an old man's wishes; but youth must be served, and God forbid that I should rob you of the joy of the conflict, my boy. When you're busted flat and need some more money, you may have it up to the amount to your credit on our books. And when that's gone I guess you'll make a better port captain than you will this morning. Does that program suit you better than the one I originally outlined?"

Matt flushed and hung his head in embarrassment, but answered truthfully: "Yes, sir."

"Very well," said Cappy, relapsing into one of his frequent colloquialisms, "go to it, boy. Eat it up."

CHAPTER XXXVI.
CAPPY FORBIDS THE BANS—YET

Cappy Ricks sat at breakfast, tapping meditatively on the apex of a boiled egg, when his daughter swished into the room, saluted her interesting parent by depositing a light kiss on his bald and ingenuous head, and took her place at the table.

Florence Ricks was a radiant vision in a filmy pink breakfast gown and cap, and as she smiled perkily at Cappy he returned her bright look with one a trifle sad and yearning.

"Florence, my love," said Cappy gently, "have you, by any chance, talked with that big, two-fisted sailor of yours within the past twelve hours?"

She shook her head negatively, tilting her nose and pursing her lips in an adorable grimace of disapproval.

"Since Matt Peasley has been master of that tug I see him only when his owners cannot find something more important for him to do. Why do you pop that question at me so suddenly? Did you want to see him about something?"

"No. I saw him yesterday forenoon, and we went into a clinch and fought each other all over my private office. Matt got the decision. I thought he might have called you up to discuss with you his plans for the future. When he left me yesterday he was on his way back to the office of the Red Stack Tugboat Company to tell the port captain he could stick some other skipper on the tug Sea Fox."

Florence clapped her hands ecstatically. "Oh, goody, goody!" she cried.

"Well, it might be worse."

"Why is he resigning? To go to work for you, as I wanted him to do six months ago?"

"Well, I'll tell you, Florry," Cappy began. "I know you're going to be disappointed, but the fact of the matter is we've just got to let that boy paddle his own canoe—though, to hear him talk, he's going to operate his own line of steamers! Matt doesn't think in canoes when the subject of the merchant marine is up for discussion any more than I think in cent pieces when I'm wrestling with a banker for a loan. He has resigned from the tug Sea Fox to go into business for himself!"

"But how can he? He hasn't any money, you silly man!"

"Oh, yes, he has. I gave him twenty thousand dollars yesterday. He had that much credit on the Blue Star books from his share of the recharter of the steamer Unicorn nearly two years ago."

"But I thought you weren't going to give him any of that money," Florence protested.

"I thought so, too," Cappy answered dryly; "but the scoundrel put up a low-down job on me and pried the twenty thousand loose," and Cappy proceeded to relate to Florry the sad tale of the salvage of the Retriever.

Florence was gifted with the same lovable sense of humor that distinguished her father; and, somewhat to his annoyance, she laughed long and heartily at this tale of how her fiance had vanquished him.

"And then what?" she queried with childish insouciance.

"Why, then he made friends with Skinner and, to my complete amazement, surrendered without firing a shot. He said he'd be my port captain now; whereas six months ago he said it was against his religion to work for a relative, and that he wanted to go into business for himself. And only the day before he'd reiterated those sentiments."

"Oh, I'm so glad!" said Florry, much relieved.

"Wait!" said Cappy dramatically. "Don't cheer yet. I've upset your apple cart, my dear. I rejected the young man's proposition and condemned him to a business of his own."

"But you wanted him for your port captain, Daddy dear. You wanted him the very worst way."

"And that's just how I got him, Florry. I don't want any man whose heart is not in his job, and a business man should never surrender for sentimental reasons. You cannot mix sentiment and business, daughter; if you do you'll get chaos. Matt Peasley surrendered to me—not because he wanted to, but to please you. You've been picking on him rather hard lately, haven't you?"

Florry admitted it.

"I knew it," Cappy declared. "I knew it—and that's why I exercised the veto on you, Florry."

Florry's eyes dropped, and in the corners of them her father thought he detected a glint of tears; whereupon he attacked his egg vigorously. After a brief silence he said:

"Of course that means a slight delay in your plans for a June wedding—"

A tear crept through Florry's long lashes and dropped unheeded into her grapefruit. Cappy saw it drop, but resolved to be cruel and ignore it.

"The infernal schemer couldn't resist the temptation to take a fall out of your old man, Florry; so naturally I had to take a fall out of him; though, at that, I have doubts whether I succeeded. I think I played into his hand; and now I'm telling you about it to save him the trouble and grief of an explanation he couldn't make and which you wouldn't understand—from him. Some day my affairs will all be yours, Florry—yours and Matt's; and he'll have to manage them for you. To manage them well, he must have experience; hence, I decided, in about two flips of a humming-bird's tail, that it would be a mighty good thing for you and Matt if I forced him into business for himself and, as I informed him, let him pay for that experience with his own money; for that is the only kind of money that will buy him any experience worth while. No young man ever learned a great deal when some sentimental old fool footed the bill for his tuition fees in the college of hard knocks."

"Poor Matt!" Florry sobbed. "He hasn't—had anything—except hard knocks since he was—fourteen years—old."

"Yes," shrilled Cappy; "and just look at the difference between him and these la-di-da boys that never had any hard knocks! Hard knocks! Why, hard knocks keep that devilish fellow in condition!"

"But I'd planned—we didn't want to have too long an—engagement—"

"I'll guarantee you, little daughter, you will not have to wait longer than six months. Please wait—for my sake." And Cappy rose, made his way round the breakfast table and placed his old arms about the light and joy of his existence. "So, so, now!" he soothed. "Don't you cry, honey, until you hear what the old man has to say. Why, haven't I always given my little daughter everything she wanted? You wanted that big sailor, Florry; I saw he wanted you; and he looked awful good to me. I knew he was man, every inch of him; he was our kind of people and he knew ships and loved them, and so I wanted him for you. What if he was a big hunk of a sailor with hardly enough money saved up to buy you half a dozen party dresses? None of the Ricks tribe was ever born or bred in the purple—and I have money enough for all practical purposes. So I went after him for you, Florry, and you're going to get him; so don't cry about it."

"Life is so filled with disappointments," Florry sobbed, notwithstanding this was the first she had ever known.

Cappy smiled a still small smile as he bent over her.

"Fiddlesticks!" he replied. "Only the day before yesterday Matt told me he didn't want to work for me; that he didn't want a relative handing him any favors; and that he wasn't marrying you to ease himself into a soft job for life. He said he wanted to make the fight himself. And do you know, Florry, if he had been my own boy I couldn't have been prouder of him than when he told me that! When old What-you-may-call-him in Shakespeare's play said: 'Let me have men about me that are fat,' it showed how blamed little Shakespeare knew about men. He should have said: 'Let me have men about me who are long and tough, and fairly thick in the middle; let me have scrappy boys about me with backbone!'

"Well, in a way, Florry, I was disappointed, and perhaps, in the heat of the moment, I showed it, as I have a habit of doing; but after Matt had left the office, and I got to thinking it over, away down low I was proud of him. Consequently when he reversed his decision yesterday I knew why, for I lived twenty-five years with your mother. But a woman's love is selfish sometimes, and I knew that Matt had surrendered, not to me, but to you; though he came across like a sport, he didn't want to, for you'd roweled him and roped him with your love, my dear—and, though you do not know it, that's a terrible thing to do to a free-running colt like Matt Peasley. He has his code, and it's a bully code; and I don't want you to tie knots in it, Florry. Won't you be as spunky and independent as he is, and give him his head for six months more? He'll probably call sometime to-day, or ring up, to tell you how I picked holes in the program; and when he does I want you to smile and tell him you're glad of it, and suggest a postponement of the wedding until he has demonstrated to me that he is a business man."

Florence looked up and bravely smiled a forgiving smile through her tears.

"You're a dreadful Buttinsky, Daddy Ricks!" she protested.

He kissed her hungrily.

"Oh, I'm a devil in my own home town!" he replied, and trotted back to his neglected breakfast. "If Matt hasn't made good as a business man within six months, or has lost his bank roll—and I intend to see to it that he does lose it, if I ever get a hack at him—we'll pull off this wedding anyhow. I guess there's room enough in this house for three."

At nine o'clock Cappy Ricks, with a lilt in his heart, drove down to his office behind his team of high-stepping bays. At the corner of California and Drumm Streets he saw Matt Peasley and hailed him. The latter came to the carriage door and looked in.

"It's all right, Matt," Cappy said with a cunning wink. "I've fixed Florry's clock for her. There won't be the slightest trouble."

Matt Peasley wrung his hand gratefully.

"I quit the Sea Fox last night," he announced gladly.

"Going into business this morning, I suppose?"

"Yes, sir."

"What line?"

"Ship, freight and marine insurance broker."

"Well, that's a line that will keep you hustling for your wheatcakes until you get well acquainted. However, just to give you a shove in the right direction, you might scout round the market and see whether you can dig up a cargo for our steamer Tillicum. Usual commission of two and a half per cent."

"Thank you, Mr. Ricks. I ought to be able to scare up something in the way of a foreign lumber cargo for her."

"We've tried and failed. Moreover, her fuel-oil tankage isn't sufficient to take her too far foreign and back; added to which she is under American registry, employing American seamen, and I'd rather lay her up than put a coolie crew aboard and compete with the British tramps, with their Lascar and Chinamen, at six and seven dollars a month. We've been running her in our own trade; but the lumber market is very dull and she has but one more cargo in sight; after that is freighted, unless we can find outside business for her, she'll have to lay up in Oakland Inner Harbor until the Panama Canal opens—when, of course, we can load her for the Atlantic seaboard. She carries nearly two million feet, and that's what makes it so hard for us to keep her busy coastwise."

"How about some Mexican or Central American business—general cargo?" Matt suggested.

"Pretty hard stuff to get. The Pacific Mail has most of the Central American business; and, owing to the political situation in Mexico, that trade is practically killed. Every vessel that gets in there has trouble with one faction or the other; they're liable to confiscate, and then we'd have to call on the navy to get our ship back for us."

"I'll look round for a grain charter to Honolulu and return with sugar or general cargo."

"We might do that," Cappy suggested, brightening. "Good luck to you, Matt—and don't be a stranger."

CHAPTER XXXVII.
MATT PEASLEY BECOMES A SHIPOWNER

A youth thrust a wary nose into Cappy Ricks' private office and announced Captain Matt Peasley was desirous of admittance.

"Show him in," Cappy ordered, and Matt entered.

"Well, young man," said Cappy briskly, "sit down and tell me of your adventures during your first week as a business man. Of course, I hear from Florry that you have opened a dink of an office somewhere—got desk space with the Alaskan Codfish Corporation, haven't you, with the use of their telephone, stenographer and general office boy?"

"Yes, sir. The manager, Slade, is a native of Thomaston—never knew anything but fish all his life; and, inasmuch as I was raised on the Grand Banks, I got in the habit of drifting round there occasionally, and Slade offered me the privilege of making it my headquarters. Ten dollars a month—cheap enough."

"Yes, considering the aroma of codfish that goes with it, free-gratis," Cappy admitted dryly; "but then I suppose that's what attracted you in the first place. But have you done any real business, Matt?"

"Well, I've arranged with several good old-line insurance companies to accept any marine-insurance business I may bring in, though I haven't sold any yet; neither have I been able to find a load for your Tillicum. By the way, you have a little old three-legged schooner laid up in Oakland Inner Harbor."

"I have three of them—more's the pity!" Cappy replied—"the Ethel Ricks, the Nukahiva and the Harpoon. Which one do you mean?"

"The Ethel Ricks. She's the only one I examined closely. Would you consider selling her?"

"Ah," said Cappy, "I perceive. Your friend Slade wants her for a codfisher, eh?"

"That's all she's good for now, Mr. Ricks. She has had her day in the lumber trade; the steam schooners have relegated her to a final resting place in the ooze of Oakland Inner Harbor; her class of windjammers is a thing of the past for general cargo. She's been laid up now for three years. True, her bottom is coppered and you dry-dock her every year; but that's an expense. And then you must consider taxes and depreciation, and sooner or later, if she lies in the mud long enough, the Teredo will eat her up; so it occurred to me that you might be glad to sell. She was built in 1883, but she was built to last—"

"Never built a cheap ship in my life and never ran 'em cheap," Cappy challenged proudly. "The Ethel Ricks is in the discard, but she's as sound a little packet as you'll find anywhere. She's had the best of care. The same is true of the Harpoon and the Nukahiva."

"What do you want for her?"

"Four thousand dollars," Cappy answered promptly.

"I was offered the Dandelion for three thousand; she's ten years younger than the Ethel Ricks and in very good condition. Sorry, but I guess you'll have to keep the Ethel—and let me tell you, the longer you keep her the less she's worth. However, I guess she doesn't owe you anything."

"No; she paid for herself more'n twice," Cappy replied.

"Then if you get three thousand for her it's like finding the money and losing a worry."

"Sold!" said Cappy.

"I didn't say I'd buy," Matt warned him. "What do you want for the Harpoon and the Nukahiva?"

"They're all sister ships. Three thousand each."

"I am empowered to make you an offer of twenty-seven hundred and fifty dollars each for the three!" Matt shot at him.

"Net? The three of them?" Cappy was all attention now; for selling schooners in lots of three was decidedly new and interesting.

"Hardly! Five per cent to me. Remember I'm a ship, freight and marine insurance broker, and I'm not working for my health. Why, I haven't even suggested any other vessels to my clients—and, by the way, they are not codfish people either. I knew you'd want to get rid of these little hookers, so I'm giving you first crack at the bargain."

"Who wants them?" Cappy demanded craftily.

"If I told you that you'd do me the way you did that Seattle broker who tried to put through the charter of the Lion and the Unicorn. When you knew who his clients were you were in position to defy him—and you did!"

"No offense," Cappy retorted innocently. "Don't be so touchy! Is this a cash proposition, Matt?"

"In the hand."

"I accept."

"Then give me a written option," Matt warned him. "No more word-of-mouth business for me with you."

Cappy laughed; and, calling in a stenographer, he dictated the option.

"Now, then, Matt," he said as he signed the option five minutes later and handed it to Matt, "who shall we make out the bills of sale to?"

"To the Pacific Shipping Company. When you're ready telephone me and I'll bring the check round."

"Go get your check now," Cappy ordered. "Skinner will have the bills of sale ready by the time you return. And I do wish to heaven," he added, "that you had called round with this proposition four days ago. I've just had those three schooners dry-docked, cleaned and painted."

"Which is the very reason why I didn't call round until to-day, Mr. Ricks. You can afford that dry-dock bill so much better than—er—the Pacific Shipping Company."

He left, laughing, and proceeded to the office of the Pacific Shipping Company, where he procured a check for eighty-two hundred and fifty dollars and returned to the Blue Star Navigation Company's office. Mr. Skinner had in the meantime prepared proper bills of sale; a notary, with offices in the building, had been called in to attest the signatures of Cappy Ricks and Mr. Hankins, president and secretary respectively of the Blue Star Navigation Company; and when Cappy Ricks handed over the bills of sale to Matt Peasley, together with the Blue Star check for four hundred and twelve dollars and fifty cents—Matt's commission—the latter handed him the certified check of the Pacific Shipping Company.

"Who is the Pacific Shipping Company, Matt?" Cappy queried. "I never heard of them before."

"It's a new company, sir," Matt replied; and, gathering up his bills of sale and the check for his commission, he fled precipitately, leaving Cappy Ricks to adjust his spectacles and examine the check. It was signed: "Pacific Shipping Company, by Matthew Peasley, President."

For a long time Cappy Ricks sat staring at that check. Finally he looked up and saw Mr. Skinner gazing at him. He held out the check and tapped Matt Peasley's signature.

"Get on to that, Skinner, my boy," he said; "get on to that! Matt's gone into the shipping business, and he's making an humble start with three little old antiquated schooners, for which he has paid me more than eight thousand dollars. Now he will go broke!"

"I do not agree with you, Mr. Ricks," Mr. Skinner replied dryly, "for I notice he didn't forget to stick us four hundred and twelve dollars and fifty cents for the privilege of selling him those three schooners! This is the first time I ever heard of anybody's paying the purchaser a commission!"

"The infernal scoundrel!" Cappy shrilled angrily, for Mr. Skinner's assertion carried the hint that Cappy had been outgeneraled. "The Yankee thief!—acting as broker for a company in which he owns all the capital stock! In business a week and he's made over four hundred dollars already, neat and nice, and as clean as a hound's tooth! Can you beat it?"

"It's better than being a port captain for the Blue Star Navigation Company at three hundred a month," Mr. Skinner suggested wistfully.

He had worked for a salary all his days, and after passing the thirty mark he had lost the courage to leap into the commercial fray and be his own man. He wished he might have been endowed at birth with a modicum of Matt Peasley's courage and reckless disregard of consequences.

CHAPTER XXXVIII.
WORKING CAPITAL

It was nearly ten weeks before Cappy Ricks laid eyes on Matt Peasley again. Inquiry from Florry elicited the information that Matt had gone to Mexico as skipper of his own schooner, the Harpoon, bound on some mysterious business.

"He's taken the old Harpoon down there to stick a Mexican—I'll bet a hat on that!" Cappy reflected. "I'll bet he'll have a tale to tell when he gets back."

There came a day when Matt, looking healthy and happy, dropped in for a social call.

"Well, young man," Cappy greeted him, "give an account of yourself. How do you find business?"

"The finest game in the world," Matt replied heartily. "I had the Ethel Ricks snaked out of the mud and hauled out on the marine railway, where I bossed a gang of riggers and sailmakers for a week, getting her gear in shape while she was having a gas engine and tanks for the distillate installed. Then I gave her a dab of paint here and there, sweetened her up, and sold her to Slade, of the Alaska Codfishing Corporation, at a net profit of fifteen hundred dollars over her total cost to me. Nearly two thousand for my first month in business. Not so bad, eh?"

"You'll do better after a while," Cappy remarked dryly. "I hear you've been to Mexico. How about it, boy?"

"I took the Harpoon down myself, and hired a skipper to take the Nukahiva. Before doing so, however, I overhauled their gear and installed gas engines in them also—only I'd learned something by this time. I bought second-hand engines, rebuilt, but with a guaranty, and they cost me a thousand dollars less than new engines. In conversation with Captain Kirk, of the steamer San Blas, I had heard that a company in Guaymas was thinking of buying a couple of little coasting schooners, putting gas engines in them, and adding these crafts to their fleet running out of Guaymas to Mazatlan, Topolobampo, and way ports. So I went down, put my schooners under the Mexican flag, and started opposition. The old-established company went to the local military commander and tried to get him to commandeer my vessels for the use of the government, which pays in depreciated shinplasters that may be worth something some day a hundred years from now."

"Whew-w-w!" Cappy whistled. "That was a narrow squeak, Matt. How did you dodge it?"

"I had the local military commander on my payroll, with good American gold, before I ever started anything. I knew he'd come to shake me down; so I anticipated him and made a monthly donation to the cause of liberty. I do not know for certain, but I imagine he went south with it himself, though I do not begrudge the amount. I only paid him for one month anyhow. By that time I had an offer to sell out; and I did, reluctantly, but for real money and at a much better figure than if I had not made it an object for them to buy. I got out with a net profit of seventy-four hundred and fifty dollars on the two schooners. Not so bad, eh, Mr. Ricks? Over nine thousand dollars in less than three months? Of course, I realize I could not have made that much if I hadn't had the funds with which to speculate."

Cappy nodded. Words were beyond him for the time being. Finally he said:

"Matt, that was pure gambling, though you think it was a speculation. It was mighty poor business, even if you did emerge with a fancy profit. You might have been cleaned out."

"Yes; and if the hare hadn't stopped to take a nap the tortoise would not have won the race," Matt replied. "So far as I can see, all business is a gamble and every investment is a bet; hence, a good business man is a good gambler."

Cappy Ricks sighed.

"There is a special providence," he said, "that looks after fools, drunken men and sailors."

CHAPTER XXXIX.
EASY MONEY

Captain Matt Peasley's first act after consummating his first successful deal was to purchase for the Pacific Shipping Company a membership in the Merchants' Exchange, on the floor of which he knew he would meet daily all the shipping men of San Francisco, and thus be enabled to keep in touch with trade conditions.

He had been a member less than a week when the wisdom of spending five hundred dollars for his membership was made delightfully apparent. While he stood watching the secretary chalk on the blackboard the record of the latest arrivals and departures, he heard a man behind him speaking:

"Heyfuss, I'm in the market to charter another freighter for the Panama run. You might look round and see whether you can line something up for us. I'd like about a two-thousand-ton boat; and we could charter her for a year."

"There's only one vessel available," the man addressed as Heyfuss answered; "and that's the Tillicum. Cappy Ricks had her laid up in Oakland Creek—"

Matt moved away and approached a clerk at the desk.

"That dark-haired man with the thick glasses, talking with Mr. Heyfuss," he said—"who is he?"

"That is Mr. Henry Kelton, manager of G. H. Morrow Company," the clerk answered. "They operate a line of sailing vessels foreign and half a dozen steamers to South American ports."

Matt thanked him, entered a telephone booth and on consulting the telephone directory, discovered that J. O. Heyfuss was a broker.

"I'll have to step lively to beat Heyfuss to it," he soliloquized, and forthwith hastened down to the office of the Blue Star Navigation Company.

"Well, young man!" Cappy greeted him genially. "How about you?"

"Never mind me. How about the Tillicum?"

"Laid up in Oakland Inner Harbor waiting for better times."

"I think I can give her some business. Would you charter her to the Pacific Shipping Company?"

"Well," Cappy replied, "I might be induced to take a chance in these hard times. How much money have you in bank to-day?"

"In a pinch I could lay my hands on thirty thousand, cash."

"Well," said Cappy thoughtfully, "that little roll, plus an established credit and a reputation for business experience, might carry you far with some people — but not with me. You're not a safe bet — yet; but we can make it safe."

"How?"

"You can pay the charter money in advance," Cappy answered smilingly.

"I have decided not to do any more gambling, Mr. Ricks. Hereafter, as near as such a thing may be humanly possible, I'm going to play a sure thing. Therefore, all things being equal, if I can guarantee you your price for the steamer, on a year's charter, you do not care what I do with the vessel, provided that I do not injure her?"

"Certainly."

"Well, then, in order to play safe and protect you, suppose I charter her from you, contingent on my ability to recharter her to some responsible shipping firm. Under those conditions would you exact the charter money in advance? You know very well that when I collect my money from the charterers you'll get yours right away."

"Without question, Matt; but sometimes a fellow cannot collect his money from the charterers, and then the owner has to wait. I'm taking no chances to speak of on you, Matthew, my son; but for the sake of making it a sporting proposition I'll talk business on the basis of fifty per cent. of the charter money, payable monthly in advance."

"That's cold-blooded, but I can stand it. What is the Tillicum going to cost me a day?"

"What kind of charter do you want—government form or bare boat?"

"You might give me an option with a price based on each form. I haven't the slightest idea what form my prospective victim prefers, though I prefer a bare-boat charter. I will close with you on whatever basis he prefers, if that is satisfactory."

"I'll make many concessions to get that vessel out of the mud and to sea, and paying a reasonable rate on the money invested in her. I hate to keep a good skipper and a good chief engineer on the beach, and I want them to begin drawing their salaries again."

Cappy reached into his desk and produced a little loose-leaf memorandum book, and from certain figures therein contained he commenced to figure what he should charge Matt for the ship. On his part, Matt, whose apprenticeship under the Blue Star had made him tolerably familiar with every steamer in the fleet, got out a pad and pencil and commenced to figure the cost of operation himself. Not knowing the cost of the steamer or the ratio of profit Cappy might expect on the investment, however, he was more or less at sea until Cappy had named his figures; whereupon Matt pretended to do some more figuring. Finally he frowned and said:

"Fifty dollars a day too much."

He did not know a thing about it, but he knew Cappy Ricks well enough to know that Cappy would first decide on his minimum price and then add a hundred dollars a day for good measure; hence, Yankeelike, Matt commenced to chaffer, with the result that before he left the office Cappy had abated his price fifty dollars a day and given Matt a forty-eight-hour option on the vessel, agreeing to charter her to him at the figures specified, contingent on Matt's ability to recharter her to a responsible firm.

Cappy chuckled as Matt Peasley left the office.

"You're taking a pretty big bite, Matt," he soliloquized; "so I'll handicap you. And if anything goes wrong, and you fail to collect from your people, I'll give you a lesson in high finance that you'll never forget, young man! I'll bet my immortal soul you're going to try to do business with Morrow & Company; and if that outfit isn't scheduled for involuntary bankruptcy, then I'm a Chinaman. A charter for a year, eh? They'll never last a year. They'll bust, owing you a month's charter money, Matthew, and the vessel will be at sea, most likely, or in a South American port, when that happens; and you can't throw her back on me until you deliver her in her home port. And meantime your charter to me keeps rambling right along, and I'll attach your bankroll if you're a day late with your payment in advance. Yes, sir; I'll break you in two for the good of your immortal soul. Matt—Matt, my son—something tells me you're monkeying with fire and liable to get burned."

From Cappy Ricks' office Matt Peasley called on Kelton of Morrow & Company. Kelton, a shrewd, double-action sort of person and the smartest shipping man on the street, looked with frank curiosity at Matt's modest card.

"Pacific Shipping Company, eh? That's a new one on me, Captain Peasley," he said.

"It's a new one on me also," Matt replied humorously; "in fact, it is too recent to be very well known. We've been operating a fleet of windjammers, with auxiliary power, down on the Mexican Coast," he added truthfully, calm in the knowledge that two schooners constitute a fleet if one be not inclined to split conversational hairs; "but we sold them and decided to go into the steamship business. We hope to buy or build a line of freighters to run to Atlantic Coast ports via the Panama Canal."

"What steam vessels have you got now?" Kelton queried interestedly.

"Only one at present, Mr. Kelton. We've acquired the Tillicum, late of the Blue Star fleet."

"Indeed!" replied Kelton.

He was all attention now; for, though Matt Peasley did not know it, less than ten days previous Kelton had tried to charter the Tillicum direct from Cappy Ricks, who, knowing something of the financial condition of Morrow & Company, had declined to consider a charter unless under a guaranty of payment other than that of Morrow & Company. Kelton was in urgent need of a steamer to cope with the congestion of freight, and the Tillicum suited the purpose of his company admirably; hence, the news that he might still be able to acquire her filled him with sudden hope.

"Indeed!" he reiterated. "I had no idea Cappy Ricks contemplated selling her, though it has been common talk on the street that he made a mistake in building such a big boat as the Tillicum for the coastwise lumber trade. She was too hard to find business for, and I dare say he was sick of his bargain."

"Well, I thought we'd take a chance on her," Matt replied, not taking the trouble to disabuse Kelton of the impression to which he had apparently jumped — to wit, that the Pacific Shipping Company had purchased the Tillicum.

"What do you intend doing with her?" Kelton continued.

"They tell me business is good on the Panama run, and it will be better when the Canal is opened. However, until the Canal does open, we would prefer to keep out of the Pacific Coast trade. Competition always means a rate war, with consequent loss to both parties to the struggle; so we'd rather charter the Tillicum for a year if we could. I heard you were in the market for a boat."

"I think we might use the Tillicum," Kelton replied. "What are you asking for her?"

Matt named a figure considerably in advance of what he expected to receive and stipulated a bare-boat charter — that is to say, Kelton's company should pay the entire cost of operating the vessel, and select her crew and officers with the exception of the captain and chief engineer, it being customary among many owners, when chartering a vessel, to stipulate that their own captain, in whom they have confidence, shall command her. Cappy Ricks always specified his own skipper and chief engineer.

When Matt named his figure Kelton promptly shouted "Thief!" but made the mistake of shouting too loud — whereat Matt Peasley knew he was not sincere and promptly decided to outgame him. At the end of half an hour of argument and much futile figuring, which deceived nobody, Matt abated his price twenty-five dollars a day and Kelton said he would think it over. Matt knew the charter was as good as closed, and when he left Morrow & Company's office he repaired straight to that of Cappy Ricks.

"I think I'll be able to recharter, Mr. Ricks," he said confidently. "Have you any objection to Morrow & Company as recharterers?"

Cappy started slightly, hesitated a fraction of a second, and replied that he had no objection whatsoever.

"Very well, sir," Matt replied. "Will you please have Mr. Skinner prepare the charter parties right away, sign them, and send them over to my office for my signature? I can't wait to sign them now. And about the captain—I suppose you'll want to put in your own skipper, of course. Who is he?"

"Captain Grant."

"Have you any objection to inserting a clause in the charter party stipulating that, if for any reason Captain Grant proves objectionable to the charterers, I may take command of the vessel myself? As charterer I will have a very vital interest in the vessel and I might feel called on to protect that interest personally."

"Matt," said Cappy earnestly, "I'll trust you in preference to most men with any ship of mine. Still, Grant is a very able man."

"He might be too slow for me, Mr. Ricks. I prefer to have a spare anchor in case of necessity."

"Well, have it your own way," Cappy acquiesced, and summoned Mr. Skinner to prepare the charter parties, while Matt went back to his own office and gave instructions that he was not to be called to the telephone.

Something told him that Kelton would be ringing up before the day was over to accept his price on the Tillicum, and he did not want to be placed in the position of having to give a yes or no answer until he had seen Cappy Ricks' charter parties, with Cappy's signature attached. He would then close up his deal with Morrow & Company, after which he would sign Cappy's charter parties and turn two copies over to Cappy. In this way he would be enabled to play safe and save his face in case any hitch occurred at the last minute.

The charter parties, duly signed and in triplicate, arrived from Cappy Ricks in the morning's mail, with a request from Cappy for Matt to append his signature to two copies and return them to the Blue Star Navigation Company. Matt, after first assuring himself that the instrument was in order, called up Kelton, who informed him that he would accept Matt's offer for a year's charter of the Tillicum. Within half an hour Matt had his charter parties ready for Kelton's signature and the deal was closed; whereupon Matt signed the charter party Cappy Ricks had sent him and handed it to Cappy, together with a check for nine thousand dollars—one half the monthly rental of the Tillicum.

Cappy whistled softly through his teeth as he handed the documents to Mr. Skinner and instructed him to put the Tillicum in commission at once.

CHAPTER XL.
THE CATACLYSM

For two voyages all went well. The Tillicum was engaged in carrying general cargo to Panama for reshipment over the Panama Railroad to Colon, at which point it was reshipped in steamers to ports along the Atlantic seaboard. Following the universal custom, Matt's charter with Morrow & Company stipulated settlement in full every thirty days, whereas his charter with Cappy Ricks, for reasons best known to Cappy, stipulated payment in full every fifteen days; which arrangement operated to keep nine thousand dollars of Matt's money in Cappy's hands continuously. This fact graveled Matt whenever he reflected that money was worth at least seven per cent.; but, since he was making sixty dollars a day profit as the result of his deal, he concluded not to mention this point to Cappy Ricks.

Morrow & Company met the first monthly payment with cash on the nail. At the second settlement, however, when Matt called for his check, Kelton requested, as a special favor, that Matt allow him four days' time. A clever talker, with a peculiarly winning way about him, he disarmed suspicion very readily, and Matt assured him he would be very glad indeed to extend him such a slight courtesy.

Meantime, however, Cappy Ricks had to be reckoned with; so, in order not to keep him waiting, Matt sent him another check for nine thousand dollars. Cappy now had eighteen thousand dollars of Matt's money; and on the fourth day, when the latter called on Kelton for his check, the latter actually made him feel ashamed of himself for calling and sent him away with one-half of the sum now overdue! This perturbed Matt somewhat, but when he showed some slight indication of it Kelton playfully picked up a glass paper weight and threatened to destroy him if he did not get out of the office at once; so, because it is difficult to be serious with a man who declines to take one seriously, Matt forced a grin and departed, with the light intimation that he would return in three days, and if the check was not forthcoming then he would fresco Kelton's office with the latter's life-blood.

"Get out!" shouted Kelton laughingly. "I know money is tight and I don't blame you for being Fido-at-the-rat-hole; but if you bother me about that check for a week I'll not speak to you."

So Matt waited a week, and then the check reached him by mail, with a courteous note from Kelton thanking him for his leniency. It seemed to Matt he had scarcely acknowledged the receipt of that check before he had to give Cappy Ricks another nine thousand dollars!

Morrow & Company were late again on the third month, but this time they did not wait to be dunned. On the day before the payment was due Kelton took Matt Peasley to luncheon and in the course of the meal he informed Matt, quite casually, that he would be a little late with his check. With two dollars' worth of his genial host's food under his belt, Matt felt that it would be rude, to say the least, if he insisted on settlement; so he said:

"Oh, don't worry about that, old man! Give it to me as soon as you can, because I'm a little pinched myself."

Nevertheless, Matt was beginning to worry, for his acquaintance throughout the trade had extended rapidly, due to his propensity for making friends, and he had heard one or two little rumors that Morrow & Company had bitten off more than they could chew in a few big deals of late and had been badly pinched; in fact, to such an extent did Matt ponder on the possibility of the company's going into the hands of the receiver, leaving his thirty thousand dollars to disappear into the ravening maw of the Blue Star Navigation Company, that he forgot to send Cappy his check for nine thousand dollars the day it was due. And the next morning Cappy himself called up and, in a voice that seemed to come straight from a cold-storage plant, asked him what he meant by it, and requested him—though to Matt it sounded like a peremptory demand—to send the check over at once. So angry and humiliated did Matt feel as a result of this dun, he could not trust himself to call with the check but sent it by special delivery.

The Tillicum had returned from her second voyage to Panama and was about to commence loading her third cargo when another payment fell due. To Matt's chagrin Kelton again pleaded for delay; and again Matt settled with Cappy Ricks prior to collecting from Morrow & Company. Kelton had promised a check on the following Wednesday, and on the appointed day Matt called, only to be met with a request for further delay. Kelton explained that Mr. Morrow had been taken very ill and things were at sixes and sevens in the office as a result. Could not Matt wait until Saturday, when Mr. Morrow would be back to sign a check?

"What's wrong with Morrow?" Matt demanded pointedly. "Has he got paralysis of the right hand?"

"Worse than that," Kelton answered seriously. "He's on the verge of nervous prostration."

"But can't you sign a check?"

"Y-e-s; but Mr. Morrow generally attends to all financial details."

"Well, we'll excuse him from attending to this detail," Matt replied. "I want a check and I want it now, because it is a week overdue; the vessel is nearly loaded and about to go to sea, and if I do not get my money—"

"Well, suppose I give you half of it now and the other half in a day or two?" Kelton suggested.

He looked worried and unhappy, and Matt felt sorry for him; for, indeed, Kelton was a likable chap and perfectly trustworthy, and Matt sensed some of the worry that was falling on the manager in his desperate efforts to run a business on short capital. However, Matt's own financial shoestring was too short for him to afford any sentiment, though, for the reason that he was naturally kind-hearted and considerate, he consented to accept a check for half the amount due and left Kelton to the society of the many devils which seemed to be tormenting him.

On the sidewalk he paused suddenly. So Morrow was on the verge of nervous prostration, eh? That was bad. It had been Matt's experience that, as a usual thing, but two things conduce to bring about nervous prostration—overwork and worry; and in Morrow's case it must be worry, for Kelton did all the work! Kelton, too, looked haggard and drawn.

"I must be very careful," Matt told himself, "for if that concern should go broke while the Tillicum is en route to Panama my charter to Morrow & Company may be considered to have terminated automatically; and if they go under owing me from ten to twenty thousand dollars, I'm still responsible to Cappy Ricks for my charter of the Tillicum until I can bring her back to her home port and turn her back to him. Thank God for that clause in the charter which gives me the privilege of terminating my charter with Cappy in case Morrow & Company terminate their charter with me! It will be all right if they terminate it while the vessel is in San Francisco; but if she's very far from home I'll most certainly be eaten alive while I'm getting her back to Cappy!"

He returned to his office and went into a long executive session with himself, from which he aroused presently and went down to the dock where the cargo was pouring into the hold of the Tillicum. Here he consulted with the captain and the purser, and obtained a list of all persons, firms or corporations which had furnished supplies of any kind to the deck department of the steamer. From the chief engineer he procured a similar list of those who had furnished supplies to the engine department; and, armed with this information, he returned to his office and dictated the following form letter:

> *Gentlemen: — Please take notice that we as charterers of the steamer Tillicum from the Blue Star Navigation Company, and as recharterers to Messrs. G. H. Morrow & Company, will not be responsible for the payment to you of any bills for supplies or stores, of any nature whatsoever, furnished to the said steamer Tillicum since she has been under charter to said G. H. Morrow & Company. Any bills contracted with you by G. H. Morrow & Company for account of the Tillicum must be paid to you by G. H. Morrow & Company. This notice is hereby given you in order that we may go on record as disclaiming any responsibility as charterers prior to the departure of the said steamer Tillicum on her next voyage.*
>
> Yours very truly,
PACIFIC SHIPPING COMPANY,
By Matthew Peasley, President.

A copy of this letter Matt sent by registered mail, with a request for a return registry receipt, to each of the creditors of the Tillicum of whom he could get track. He had all the receipts in hand by the last mail delivery the next day, and at eight o'clock that night the Tillicum, having cleared the customs the same afternoon, departed for Panama. Two days later Matt again called on Morrow & Company for the money due him and, after much argument, succeeded in getting it. He hastened at once to the bank on which it was drawn and asked the paying teller to certify it. This the latter declined to do—neither would he cash the check; so Matt took it back to Kelton.

"Kelton," he said, "the bank will not honor your check."

Kelton looked desperate.

"Confound you!" he growled. "I stalled you until five minutes before the bank closed, thinking you would deposit it in your own bank to-morrow morning and I'd have a deposit to cover it by that time. It will be all right first thing in the morning, Peasley."

"It had better be!" Matt told him bluntly. "Your charter provides for cancellation in the event that payments are not made as stipulated, and I'm not in a position to carry you or to take any chances on you— and I'm not going to."

"I can't blame you a bit," Kelton answered regretfully. "I tell you, with the money market as tight as it is, we're beating the devil round the stump these days. Confound it, Peasley, a man has to do some scheming and stalling when everybody is crowding him for money, doesn't he?"

The check was not paid when Matt presented it the next morning. As he came out of the bank a newsboy, crying his daily sensation, accosted him with the first afternoon edition, and Matt's glance caught a smear of red ink seven columns wide across the front page:

SHIPPING MAN A SUICIDE!

It was Morrow!

For about a minute Matt Peasley stood on the corner, doing some of the fastest thinking he had ever done. Morrow had taken a short cut out of his financial worries, and Matt realized that the tragedy would undoubtedly bring an avalanche of creditors down on the unhappy Kelton and ruin the firm. At any rate, the concern would doubtless go into the hands of a receiver, and Matt Peasley might or might not hope for his in the sweet by and by, according to the amount of salvage reported. The Tillicum was seventy-six hours at sea!

"Matthew," Matt Peasley murmured to himself, "'theirs not to reason why, theirs but to do and die'—and all in one thundering big hurry!"

CHAPTER XLI.
WHEN PAIN AND ANGUISH WRING THE BROW

Cappy Ricks was having his siesta, with his feet on top of his desk, when Matt Peasley came bounding in, seized him by the shoulder and shook him wideawake.

"Well, young man," Cappy snapped querulously, "what's all the excitement about?"

"Morrow has committed suicide, and I know the firm is in financial difficulties. I'll not be able to collect now — I'll have to wait with the rest of the creditors; and meantime the Tillicum, fully loaded, is somewhere down off the Mexican coast. Good gracious, Mr. Ricks, there's the very devil to pay!"

"We will, if you please, not include outsiders in this argument for the present, Matt," Cappy retorted dryly. "The unfortunate devil does not pay! You do, Matt. I should worry!"

"But you can help me save something from the wreck!" Matt pleaded desperately. "It's going to clean me of my last dollar to make good with you on my charter, even if Morrow & Company do not make good with me on theirs; and — "

Cappy Ricks held up his hand.

"My dear boy," he said with maddening calm, "listen to me! I had a hunch this would happen. As a matter of fact, I declined to charter to Morrow & Company direct ten days before you came prancing in with your head all swelled up with a brand-new idea for making a lot of easy money in a hurry. Me charter to them — me!" In his superb scorn Cappy waxed ungrammatical. "I should kiss a pig! Why, if sawmills were selling for six bits each I wouldn't trust that concern with a hatful of sawdust—not that they weren't honest and capable, but they haven't got any money to speak of any more!"

"But—but—Why, dad burn it, sir, you said it was perfectly agreeable to you to have me charter the Tillicum to them!" Matt roared, angry, hurt and amazed.

"Why should I worry what you do? I have all I can do to attend to my own business. Why should I tell you yours?"

"But—"

"No ifs or buts, Matt. I played safe; but you're caught away off third base and now you're out! You've got to settle with me for every day you have that vessel under charter until you deliver her back here in San Francisco Bay and formally surrender her to me. You've got to pay me—and what's more, I'm going to see to it that you do! Business is business, my boy."

"Well, I'll pay you all the cash I can and give you my note for the remainder."

"Your note!" Cappy jeered. "Your note! What do I want with your note! Is it hockable at any bank? Huh! Answer me that."

"You needn't insult me!" Matt growled wrathfully.

"Bah!" Cappy sneered. "You think you're mighty smart, don't you, Matt? Do you remember what I told you when you declined to go to work for me and insisted on going into business for yourself? I told you you'd go bust—and you're going right now. All you'll have left in thirty days will be the clothes you stand in and the corporation seal of the Pacific Shipping Company. Ho-ho! Isn't that funny? The idea of a man's paying thirty thousand dollars for a dinky old corporation seal worth two and a half!"

Matt Peasley's face went white with suppressed fury.

"Yes," he said quietly. "I seem to remember some such prophecy; also, some conversation to the effect that I'd be a better business man if I purchased my business experience with my own money. You said there were wolves along California Street that would take my roll away from me so fast it'd surprise me. I must confess, however, that I had no idea you would lead the pack! However, I didn't come here to argue, Mr. Ricks—"

"What did you come for? Sympathy?" Cappy queried. "Because, if you did, you've come to the wrong shop, my boy. Business is business, Matt; I never mix sentiment with it and I advise you never to do it either. Pay your way and take your beating like a sport—that's my policy, Matt."

"Do you want to save the Blue Star Navigation Company some money?" Matt managed to articulate.

"Certainly! Now you're talking business; so I'll listen."

"As charterer of your steamer Tillicum, I find that Captain Grant, the master you installed there, is offensive to me. I object to the way he parts his hair and knots his necktie, and I want a new skipper on the ship."

Cappy Ricks slid out to the edge of his swivel chair, placed a hand on each knee and eyed Matt suspiciously over the rims of his spectacles. After a long silence he shook his head negatively.

"Then I'll sue you!" Matt replied. "There's a clause in the charter party. You've got to do it."

Cappy's mouth flew open.

"Oh, by Judas Priest, that's right," he said, and laughed. "So you're providing a job for yourself after the smoke clears away, eh?" he quizzed. "Well, you can skipper the Tillicum while you keep up the payments of the charter money, Matt; but I give you my word that the day you slip up on a payment, out you go and back Captain Grant goes into the ship. Meantime, however, I think I see now why you inserted that clause. In the event of just such a contingency as the present you wanted the privilege of jumping in and taking command yourself."

Matt nodded.

"Captain Grant is a good man, but old. He can't drive a crew like I can, Mr. Ricks—and, with me on the job, that steamer will be discharged and back in San Francisco Bay from three to five days sooner that she would ordinarily. It means six hundred dollars a day to me, sir, and every day saved is worth that much cash in hand to you, since you profess to think so lightly of my promissory note."

"Enough!" Cappy commanded. "I'll admit that the thought does you credit. It was a mighty bright idea, Matt, and showed fine forethought. Now, then, what are you going to do to save your roll?"

"The City of Para leaves for Panama to-morrow. Give me a letter to Captain Grant, commanding him to turn his ship over to me on presentation of this letter. I will furnish him the funds to pay his transportation back to San Francisco."

"Fair enough," said Cappy; and, calling in a stenographer, he dictated the desired letter.

Ten minutes later Matt Peasley had left the office without the formality of saying good-by to Cappy Ricks, and was in a taxicab en route to his lodgings to pack his steamer trunk and hand baggage. Cappy Ricks chuckled as Matt went angrily out.

"Ah—that first time a man goes broke!" he soliloquized. "What a blow to one's pride! What a shock to the nervous system!" He sighed. "Poor old Matt! Nobody knows better than Cappy Ricks how you feel, because he's been there twice and it blamed near broke his heart each time it happened."

He shook his head with an air of satisfaction, for things were going well with him. He had made a prophecy and it was in a fair way of being fulfilled—nay, its fulfillment was inevitable; whereat Cappy, after the habit of the aged in their conflict with Youth, felt very much like shaking hands with himself. Indeed, so pleased was he that presently he called in Mr. Skinner and related the story in meticulous detail to the general manager.

Mr. Skinner was delighted. More—he was overcome. He sat down and permitted himself the most soul-satisfying laugh he had had in years.

CHAPTER XLII.
UNEXPECTED DEVELOPMENTS

Mr. Skinner thrust his head into Cappy Ricks' office and said:

"I've just had a telephone message from the Merchants' Exchange. The Tillicum is passing in."

"Then," said Cappy Ricks, "in about two hours at the latest we may expect a mournful visit from Captain Matt Peasley."

"If you don't mind, Mr. Ricks," said Skinner with a smirk, "I should dearly love to be present at the interview."

Cappy smiled brightly.

"By all means, Skinner, my dear boy; by all means, since you wish it. It just about breaks my heart to think of the cargo of grief I'm going to slip that boy; but I have resolved to be firm, Skinner. He owes us eighteen thousand dollars and he must go through with his contract to the very letter, and pay the Blue Star Navigation Company every last cent due it. He will, doubtless, suggest some sort of settlement—ten cents on the dollar—"

"Don't agree to it," Mr. Skinner pleaded. "He has more than a thousand dollars a month going to his credit on our books from the Unicorn charter, and if that vessel stays afloat a year longer we'll be in the clear. Be very firm with him, Mr. Ricks. As you say, it is all for his own benefit and the experience will do him a whole lot of good."

"I love the boy," said Cappy; "but in the present case, Skinner, I haven't any heart. A chunk of anthracite coal is softer than that particular organ this morning. Be sure to show Matt in the minute he comes up from the dock."

Mr. Skinner needed no urging when, less than two hours later, Captain Matt Peasley arrived. Mr. Skinner greeted him courteously and followed him into Cappy's office.

"Well, well, well!" Cappy began unctuously. "How do you do, Matt, my dear boy? Glad to see you; in fact, we're extra glad to see you," he added significantly and winked at Mr. Skinner, who caught the hint and murmured loud enough for Matt Peasley to hear:

"Eighteen thousand dollars to-morrow!"

Cappy extended a hand, which Matt grasped heartily.

"You're looking fit as a fiddle," Cappy continued. "Doesn't look a bit worried — does he, Skinner?"

"I must admit he appears to carry it off very well, Mr. Ricks. We had thought, captain," Skinner continued, turning to Matt Peasley, "that, when Mr. Ricks agreed to permit you to assume command of the Tillicum when she reached Panama, we might have been treated to an exhibition of speed; but the fact of the matter is that instead of economizing on time you are about ten days in excess of the period it would have taken for Captain Grant to have discharged his cargo and gotten back to San Francisco." He winked at Cappy Ricks, who returned the wink.

"You mean in ballast," Matt suggested. Skinner nodded. "Oh, well, that accounts for it," Matt continued serenely. "I came home with a cargo of steel rails."

Cappy Ricks slid out to the extreme edge of his swivel chair; and, with a hand on each knee, he gazed at Matt Peasley over the rims of his spectacles. Mr. Skinner started violently.

"You came home with a cargo of steel rails?" Cappy demanded incredulously.

"Certainly! Do you suppose I would go to the expense of hiring somebody else to skipper the Tillicum while I was there with my license? Not by a jugful! I was saving every dollar I could. I had to."

"Er — er — Where is Captain Grant?" Skinner demanded.

"Captain Grant is free, white and twenty-one. He goes where he pleases without consulting me, Mr. Skinner. He means nothing in my life — so why should I know where he is?"

"You infernal scoundrel!" shrilled Cappy Ricks. "You whaled hell out of him and threw him out on the dock at Panama — that's what you did to him! You took the Tillicum away from him by force."

"Captain Grant is a fine, elderly gentleman, sir," Matt interrupted. "I would not use force on him. He left the ship of his own free will at San Diego, California."

"At San Diego?" Cappy and Skinner cried in unison.

"At San Diego."

"But you said you were going to Panama on the City of Para, the regular passenger liner," Cappy challenged.

"Well, I wasn't committed to that course, sir. After leaving your office I changed my mind. I figured the Tillicum was somewhere off the coast of Lower California; so I wirelessed Captain Grant, explained to him that the ship was back on my hands by reason of the failure of Morrow & Company, and ordered him to put into San Diego for further orders. He proceeded there; I proceeded there; we met; I presented your letter relieving him of his command. Simple enough, isn't it?"

"But what became of him?"

"How should I know, sir? I've been as busy as a bird dog down in Panama. Please let me get on with my story. I had just cleared Point Loma and was about to surrender the bridge to my first mate when an interesting little message came trickling out of the ether—and my wireless boy picked it up, because it was addressed to 'Captain Grant, Master S. S. Tillicum.'"

Cappy Ricks quivered and licked his lower lip, but said nothing.

"That message," Matt continued, "was brought to me by the operator, who really didn't know what to do with it. Captain Grant had left the ship and Sparks didn't know what hotel in San Diego the late master of the Tillicum would put up for the night; so I read the message to see whether it was important, for I felt that it had to do with the ship's business and that I was justified in reading it."

Again Cappy Ricks squirmed. Mr. Skinner commenced to gnaw his thumb nail.

"That message broke me all up," Matt continued sadly. "It destroyed completely my faith in human nature and demonstrated beyond a doubt that there is no such thing in this world as fair play in business. It's like a waterfront fight. You just get your man down and everything goes—kicking, biting, gouging, knee-work!" Matt sighed dolorously and drew from his vest pocket a scrap of paper. "Just listen to this for a message!" He continued. "Just imagine how nice you'd feel, Mr. Ricks, if you were skippering a boat and picked up a message like this at sea:

> "'Grant, Master Steamer Tillicum: Gave Captain Matt Peasley a letter to you yesterday ordering you to turn over command of Tillicum to him on presentation or demand. This on his request and on his insistence, as per clause in charter party, copy of which you have. Peasley leaves to-day for Panama on City of Para. This will be your authority for declining to surrender the ship to him when he comes aboard there. Stand pat! Letter with complete instructions for your guidance follows on City of Para.
>
> "Ricks."'

Cappy Ricks commenced tapping one foot nervously against the other, Mr. Skinner coughed perfunctorily, while Matt withered each with a rather sorrowful glance.

"Of course you can imagine the shock this gave me. I give you my word that for as much as five seconds I didn't know what to do; but after that I got real busy. I swung the ship and came ramping back to San Diego harbor, slipped ashore in the small boat and found Captain Grant at the railroad station buying a ticket for San Francisco. I had to wait and watch the ticket office for an hour before he showed up, and when he did I made him a proposition. I told him that if he would agree to keep away from the office of the Blue Star Navigation Company you might think he was peeved at being relieved of his command so peremptorily, and hence would not attach any importance to his failure to report at the office.

"In consideration of this I gave him my word of honor that he would be restored to his command as soon as I could bring the Tillicum back from Panama, and meantime his salary would continue just the same—in proof of which I gave him a check for two months' pay in advance. He said he thought it all a very queer proceeding; but, since he was no longer in command of the Tillicum, it wasn't up to him to ask questions, and he agreed to my proposition. However, he said he thought he ought to wire the company acknowledging receipt of their instructions with reference to surrendering his command—and I agreed with him that he should. 'But,' I said, 'why bother sending such a message, collect, ashore, when we pay a flat monthly rate to the wireless company for the plant and operator aboard the ship, no matter how many messages we send? Give me your message to Mr. Ricks and when I get back aboard the Tillicum I'll wireless it to him for you, and it won't cost the ship a cent extra.'

"Well, you know your own captains, Mr. Ricks. They'll save their ships a dollar wherever they can; and simple, honest Old Man Grant agreed to my suggestion. Before he had an opportunity to consider I stepped to the telegraph office and wrote this message for him." Matt produced another telegram and read:

"'Blue Star Navigation Company,

"'258 California Street, San Francisco.

"'Instructions with reference to change of masters received.

"Would feel badly if I thought any act of mine necessitated change; but since my conscience is clear I shall not worry. I always have done and always shall do my duty to my owners without thought of my personal interests, and you may rely fully on that in the present emergency.'"

"Well, sir, that sounded so infernally grandiloquent to Old Man Grant that his hand actually trembled with emotion as he signed it—at my suggestion. You know I'd hate to be tried for forgery. Then I shook hands with him and started for Panama once more—only this time I kept right on going; and I didn't spare the fuel oil either. Why should I? It wasn't costing me anything."

Both Cappy and Mr. Skinner winced, as from a blow. Matt waited for them to say something, but they didn't; so after a respectful interval he resumed:

"Off the Coronado Islands I sent you Captain Grant's diplomatic message. I was very glad to send it to you, Mr. Ricks, because I knew its receipt would make you very happy, and I like to scatter happiness wherever I can. The Scriptures say we should return good for evil."

Cappy Ricks bounded to his feet and shook a skinny fist under Matt Peasley's nose.

"You're a damned scoundrel!" he piped, beside himself with rage. "Be careful how you talk to me, young man, or I'll lose my temper; and if I ever do—"

"That would be terrible, wouldn't it?" Matt laughed. "I suppose you'd just haul off and biff me one, and I'd think it was autumn with the leaves falling!"

Cappy choked, turned purple, sat down again, and glanced covertly at Mr. Skinner, who returned the glance with one that seemed to shout aloud: "Mr. Ricks, I smell a rat as big as a Shetland pony. Something has slipped and we're covered with blood. Incredible as it may seem, this rowdy Peasley has outthought us!"

"Did you get the letter we sent Captain Grant at Panama?" Skinner managed to articulate presently.

Matt nodded affirmatively.

"Opened it, I suppose!" Cappy accused him.

Matt nodded negatively, produced the letter from his pocket and handed it to Cappy.

"Where I was raised," he said gently, "they taught boys that it was wrong to read other people's private correspondence. You will note that the seal is unbroken."

"Thank God for that!" Cappy Ricks murmured, sotto voice, and tore the letter into tiny bits. "Now, then," he said, "we'll hear the rest of your story."

"When did a doctor look you over last?" Matt queried. "I'm afraid you'll die of heart disease before I finish."

"I'm sound in wind and limb," Cappy declared. "I'm not so young as I used to be; but, by Jupiter, there isn't any young pup on the street who can tell me where to head in! What next?"

"Of course, Mr. Ricks, very shortly after I had rechartered the Tillicum to Morrow & Company I began to suspect they were shy of sufficient capital to run their big business comfortably. I found it very hard to collect; so, fully a month before they went up the spout, I commenced to figure on what would happen to me if they did. Consequently, I wasn't caught napping. On the day Morrow committed suicide the company gave me a check that was repudiated at the bank. I protested it and immediately served formal notice on Morrow & Company that their failure to meet the terms of our charter party necessitated immediate cancellation; and accordingly I was cancelling it."

"Did you send that notice by registered mail?" Skinner demanded.

"You bet! — with a return registry receipt requested."

Cappy nodded at Skinner approvingly, as though to say: "Smart of him, eh?" Matt continued:

"After sending my wireless to Captain Grant aboard the Tillicum I sent a cablegram to the Panama Railroad people informing them that, owing to certain circumstances over which I had no control, the steamer Tillicum, fully loaded and en route to Panama to discharge cargo, had been turned back on my hands by the charterers. I informed them I had diverted the steamer to San Diego for orders, and in the interim, unless the Panama Railroad guaranteed me by cable immediately sixty per cent. of the through-freight rate for the Tillicum, and a return cargo to San Francisco, I would decline to send the Tillicum to Panama, but would, on the contrary, divert her to Tehuantepec and transship her cargo over the American-Hawaiian road there. I figured —"

"You infernal scoundrel!" Cappy Ricks murmured. "You — slippery — devil!"

"Of course," Matt went on calmly, "I had no means of knowing what freight rate Morrow & Company received; but I figured that they ought to get about forty per cent., the Panama Railroad about twenty per cent., and the steamer on the Atlantic side the remaining forty. So I decided to play safe and ask sixty per cent. of the through rate, figuring that the Panama Railroad would give it to me rather than have the Tillicum's cargo diverted over their competitor's road at Tehuantepec. In the first place they were depending on business from Morrow & Company's ships; and, with Morrow & Company gone broke and a new company liable to take over their line, it would be a bad precedent to establish, to permit one cargo to go to the competitor. Future cargoes might follow it!

"Then, too, the schedule of the ships on the Atlantic side of the Canal doubtless had been made up already, with a view to handling this cargo ex-Tillicum, and to lose the cargo would throw that schedule out of joint; in fact, from whatever angle I viewed the situation, I could see that the railroad company would prefer to give up its twenty per cent. rather than decline my terms. They might think their competitor had already made me an offer! Of course, it was all a mighty bluff on my part, but bluffs are not always called, particularly when they're made good and strong; and, believe me, my bluff was anything but weak in the knees. I told the Panama people to wire their reply to me at San Diego, and when I got to that city, twenty-four hours later, their answer was awaiting me."

"They called your bluff?" Mr. Skinner challenged.

"Pooh-pooh for you!" Matt laughed. "God is good and the devil not half bad. I got the guaranties I asked for, old dear! Don't you ever think I'd have been crazy enough to go to Panama without them."

Cappy jerked forward in his chair again.

"Matt," he said sternly, "you have defaulted in your payments to the Blue Star Navigation Company to the tune of eighteen thousand dollars, and I'd like to hear what you have to say about that."

"Well, I couldn't help it," Matt replied, "I was shy ten thousand dollars when Morrow & Company defaulted on me, and I was at sea when the other payment fell due. However, you had your recourse. You could have canceled the charter on me. That was a chance I had to take.

"Why didn't you grab the ship away from me? If you had done that you would be in the clear to-day instead of up to your neck in grief."

"We'll grab her away from you to-day—never fear!" Cappy promised him. "I guess we'll get ours from the freight due on that cargo of steel rails you came home with."

"You have another guess coming, Mr. Ricks. You'll not do any grabbing to-day, for the reason that somebody else has already grabbed her."

"Who?" chorused Cappy and Skinner.

"The United States Marshal. Half an hour ago the Pacific Shipping Company libeled her."

"What for, you bonehead? You haven't any cause for libel, so how can you make it stick?"

"The Pacific Shipping Company has cause, and it can make the libel stick. The first mate of the Tillicum assigned to the Pacific Shipping Company his claim for wages as mate—"

"Matt, you poor goose! The Pacific Shipping Company OWE him his wages. Your dink of a company chartered the boat, and we will not pay such a ridiculous claim."

"I do not care whether you do or not. That libel will keep you from canceling my charter, although when you failed to cancel when I failed to make the payments as stipulated, your laxity must be regarded in the eyes of the law as evidence that you voluntarily waived that clause in the charter; and after you have voluntarily waived a thing twice you'll have a job making it stick the third time."

"If I had only known!" groaned Skinner miserably.

"Besides," Matt continued brightly, "I have a cargo in that vessel, and she's under charter to my company at six hundred dollars a day. Of course you know very well, Mr. Ricks, that while the United States Marshal remains in charge of her I cannot discharge an ounce of that cargo or move the ship, or—er—anything. Well, naturally that will be no fault of the Pacific Shipping Company, Mr. Ricks. It will be up to the Blue Star Navigation Company to file a bond and lift that libel in order that I may have some use of the ship I have chartered from you. If you do not pull the plaster off of her of course I'll have to sue you for heavy damages; and I can refuse to pay you any moneys due you."

"We'll lift the libel in an hour," Mr. Skinner declared dramatically; and he took down the telephone to call up the attorney for the Blue Star.

"Wait!" said Matt. "I'm not through. Before I entered the harbor I called all hands up on the boat deck and explained matters to them. They had been engaged by Morrow & Company, and the firm of Morrow & Company was in the bankruptcy court; so the prospects of cash from that quarter did not seem encouraging. The Pacific Shipping Company had made a bare-boat charter from the Blue Star Navigation Company, and had then made a similar charter to Morrow

& Company; consequently the Pacific Shipping Company would repudiate payment, and, as president and principal stockholder of that company, I took it on myself to repudiate any responsibility then and there.

"Then the crew wanted to know what they should do, and I said: 'Why, seek the protection of the law, in such cases made and provided. A seaman is not presumed to have any knowledge of the intricate deals his owners may put through. All he knows is that he is employed aboard a ship, and if he doesn't get his money from the charterers at the completion of the voyage he can libel the ship and collect from the owners. This is a fine new steamer, men, and I, for one, believe she is good for what is owing you all; and if you will assign your claims to the Pacific Shipping Company I will pay them in full and trust to the Blue Star Navigation Company to reimburse me.' So they did that.

"Now go ahead, Mr. Skinner, and lift the libel I put on the vessel for my first mate's account, and the instant you get it lifted I'll slap another libel on her for account of the second mate. Get rid of the second mate's claim and up bobs the steward, and so on, ad libitum, e pluribus unum, now and forever, one and inseparable. I care not what course others may pursue, but as for me, give me liberty or give me death!"

Mr. Skinner quietly hung up the telephone receiver.

"And, by the way," Matt continued, "I forgot to mention that I requested the steward to stay aboard and make the United States Marshal comfortable as soon as he arrived. In these little matters one might as well be courteous, and I should hate to have the Tillicum acquire a reputation for being cheap and inhospitable."

"You dirty dog!" cried Cappy Ricks hoarsely.

"Really, my dear Peasley, this matter has passed beyond the joke stage," Mr. Skinner began suavely.

"Let me get along with my story," said he. "The worst is yet to come. My attorney informs me—"

"Matt Peasley," said Cappy Ricks, "that's the first lie I ever knew you to tell. You don't have to hire an attorney to tell you where to head in, you infernal sea lawyer!"

"I thank you for the compliment," Matt observed quizzically. "Perhaps I deserve it. However, 'we come to bury Caesar, not to praise him;' so, if you will kindly hold over your head, Mr. Ricks, I'll be pleased to hit it another swat."

"Well, I'll admit that the failure of Morrow & Company and the Pacific Shipping Company to pay the crew of the Tillicum puts the buck up to me, and I dare say I'll have to pay," Cappy admitted, his voice trembling with rage.

"Well, that isn't the only bill you'll have to pay. Don't cheer until you're out of the woods, Mr. Ricks. You'll have to pay for a couple of thousand barrels of fuel oil, and a lot of engine supplies, and sea stores, and laundry, and water—why, Lord bless you, Mr. Ricks, I can't begin to think of all the things you're stuck for!"

"Not a bit of it!" Cappy cried triumphantly. "It was an open-boat charter, my son, and you rechartered on the same basis; and, though Morrow & Company were originally responsible you'll find that the creditors, despairing of collecting from them, will come down on the Pacific Shipping Company like a pack of ravening wolves, by thunder! Don't YOU cheer until YOU'RE out of the woods!"

"Well, I have a license to cheer," Matt replied, "because I got out of the woods a long time ago. Before the vessel sailed from this port, I sent this letter to all her creditors!" And Matt thrust into Cappy Ricks' hand a copy of the letter in question.

"That will not help you at all," Mr. Skinner, who had read the letter over Cappy's shoulder, declared.

"It wouldn't—if I hadn't sent it by registered mail and got a return receipt," Matt admitted; "but, since I have a receipt from every creditor acknowledging the denial of responsibility of the Pacific Shipping Company, I'm in the clear. It was up to the creditors to protect their hands before the vessel went to sea! They had ample warning—and I can prove it! I tell you, Mr. Ricks, when you begin to dig into this matter you will find these creditors will claim that every article furnished to the Tillicum while Morrow & Company had her was ordered on requisitions signed by Captain Grant, your employee, or Collins, your chief engineer. They were your servants and you paid their salaries."

"All right then," Cappy challenged. "Suppose we do have to pay. How about that freight money you collected in Panama—eh? How about that? I guess we'll have an accounting of the freight money, young man."

"I submit, with all due respect, that what I did with that freight money I collected in Panama is none of your confounded business. I chartered a vessel from you and she was loaded with a cargo. The only interest you can possibly have in that cargo lies in the fact that the Pacific Stevedoring Company stowed it in the vessel and hasn't been paid some forty-five hundred dollars for so stowing it, and eventually, of course, you'll have to foot the bill as owner of the vessel. That vessel and cargo were thrown back on my hands, not on yours; so why should you ask questions about my business? You've got your nerve with you!"

"But you'll have to render an accounting to Morrow & Company," Cappy charged.

"I'll not. They gave me a check that was returned branded 'Not sufficient funds;' they didn't keep their charter with me, and if I hadn't been a fly young fellow their failure would have ruined me, and then a lot they'd care about it! If I spoke to them about it they'd say: 'Well, these things will happen in business. We're sorry; but what can we do about it?' No, Mr. Ricks; I'm in the clear with Morrow & Company, and their creditors will be lucky if I do not present my claim for ten thousand dollars because of that worthless check I hold. When I collected from the Panama Railroad Company for the freight on that southbound cargo I paid myself all Morrow & Company owed me, and the rest is velvet if I choose to keep it. If I do not choose to keep it the only honorable course for me to pursue will be to send a statement and my check for the balance to the receiver for Morrow & Company."

"What!" demanded Mr. Skinner. "And leave the Blue Star Navigation Company to pay the crew?"

"Yes—and the fuel bill, and the butcher and the baker and the candlestick maker, and the stevedoring firm, and the whole infernal, sorry mess!"

Cappy Ricks motioned to Mr. Skinner to be silent; then he rose and placed his hand on Matt's shoulder.

"Matt," he said kindly, "look me in the eyes and see if you can have the crust to tell me that, with all that freight money in your possession, you do not intend to apply the residue to the payments of these claims against the Tillicum."

Matt bent low and peered fiercely into Cappy's face, for all the world like a belligerent rooster.

"Once more, my dear Mr. Ricks," he said impressively, I desire to inform you that, so far as the steamer Tillicum is concerned, I venerate you as a human Christmas tree. I'm the villain in this sketch and proud of it. You're stabbed to the hilt! Why should I be expected to pay the debts of your steamer?"

"But you used all the materials placed aboard her for your own use and benefit."

"That, Mr. Ricks, constitutes my profit," Matt retorted pleasantly. "She had fuel oil aboard when she was turned back on me sufficient to last her to Panama and return—she had engine supplies, gear, beef in the refrigerator, provisions in the storeroom, and clean laundry in the linen lockers; in fact, I never went to sea in command of a ship that was better found."

"Matt Peasley," said Cappy solemnly, "you think this is funny; but it isn't. You do not realize what you are doing. Why, this action of yours will be construed as highway robbery and no man on the Street will trust you. You must think of your future in business. If this leaks out nobody will ever extend you any credit—"

"I should worry about credit when I have the cash!" Matt retorted. "I'm absolutely within the law, and this whole affair is my picnic and your funeral. Moreover, I dare you to give me permission to circulate this story up and down California Street! Yes, sir, I dare you—and you aren't game! Why, everybody would be cheering for me and laughing at you, and you'd get about as much sympathy as a rich relative with arterial sclerosis. I haven't any sympathy for you, Mr. Ricks. You got me into this whole mess when a kind word from you would have kept me out of it. But, no; you wouldn't extend me that kind word. You wanted to see me get tangled up and go broke; and when you thought I was a dead one you made fun of me and rejoiced in my wretchedness, and did everything you could to put me down and out, just so you could say: 'Well, I warned you, Matt; but you would go to it. You have nobody to blame but yourself.'

"Of course I realize that you didn't want to make any money out of me; but you did want to manhandle me, Mr. Ricks, just as a sporting proposition. Besides, you tried to double-cross me with that wireless message. I knew what you were up to. You thought you had pulled the same stunt on me I pulled on you, and that letter to Captain Grant contained full instructions. However, you wanted to be so slick about it you wouldn't get caught with your fingers in the jam; so you forbore to cancel my charter. You figured you'd present me with my troubles all in one heap the day I got back from Panama. I'm onto you!"

"Well, I guess we've still got a sting in our tail," Cappy answered pertly. "Slap on your libels. We'll lift 'em all, and to-morrow we'll expect eighteen thousand dollars from you, or I'm afraid, Matthew, my boy, you're going to lose that ship with her cargo of steel rails, and we'll collect the freight."

"Again you lose. You'll have to make a formal written demand on me for the money before you cancel the charter; and when you do I'll hand you a certified check for eighteen thousand dollars. Don't think for a minute that I'm a pauper, Mr. Ricks; because I'm not. When a fellow freights one cargo to Panama and another back, and it doesn't cost him a blamed cent to stow the first cargo and cheap Jamaica nigger labor to stow the second, and the cost of operating the ship for the round trip is absolutely nil—I tell you, sir, there's money in it."

Cappy Ricks' eyes blazed, but he controlled his temper and made one final appeal.

"Matt," he said plaintively, "you infernal young cut-up, quit kidding the old man! Don't tell me that a Peasley, of Thomaston, Maine, would take advantage of certain adventitious circumstances and the legal loopholes provided by our outrageous maritime laws—"

"To swindle the Blue Star Navigation Company!" Mr. Skinner cut in.

"Swindle is an ugly word, Mr. Skinner. Please do not use it again to describe my legitimate business—and don't ask any sympathy of me. You two are old enough and experienced enough in the shipping game to spin your own tops. You didn't give me any the best of it; you crowded my hand and joggled my elbow, and it would have been the signal for a half holiday in the office if I had gone broke."

"But after all Mr. Ricks has done for you—"

"He always had value received, and I asked no favors of him—and received none."

"But surely, my dear Matt," Skinner purred, for the first time calling his ancient enemy by his Christian name—"surely you're jesting with us."

"Skinner, old horse, I was never more serious in my life. Mr. Alden P. Ricks is my ideal of a perfect business man; and just before I left for Panama he informed me—rather coldly, I thought—that he never mixed sentiment with business. Moreover, he advised me not to do it either. To surrender to him now would mean the fracturing, for the first time in history, of a slogan that has been in the Peasley tribe for generations."

"What's that?" Cappy queried with shaking voice.

"Pay your way and take your beating like a sport, sir," Matt shot at him. He drew out his watch. "Well," he continued, "I guess the United States Marshal is in charge of the Tillicum by this time; so get busy with the bond and have him removed from the ship. The minute one of those birds lights on my deck I just go crazy!"

"Yes, you do!" screamed Cappy Ricks, completely losing his self-control. "You go crazy—like a fox!"

And then Cappy Ricks did something he had never done before. He swore, with a depth of feeling and a range of language to be equalled only by a lumberjack. Matt Peasley waited until he subsided for lack of new invective and then said reproachfully:

"I can't stand this any longer, Mr. Ricks. I'll have to go now. Back home I belonged to the Congregational Church—"

"Out!" yelled Cappy. "Out, you vagabond!"

CHAPTER XLIII.
CAPPY PLANS A KNOCK-OUT

The morning following Matt Peasley's triumphant return from Panama with the steamer Tillicum, Cappy Ricks created a mild sensation in his offices by reporting for duty at a quarter past eight. Mr. Skinner was already at his desk, for he was a slave driver who drove himself fully as hard as he did those under him. He glanced up apprehensively as Cappy bustled in.

"Why, what has happened, Mr. Ricks?" he queried.

"I have an idea," said Cappy. "Skinner, my boy, a word with you in private."

Mr. Skinner rose with alacrity, for instinct warned him that he was in for some fast and clever work. Cappy sat in at his desk, and Skinner, drawing up a chair, sat down beside him and waited respectfully for Cappy to begin.

"Skinner," Cappy began impressively, "for many years you and I have been harboring the delusion that we are business men, whereas, if we can stand to hear the truth told about ourselves, we handle a deal with the reckless abandon of a pair of bear cubs juggling hazel nuts."

"I have sufficient self-esteem," Skinner replied stiffly, "not to take that pessimistic view of myself. If you refer to the inglorious rout we suffered yesterday in our skirmish with Captain Matt Peasley, permit me to remind you, in all respect, that you handled that entire deal yourself."

"Bah!" said Cappy witheringly. "Why, you aided and abetted me, Skinner. You told me my strategy was absolutely flawless."

"I am not the seventh son of a seventh son, sir. I did not see the flaw in your strategy. You lost by one of those strange accidents which must be attributed to the interference of the Almighty in the affairs of men."

"Lost!" Cappy jeered. "Lost! Skinner, you infuriate me. I haven't lost. Like John Paul Jones, I haven't yet commenced to fight. Skinner, listen to me. When I get through with that Matt Peasley you can take it from me he'll be sore from soul to vermiform appendix."

"If I may be permitted a criticism, sir, I would suggest that you let this matter rest right where it is. Surely you realize the delicate position you are in, quarreling with your future son-in-law—"

"Agh-h-h! Pooh!" snapped Cappy. "That's all outside office hours. I haven't any grudge against the boy and he knows it. I don't want his little old bank roll—that is, for keeps. When I went into this deal, Skinner, I was actuated by the same benevolent intentions as a man that desires to cure a hound pup of sucking eggs. He fills an egg with cayenne pepper and leaves it where the pup can find it—and after that the pup sucks no more eggs. I love this boy Matt like he was my own son, but he's too infernally fresh! He holds people too cheap; he's too trustful. He's made his little wad too easily, and easy money never did any man any good. So I wanted to teach him that business is business, and if I could take his roll away from him I was going to do it. Of course, Skinner, I need not remind you that I would have loaned him the next minute, without interest and without security, every cent I'd taken from him in this deal—"

"But why peeve over it, Mr. Ricks? If Captain Matt—"

"At my age—to take a beating like that?" Cappy shrilled. "Impossible! Why, he'll tell this story on the Merchants' Exchange, and I can't afford that. Not at my age, Skinner, not at my age! I have a reputation to sustain, and, by the Holy Pink-toed Prophet, I'm going to sustain it. I'm going down fighting like a bear cat. I know he scalded us yesterday, Skinner, but every dog must have his day—and that dog-gone Matt's day dawned this morning."

"The only tactical error, if I may appear hypercritical," Skinner said suavely, "was your failure to cancel the charter on the very day that Matt slipped up on his first advance payment. If you had done that you would have had him. Don't say I didn't call your attention to the fact that his payment was overdue!"

"Yes, if I had done that I would have had him, but how much would I have had him for? Paltry nine thousand dollars! I wanted him to get into the financial quicksands up to his chin—and then I'd have had him! Besides, Skinner, I had to go slow. Just think what would have happened if Florry found me out! Why, I would have had to call off the dogs before I was half through the job."

"He's probably told her all about it by now," Skinner suggested.

"Don't get him wrong," Cappy protested. "He's no tattle-tale. He'll fight fair. However, as I was saying, I couldn't do anything raw, Skinner. I had planned, when Matt reached Panama and discovered he had been double-crossed to pass the buck up to you!"

Mr. Skinner started, but Cappy continued serenely:

"I planned to be away from the office when the blow-off came, and you were to have borne the brunt of Matt's fury and despair. Why, what the devil do I have a general manager for if not to help me out in these little affairs? And besides, Skinner, when he blew in here the day Morrow & Company hit the ceiling, he was so excited and worried I felt positive he was busted then; so what was the use calling him for his overdue payment when if I let him run on I'd have his young soul in hock for the next ten years?" Cappy leaned forward and laid an impressive hand on Mr. Skinner's knee. "You know, Skinner, we really need that boy in this office, and it would have been a fine thing to have gotten him and gotten him right. Then he wouldn't be leaving the reservation to chase rainbows. However, as the boys say, I overlooked a bet, but I'll not overlook another."

"You said you had an idea," Mr. Skinner suggested.

"I have. Just at present there is a libel on the Tillicum, and when we lift it Matt Peasley is prepared to plaster another libel on her, and another, and still another. Now, as a result of our conversation with Matt yesterday, he thinks we'll lift the libel to-day—in fact, settle with him for what he paid the crew when they assigned their wage claim to his company, and thus prevent any further libels. Now, if we do that it leaves Matt in the clear to commence discharging his cargo, but at the same time it makes it incumbent upon him to slam a certified check for eighteen thousand dollars down on the Blue Star counter, in order to hold the vessel long enough to discharge her and collect the freight. Then he'll turn the vessel back on our hands with many thanks—rot him!"

"I have no doubt that such are his intentions, Mr. Ricks; in which event he will, of course, be ready with the certified check the instant we make formal, written demand upon him for our money. I believe I have already warned you, sir, that we cannot cancel the charter without first making formal, written demand for our charter money."

"Well," said Cappy, "we'll get round that all right."

"Pray, how?"

"What time did Matt Peasley leave this office after the battle yesterday?"

"I should say in the neighborhood of half after three."

"Hum! Ahem! Harump-h-h! The banks close at three, and they do not reopen for business until ten this morning. It is now exactly a quarter of nine. Has Matt Peasley had time to procure a certified check since he arrived from Panama—or has he not?"

"The situation admits of no argument," Mr. Skinner admitted.

"Exactly! He didn't have time yesterday, and he sha'n't have time to-day, and to-morrow will be too late, because his money is due us to-day! We shall lift all those libels and free the Tillicum for him; then we shall make formal demand upon him for eighteen thousand dollars, in cash or certified check—we can legally decline his check unless certified—and when he fails to make good we formally cancel the charter. Then what happens? I'll tell you. We grab the boat with a full cargo from him as he grabbed it from Morrow & Company with a full cargo. Then we collect the freight on that northbound cargo as he collected the freight on the southbound cargo, and," Cappy continued calmly, "I dare say that freight money will put us in the clear on all those bills we're stuck for."

"And to do all this," Skinner remarked sententiously, "it is necessary to tie up Matt Peasley's bank account the instant the bank opens this morning."

"Skinner," said Cappy feelingly, "you get me almost before I get myself. Now listen, while I give you your orders: Go right up to our attorney's office, take our copy of the charter with you, explain that Matt has defaulted in his payments, and instruct our attorney to enter suit to collect. Tell him to get the complaint out and filed within three-quarters of an hour, and then, the instant he has filed the suit, he is to get out a writ of attachment on the Pacific Shipping Company's bank account."

"But we cannot do that, Mr. Ricks. We must make formal, written demand for the payments in arrears before we can proceed to force collection—"

"Certainly. We'll do that after we've tied up his bank account."

"But when we get into court we'll be nonsuited because we didn't do that first."

"I sincerely hope so. But in the meanwhile we've tied up Matt's bank account, and while we're arguing the merits of our action in so doing, another sun will have set, and when it rises again"—Cappy kissed his hand airily into space—"the good ship Tillicum will be back under the Blue Star Flag—"

"But Matt Peasley will allege conspiracy and a lot of things, and he can sue us and get the boat back and force us to render an accounting of that freight money."

"That situation will admit of much argument, Skinner. However, Matt will not sue me. Florry wouldn't let him! He'll make us lift the attachment on his bank account, and then he'll protect himself and tell us to whistle for the eighteen thousand dollars he owes us. Whichever way the cat jumps he wins. What I want to do is break even and with a modicum of my self-respect left intact."

"He'll promptly file a bond to lift the attachment—"

"Will he? Who in this city will go on his bond? Who does he know?"

"There are bonding companies in business, and for a cash consideration—"

"Rot! They will investigate and ponder before granting his application for a bond. It takes a day or two to get a bond through a bonding house, and all I want to do is to tie Matt up for a day. Now, listen! You see to it that the suit is filed and an attachment levied on Matt Peasley's bank account in the Marine National. That's where he keeps his little wad, because I took him over and introduced him there myself. Well, sir, in the meantime I'll call up Matt and precipitate a devil of a row with him over the phone. I'll tell him I've made up my mind to fight him to the last ditch and that those libels will not be lifted until he lifts them himself. Of course, he'll figure right away that he won't need a certified check to-day, and maybe he'll neglect to provide himself with one; or he may be chump enough to figure we'll take his check uncertified, and if he does that will teach him something."

"Well, I'm betting he'll not be caught napping," Mr. Skinner declared, "and if you want my opinion of this new proceeding I will state frankly that I am not in favor of it. It savors too much of assination. Of course, you may do it and get away with it—"

"Pooh!" snorted Cappy. "Forget it. At ten minutes of three this afternoon the libel on the Tillicum will be lifted, and Matt Peasley will be paid in cash the sum he advanced his crew for wages. That will block him from slapping any more libels on her and holding us up. Then we'll make formal, written demand upon him for eighteen thousand dollars; he won't have it where he can lay his hands on it, and he'll be up Salt Creek without a paddle."

"I am not in favor of it," Mr. Skinner reiterated firmly.

"Neither am I, Skinner, but I've got to do something. Can't let that young pup cover me with blood. No, sir, not at my age, Skinner. I can't afford to be laughed off California Street. And by the way, since when did you become a champion of Matt Peasley?"

Mr. Skinner did not answer.

"Since when?" Cappy repeated.

"Since he administered such a thorough thrashing to the Blue Star Navigation Company," Mr. Skinner answered, "and did it without prejudice. He swatted us, and we deserved it, but he didn't get angry. Every time he banged us, he'd look at me as much as to say: 'I hate to swat you two, but it's got to be done.' Bang! 'This hurts me more than it does you.' Biff! And then he went out smiling. I used to think he was an—an—interloper, I thought he had designs on the Blue Star Navigation Company and the Ricks Lumber and Logging Company, but he hasn't. He doesn't give a hoot for anything or anybody except for what he can be to them; not for what they can be to him. He's brainy and spunky and, by thunder, I'm for him, and if you're going to hand him a clout when he isn't looking you'll have to do it yourself."

"Skinner," said Cappy Ricks impressively. "Look me square in the eye. Do you refuse orders?"

"I do, sir," Skinner replied, and looked Cappy in the eye so fiercely that the old schemer quailed. "This is an unworthy business, Mr. Ricks. You're trying to teach Matt Peasley some business tricks, and he's taught you a few, so be a sport, sir, and pay for your education."

"All right," Cappy replied meekly. "When my own general manager goes back on me, I suppose there's nothing to do but quit. The program appears to be impracticable, so we'll say no more about it."

"I am glad to hear you say that, Mr. Ricks," Skinner answered feelingly, and forthwith repaired to his own office.

Cappy Ricks gazed after him almost affectionately, and as the door closed behind the general manager, Cappy murmured sotto voce:

"Skinner, I've been twenty-five years wondering why the devil I liked you, and now I know. Why, you cold-blooded, efficient, human automaton, you've actually got a heart! Bow! wow! Faithful Fido Skinner was just a-tugging at the chain and dragging the dog house after him in his efforts to eat me up! I hope I go bankrupt if I don't raise his salary!"

He turned to a pigeonhole in his desk and drew forth the charter he had negotiated months before with Matt Peasley for the Tillicum. He read it over carefully, tucked it in his breast pocket and slipped quietly out the door. One hour later a suit against the Pacific Shipping Company was filed in the county clerk's office, and at five minutes after ten a deputy-sheriff appeared at the paying-teller's window in the Marine National Bank and filed a writ of attachment on the funds to their credit.

CHAPTER XLIV.
SKINNER DEVELOPS INTO A HUMAN BEING

Cappy Ricks was having his mid-afternoon siesta in his office when Captain Matt Peasley appeared at the counter of the general office and, without awaiting an invitation to enter, swung through the office gate and made straight for Cappy's office. En route he had to pass through Mr. Skinner's lair, and the general manager looked up as Matt entered.

"Well, Captain," he said pleasantly, "how goes it?"

"Fine," Matt answered with equal urbanity. "That was a slick piece of work tying up my bank account. I can't get a bond to-day, the bank is closed, and I suppose you're going to insist upon payment of that eighteen thousand dollars before midnight to-night or take the Tillicum and her cargo away from me."

Mr. Skinner started in genuine amazement.

"Attached your bank account, Matt? I give you my word of honor I had nothing to do with it."

"Well, it's tied up by the Blue Star Navigation Company, and Cappy Ricks has served notice on me to call here and pay up or suffer cancellation of my charter. Of course, for all the good my bank account is to me this minute he might as well ask me to give him the moon."

"I'm truly sorry," said Skinner. "I protested to Mr. Ricks against this action. I assure you I would not have taken such a course myself — under the circumstances."

"Cappy wants cash or a certified check," Matt complained, "and he's made it impossible for me to go to my bank and get either — to-day. What am I going to do?"

"I'm afraid you're going to lose the Tillicum and her cargo. The Blue Star Navigation Company will doubtless collect the freight on that northbound cargo. Besides, Mr. Ricks has some business offered for the Tillicum and wants her back—"

"But I was going to give her back to him as soon as I discharged her cargo. Now, just for that he'll not get her back. I'll keep her the full year."

"But how?" Mr. Skinner queried kindly.

"By paying the Blue Star Navigation Company eighteen thousand dollars in good old U. S. yellow-backs." Matt laughed and drew from his hip pocket a roll that would have choked a hippopotamus. "Skinner, this is so rich I'll have to tell you about it, and then if you're good I'll let you be present when I put the crusher on Cappy. His plan was without a flaw. He had me right where he wanted me—only something slipped."

"What?" Mr. Skinner demanded breathlessly.

"Why, as soon as my account was attached, the bank called me up and told me about it. I was just about to start for the bank to make a deposit of all that freight money I had collected in Panama—about twenty-four thousand dollars, more or less—the Panama Railroad gave it to me in a lump—exchange on San Francisco, you know—"

"So you cashed that draft at the bank upon which it was drawn—"

"And I'm here with the cash to smother Cappy Ricks! I'll cover him with confusion, the old villain! Skinner, I give you my word, if he hadn't tried to slip one over on me I would never have stuck him with all those bills Morrow & Company didn't pay, but now that he's gone and attached my bank account—"

Mr. Skinner rose and took Matt Peasley by the arm.

"Matt," he said in the friendliest fashion imaginable. "You and I have clashed since the first day I learned of your existence, but we're not going to clash any more." He pointed to the door leading to Cappy Ricks' office. "One of these days, Matt, whether you want to or not, you're going to be occupying that office and giving orders to me, and when you do I want to tell you here and now I shall accord you the same measure of respect I now accord Mr. Ricks. I've worked twenty-five years for Mr. Ricks. I—I'm—absurdly fond of him, for all his er—er—"

Cappy Ricks: OR, the Subjugation of matt Peasley | 243

"Why, so am I, Skinner. I'd do anything to please him—"

"Then do it," Skinner pleaded. "Give him a cheap victory. He's an old man and he'll enjoy it. He didn't sleep a wink last night, just scheming a way to get a strangle hold on you—it's hard for the old to give way to the young, you know—and now he's inside there, just hungering for you to arrive so he can jeer at you and lecture you and make fun of you. He doesn't want your money. Why, he loves you as if you were his own boy—"

"But how can I let him get away with this deal?" Matt queried soberly.

"By rushing in on him now and simulating a terrific rage. Just imagine you're on the bridge of a steamer making up to a dock against a strong flood tide, with stupid mates fore and aft, and rotten lines that won't hold when you get them over the dolphins, and the tide has grabbed you and slammed you into the dock and done five hundred dollars' worth of damage—just feel like that, Matt—"

"If I do I'll cuss something scandalous," Matt warned him.

"The harder the better."

"And I'm to keep this money in my pocket, and let him cancel my charter, and take that northbound cargo away from me, and collect the freight on me—"

"Exactly that! He'll withdraw his suit against you to-morrow and release your bank account, and then you decline to pay him the eighteen thousand dollars you owe him until he gives an accounting of the freight money he's collected. He'll tell you to go to Halifax, but you mustn't mind. It's going to make him as happy as a fool to think he beat you in the end."

A slow smile spread over Matt's face.

"Skinner," he said. "You're a good old wagon, that's what you are. I'm sorry we ever had any mix-up, and we'll never have another—after this one—and this is going to be a fake. You see, Skinner, if we're going to put one over on Cappy let's have it one worth while—so this is the program. I've just arrived, with blood in my eye, to clean out the Blue Star office, and I'm starting in with the general manager. Clinch me now, and we'll wrestle all over the office and bang against the furniture and that door there—"

As Cappy Ricks was wont to remark, Mr. Skinner could "get" one before one could "get" one's self.

"Get out of my office, you infernal rowdy," he yelled loud enough to awaken Cappy Ricks next door. Then he clinched with Matt Peasley.

"A good fight," said Cappy Ricks half an hour after Matt Peasley had been pried away from Mr. Skinner and forced to listen to reason, "is the grandest thing in life. Now there's that crazy boy gone out in a rage just because he had the presumption to tangle with me in a business deal and get dog-gone well licked! He put it all over me yesterday, thinking I couldn't protect myself. Well, he knows better now, Skinner; he knows better now! In-fer-nal young scoundrel! Wow, but wasn't he a wild man, Skinner? Wasn't he though?" And Cappy Ricks chuckled.

"You have probably cured him of sucking eggs," Mr. Skinner observed enigmatically.

"Well, I handed the young pup a dose of cayenne pepper, at any rate," Cappy bragged, "and I wouldn't have missed doing it for a cool hundred thousand. Why, Skinner, a man might as well retire from business when he gets so weak and feeble and soft-headed he doesn't know how to protect himself in the clinches and break-aways."

Mr. Skinner smiled. "The old dog for the cold scent," he suggested.

"You bet," Cappy cackled triumphantly. "Skinner, my dear boy, what are we paying you?"

"Ten thousand a year, sir."

"Not enough money. Hereafter pay yourself twelve thousand. Tut, tut. Not a peep out of you, sir, not a peep. If you do, Skinner, you'll spoil the happiest day I've known in twenty years."

CHAPTER XLV.
CAPPY PULLS OFF A WEDDING

About a week later, Captain Matt Peasley was studying the weather chart at the Merchants' Exchange when he heard behind him a propitiatory "Ahem! Hum-m-m! Harump-h-h-h!"—infallible evidence that Cappy Ricks was in the immediate offing, yearning for Matt to turn round in order that he might hail the boy and thus re-establish diplomatic relations. Matt, however, elected to be perverse and pay no attention to Cappy; instead, he moved closer to the chart and affected greater interest in it.

"Hello, you big, sulky boob!" Cappy snapped presently, unable to stand the silence any longer. "Come away from that weather chart. It's blowing a fifty-mile nor'west gale off Point Reyes, and that's all any shipping man cares to know to-day. You haven't got any ships at sea!"

"No; but you have, sir," Matt replied, unable longer to simulate indifference to Cappy's presence. "The Tillicum is bucking into that gale this minute, wasting fuel oil and making about four miles an hour. I'm glad you're paying for the oil. Where are you loading her?"

"At Hinch's Mill, in Aberdeen, Grays Harbor; discharge at Honolulu and back with sugar." Cappy came close to Matt and drew the latter's great arm through his. "Say, Matt," he queried plaintively, "are you still mad over that walloping I gave you?"

"Well-l, no. I think I've recovered. And I'm not willing to admit I was walloped. The best you got out of our little mix-up with the Tillicum was a lucky draw."

"I'm still out a lot of money," Cappy admitted. "You owe me eighteen thousand dollars on that charter I canceled on you, Matt, and you ought to pay it. Really, you ought."

"That being tantamount to an admission on your part you cannot go into court with clean hands and force me to pay it," Matt flashed back at him, "I'll make you a proposition: You render me an accounting of the freight you collected on the cargo you stole from me, and I'll render you an accounting for the freight on the cargo I stole from you; then we'll get an insurance adjuster in and let him figure out, by general average, how much I would owe you if I had a conscience; then I'll give you my note, due in one year, at six per cent. for whatever the amount may be."

"Why not give me the cash?" Cappy pleaded. "You've got the money in bank."

"I know; but I want to use it for a year."

"Your note's no good to me," Cappy protested. "I told you once before it wasn't hockable at any bank."

"Then I'll withdraw my proposition."

"And present a substitute?"

"No, sir."

"I guess I'll take your note," Cappy said eagerly.

"I thank you for the compliment," Matt laughed; and Cappy, no longer able to dissemble, laughed with him — and their feud was over. Consequently, post-mortems being in order, Matt went on: "I feel pretty sneaky about sticking you with all those bills on the Tillicum that Morrow & Company defaulted on, just because the law enabled me to do so — but you did your best to ruin me; you wouldn't have showed me any pity or consideration."

"Not a dog-goned bit!" Cappy declared firmly. "I was out to bust you wide open for the good of your immortal soul. I would have taken your roll away from you, my son, by fair means — or — er — legal, if I could." He looked up at Matt, with such a smile as he might have applied to a lovable and well-beloved son. "I hope you've got sporting blood enough in you to realize I didn't really want your little bank roll, Matt," he said half pleadingly. "I don't know just why I did it — except that I'm an old man and I know it; and I hate to be out of the running. I suppose, just because I'm old, I wanted to take a fall out of you — you're so young; and — oh, Matt, you do make a scrap so worth while!"

"And, because I've lived longer in this world and fought harder for what I've got than you'll ever have to fight, I wanted to put about six feet of hot iron into your soul. You're a little bit too cocksure, Matt. I tell you it's a mistake to hold your business competitor cheap. I want you to know that the fine gentleman who plays cribbage with you at your club to-night will lift the hair off your head down here on the Street to-morrow, because that's the game; and nobody shakes hands with you before giving you the poke that puts you to sleep. There are a lot of old men out in the almshouse just because they trusted too much in human nature; and I wanted to show you how hard and cruel men can be and excuse their piracy on the plea that it is business! I tell you, Matt Peasley, when you've lived as long as I have you'll know men for the swine they are whenever they see some real money in sight."

"Well, I shouldn't be surprised if you got the lesson over after all," Matt replied gravely. "You certainly made me step lively to keep from getting run over. You scared me out of a year's growth."

Cappy laughed contentedly.

"And what are you going to do with all this money you admit you owe me and decline to let me see the color of for a year?"

"Do you really want to know?" Matt queried.

"I'll take you to luncheon up at the Commercial Club if you'll tell me."

Matt bent low and whispered in Cappy's ear:

"I'm going to marry your daughter. I'll have to furnish a home and—"

"No excuse!" said Cappy fiercely. "Son, all you've got to buy is the wedding ring and the license, and some clothes. I'm stuck for the wedding expenses and you don't have to furnish a home. My house is big enough for three, isn't it?"

"But this thing of living with your wife's relations—" Matt began mischievously, until he saw the pain and the loneliness in Cappy's kind old eyes. "Oh, well," he hastened to add, "pull it off to suit yourself; but don't waste any time."

"In-fer-nal young scoundrel!" Cappy cried happily. "We've waited too long already."

Florry was a June bride, and the proudest and happiest man present, not excepting the groom, was old Cappy Ricks. He looked fully two inches taller as he walked up the church aisle, with Florry on his arm, and handed her over to Matt Peasley, waiting at the altar. And when the ceremony was over, and Matt had entered the waiting limousine with his bride, Cappy Ricks stood on the church steps among a dozen of his young friends from the wholesale lumber and shipping trade and made a brief oration.

"Take a good look at him, boys," he said proudly. "You fresh young fellows will have to tangle with him one of these bright days; and when you do he'll make hell look like a summer holiday to you. See if he doesn't!"

Later, when Matt and Florry, about to leave on their honeymoon, were saying good-bye, Matt put his huge arm round Cappy and gave him a filial hug. Cappy's eyes filled with tears.

"I guess we understand each other, sonny," he said haltingly. "I've wanted a son like you, Matt. Had a boy once—little chap—just seven when he died—might have been big like you. I was the runt of the Ricks' tribe, you know—all the other boys over six feet—and his mother's people—same stock. I—I—"

Matt patted his shoulder. Truly he understood.

CHAPTER XLVI.
A SHIP FORGOTTEN

The Blue Star Navigation Company's big steam schooner Amelia Ricks, northbound to load lumber at Aberdeen in command of a skipper who revered his berth to such an extent that he thought only of pleasing Mr. Skinner by making fast time, thus failing to take into consideration a two-mile current setting shoreward, had come to grief. Her skipper had cut a corner once too often and started overland with her right across the toe of Point Gorda. Her wireless brought two tugs hastening up from San Francisco; but, before they could haul her off at high tide, the jagged reef had chewed her bottom to rags, and in a submerged condition she was towed back to port and kicked into the dry dock at Hunters Point.

Cappy Ricks, feverishly excited over the affair, was very anxious to get a report on the condition of the vessel as soon as possible. He had planned to hire a launch and proceed to Hunters Point for a personal appraisal of the damage to the Amelia Ricks, but the northwest trades were blowing half a gale that day and had kicked up just sufficient sea to warn Cappy that seasickness would be his portion if he essayed to brave it in a launch. It occurred to him, therefore, to stay in the office and send somebody in whose knowledge of ships he had profound confidence. He got Matt Peasley on the phone at once.

"Matt," he said plaintively. "I want you to do the old man a favor, if you will. You heard about our Amelia Ricks, didn't you? Well, she's in dry dock at Hunters Point now, and they'll have the dock pumped out in two hours so we can see what her bottom looks like. I know she's ripped out clear up to the garboards and probably hogged, and I can hardly wait to make sure. The marine surveyor for the Underwriters will go down this afternoon to look her over, and then he'll take a day to present his long, typewritten report—and I can't wait that long. Will you skip down to Crowley's boathouse, hire a launch and charge it to us, and go down to see the Amelia? She'll be shored up by the time you get down there. Make a good quick examination of the damage and hurry back so I can talk it over with you. I go a heap on your judgment, Matt."

"I'll start right away, sir," Matt promised, glad of any opportunity to favor Cappy.

Two hours later, on his way back to the Mission Street bulkhead, he passed, in Mission Bay, a huge, rusty red box of a steel freighter, swinging at anchor. Under ordinary weather conditions Matt would have paid no attention to her; but, as has already been stated, the northwest trades were blowing a gale and had kicked up a sea; hence the steamer was rolling freely at her anchorage, and as the launch bobbed by to windward of her she rolled far over to leeward—and Matt saw something that challenged his immediate attention and provoked his profound disgust. The sides of the vessel below the water line were incrusted with barnacles and eelgrass fully six inches thick!

No skipper that ever set foot on a bridge could pass that scaly hulk unmoved. Matt Peasley said uncomplimentary things about the owners of the vessel and directed the launchman to pass in under her stern, in order that he might read her name. She proved to be the Narcissus, of London.

He stood in the stern of the launch, staring thoughtfully after the Narcissus, and before his mind there floated that vision of the barnacles and eelgrass, infallible evidence that the years had been long since the Narcissus had been hauled out.

"Do you know how long that steamer has lain there?" he queried of the launchman.

"I been runnin' launches to and from Hunters Point for seven years an' she was there when I come on the job," the latter answered.

"It's no place for a good ship," Matt Peasley murmured musingly. "She ought to be out on the dark blue, loaded and earning good money for her owners. I must find out why she isn't doing it."

Having rendered a meticulous report to Cappy on the condition of the Amelia Ricks, Matt, his brain still filled with thoughts of that lonely big steamer swinging neglected in Mission Bay among the rotting oyster boats and old clipper ships waiting to be converted into coal hulks, proceeded to the Merchants' Exchange where Lloyds' Register soon put him in possession of the following information:

The steamer Narcissus had been built in Glasgow in 1894 by Sutherland & Sons, Limited. She was four hundred and fifty-five feet long, fifty-eight feet beam and thirty-one feet draft. She had triple-expansion engines of two thousand indicated horse power, two Scotch boilers, and was of seventy-five hundred tons net register.

"Huh!" Matt murmured. "She'll carry forty per cent. more than her registered tonnage; if I had the loading of her she'd carry fifty per cent. more, at certain seasons of the year. I wonder why her owners have let her lie idle for eight years? I'll have to ask Jerry Dooley. He knows everything about ships that a landsman can possibly know."

Jerry Dooley had presided over the desk at the Merchants' Exchange for so many years that there was a rumor current to the effect that he had been there in the days when the water used to come up to Montgomery Street. Before Jerry's desk the skippers of all nations came and went; to him there drifted inevitably all of the little, intimate gossip of the shipping world. If somebody built a ship and she had trouble with her oil burners on the trial trip, Jerry Dooley would know all about it before that vessel got back to her dock again. If somebody else's ship was a wet boat, Jerry knew of it, and could, moreover, give one the name of the naval architect responsible; if a vessel had been hogged on a reef, Jerry could tell you the name of the reef, the date of the wreck, the location of the hog, and all about the trouble they had keeping her cargo dry as a result. To this human encyclopedia, therefore, did Matt Peasley come in his still-hunt for information touching the steamer Narcissus.

He opened negotiations by handing Jerry Dooley a good cigar. Jerry examined it, saw that it was a good cigar, and said: "I don't smoke myself, but I have a brother that does." He fixed Matt Peasley with an alert, inquisitive eye and said: "Well, what do you know, Captain?"

"Nothing much. What do you know about the steamer Narcissus?"

Jerry Dooley scratched his red head.

"Narcissus!" he murmured. "Narcissus! By George, it's a long time since I heard of her. Has she just come into port?" And he glanced apprehensively at the register of arrivals and departures, wondering if he hadn't overlooked the Narcissus.

"She's been in port eight years at least," Matt answered; "tucked away down in Mission Bay, with a watchman aboard."

"Oh, I remember now," Jerry replied. "She belongs to the Oriental Steamship Company. Old man Webb, of the Oriental Company, got all worked up about the possibilities of the Oriental trade right after the Spanish War. He had a lot of old bottoms running in the combined freight and passenger trade and not making expenses when the war came along, and the Government grabbed all his boats for transports to rush troops over to the Philippines. That was fine business for quite a while and the Oriental got out of the hole and made a lot of money besides. About that time Old Webb saw a vision of huge Oriental trade for the man who would go after it, and in his excitement he purchased the Narcissus. She carried horses down to the Philippines, and to China during the Boxer uprising; and when that business was over, and while old Webb was waiting for the expected boom in trade to the Orient, he got a lumber charter for her from Puget Sound to Australia. But she was never built for a lumber boat, though she carried six million five hundred thousand feet; she was so big and it took so long to load and discharge her that she lost twenty-five thousand dollars on the voyage. Run her in the lumber trade and the demurrage would break a national bank.

"Well, sir, after that lumber charter, old man Webb had a fit. He tried her out on a few grain charters, but she didn't make any money to speak of; and about that time the P. & S. W., with a view to grabbing some Oriental freight for their road, got the control of the steamship company away from Webb. The Oriental trade boom never developed, and the regular steamers, carrying freight and passengers, were ample to cope with what business the company was offered; so they didn't need the Narcissus.

"As I remember it, she was expensive to operate. She had a punk pair of boilers or she needed another boiler—or something; at any rate, she was a hog on coal, and they laid her up until such time as they could find use for her. I suppose after she was laid up a few years the thought of all the money it would cost to put her in commission again discouraged them—and she's been down in Mission Bay ever since."

"But the Canal will soon be open," Matt suggested. "One would suppose they'd put her in commission and find business for her between Pacific and Atlantic coast ports."

"You forget she's a foreign-built vessel and hence cannot run between American ports."

"She can run between North and South American ports," Matt replied doggedly. "I bet if I owned her I'd dig up enough business in Brazil and the Argentine to keep her busy. I'd be dodging backward and forward through the Canal."

"You would, of course," Jerry answered placidly; "but the Oriental Steamship Company cannot."

"Why?"

"Fifty-one per cent. of their stock is owned by a railroad—and under the law no railroad-owned ship may use the Canal."

Matt's eyebrows arched.

"Ah!" he murmured. "Then that's one of the reasons why she's a white elephant on their hands."

"Got a customer for her?" Jerry queried shrewdly. "A fellow ought to be able to pick the Narcissus up rather cheap."

Matt shook his head negatively.

"Happened to pass her in a launch a couple of hours ago, and the sight of the barnacles on her bottom just naturally graveled me and roused my curiosity. Much obliged for your information." And Matt excused himself and strolled over to the counter of the Hydro-graphic Office to look over the recent bulletins to masters.

The information that the whistling buoy off Duxbury Reef had gone adrift and that Blunt's Reef Lightship would be withdrawn for fifteen days for repairs and docking interested him but little, however. In his mind's eye there loomed the picture of that great red freighter, with her foul bottom, rusty funnel and unpainted, weather-beaten upper works.

"Her bridge is pretty well exposed to the weather," he murmured. "I'd build it up so the man on watch could just look over it. I noticed they'd had the good sense to house over her winches, so I dare say they're in good shape; her paint will have prevented rust below the water line, and I'll bet she's as sound as the day she was built. I think

254 | Cappy Ricks: OR, the Subjugation of matt Peasley

I'd paint her dead black, with red underbody and terra-cotta upper works." He pondered. "Yes, and I'd paint her funnel dead black, too, with a broad red band; and on both sides of the funnel, in the center of this red band, I'd have a white diamond with a black P in the center of it. By George, they'd know the Peasley Line as far as they could see it!"

He would have dreamed on had he not bethought himself suddenly of his modest capital—fifty thousand-odd dollars, out of which he owed Cappy Ricks a considerable sum on a promissory note due in one year. On such a meager bank balance it would not do to dream of buying a vessel worth nearly four hundred thousand dollars. Why, it would require twenty thousand dollars to put her in commission after all these years of idleness, and she had to have another boiler because she was a hog on coal; and, in addition, her operating cost would be between nine and ten thousand dollars a month.

Matt shook his head and looked round the great room as though in search of inspiration. He found it. His wandering glance finally came to rest on Jerry Dooley's alert countenance. Jerry crooked a finger at him and Matt strolled over to the desk.

"I've been watching you milling the idea round in your head," said Jerry. "I saw you reject it. You're crazy! It can be done."

"How?" Matt queried eagerly.

"Go get an option on her for the lowest price you can get—then form a syndicate and sell her to them at a higher price; or, if you don't want to do that, form your syndicate to buy her at the option price, and if you work it right you can get the job of managing owner. I want to tell you that two and one-half per cent. commission on her freight earnings would make a nice income."

"I wonder whom I could get into the syndicate?" Matt queried.

Jerry scratched his head.

"Well," he suggested, "you're mighty close to old Cappy Ricks. If you could hook him for a piece of her, the rest would be easy. Any shipping man on the Street will follow where Cappy Ricks leads. I'd try Pollard & Reilly; Redell, of the West Coast Trading Company; Jack Haviland, the ship chandler; Charley Beyers, the ship's grocer and butcher; A. B. Cahill & Co., the coal dealers; Pete Hansen, of the

Bulkhead Hotel down on the Embarcadero—he's always got a couple of thousand dollars to put into a clean-cut shipping enterprise. Then there's Rickey, the ship-builder, and—yes, even Alcott, the crimp, will take a piece of her. I'd look in on Louis Wiley, the chronometer man, and Cox, the coppersmith—why I'd take in every firm and individual who might hope to get business out of the ship; and, you bet, I'd sell 'em all a little block of stock in the S. S. Narcissus Company."

"It might be done," Matt answered evasively. "I'll think it over."

He did think it over very seriously the greater portion of that night. As a result, instead of going to his office next morning he went to Mission Street bulkhead and engaged a launch, and forty minutes later, in response to his hail, the aged watchman aboard the Narcissus came to the rail and asked him what he wanted.

"I want to come aboard!" Matt shouted.

"Got a permit from the office?"

"No."

"Orders are to allow nobody aboard without a permit."

"How do you like the color of this permit?" Matt called back, and waved a greenback.

The answer came in the shape of a Jacob's ladder promptly tossed overside and Matt Peasley mounted the towering hulk of the Narcissus.

"What do you want?" the watchman again demanded as he pouched the bill Matt handed him.

"I want to examine this vessel from bilge to truck," Matt answered. "I'll begin with a look at the winches."

As he had surmised, the winches had been housed over and fairly buried in grease when the ship laid up; hence they were in absolutely perfect condition. The engines, too, had received the best of care, as nearly as Matt could judge from a cursory view. Her cargo space was littered up with a number of grain chutes, which would have to come out; and her boats, which had been stored in the empty hold aft, away from the weather, were in tiptop shape. She had a spare anchor, plenty of chain, wire cable and Manila lines, though these latter would doubtless have to be renewed in their entirety, owing to deterioration from age.

Her crew quarters were commodious and ample, and the officers' quarters all that could be desired; her galley equipment was complete, even to a small auxiliary ice plant. What she needed was cleaning, painting and scraping, and lots of it, also the riggers would be a few days on her standing rigging; but, so far as Matt could discern, that was all. From the watchman he learned that one Terence Reardon had been her chief engineer in the days when the Oriental Steamship Company first owned her.

From the Narcissus, Matt Peasley returned to the city and went at once to the office of the Marine Engineers' Association, where he made inquiry for Terence Reardon. It appeared that Terence was chief of the Arab, loading grain at Port Costa; so to Port Costa Matt Peasley went to interview him. He found Reardon on deck, enjoying a short pipe and a breath of cool air, and introduced himself.

"I understand you were the chief of the Narcissus at one time, Mr. Reardon," Matt began abruptly. "I understand, also, that under your coaxing you used to get ten miles out of her loaded."

Parenthetically it may be stated that Matt Peasley had never heard anything of the sort; but he knew the weaknesses of chief engineers and decided to try a shot in the dark, hoping, by the grace of the devil and the luck of a sailor, to score a bull's-eye. He succeeded at least in ringing the bell.

"Coax, is it?" murmured Terence Reardon in his deep Kerry brogue. "Faith, thin, the Narcissus niver laid eye on the day she could do nine an' a half wit' the kindliest av treatment. Wirrah, but 'tis herself was the glutton for coal. Sure, whin I'd hand in me report to ould Webb, and he'd see where she'd averaged forty ton a day, the big tears'd come into the two eyes av him—the Lord ha' mercy on his sowl!"

"You never had any trouble with her engines," Matt suggested.

"I had throuble keepin' shteam enough in the b'ilers to run thim; but I'll say this for her ingines: Give them a chancet an' they'd run like a chronometer."

"Would you consider an offer to leave the Arab and be chief of the Narcissus?" Matt queried. "I'm thinking of buying her, and if I do I'll give you twenty-five dollars a month above the regular Association scale."

"I'll go ye," murmured Reardon, "on wan condition: Ye'll shpend some money in her ingine room, else 'tis no matther av use for ye to talk to me. I'll not be afther breakin' me poor heart for the sake av twenty-five dollars a month. Sure, 'twould be wort' that alone to see the face av ye, young man, afther wan look at the coal bill."

"What repairs would you suggest? Do you think she needs another boiler? I noticed she has two. We could move those two over and make room for another."

"Do nothing av the sort, sir. Before ould Webb got her she'd been usin' bad wather down on the East African Coast, I'm thinkin', and it raised hell wit' her. 'Tis the expinse av retubin' her condensers that always frightened ould Webb, and whin he lost conthrol the blatherskite booby av a port ingineer the new owners app'inted come down to the ship, looked her over, wit' niver a question to me that knew the very sowl av her, and reported to the owners that what she needed was another b'iler." And Terence Reardon laughed the short, mirthless chuckle of the man who knows.

"Then," Matt continued, "the money should be spent—"

"In retubing her condensers," declared the engineer emphatically. "Do that an' do a good job on her, an' she'll have shteam enough for thim fine big ingines av hers on thirty-two ton a day, an' less. An' have a care would ye buy her until she ships a new crank shaft. She's a crack in the web av the afther crank shaft ye could shtick a knife blade into. She may run for years, but sooner or later some wan'll have a salvage claim agin ye if ye neglect it now. An', for the love av heaven, have nothin' to do wit' her big motor. 'Twas bur-rnt out by him that had her ahead av me—bad cess to him, whereiver he is! An' they did a poor, cheap job av windin' the armature agin. Ye'll be in hot wather wit' the electric-light system until ye put in a new motor.

"The rheostat on the searchlight niver was any good; and she may or may not need a new whistle—I dunno. Sure, the skipper niver blew it good an' long but the wanst; an', so help me, young man, I was lookin' at the shteam gauge whin he shtarted that prolonged blast—an' whin he finished the gauge had dhropped tin pounds! So up I go on the bridge to the ould man, an' says I to him, says I: 'Clear weather or thick fog, I'm tellin' ye to lave that whistle alone if ye expect to finish the voyage. Wan toot out av it means a ton av coal gone to hell an' a dhrop av blood out av the owner's heart! An' from that time on the best I iver hearrd out av that whistle was a sick sort av a sob."

Matt laughed as Terence Reardon's natural propensity for romancing came to the front. He thanked the chief for the latter's invaluable information, and, with a mental resolve to have Terence Reardon presiding over the engines of the Narcissus at no distant date, he returned to the city.

CHAPTER XLVII.
THE TAIL GOES WITH THE HIDE

The following morning Matt called upon MacCandless, the general manager of the Oriental Steamship Company. Mr. MacCandless was a cold individual of Scotch ancestry, with a scent for a dollar a trifle keener than most; and Matt Peasley, young and inexperienced in business fencing, was never more aware of his deficiencies than when he faced MacCandless across the latter's desk. Consequently, he resolved to waste no words in vain parley. MacCandless was still looking curiously at Matt's card when the latter said:

"I called with reference to that big freighter of the Oriental Steamship Company — the Narcissus. Is she for sale?"

MacCandless smiled with his lips, but his eyes wore the eternal Show-me! look. He nodded.

"Foolish of me to ask, I know," Matt continued complacently, "since it is a matter of common gossip that you would have been delighted to have sold her any time these past eight years."

Since MacCandless did not deny this Matt assumed that it was true and returned to the attack with renewed vigor.

"What do you want for her?"

"Are you acting as a broker in this matter or do you represent principals who have asked you to interview me? In other words, before I talk business with you I want to know that you mean business. I shall waste no time discussing a possible trade unless you assure me that you have a customer in sight. I am weary of brokers. I've had forty of them after that vessel from time to time, but no business ever resulted."

"Which is not at all surprising, considering the circumstances," Matt retorted. "If you cannot use her yourself you mustn't expect other people to be over-enthusiastic about owning her. However, I think I can find business for her, and I've come to buy her myself. You seem to think a lot of your time, so I'll conserve it for you. I'm the principal in this deal, and if you really want to get rid of her we'll do business in two minutes."

"Three hundred thousand dollars," MacCandless answered promptly.

"Listen," said Matt Peasley. "I have fifty thousand dollars of my own in bank this minute, but I will have to raise two hundred and fifty thousand more before I can afford to buy your vessel, even if we agree on that price, which does not seem probable. I'll give you two hundred and fifty thousand dollars for the steamer Narcissus; but when you turn her over to me I want a ship, not a piece of floating junk. You'll have to ship a new crank shaft, rewind the main motor, renew the Manila lines, overhaul the standing rigging, retube the condensers and dock her before handing her over to me. She's as foul as any hulk in Rotten Row."

"Why, that will cost in the neighborhood of forty thousand dollars—nearer fifty!" MacCandless declared.

"I know. But for three hundred thousand dollars I can go to Sweden, build a smaller vessel than the Narcissus, have her right up to date, with two-thousand-horsepower oil-burning motors in her; and the saving in space due to motor installation, with oil tanks instead of coal bunkers, will enable me to carry fully as much cargo as the Narcissus. Also, I'll burn six tons of crude oil a day to your forty tons of coal a day in the Narcissus. I'll employ eight men less in my crew, and have a cleaner, faster and better ship. The motor ship is the freighter of the future, and you know it. Your Narcissus is out of date, and I'm only offering you two hundred and fifty thousand dollars because I can use her right away."

"Young man," said MacCandless, "you talk like a person that means business, but you overlook the fact that this company is neither bankrupt nor silly. The directors will, I feel assured, agree to do all the work you specify, but the price must be three hundred thousand. That will leave us two hundred and fifty thousand dollars net."

"I'll split the difference with you."

MacCandless shook his head.

"Well, that ends our argument," Matt answered pleasantly, and took up his hat. "You can keep your big white elephant another eight years, Mr. MacCandless. Perhaps some principal will come along then and make you another offer; and in the interim you can charge off about one hundred and fifty thousand dollars interest on the money tied up in the Narcissus. Fine business—I don't think!" He nodded farewell and started for the door.

"But you say you have but fifty thousand dollars," MacCandless protested.

"I said I'd have to get two hundred and fifty thousand dollars more. Well, I'll do it."

"Quite a sum to raise these days," MacCandless remarked doubtfully.

"Well, if you'll give me a sixty-day option on the Narcissus at two hundred and seventy-five thousand dollars and agree to do the repairs on her, including dry-docking, cleaning and painting her up to the water line, I'll take a ten-thousand-dollar chance, Mr. MacCandless, that I can raise the money."

"Do you mean you'll give the Oriental Steamship Company ten thousand dollars for a sixty-day option?"

"I do; and I'll pay for the vessel as I raise the remainder of the money. Ten thousand dollars down for the option, to apply on the purchase price, of course, if the deal goes through, and to be forfeited to you if I fail to make the next payment on time."

"What will the next payment be?" the cautious MacCandless demanded.

"Twenty thousand dollars a month, with interest at six per cent. in deferred payments. You might as well be earning six per cent. on her as have her rusting holes in her bottom down there in Mission Bay. As she lies, you're losing at least six per cent. interest on her."

"There's reason in that," MacCandless answered thoughtfully. "You to insure the vessel as our interest may appear, bill of sale in escrow; and if you default for more than thirty days on any payment before we have received fifty per cent. of the purchase price you lose out and we get our ship back."

"Sharp business, but I'll take it, Mr. MacCandless. After I've paid half the money I can mortgage her for the remainder and get out from under your clutches. Put the buck up to your directors, get their approval to the option and contract of sale, notify me, and I'll be right up with a certified check for ten thousand dollars." And, without giving MacCandless time to answer, Matt took his departure.

"If I talked ten minutes with that man," he soliloquized, "he'd have the number of my mess. He'd realize what a piker I was and terminate the interview. But—I—think he'll meet my terms, because he sees I'm pretty young and inexperienced, and he figures he'll make ten or twenty thousand dollars out of me before I discover I'm a rotten promoter. And, at that, his is better than an even-money bet!"

At five o'clock that same day MacCandless telephoned.

"I have called a special meeting of our directors, Captain Peasley," he announced, "and put your proposition up to them. They have agreed to it, and if you will be at my office at ten o'clock to-morrow I think we can do business."

"I think so," Matt answered. "I'll be there."

He hung up, reached for a telegraph blank and wrote the following message:

San Francisco, July 28, 1914.

Terence Reardon,
Chief Engineer, S. S. Arab,
Port Costa, California.

Have bought Narcissus. Offer you one hundred seventy-five a month quit Arab now and supervise installation new crank shaft, retubing condensers, and so on; permanent job as chief. Do you accept? Answer immediately.

PACIFIC SHIPPING COMPANY,
Matthew Peasley, President.

Having dispatched this message, Matt Peasley closed down his desk, strolled round to the Blue Star Navigation Company's offices, and picked up his newly acquired father-in-law. On their way home in Cappy's carriage the old gentleman, apropos of the afternoon press dispatches from Europe, remarked that the situation abroad was anything but encouraging.

"Do you think we'll have a war in Europe?" Matt queried.

"Germany seems determined to back up Austria in her demands on Serbia, and I don't think Serbia will eat quite all of the dish of dirt Francis Joseph has set before her," Cappy answered seriously. "Austria seems determined to make an issue of the assassination of the Archduke Ferdinand and his wife. If she does, Matt, there'll be the most awful war in history. All Europe will be fighting."

Matt was silent and thoughtful all the way home, but just before they left the carriage he turned to Cappy.

"If there's war," he remarked, "England will, doubtless, control the seas because of her superior navy. German commerce will absolutely cease."

"The submarine will have to be reckoned with, also," Cappy suggested. "England's commerce will doubtless be knocked into a cocked hat."

"There'll be a shortage of bottoms, and vessels will be in brisk demand," Matt predicted. "There'll be a sharp rise in freight rates on all commodities the instant war breaks out, and the American mercantile marine ought to reap a harvest."

"My dear boy," said Cappy acidly, "why speak of the American mercantile marine? There ain't no such animal."

"There will be—if the war in Europe ever starts," Matt retorted; "and, what's more, I'm going to bet there will be war within thirty days."

He did not consider it advisable to mention to Cappy that he was going to bet ten thousand dollars!

CHAPTER XLVIII.
VICTORY

At ten o'clock the following morning Matt Peasley, accompanied by an attorney, an expert in maritime law, presented himself at the Oriental Steamship Company's office. MacCandless and the attorney for his company were awaiting them, with a tentative form of contract of sale already drawn up, and after a two-hour discussion on various points the finished document was finally presented for the signatures of both parties, but not, however, until Matt Peasley had been forced to do something that brought out a gentle perspiration on the backs of his sturdy legs. Before the shrewd MacCandless would consent to begin the work of placing the vessel in commission, according to agreement, he stipulated a payment of twenty-five thousand dollars down! He estimated the cost of the docking and repair work at fifty thousand dollars, and, desiring to play safe, insisted that Matt Peasley should advance at least fifty per cent. of this preliminary outlay in cash.

Matt thereupon excused himself from the conference on the plea that he had to consult with others before taking this step. He was gone about fifteen minutes, during which time he consulted with the "others." They happened to be two newsboys selling rival afternoon editions. Matt Peasley did business with each, and after a quick perusal of both papers, he decided that war was inevitable and resolved to take the plunge. In no sense of the word, however, did he believe he was gambling. His conversation with Terence Reardon had convinced him that the Narcissus was a misunderstood ship—that she had been poorly managed and was the victim of a false financial policy.

Hence, even though the war should not materialize, he would be making no mistake in tying her up. She was a bully gamble and a wonderful bargain at the price; with Terence Reardon presiding over her engines at a salary twenty-five dollars in excess of the union scale, the orders to keep her out of the shop would be followed, so far as lay in Terence's power. Even should he not succeed in financing the enterprise Cappy Ricks would be glad to take his bargain off his hands—perhaps at a neat profit. Consequently, Matt went over to his bank, procured an additional certified check for fifteen thousand dollars and returned to MacCandless' office, where he signed the contract of sale and paid over his twenty-five thousand dollars. He trembled a little as he did it.

"I'll have the insurance on her placed this afternoon," MacCandless suggested as he handed Matt his copy of the sale contract; whereat the latter came to life with galvanic suddenness.

"Oh, no, you'll not, Mr. MacCandless," he suggested smilingly. "I'll place that insurance myself. My company has to pay for it, so I'll act as agent and collect my little old ten per cent. commission. But, passing that, do you want to know the latest—the very latest news?"

"I don't mind," MacCandless replied.

"Well, there's going to be a devil of big war in Europe and I wouldn't take four hundred thousand dollars for the Narcissus this minute. May I use your telephone? Thanks!" He called up his office. "Is there a telegram there for me?" he queried, and on being answered in the affirmative he directed his stenographer to read it to him. He turned to MacCandless.

"Mr. Terence Reardon will have entire charge of the work of retubing those condensers, and so on," he explained. "I'll give him a letter to you, which will be his authority to superintend the job. I'm going to New York tonight, but I think I'll be back in time to accept the vessel when she's ready for commission." He looked at his watch. It was just twelve-thirty o'clock. "The Overland leaves at two-thirty," he murmured. "I'll have just time to pack a suit case." And he picked up his hat and fled with the celerity and singleness of purpose of a tin-canned dog.

Cappy Ricks woke from his mid-afternoon doze to find his son-in-law shaking him by the shoulder.

"Well, young man," Cappy began severely, "so you're back, are you? Give an account of yourself. Where the devil have you been for the past two weeks? Why did you go, and why did you have the consummate nerve to leave Florry behind you? Why, you hadn't been married two months—"

"I couldn't take her with me, sir," Matt protested. "I wanted to, but she would have been in the way. You see, I knew I was going to be busy night and day."

Cappy Ricks slid out to the edge of his swivel chair; with a hand on each knee he gazed at his smiling son-in-law over the rims of his spectacles. For fully a minute he remained motionless.

"Matt," he demanded suspiciously, "what the devil have you been up to?"

Matt raised a huge forefinger.

"Number one," he began: "I bought the Oriental Steamship Company's freighter Narcissus, seventy-five hundred tons' register, for two hundred and seventy-five thousand dollars, and in a month she'll be in tiptop shape and ready for sea. I've paid twenty-five thousand dollars down on her and I'll have to make a payment of twenty thousand dollars on the twenty-sixth of September and twenty thousand dollars a month on her thereafter until she, is paid for. And if I default on a payment for more than thirty days before I've paid off half of the purchase price the Oriental Steamship Company may, at its option, take the vessel away from me."

Cappy Ricks smiled.

"Ah!" he breathed softly. "So you want help, eh? You finally did manage to get into deep water close to the shore, and now you're yelling to father to come through and save you, eh? Well, I'll do it, my boy, because I think you made a bully buy; and she's worth it. I'll take over your bargain for you and give you, say—er—ahem! we—harumph-h-h—say twenty-five thousand dollars profit. Not so bad, eh? When I was your age—" Cappy paused, open-mouthed. He had suddenly remembered something. "Oh, no," he contradicted himself; "this isn't my foolish day—not by a jugful! You owe me a lot of money on that promissory note you gave me when we settled up for that Tillicum business—so I'll not give you any money after all. I'll just take the contract of sale off your hands, give you back the money you risked in the deal—and your promissory note, cancelled." And Cappy Ricks sat back and clawed his whiskers expectantly.

"Oh, I'm not in distress," Matt answered cheerfully. "On the contrary, I'm going to take up that note before the week is out."

Once more Cappy slid out to the edge of his chair.

"Where are you going to get the money?" he demanded bluntly.

"I'm going to sell the Narcissus. The day I purchased her it was a moral certainty that Europe was to be plunged into a terrible war; so the ink wasn't dry on the contract before I was streaking it for New York. War was declared by England on Germany on the fifth of August, and while you'd be saying Jack Robinson every German freighter went into neutral ports to intern until the war should terminate. The German raiders are still out after the British and French commerce, and the deep-water shipping out of Eastern ports isn't a business any more. It's a delirium—a night-mare! Why, I was offered any number of charters for my Narcissus, but I didn't bother trying to charter her until just before I started for home; and, moreover, the longer I waited the better charter I could make. Besides, she isn't in commission yet—and I had other fish to fry."

"For instance?" Cappy inquired wonderingly.

"It is an undisputed fact that the early bird gets the worm," Matt Peasley replied brightly, "and I was the early bird. I was in New York a few days before the war became general, and for a week thereafter everybody was so blamed interested in the fighting they neglected business. But I didn't. I went to New York to charter, under the government form, as many big steel freighters as I could lay hands on—"

Cappy Ricks raised his clasped hands and gazed reverently upward.

"Oh, Lord!" he murmured. "How many? How many?"

"Fifteen," Matt Peasley murmured complacently. "I got about half of them real cheap, because business was rotten when I landed in the East. Why, I chartered the entire fleet of one shipping firm in Boston. I had to pay a stiffer rate for the others; but—"

"How long did you charter them for?" Cappy yelled. "Quick! Tell me!"

"All for a year, with the privilege of renewal at a ten per cent. advance. I had no difficulty in rechartering to the men who had been asleep on the job. I shall average a profit of two hundred dollars a day on each of the fifteen even if I do not charter them longer—"

"A day!" Cappy's voice rose to a shrill scream.

"A day! Any American bottom that will float and move through the water is worth five times what it was before war was declared, and the freight rates are going up every day. Three thousand dollars a day income—three hundred and sixty-five days in the year! Man, if the war lasts a year I'll make a million dollars net!"

"But—but—about this Narcissus?" Cappy sputtered.

"Just before I left for home I chartered her at fourteen hundred dollars a day—forty-two thousand dollars a month—on the Government form of charter."

"Impossible!" Cappy shrieked, losing all control of himself. "Dog-gone you, Matt Peasley, don't tell me such stories. You're driving me crazy!"

"It will cost me nine thousand a month to run her—and she doesn't even go near the war zone. I'm going to run her to South American ports."

"How long?"

Matt Peasley smiled. "How long?" he echoed. "Why, she's only chartered for one trip just now. You don't suppose I'd charter her for several voyages or for a year, on a freight market that's growing overnight?"

"And those fifteen vessels you chartered. You rechartered them. For what period?"

"Three months, with privilege of renewal at the going rates."

"Matt," Cappy murmured, "you're great. Damn me, sir, I could kiss you."

Matt grinned at this earnest commendation.

"Of course I can operate the Narcissus and meet my monthly payments to the Oriental Steamship Company and still be ahead of the game," he continued. "But I'm going to sell her, Mr. Ricks. I've had an offer of four hundred and fifty thousand dollars for her already—and she's still waiting to be hauled out on the marine railway and put in commission! I'll just wait one week and by that time she'll bring half a million. At that I hate to sell, but I've got to. I figure a bird in the hand is worth two in the bush."

"Why have you got to?" Cappy shrilled. "You're crazy! You don't have to."

"But the next payment will come due on her before I receive any charter money from the Steel people, and that will clean me for fair. I can't help myself. Besides, I've got these other fifteen vessels chartered; I'll have to have capital—and I've got to have it quickly or I'll be a pauper while you'd be saying Jack Robinson."

"But, Matt, you old dunderhead, you mustn't sell a good thing. Why, man, you've got a million and a half profit right in the hollow of your hand; and, oh, we mustn't let it get away, Matt—we mustn't let it get away!

"It was magnificent, Matt—perfectly magnificent. I'll help you, sonny. By golly, I'll go to the bat for you and back you for the last dollar I have. No more monkeyshines between us now, boy! We've had a lot of fun in our day, playing nip and tuck with each other; but this is real business. You've got to be saved."

"I had an idea that you would see it in that light, sir," Matt suggested smilingly. "I knew you'd back me up; so I didn't worry. But you'll have to take half the profit on the deals I've made—that's only fair."

"Profits!" Cappy Ricks sneered. "Why, what the devil do I care for profits? You keep the profits. You and Florry are young and you'll know how to enjoy them. Why, what do you think I am? A human hog? Let me sit in the game with you—let me play the game of business with you, son, down to my last buffalo nickel. I can't take the blamed money with me when I die, can I? But don't ask me to make any money out of you, my boy. I'm going to get my fun watching you in action."

Matt Peasley came close and took old Cappy Ricks' hand in both of his.

"I want to be your partner," he said wistfully. "I couldn't come into this office and sponge off you, and so I've waited until I could buy in! I wanted to bring some assets besides myself when I should come to manage the Blue Star. May I, sir? I want to turn in this big deal I've put over for stock in the Ricks Lumber and Logging Company and the

Mr. Skinner glanced at Cappy Ricks with the closest approach to downright affection he considered quite dignified to permit during business hours.

"I notice you were going to quit a minute ago to become president emeritus—and now you're including yourself in the new program of activity," he reminded Cappy Ricks. "I seem to remember that for the past few years you've been talking of the happy day when you could retire and learn to play golf."

"Golf!" Cappy glanced at Mr. Skinner witheringly. "Skinner," he continued, "don't be an ass! Golf is an old man's game—and I belong with the young fellows. Why, don't you remember the day, three years ago, when we discovered we had a sailor named Matt Peasley before the mast in the old Retriever? Why, ever since I've been having so much fun—"

"And that reminds me," Matt interrupted: "We must send a new skipper to Aberdeen to relieve Mike Murphy in the Retriever. He has his ticket for steam and I've hired him at two hundred and fifty a month to skipper the Narcissus. Mike is one of the best men under the Blue Star; he has come up from before the mast."

"The only kind I ever gave a whoop for," Cappy declared. "In effect, he once told me to go chase myself."

"But," Skinner persisted, "how about playing golf?"

Cappy Ricks raised his eyes reverently upward. "Please God," he said, "I'll die in the harness!"

"Amen!" said Mr. Skinner; and Matt Peasely re-echoed the sentiment.